CHAPTER 01

ART AND STORY BY
SEAN DILLON
@GRANDPABATS

COWRITTEN BY
STEVEN PETRIVELLI
@STEVEN_PETRO

BRYAN SEATON: PUBLISHER/CEO **SHAWN GABBORIN:** EDITOR IN CHIEF **JASON MARTIN:** PUBLISHER-DANGER ZONE
NICOLE D'ANDRIA: MARKETING DIRECTOR/EDITOR **JESSICA LOWRIE:** SOCIAL MEDIA CZAR **DANIELLE DAVISON:**
EXECUTIVE ADMINISTRATOR **CHAD CICCONI:** BAD GUY STUNT DOUBLE **SHAWN PRYOR:** PRESIDENT OF CREATOR
RELATIONS

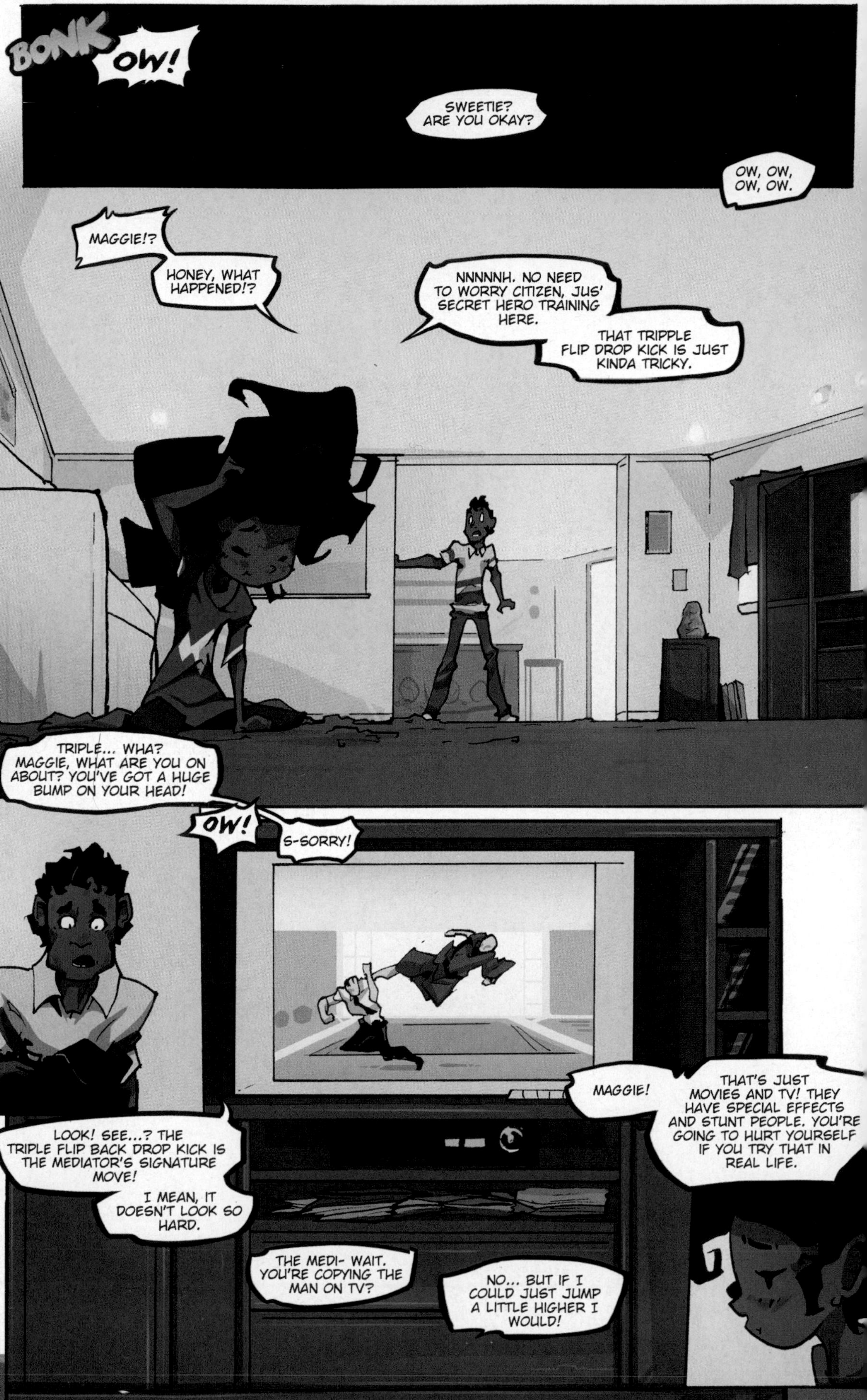
BONK
OW!
SWEETIE? ARE YOU OKAY?
OW, OW, OW, OW.
MAGGIE!?
HONEY, WHAT HAPPENED!?
NNNNNH. NO NEED TO WORRY CITIZEN, JUS' SECRET HERO TRAINING HERE.
THAT TRIPPLE FLIP DROP KICK IS JUST KINDA TRICKY.
TRIPLE... WHA? MAGGIE, WHAT ARE YOU ON ABOUT? YOU'VE GOT A HUGE BUMP ON YOUR HEAD!
OW!
S-SORRY!
LOOK! SEE...? THE TRIPLE FLIP BACK DROP KICK IS THE MEDIATOR'S SIGNATURE MOVE!
I MEAN, IT DOESN'T LOOK SO HARD.
MAGGIE!
THAT'S JUST MOVIES AND TV! THEY HAVE SPECIAL EFFECTS AND STUNT PEOPLE. YOU'RE GOING TO HURT YOURSELF IF YOU TRY THAT IN REAL LIFE.
THE MEDI- WAIT. YOU'RE COPYING THE MAN ON TV?
NO... BUT IF I COULD JUST JUMP A LITTLE HIGHER I WOULD!

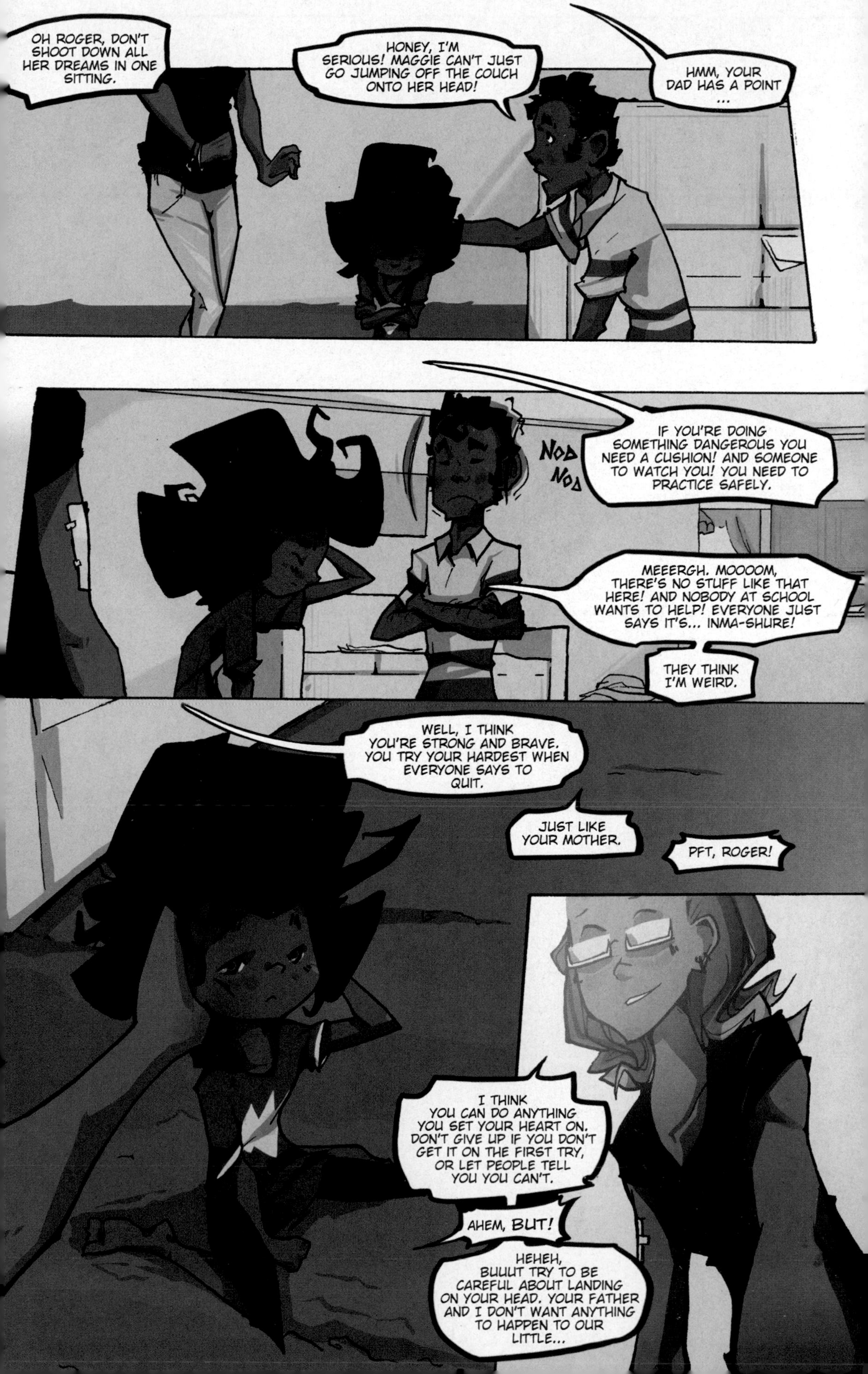
OH ROGER, DON'T SHOOT DOWN ALL HER DREAMS IN ONE SITTING.
HONEY, I'M SERIOUS! MAGGIE CAN'T JUST GO JUMPING OFF THE COUCH ONTO HER HEAD!
HMM, YOUR DAD HAS A POINT ...
NOD NOD
IF YOU'RE DOING SOMETHING DANGEROUS YOU NEED A CUSHION! AND SOMEONE TO WATCH YOU! YOU NEED TO PRACTICE SAFELY.
MEEERGH. MOOOOM, THERE'S NO STUFF LIKE THAT HERE! AND NOBODY AT SCHOOL WANTS TO HELP! EVERYONE JUST SAYS IT'S... INMA-SHURE!
THEY THINK I'M WEIRD.
WELL, I THINK YOU'RE STRONG AND BRAVE. YOU TRY YOUR HARDEST WHEN EVERYONE SAYS TO QUIT.
JUST LIKE YOUR MOTHER.
PFT, ROGER!
I THINK YOU CAN DO ANYTHING YOU SET YOUR HEART ON. DON'T GIVE UP IF YOU DON'T GET IT ON THE FIRST TRY, OR LET PEOPLE TELL YOU YOU CAN'T.
AHEM, BUT!
HEHEH, BUUUT TRY TO BE CAREFUL ABOUT LANDING ON YOUR HEAD. YOUR FATHER AND I DON'T WANT ANYTHING TO HAPPEN TO OUR LITTLE...

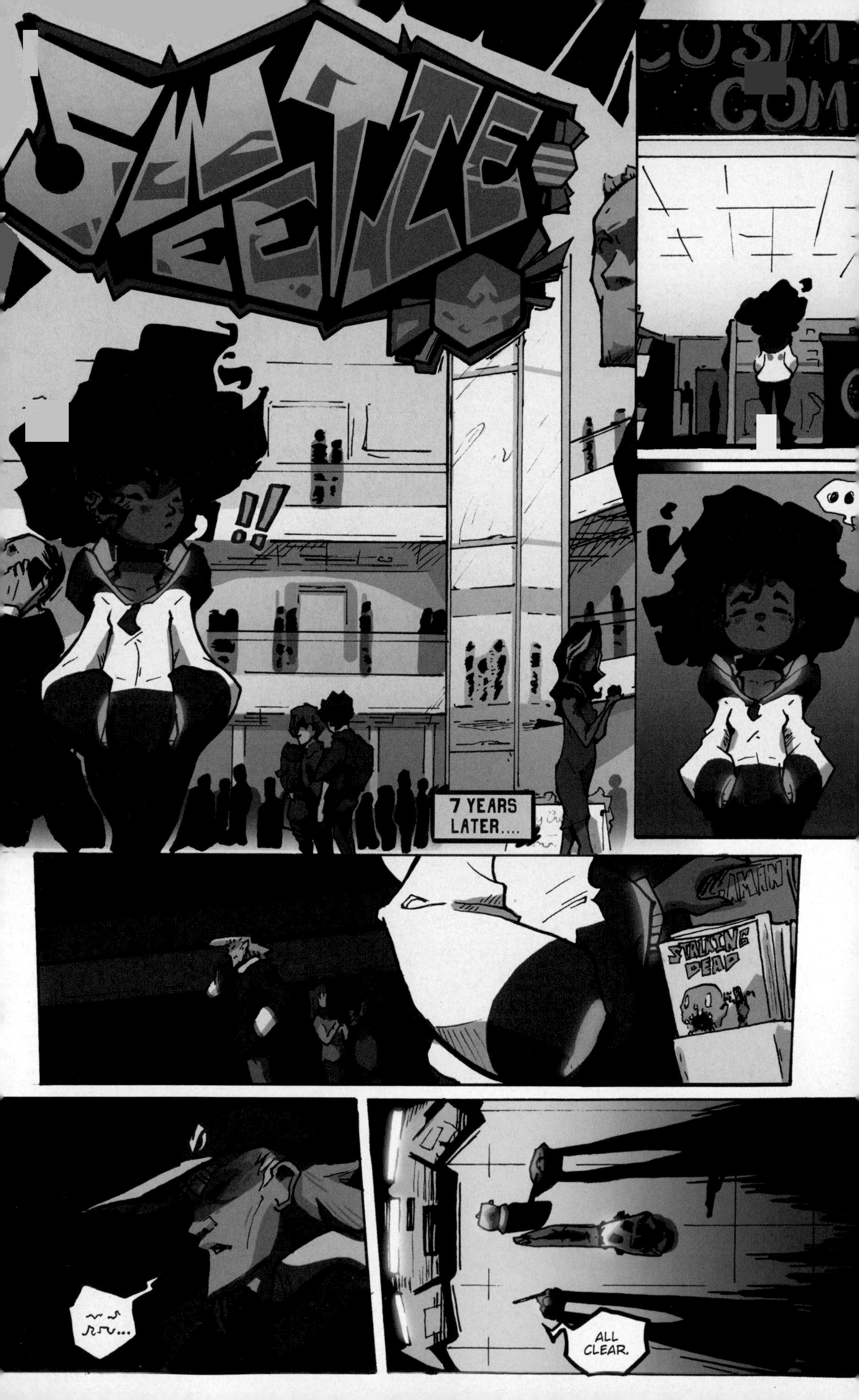
!!
7 YEARS
LATER....
STALKING
DEAD
ALL
CLEAR.

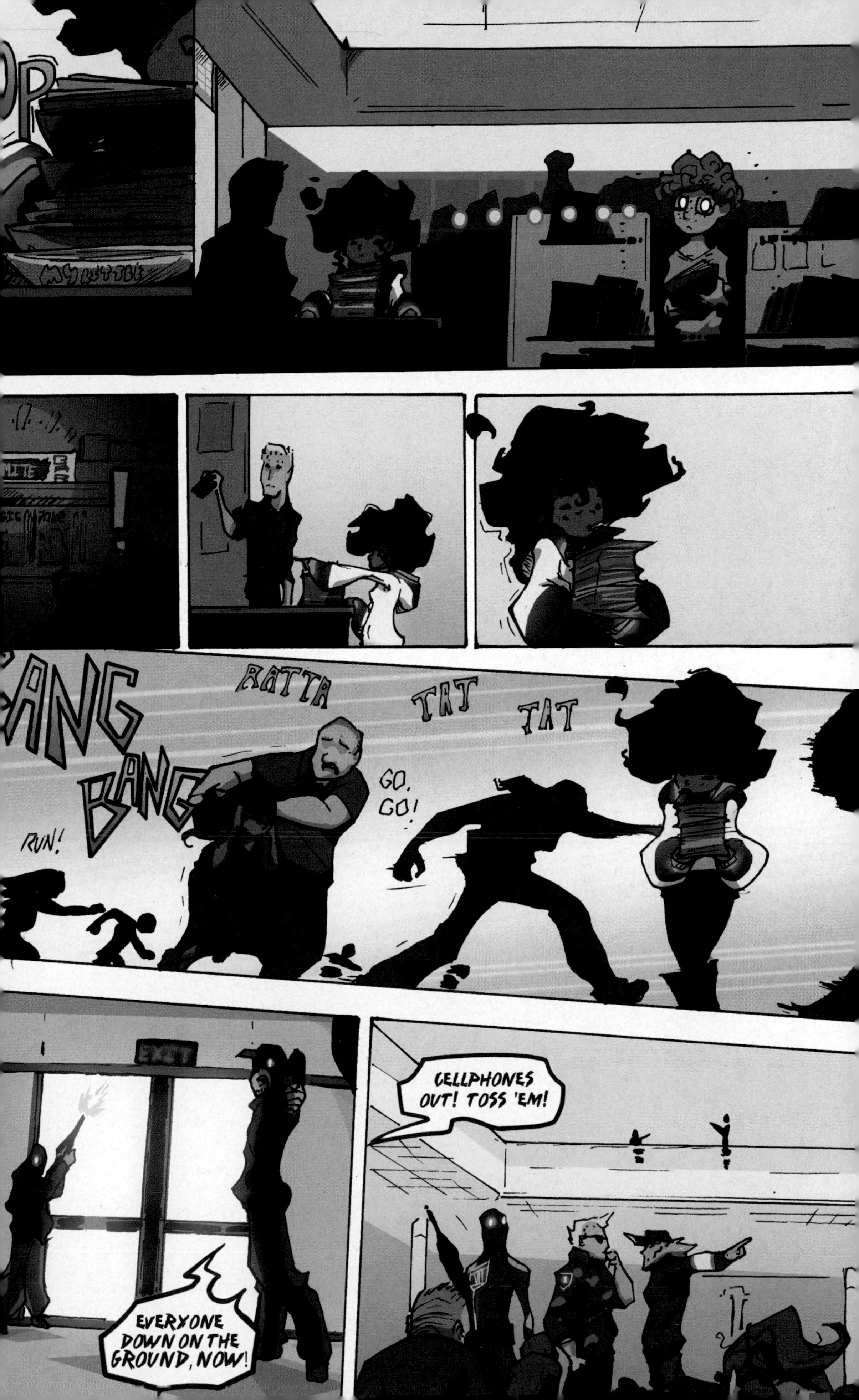
BANG
RATTA
TAT
TAT
BANG
RUN!
GO. GO!
EVERYONE DOWN ON THE GROUND, NOW!
CELLPHONES OUT! TOSS 'EM!

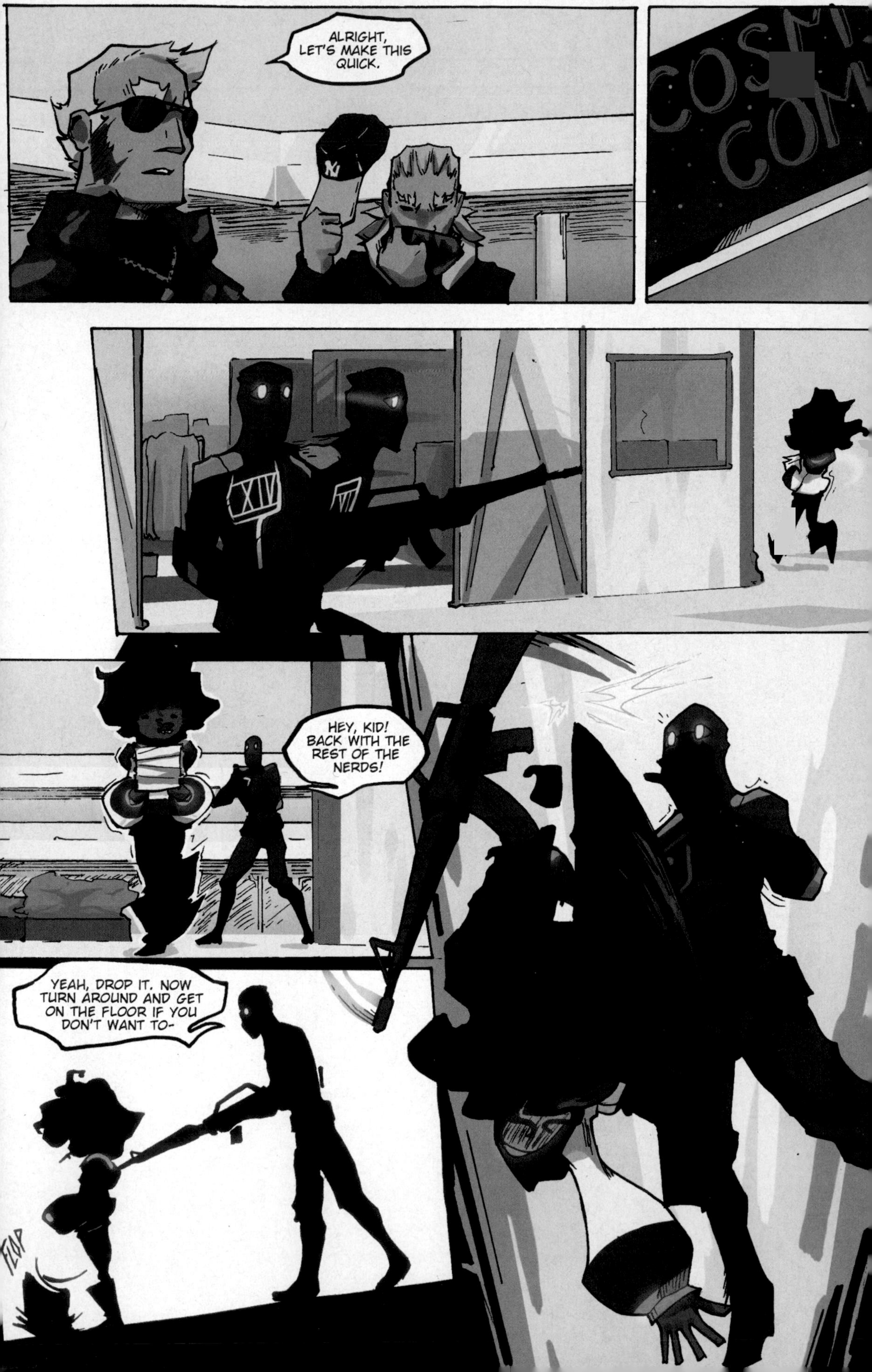
ALRIGHT, LET'S MAKE THIS QUICK.
HEY, KID! BACK WITH THE REST OF THE NERDS!
YEAH, DROP IT. NOW TURN AROUND AND GET ON THE FLOOR IF YOU DON'T WANT TO-
FLOP

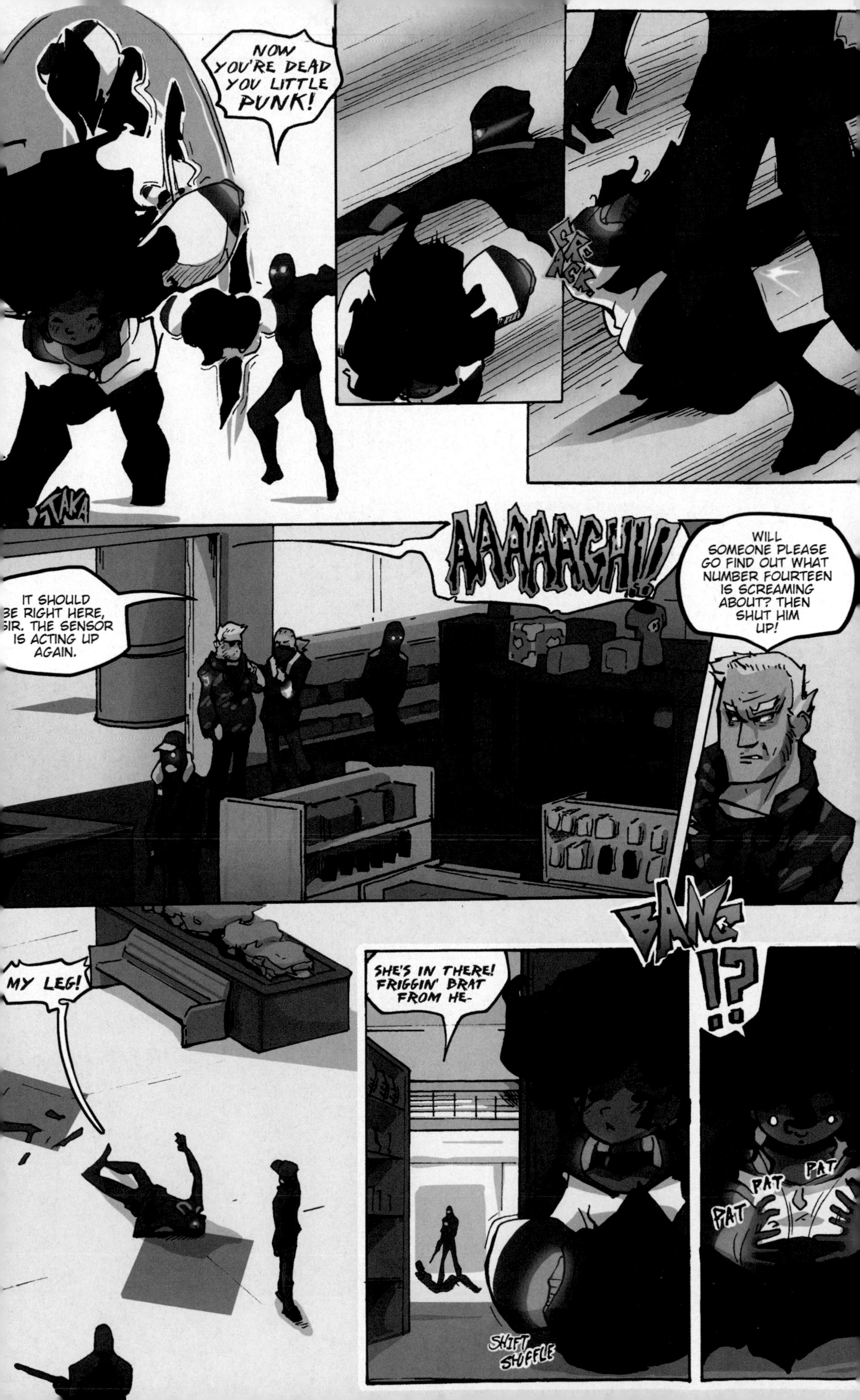
NOW YOU'RE DEAD YOU LITTLE PUNK!
TAKA
AAAAAGH!!
IT SHOULD BE RIGHT HERE, SIR. THE SENSOR IS ACTING UP AGAIN.
WILL SOMEONE PLEASE GO FIND OUT WHAT NUMBER FOURTEEN IS SCREAMING ABOUT? THEN SHUT HIM UP!
MY LEG!
SHE'S IN THERE! FRIGGIN' BRAT FROM HE-
BANG
SHIFT SHUFFLE
!?
PAT PAT PAT

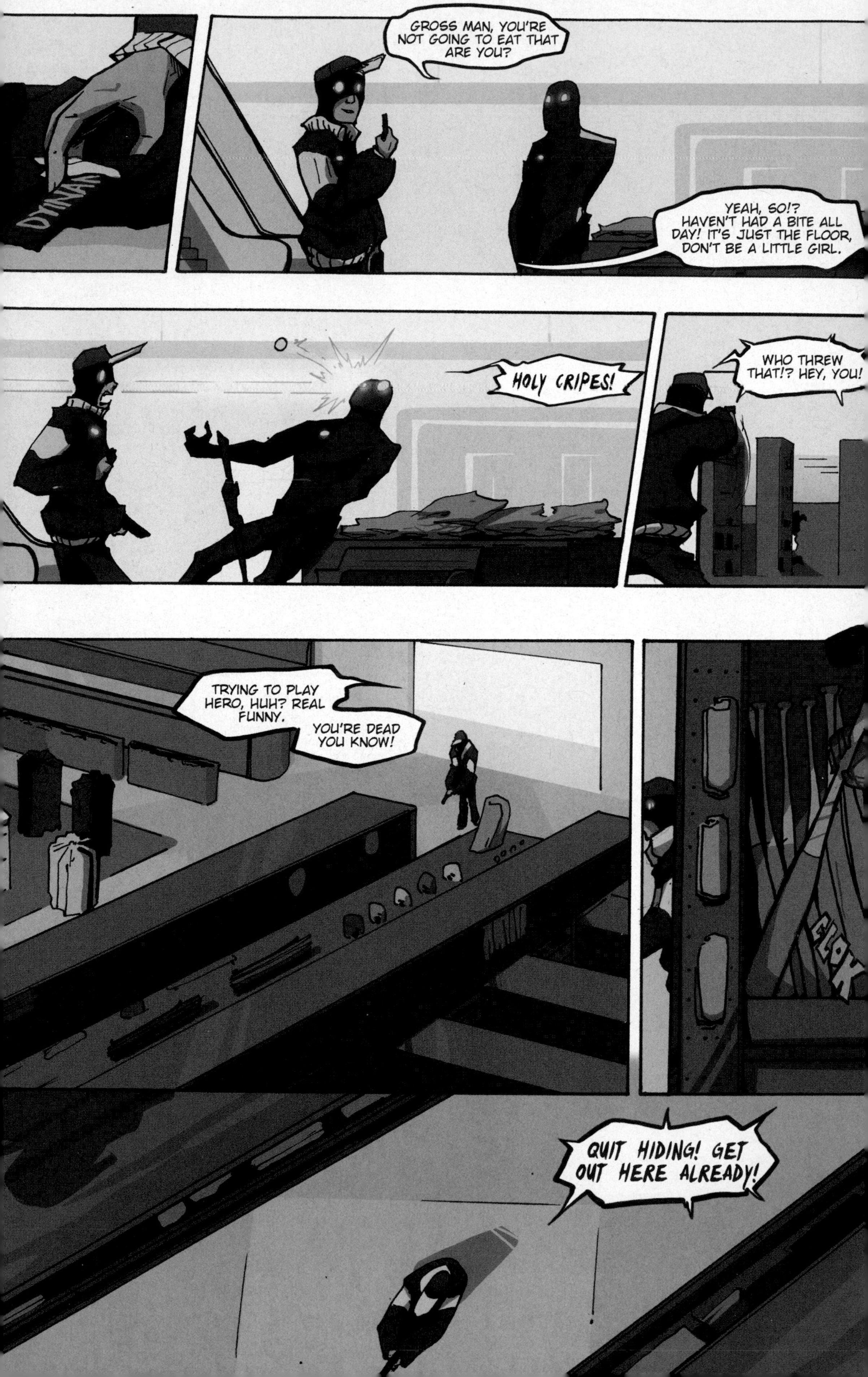
DYNAH
GROSS MAN, YOU'RE NOT GOING TO EAT THAT ARE YOU?
YEAH, SO!? HAVEN'T HAD A BITE ALL DAY! IT'S JUST THE FLOOR, DON'T BE A LITTLE GIRL.
HOLY CRIPES!
WHO THREW THAT!? HEY, YOU!
TRYING TO PLAY HERO, HUH? REAL FUNNY.
YOU'RE DEAD YOU KNOW!
GLOK
QUIT HIDING! GET OUT HERE ALREADY!

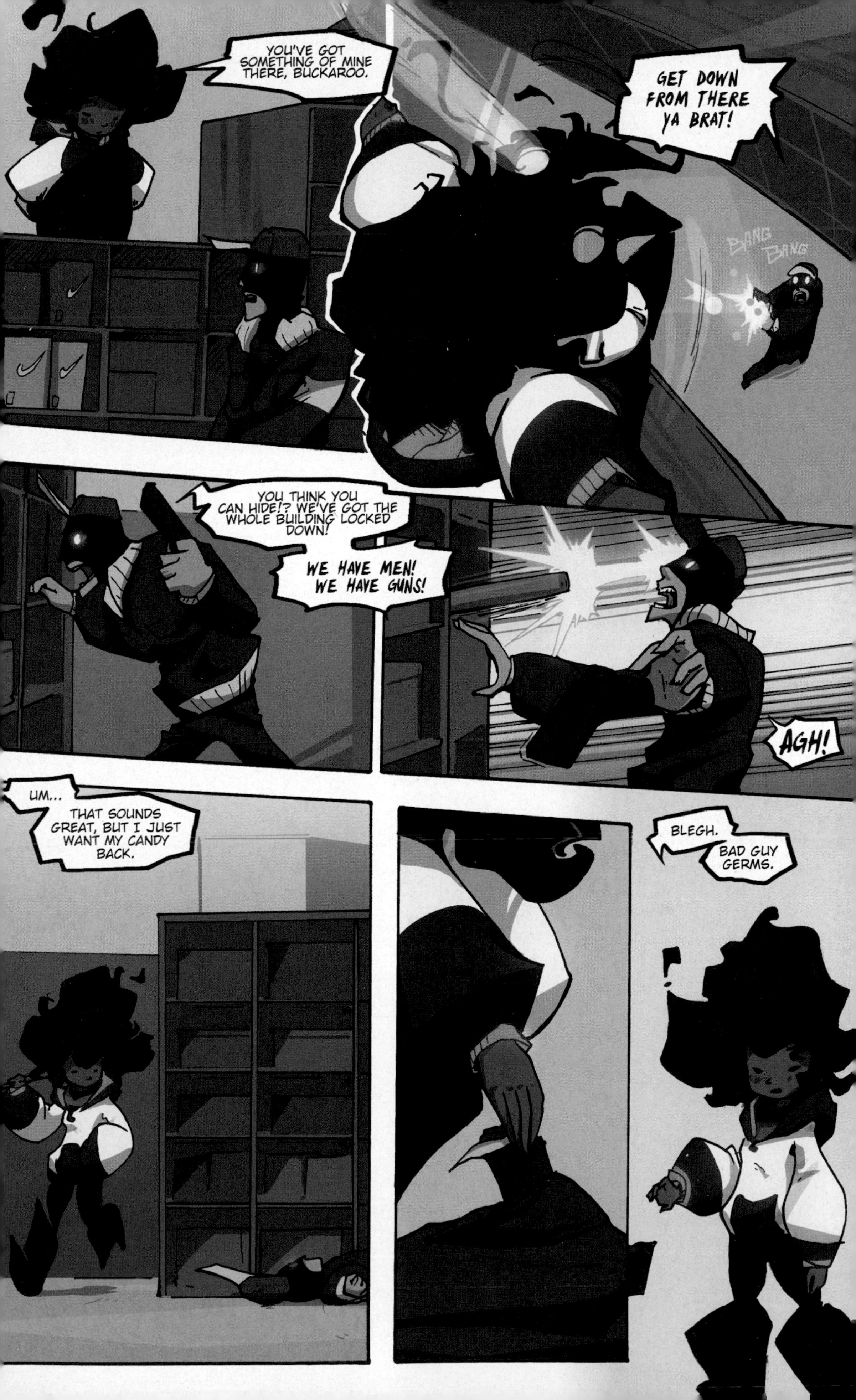
YOU'VE GOT SOMETHING OF MINE THERE, BUCKAROO.
GET DOWN FROM THERE YA BRAT!
BANG BANG
YOU THINK YOU CAN HIDE!? WE'VE GOT THE WHOLE BUILDING LOCKED DOWN!
WE HAVE MEN! WE HAVE GUNS!
AGH!
UM...
THAT SOUNDS GREAT, BUT I JUST WANT MY CANDY BACK.
BLEGH.
BAD GUY GERMS.

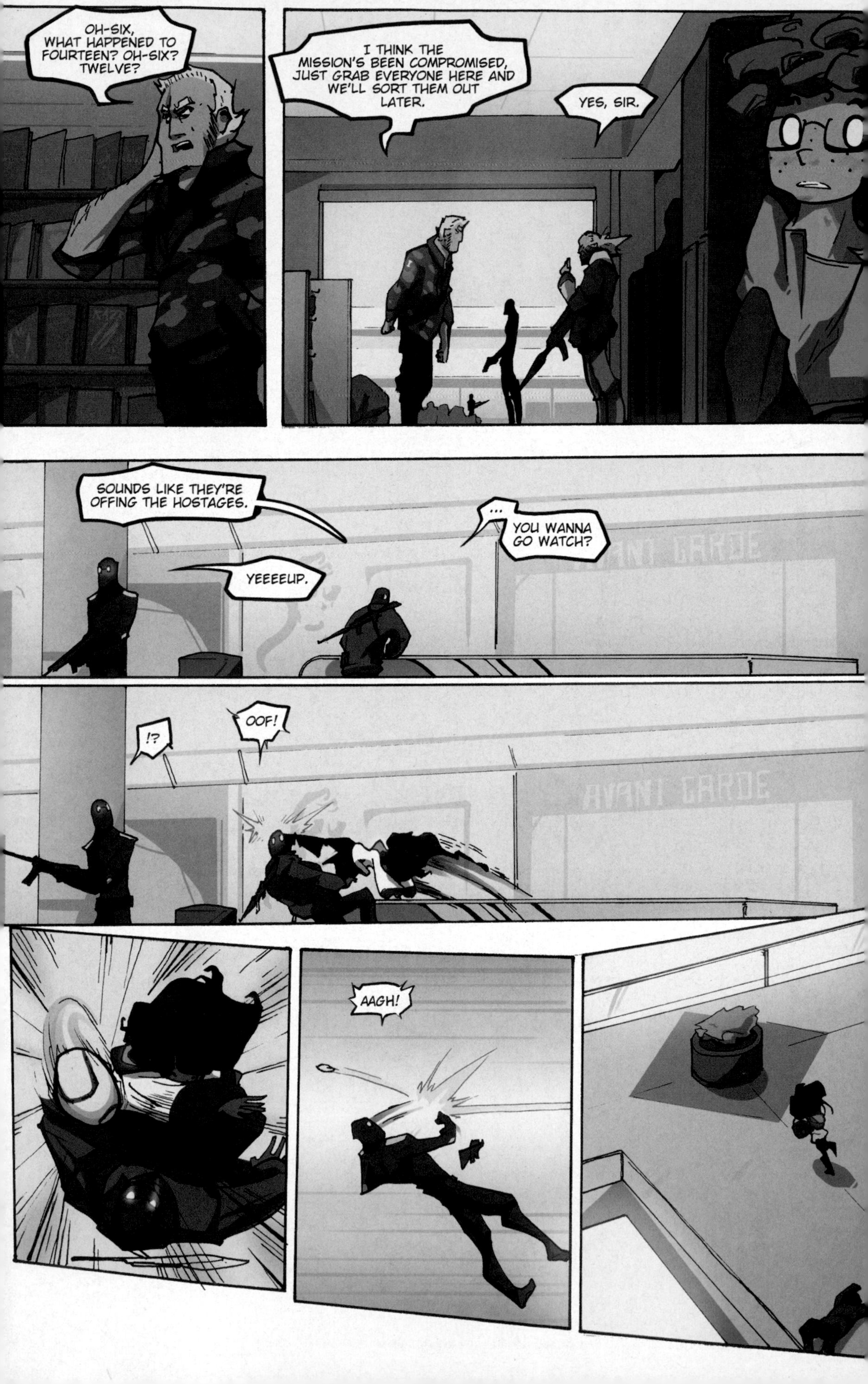
OH-SIX, WHAT HAPPENED TO FOURTEEN? OH-SIX? TWELVE?
I THINK THE MISSION'S BEEN COMPROMISED, JUST GRAB EVERYONE HERE AND WE'LL SORT THEM OUT LATER.
YES, SIR.
SOUNDS LIKE THEY'RE OFFING THE HOSTAGES.
...
YOU WANNA GO WATCH?
YEEEEUP.
AVANT GARDE
!?
OOF!
AVANT GARDE
AAGH!

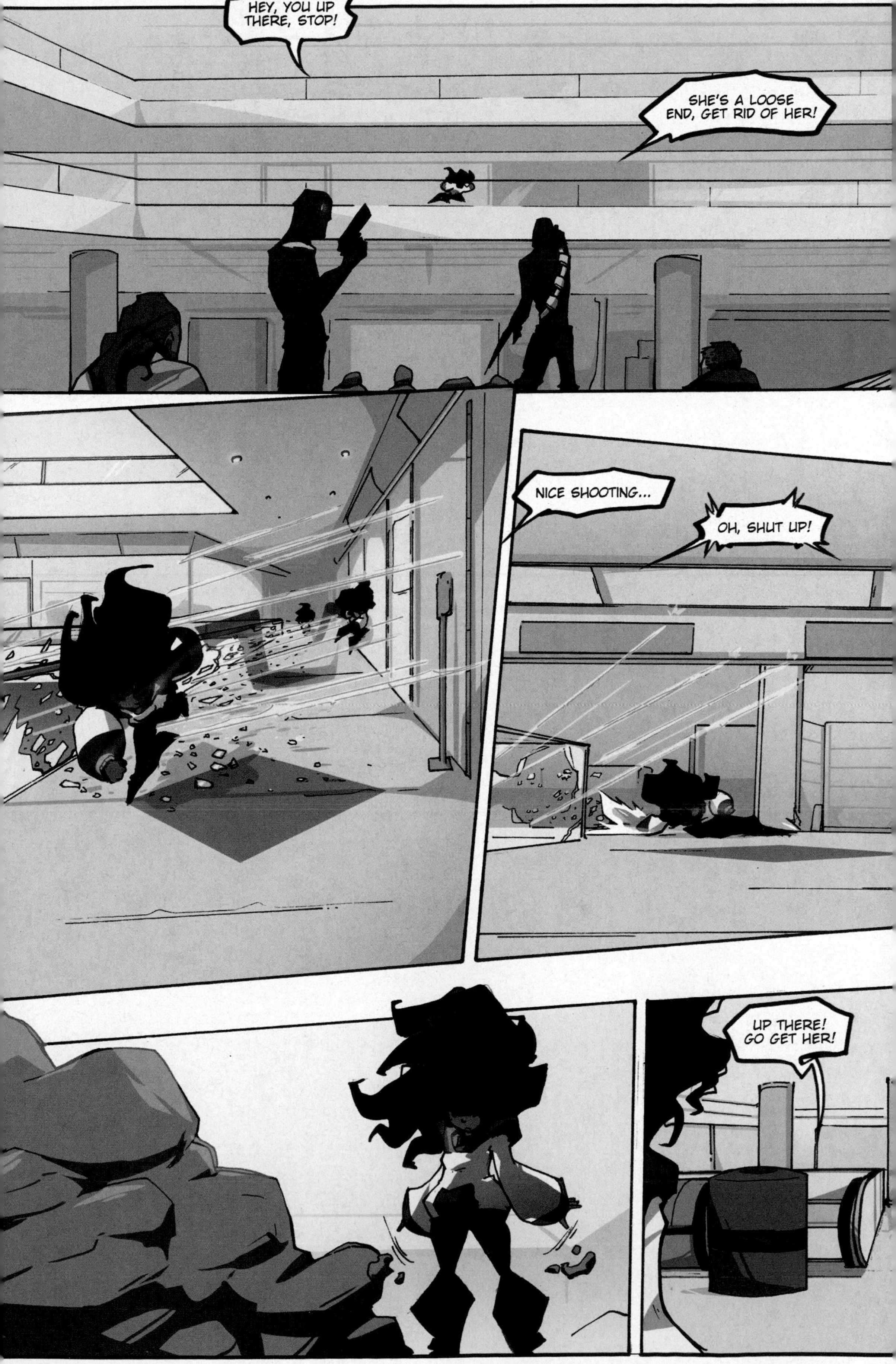
HEY, YOU UP THERE, STOP!
SHE'S A LOOSE END, GET RID OF HER!
NICE SHOOTING...
OH, SHUT UP!
UP THERE! GO GET HER!

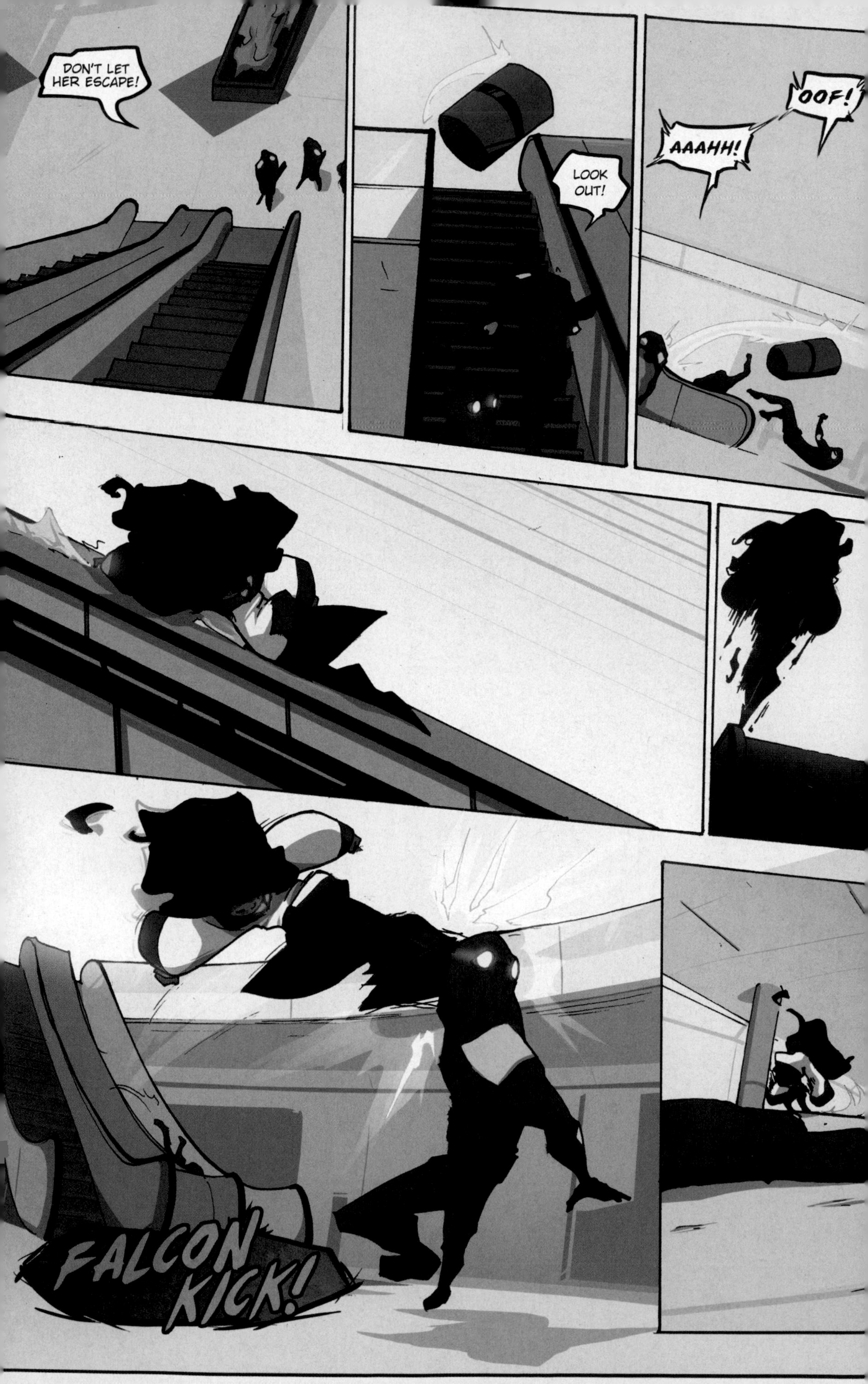
DON'T LET HER ESCAPE!
LOOK OUT!
AAAHH!
OOF!
FALCON KICK!

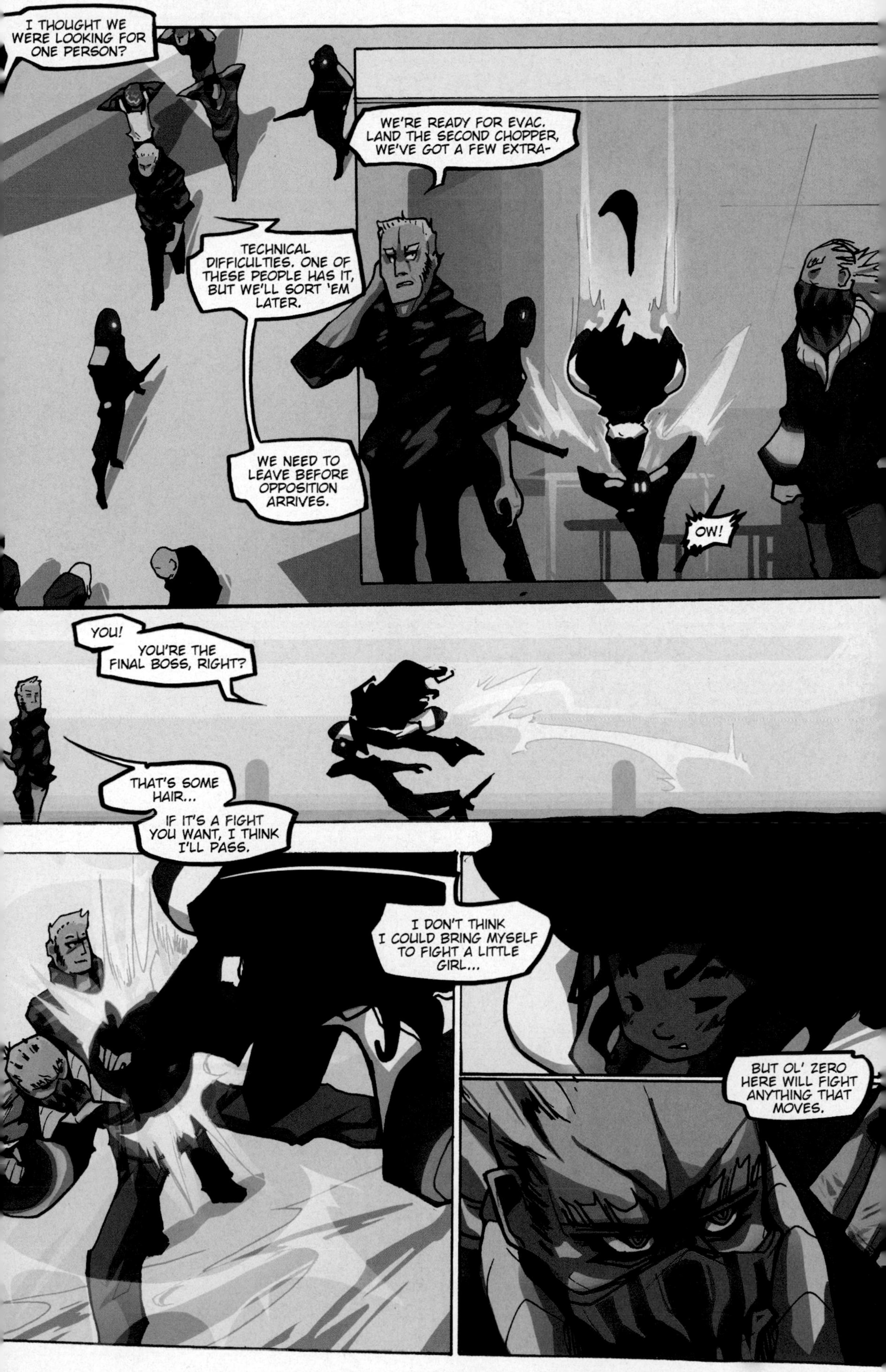
I THOUGHT WE WERE LOOKING FOR ONE PERSON?
WE'RE READY FOR EVAC. LAND THE SECOND CHOPPER, WE'VE GOT A FEW EXTRA-
TECHNICAL DIFFICULTIES. ONE OF THESE PEOPLE HAS IT, BUT WE'LL SORT 'EM LATER.
WE NEED TO LEAVE BEFORE OPPOSITION ARRIVES.
OW!
YOU!
YOU'RE THE FINAL BOSS, RIGHT?
THAT'S SOME HAIR...
IF IT'S A FIGHT YOU WANT, I THINK I'LL PASS.
I DON'T THINK I COULD BRING MYSELF TO FIGHT A LITTLE GIRL...
BUT OL' ZERO HERE WILL FIGHT ANYTHING THAT MOVES.

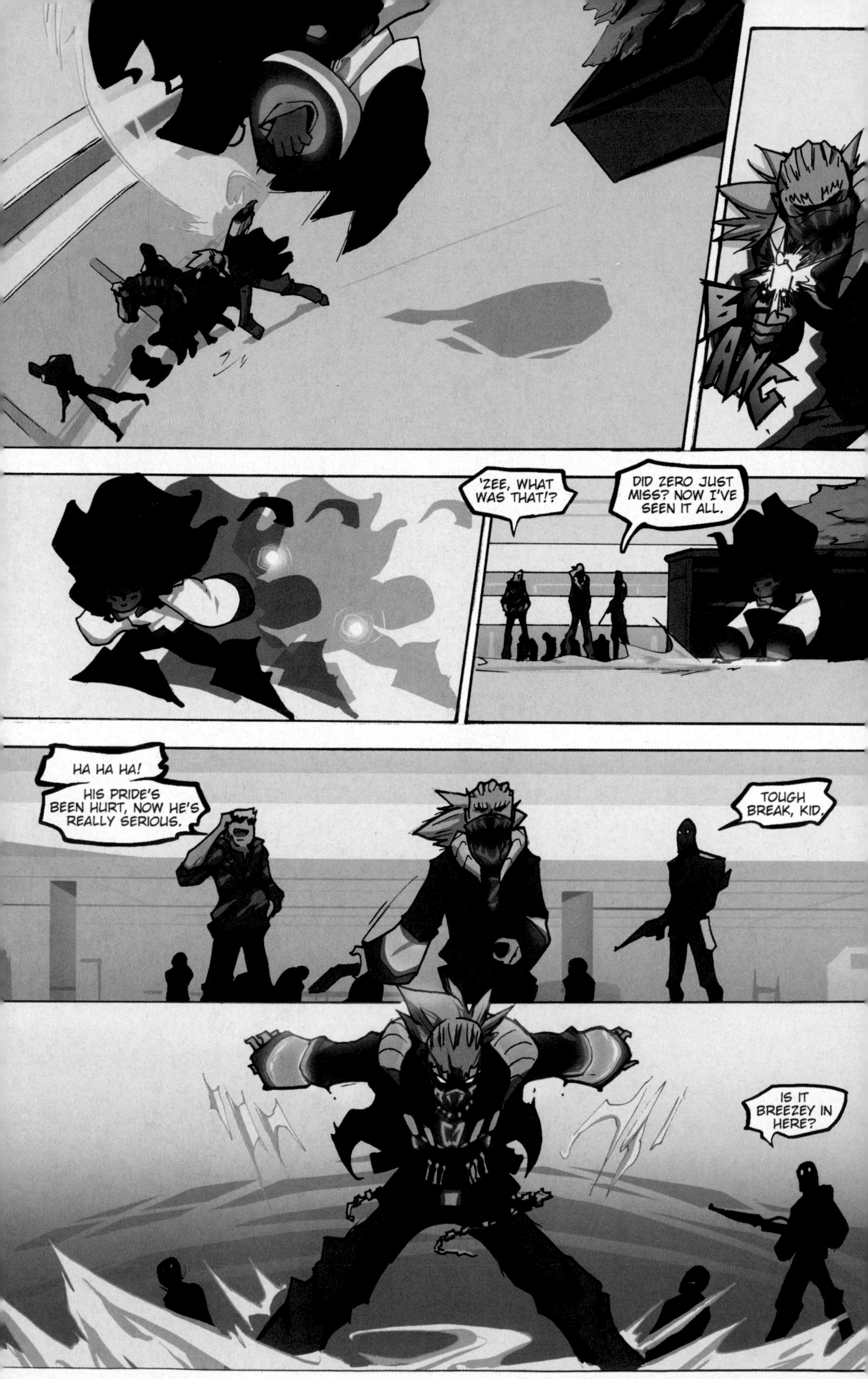
BANG
'ZEE, WHAT WAS THAT!?
DID ZERO JUST MISS? NOW I'VE SEEN IT ALL.
HA HA HA!
HIS PRIDE'S BEEN HURT, NOW HE'S REALLY SERIOUS.
TOUGH BREAK, KID.
IS IT BREEZEY IN HERE?

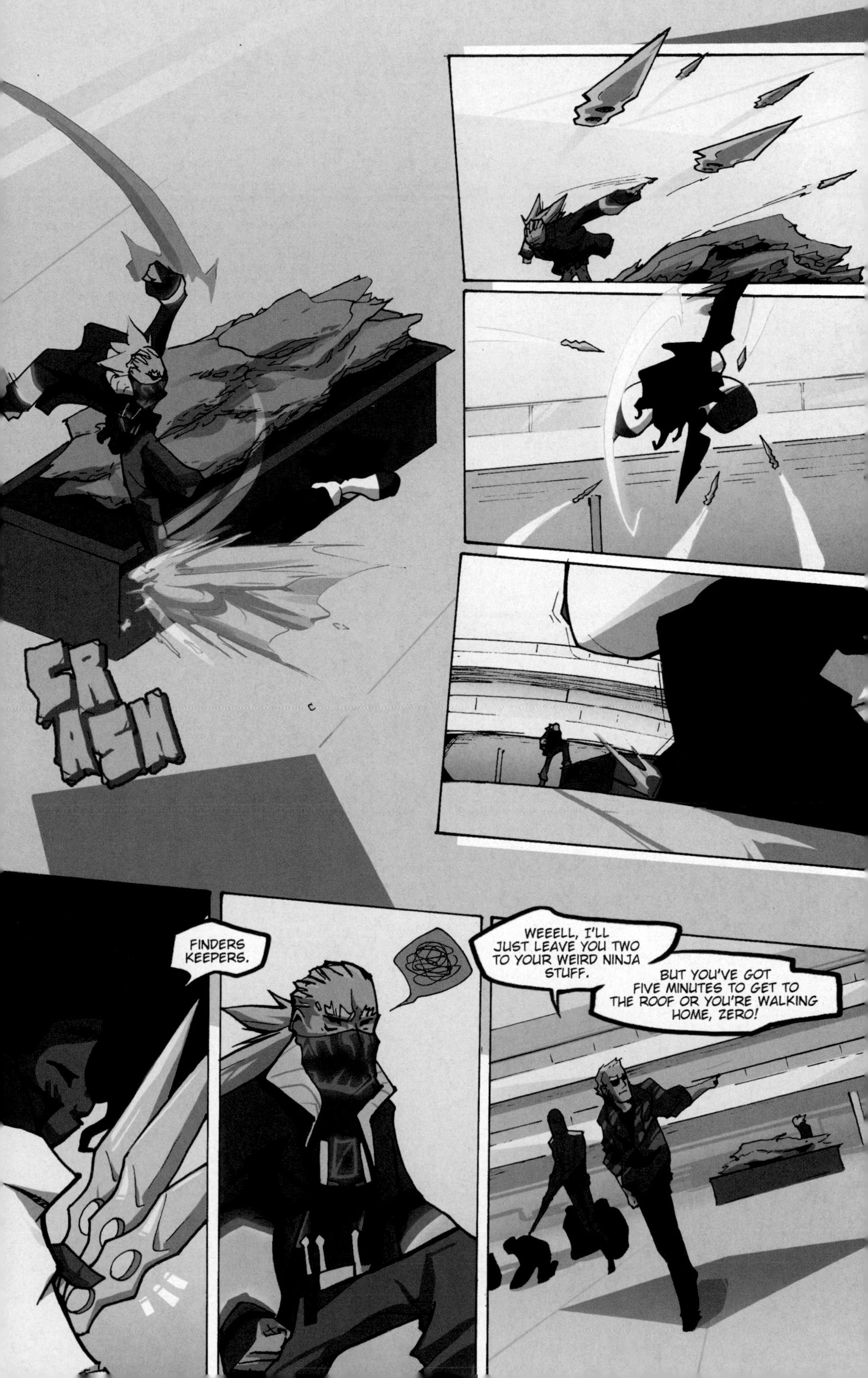
CRASH
FINDERS KEEPERS.
WEEELL, I'LL JUST LEAVE YOU TWO TO YOUR WEIRD NINJA STUFF.
BUT YOU'VE GOT FIVE MINUTES TO GET TO THE ROOF OR YOU'RE WALKING HOME, ZERO!

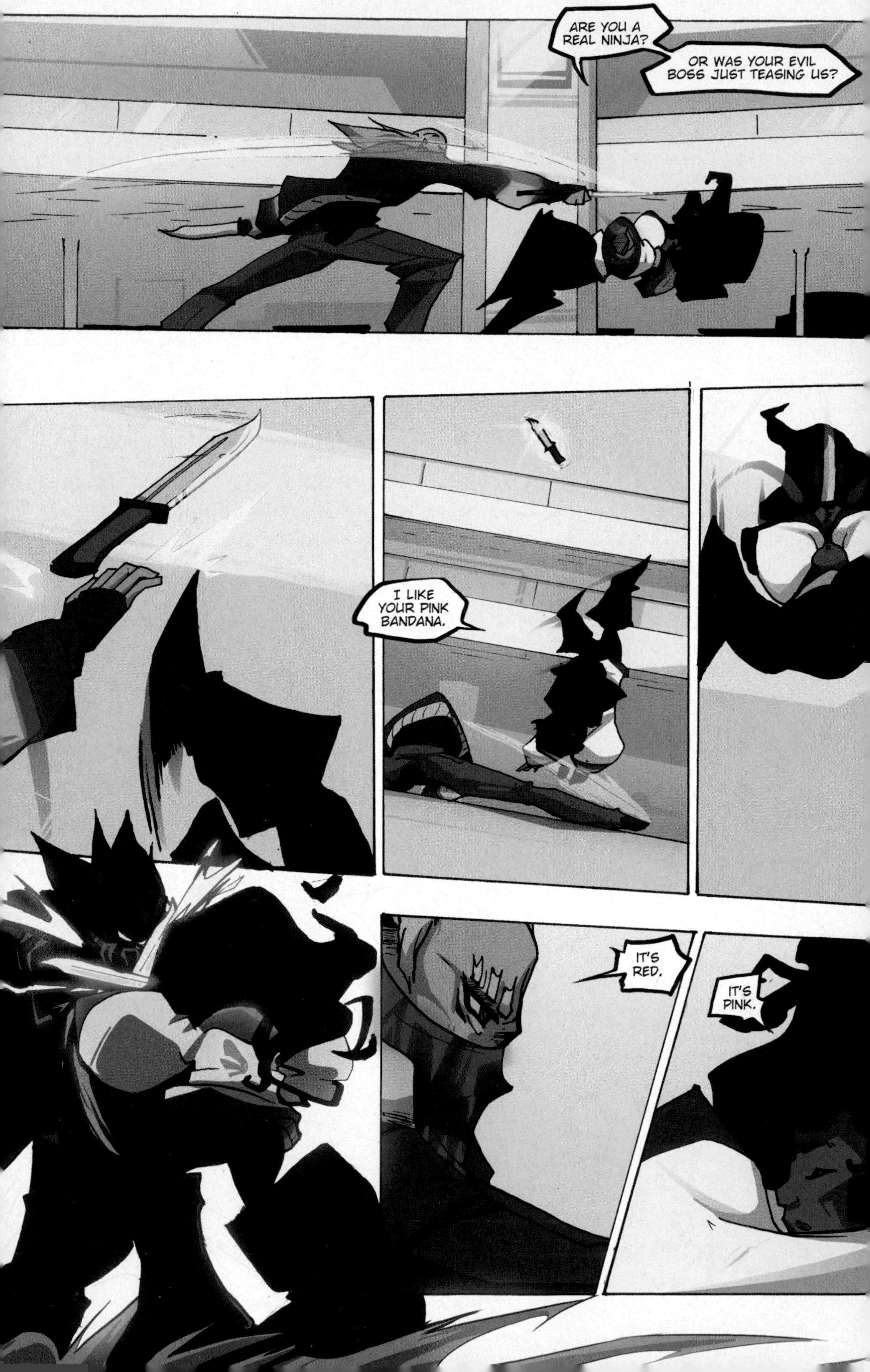
ARE YOU A REAL NINJA?
OR WAS YOUR EVIL BOSS JUST TEASING US?
I LIKE YOUR PINK BANDANA.
IT'S RED.
IT'S PINK.

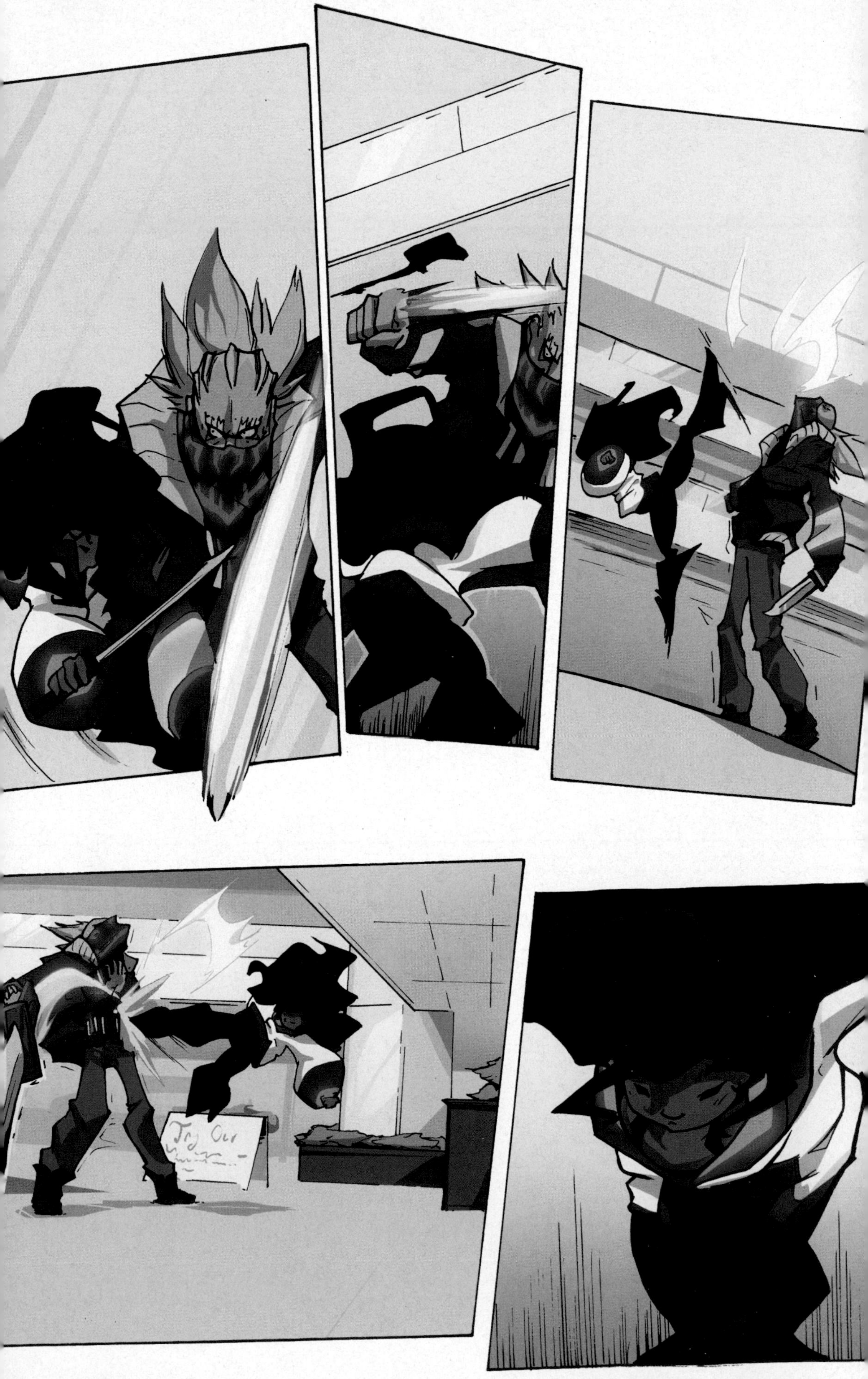
Try Our

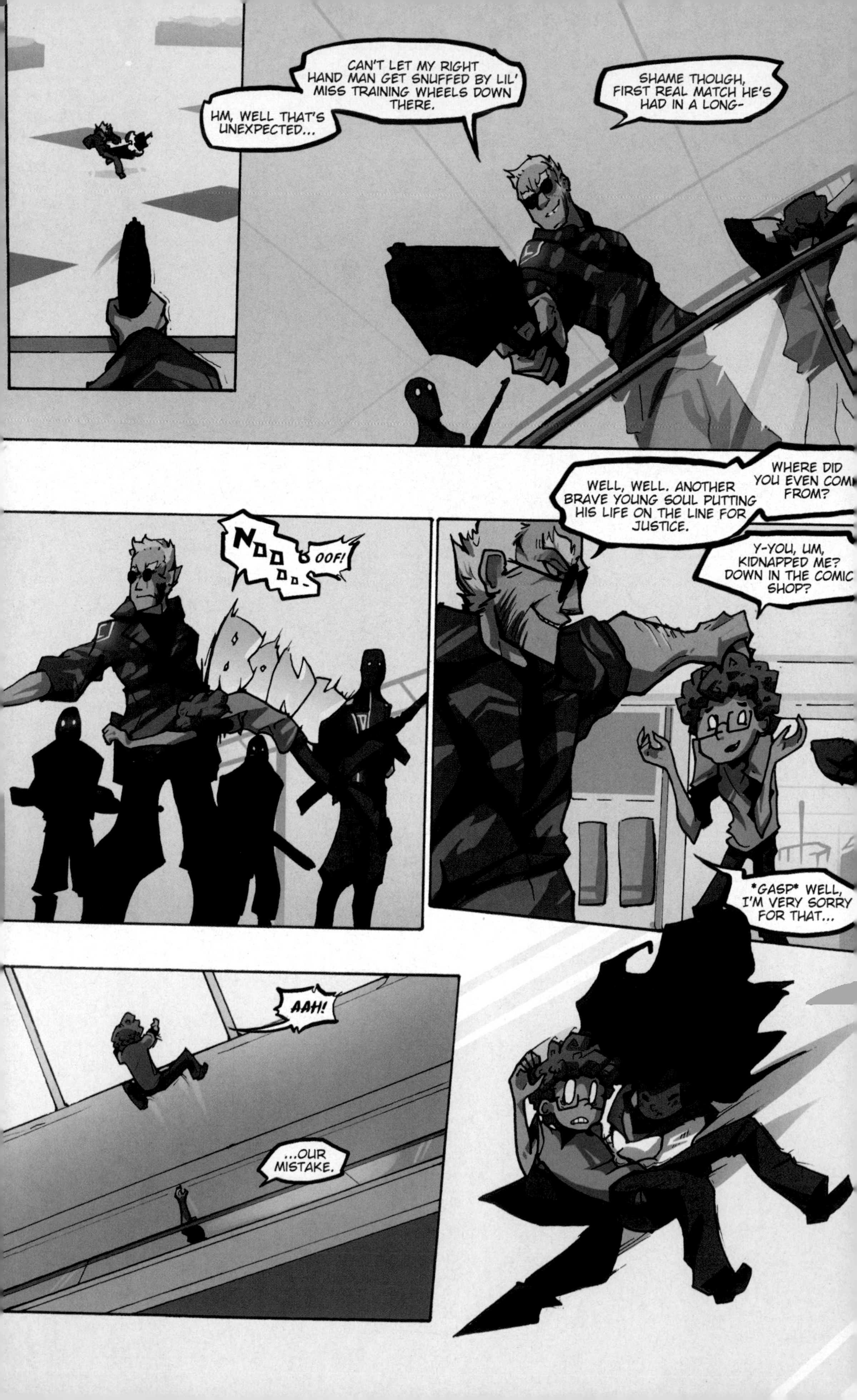
HM, WELL THAT'S UNEXPECTED...
CAN'T LET MY RIGHT HAND MAN GET SNUFFED BY LIL' MISS TRAINING WHEELS DOWN THERE.
SHAME THOUGH, FIRST REAL MATCH HE'S HAD IN A LONG-
NOOOO-
OOF!
WELL, WELL. ANOTHER BRAVE YOUNG SOUL PUTTING HIS LIFE ON THE LINE FOR JUSTICE.
WHERE DID YOU EVEN COME FROM?
Y-YOU, UM, KIDNAPPED ME? DOWN IN THE COMIC SHOP?
GASP WELL, I'M VERY SORRY FOR THAT...
AAH!
...OUR MISTAKE.

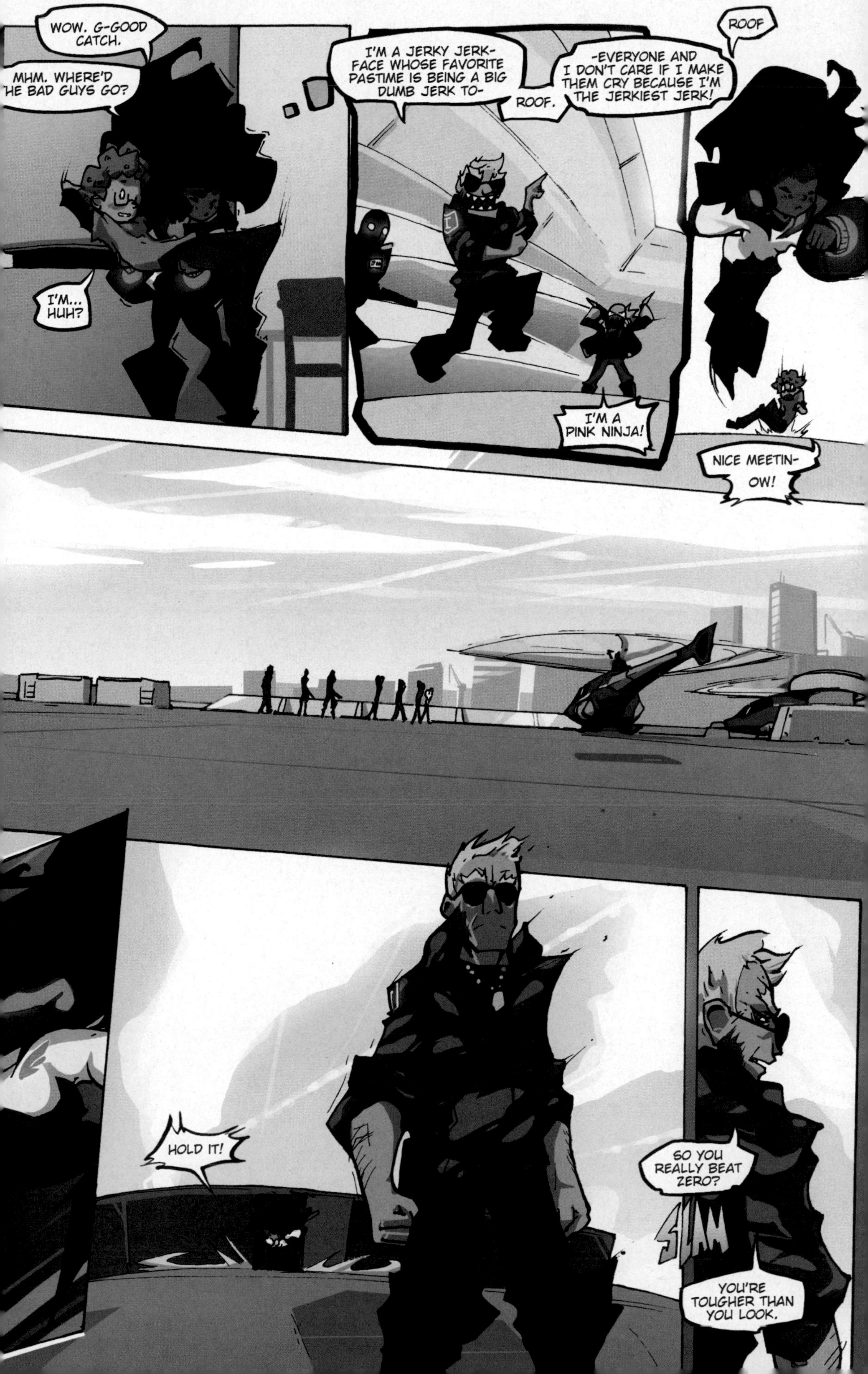
WOW. G-GOOD CATCH.
MHM. WHERE'D THE BAD GUYS GO?
I'M... HUH?
I'M A JERKY JERK-FACE WHOSE FAVORITE PASTIME IS BEING A BIG DUMB JERK TO-
ROOF.
-EVERYONE AND I DON'T CARE IF I MAKE THEM CRY BECAUSE I'M THE JERKIEST JERK!
I'M A PINK NINJA!
ROOF
NICE MEETIN-
OW!
HOLD IT!
SO YOU REALLY BEAT ZERO?
SLAM
YOU'RE TOUGHER THAN YOU LOOK.

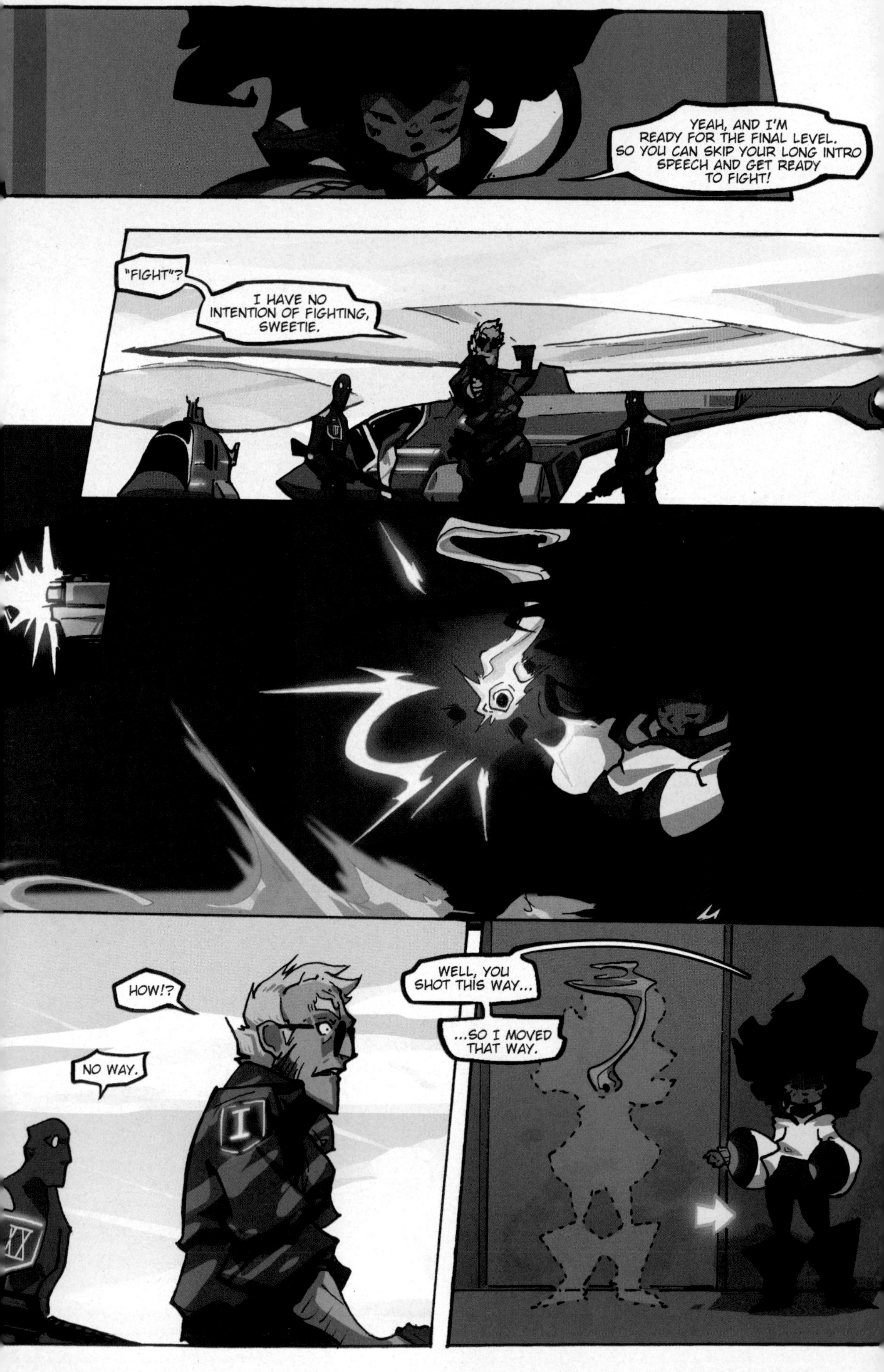

YEAH, AND I'M READY FOR THE FINAL LEVEL. SO YOU CAN SKIP YOUR LONG INTRO SPEECH AND GET READY TO FIGHT!
"FIGHT"?
I HAVE NO INTENTION OF FIGHTING, SWEETIE.
HOW!?
NO WAY.
WELL, YOU SHOT THIS WAY...
...SO I MOVED THAT WAY.

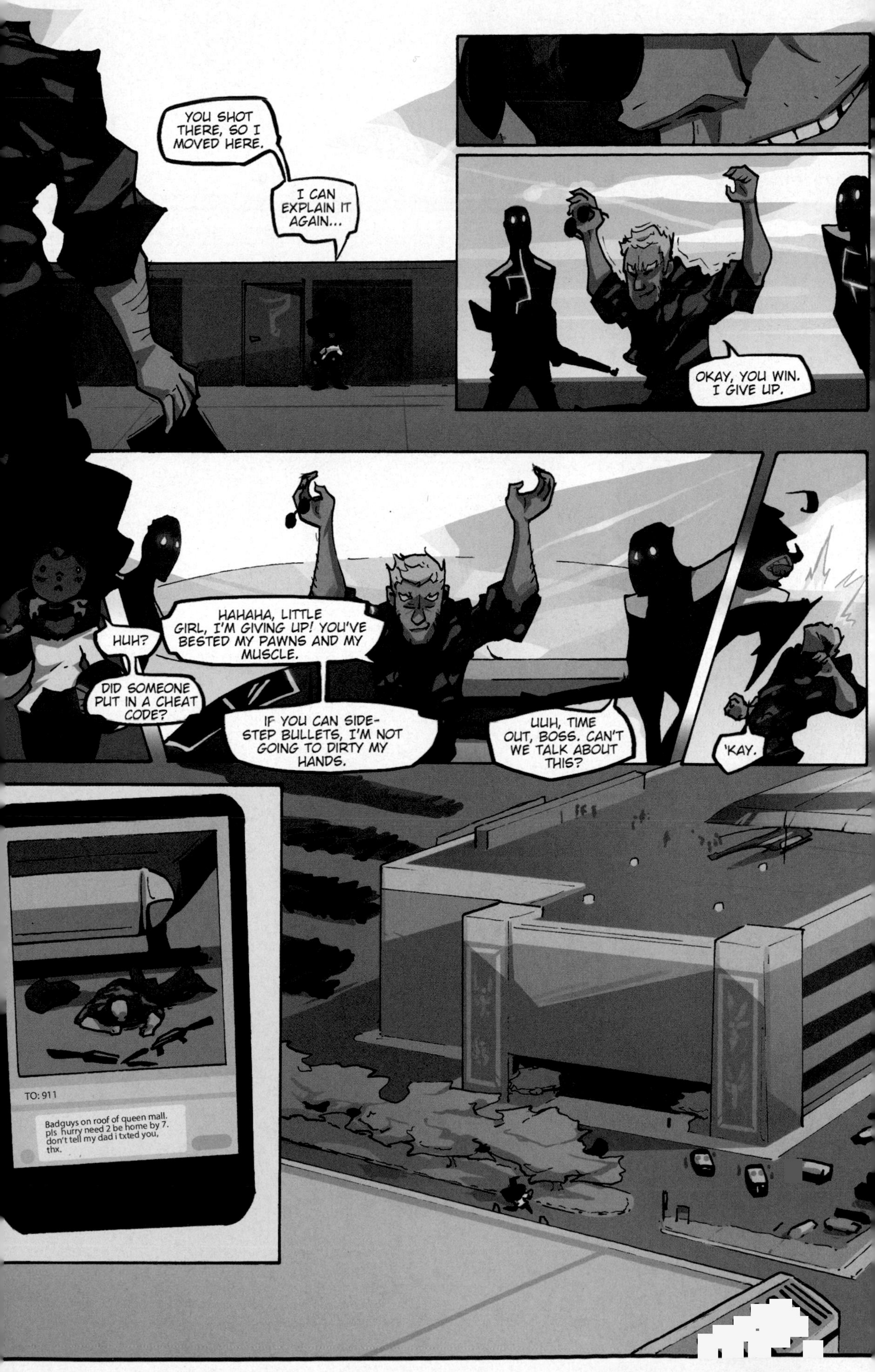
YOU SHOT THERE, SO I MOVED HERE.
I CAN EXPLAIN IT AGAIN...
OKAY, YOU WIN. I GIVE UP.
HUH?
DID SOMEONE PUT IN A CHEAT CODE?
HAHAHA, LITTLE GIRL, I'M GIVING UP! YOU'VE BESTED MY PAWNS AND MY MUSCLE.
IF YOU CAN SIDE-STEP BULLETS, I'M NOT GOING TO DIRTY MY HANDS.
UUH, TIME OUT, BOSS. CAN'T WE TALK ABOUT THIS?
'KAY.
TO: 911
Badguys on roof of queen mall. pls hurry need 2 be home by 7. don't tell my dad i txted you, thx.

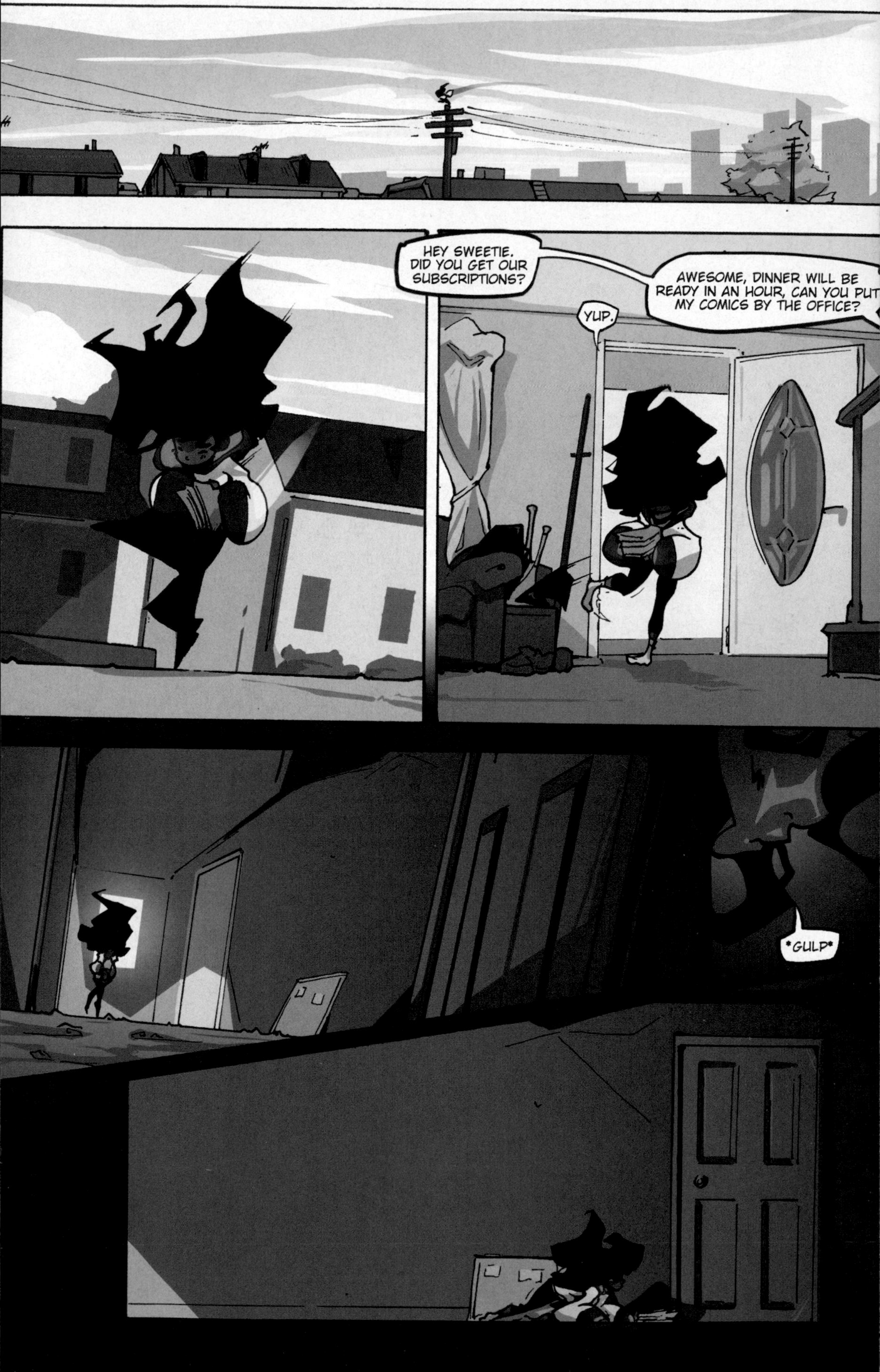
HEY SWEETIE.
DID YOU GET OUR SUBSCRIPTIONS?
YUP.
AWESOME, DINNER WILL BE READY IN AN HOUR, CAN YOU PUT MY COMICS BY THE OFFICE?
GULP

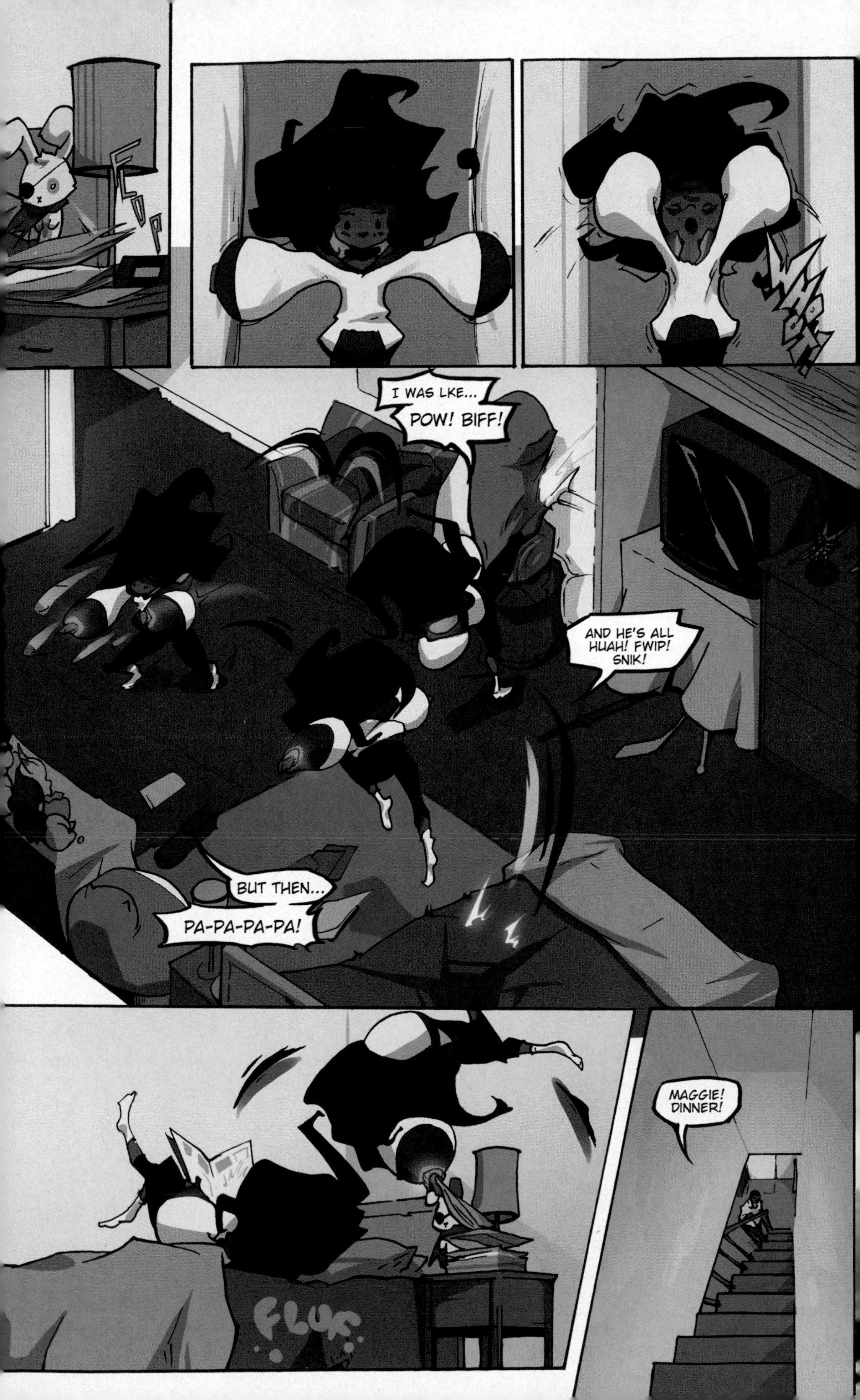
FLOP
I WAS LKE...
POW! BIFF!
AND HE'S ALL HUAH! FWIP! SNIK!
BUT THEN...
PA-PA-PA-PA!
MAGGIE! DINNER!
FLUF

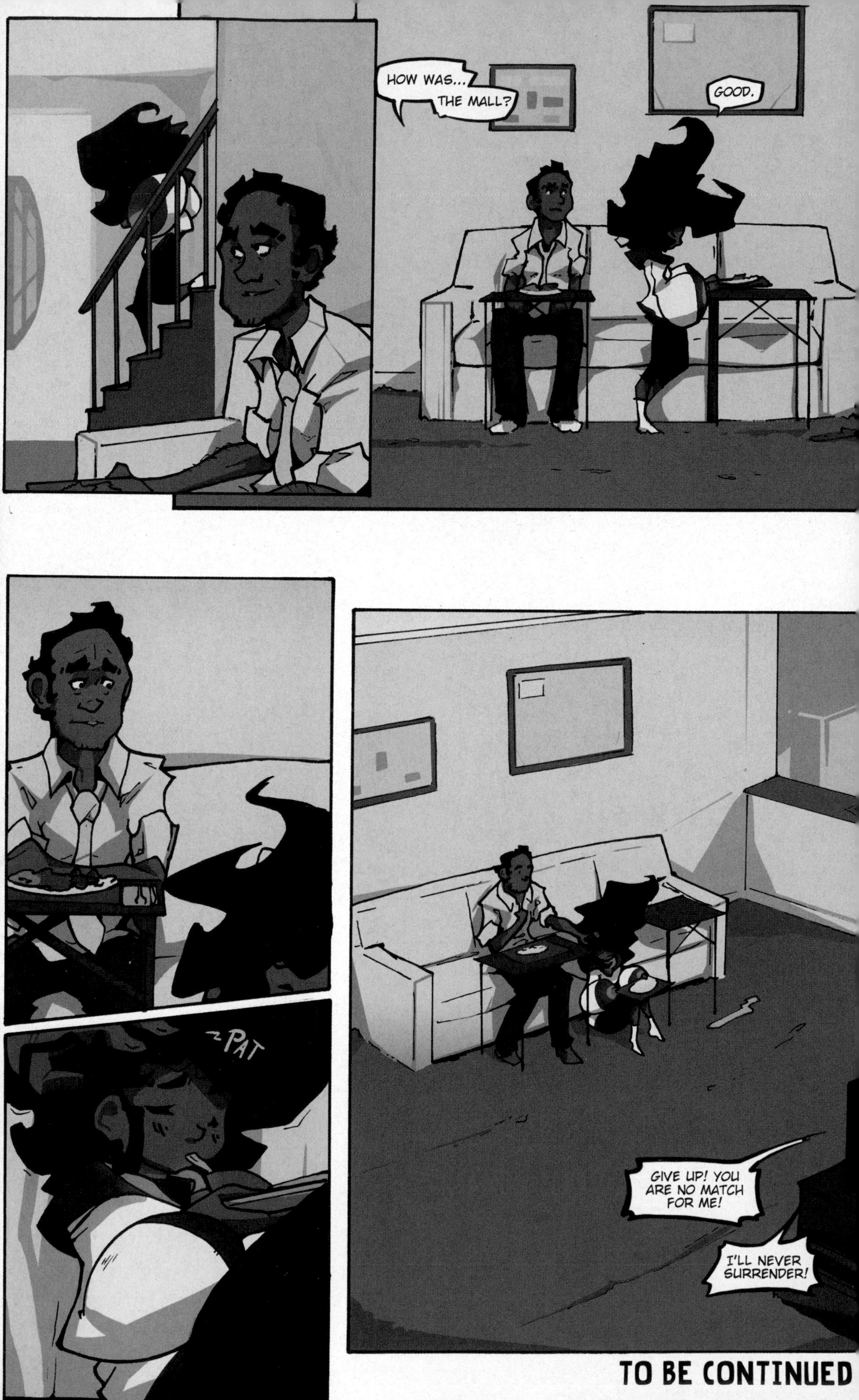
HOW WAS... THE MALL?
GOOD.
PAT
GIVE UP! YOU ARE NO MATCH FOR ME!
I'LL NEVER SURRENDER!

TO BE CONTINUED

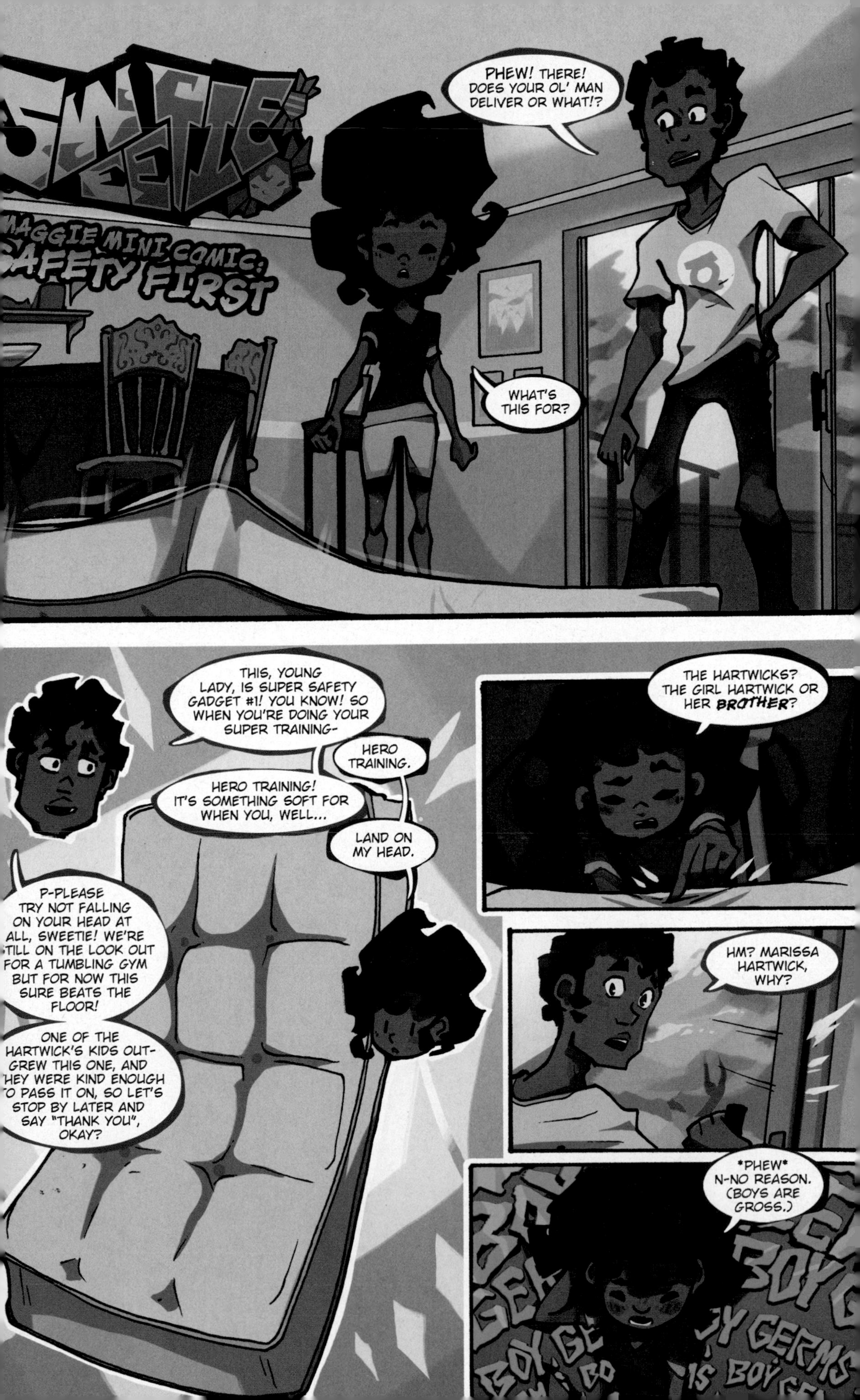
SWEETIE
MAGGIE MINI COMIC:
SAFETY FIRST
PHEW! THERE! DOES YOUR OL' MAN DELIVER OR WHAT!?
WHAT'S THIS FOR?
THIS, YOUNG LADY, IS SUPER SAFETY GADGET #1! YOU KNOW! SO WHEN YOU'RE DOING YOUR SUPER TRAINING-
HERO TRAINING.
HERO TRAINING! IT'S SOMETHING SOFT FOR WHEN YOU, WELL...
LAND ON MY HEAD.
P-PLEASE TRY NOT FALLING ON YOUR HEAD AT ALL, SWEETIE! WE'RE STILL ON THE LOOK OUT FOR A TUMBLING GYM BUT FOR NOW THIS SURE BEATS THE FLOOR!
ONE OF THE HARTWICK'S KIDS OUT-GREW THIS ONE, AND THEY WERE KIND ENOUGH TO PASS IT ON, SO LET'S STOP BY LATER AND SAY "THANK YOU", OKAY?
THE HARTWICKS? THE GIRL HARTWICK OR HER BROTHER?
HM? MARISSA HARTWICK, WHY?
PHEW N-NO REASON. (BOYS ARE GROSS.)
BOY GERMS

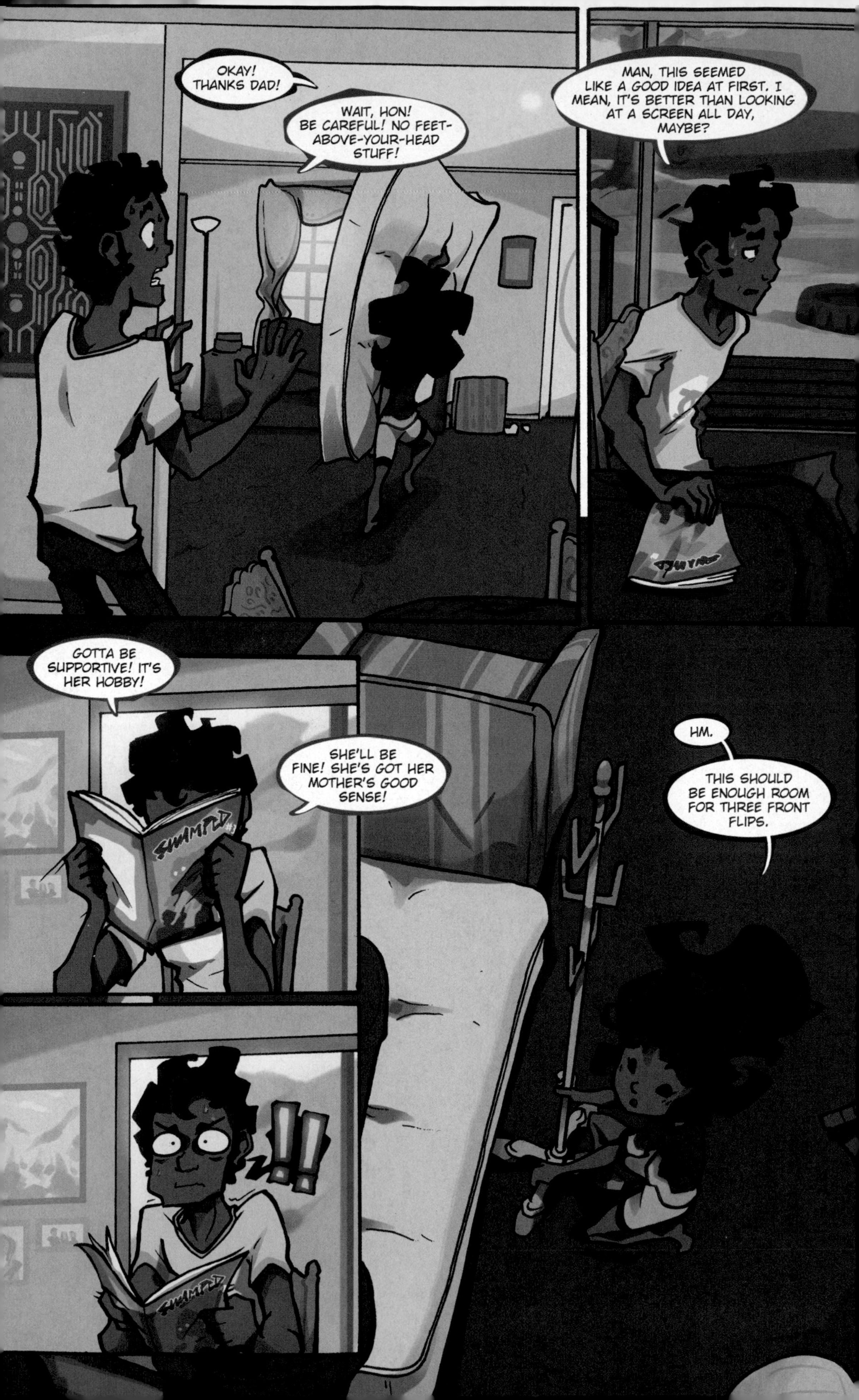
OKAY! THANKS DAD!
WAIT, HON! BE CAREFUL! NO FEET-ABOVE-YOUR-HEAD STUFF!
MAN, THIS SEEMED LIKE A GOOD IDEA AT FIRST. I MEAN, IT'S BETTER THAN LOOKING AT A SCREEN ALL DAY, MAYBE?
GOTTA BE SUPPORTIVE! IT'S HER HOBBY!
SHE'LL BE FINE! SHE'S GOT HER MOTHER'S GOOD SENSE!
SWAMPED
HM.
THIS SHOULD BE ENOUGH ROOM FOR THREE FRONT FLIPS.
!!
SWAMPED

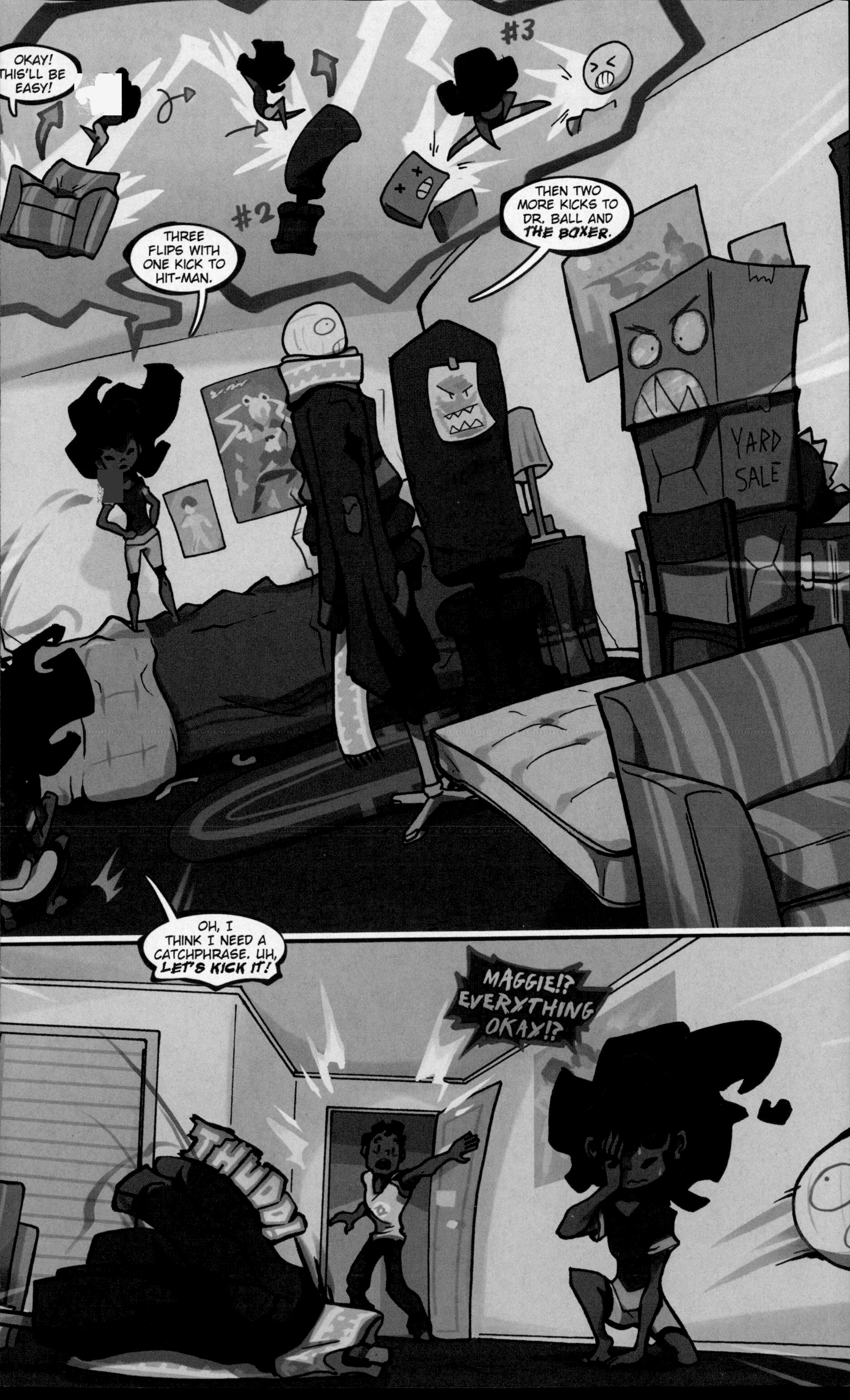

OKAY! THIS'LL BE EASY!
#2
#3
THREE FLIPS WITH ONE KICK TO HIT-MAN.
THEN TWO MORE KICKS TO DR. BALL AND **THE BOXER.**
YARD SALE
OH, I THINK I NEED A CATCHPHRASE. UH, **LET'S KICK IT!**
MAGGIE!? EVERYTHING OKAY!?
THUD!

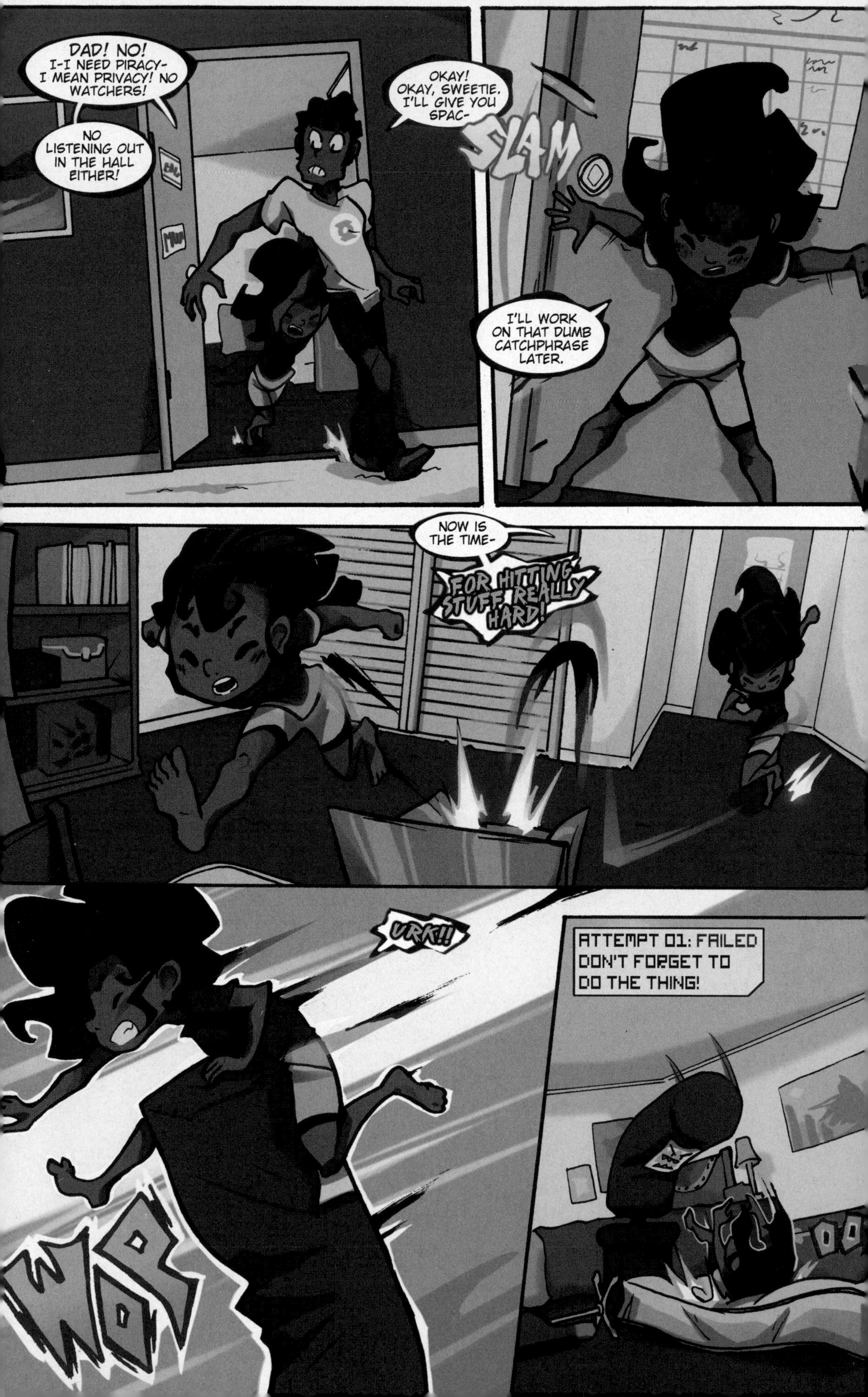
DAD! NO! I-I NEED PIRACY- I MEAN PRIVACY! NO WATCHERS!
NO LISTENING OUT IN THE HALL EITHER!
OKAY! OKAY, SWEETIE. I'LL GIVE YOU SPAC-
SLAM
I'LL WORK ON THAT DUMB CATCHPHRASE LATER.
NOW IS THE TIME-
FOR HITTING STUFF REALLY HARD!
URK!!
ATTEMPT 01: FAILED
DON'T FORGET TO DO THE THING!
WOP

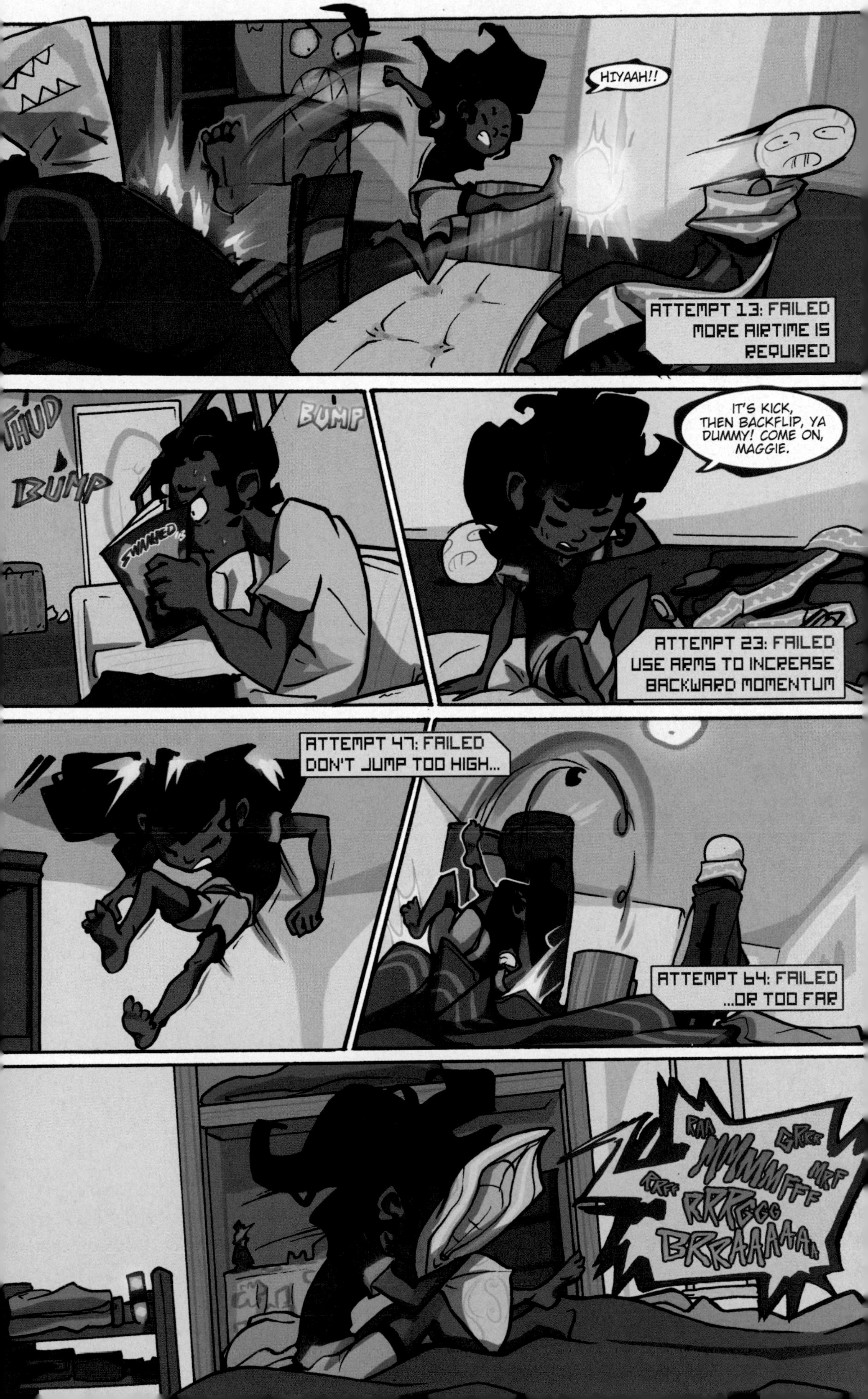
HIYAAH!!
ATTEMPT 13: FAILED
MORE AIRTIME IS
REQUIRED
THUD
BUMP
BUMP
SWAMPED
IT'S KICK, THEN BACKFLIP, YA DUMMY! COME ON, MAGGIE.
ATTEMPT 23: FAILED
USE ARMS TO INCREASE
BACKWARD MOMENTUM
ATTEMPT 47: FAILED
DON'T JUMP TOO HIGH...
ATTEMPT 64: FAILED
...OR TOO FAR
MMMMMFFF
MRF
RRRGGG
BRRAAAAA

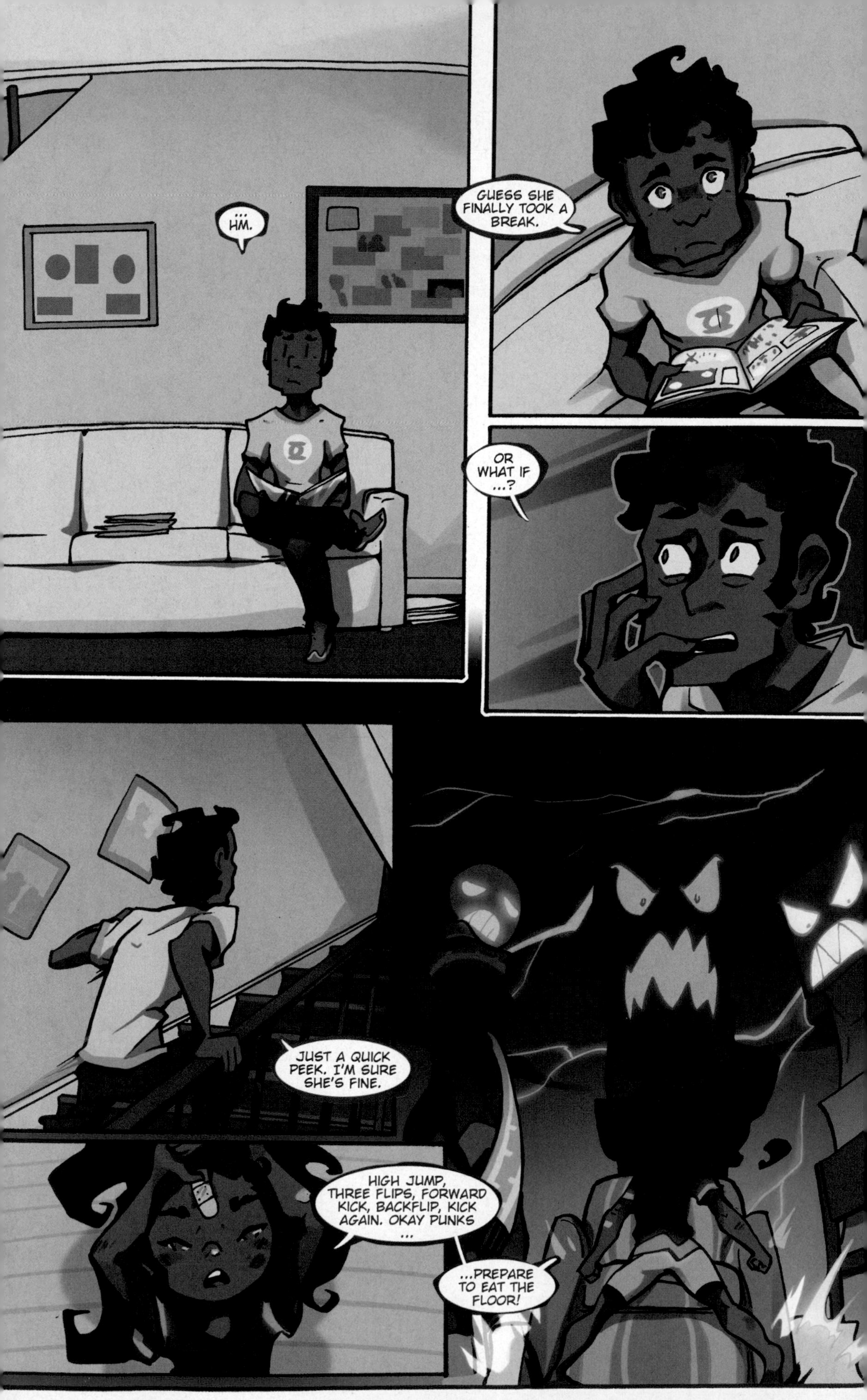
... HM.
GUESS SHE FINALLY TOOK A BREAK.
OR WHAT IF ...?
JUST A QUICK PEEK. I'M SURE SHE'S FINE.
HIGH JUMP, THREE FLIPS, FORWARD KICK, BACKFLIP, KICK AGAIN. OKAY PUNKS ...
...PREPARE TO EAT THE FLOOR!

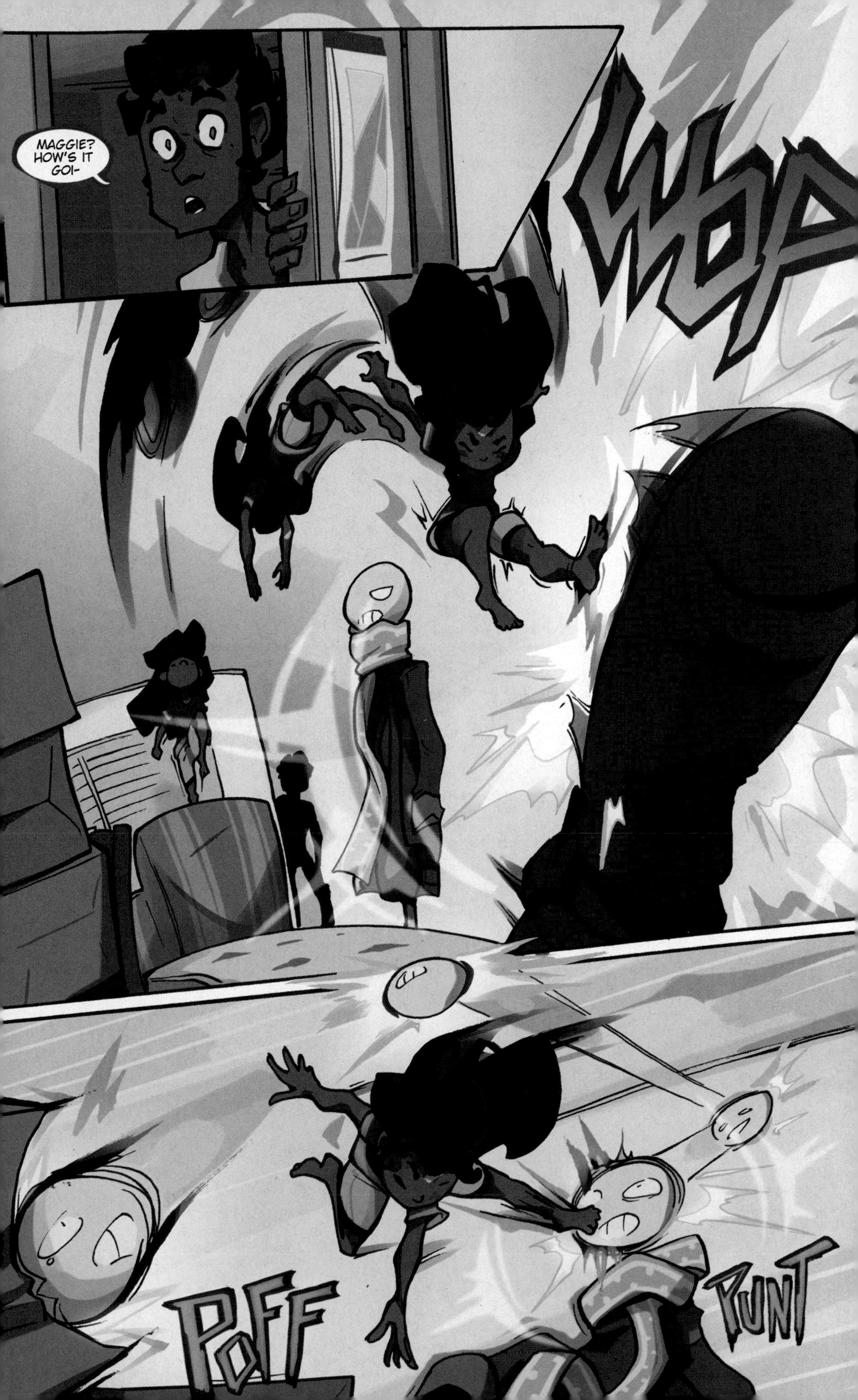
MAGGIE? HOW'S IT GOI-
WOP
POFF
PUNT

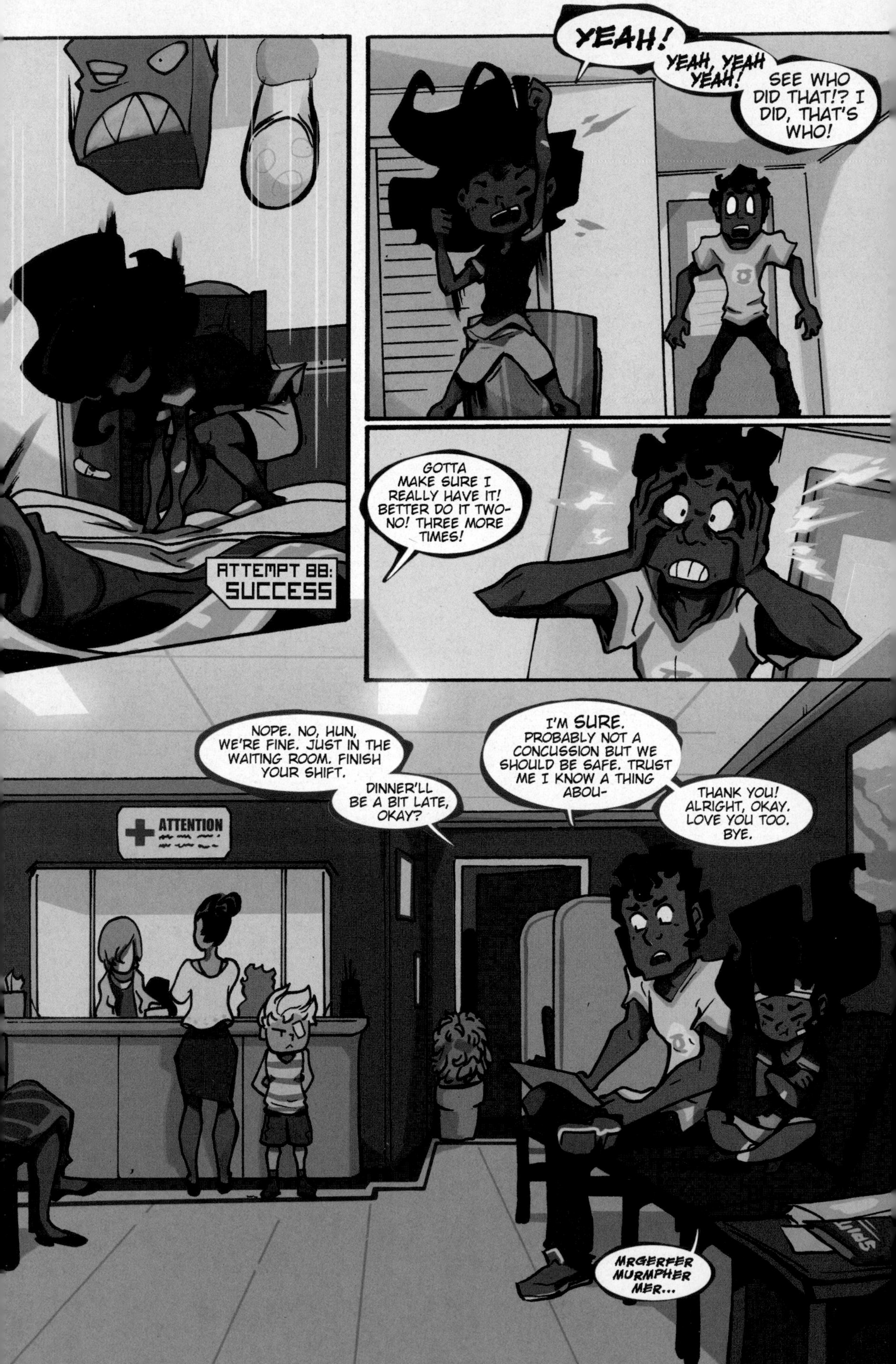
ATTEMPT 88: SUCCESS
YEAH!
YEAH, YEAH YEAH!
SEE WHO DID THAT!? I DID, THAT'S WHO!
GOTTA MAKE SURE I REALLY HAVE IT! BETTER DO IT TWO- NO! THREE MORE TIMES!
NOPE. NO, HUN, WE'RE FINE. JUST IN THE WAITING ROOM. FINISH YOUR SHIFT.
DINNER'LL BE A BIT LATE, OKAY?
I'M SURE. PROBABLY NOT A CONCUSSION BUT WE SHOULD BE SAFE. TRUST ME I KNOW A THING ABOU-
THANK YOU! ALRIGHT, OKAY. LOVE YOU TOO. BYE.
ATTENTION
MRGERFER MURMPHER MER...

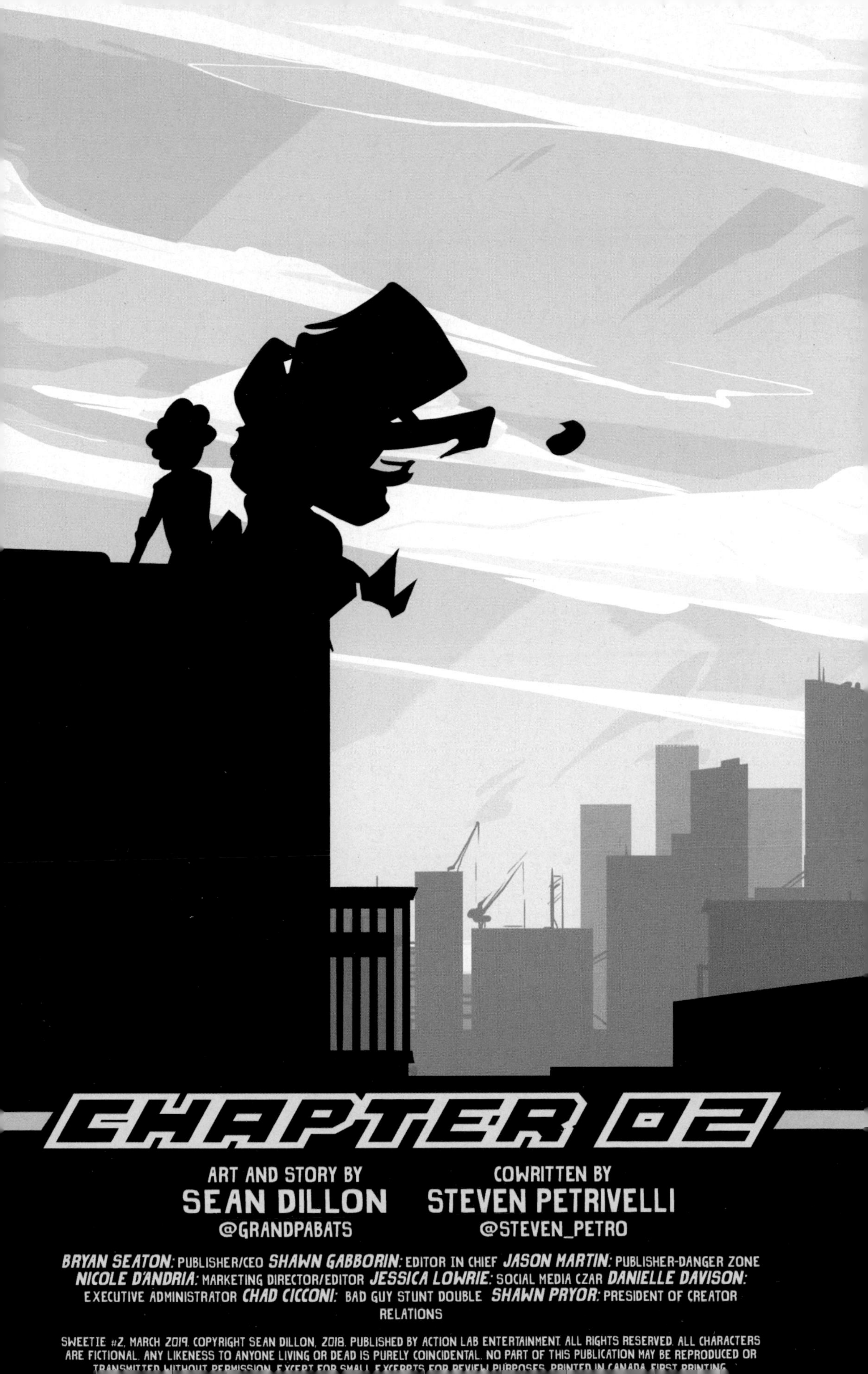

CHAPTER 02

ART AND STORY BY
SEAN DILLON
@GRANDPABATS

COWRITTEN BY
STEVEN PETRIVELLI
@STEVEN_PETRO

BRYAN SEATON: PUBLISHER/CEO ***SHAWN GABBORIN:*** EDITOR IN CHIEF ***JASON MARTIN:*** PUBLISHER-DANGER ZONE ***NICOLE D'ANDRIA:*** MARKETING DIRECTOR/EDITOR ***JESSICA LOWRIE:*** SOCIAL MEDIA CZAR ***DANIELLE DAVISON:*** EXECUTIVE ADMINISTRATOR ***CHAD CICCONI:*** BAD GUY STUNT DOUBLE ***SHAWN PRYOR:*** PRESIDENT OF CREATOR RELATIONS

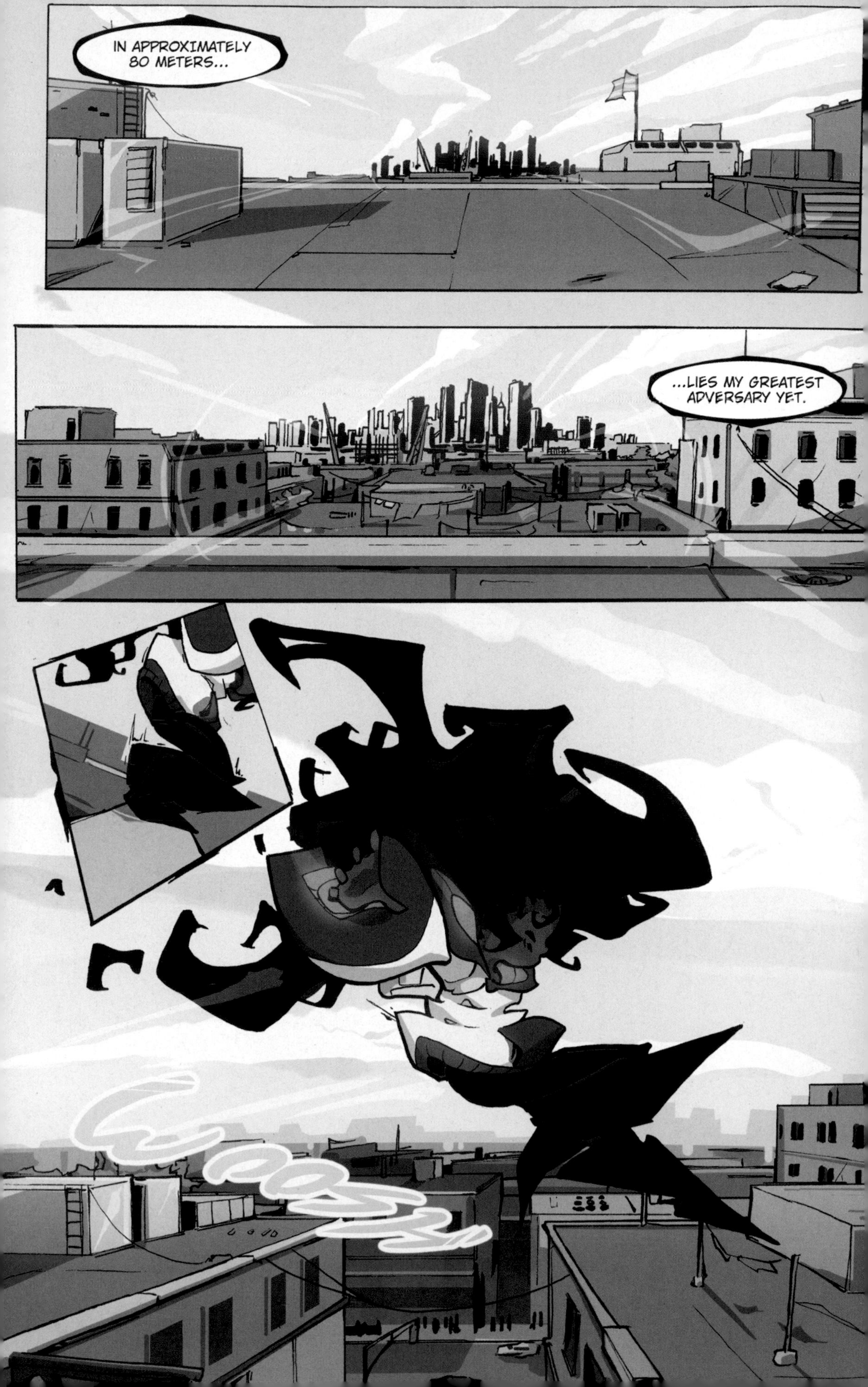
IN APPROXIMATELY 80 METERS...
...LIES MY GREATEST ADVERSARY YET.
WOOSH

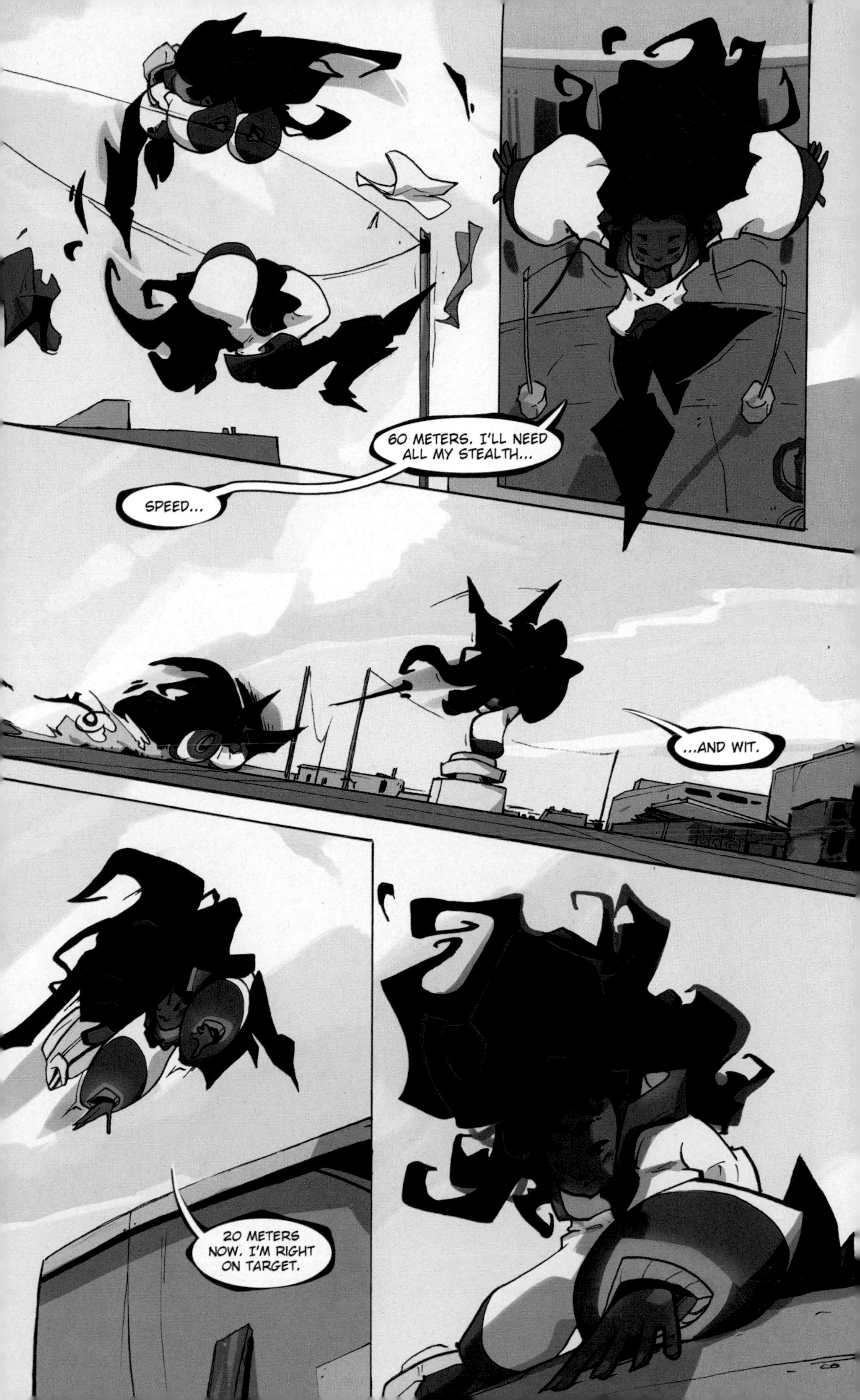
60 METERS. I'LL NEED ALL MY STEALTH...
SPEED...
...AND WIT.
20 METERS NOW. I'M RIGHT ON TARGET.

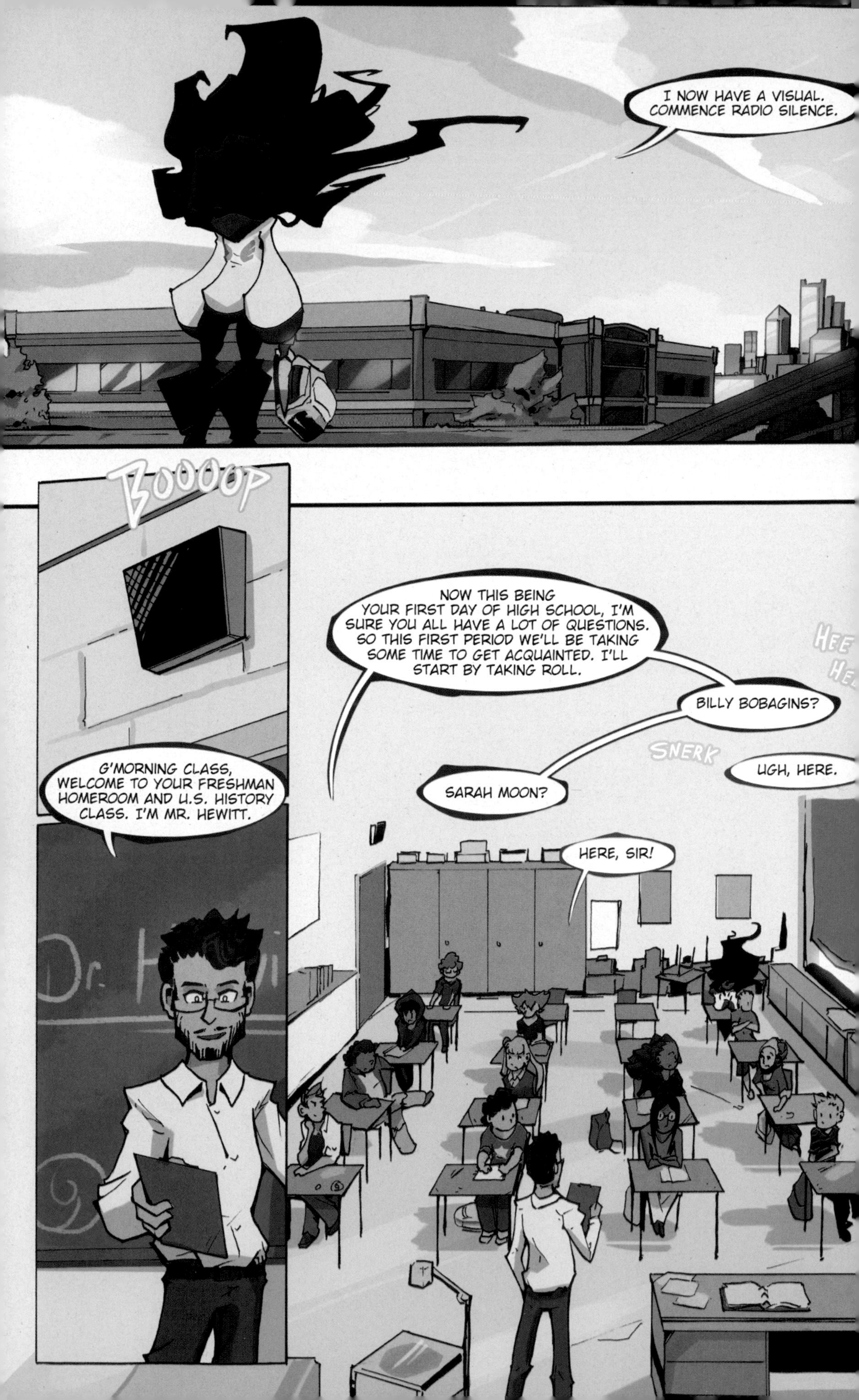
I NOW HAVE A VISUAL. COMMENCE RADIO SILENCE.
BOOOOP
G'MORNING CLASS, WELCOME TO YOUR FRESHMAN HOMEROOM AND U.S. HISTORY CLASS. I'M MR. HEWITT.
NOW THIS BEING YOUR FIRST DAY OF HIGH SCHOOL, I'M SURE YOU ALL HAVE A LOT OF QUESTIONS. SO THIS FIRST PERIOD WE'LL BE TAKING SOME TIME TO GET ACQUAINTED. I'LL START BY TAKING ROLL.
BILLY BOBAGINS?
HEE
SNERK
UGH, HERE.
SARAH MOON?
HERE, SIR!

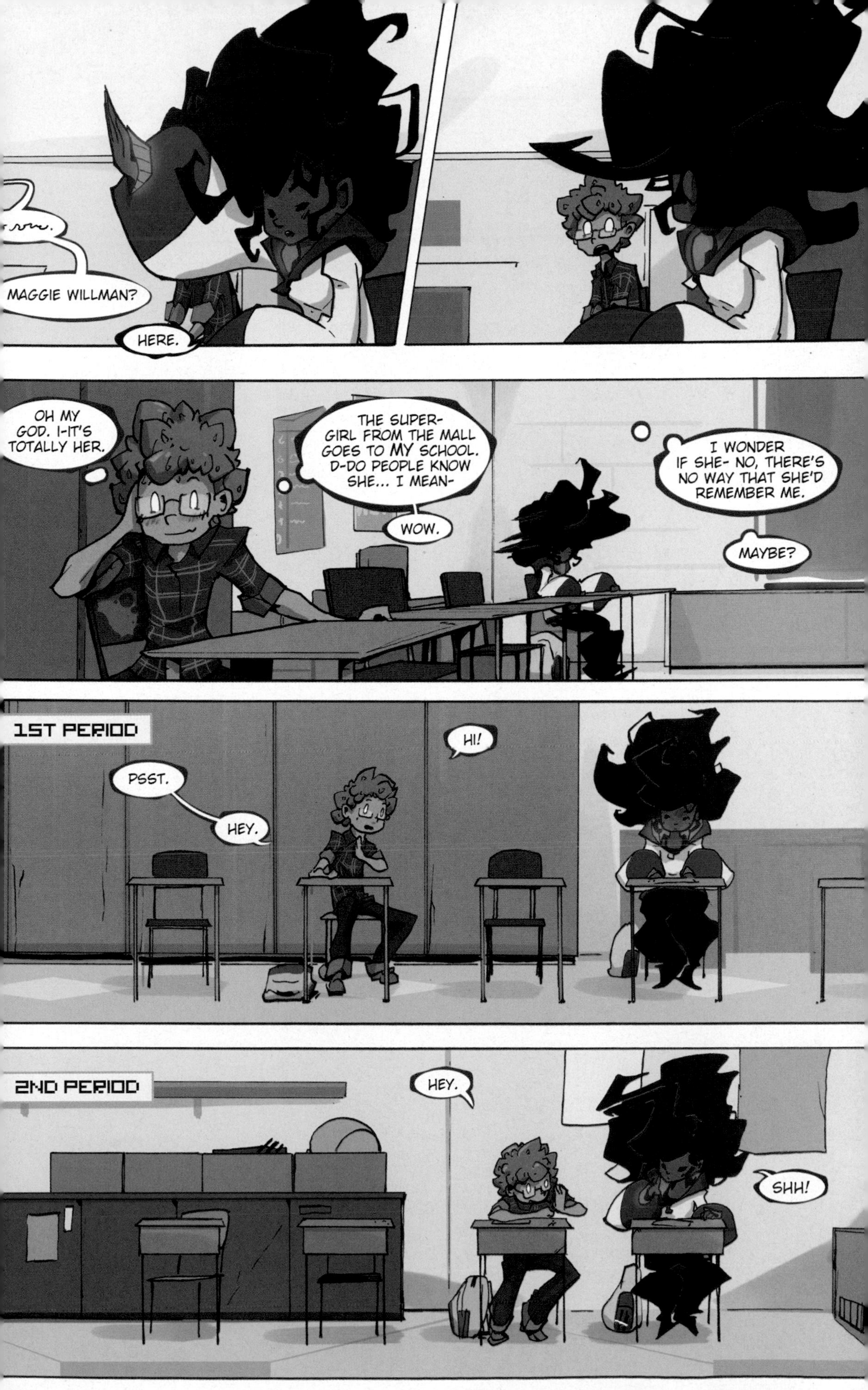
MAGGIE WILLMAN?
HERE.
OH MY GOD. I-IT'S TOTALLY HER.
THE SUPER-GIRL FROM THE MALL GOES TO MY SCHOOL. D-DO PEOPLE KNOW SHE... I MEAN-
WOW.
I WONDER IF SHE- NO, THERE'S NO WAY THAT SHE'D REMEMBER ME.
MAYBE?
1ST PERIOD
PSST.
HEY.
HI!
2ND PERIOD
HEY.
SHH!

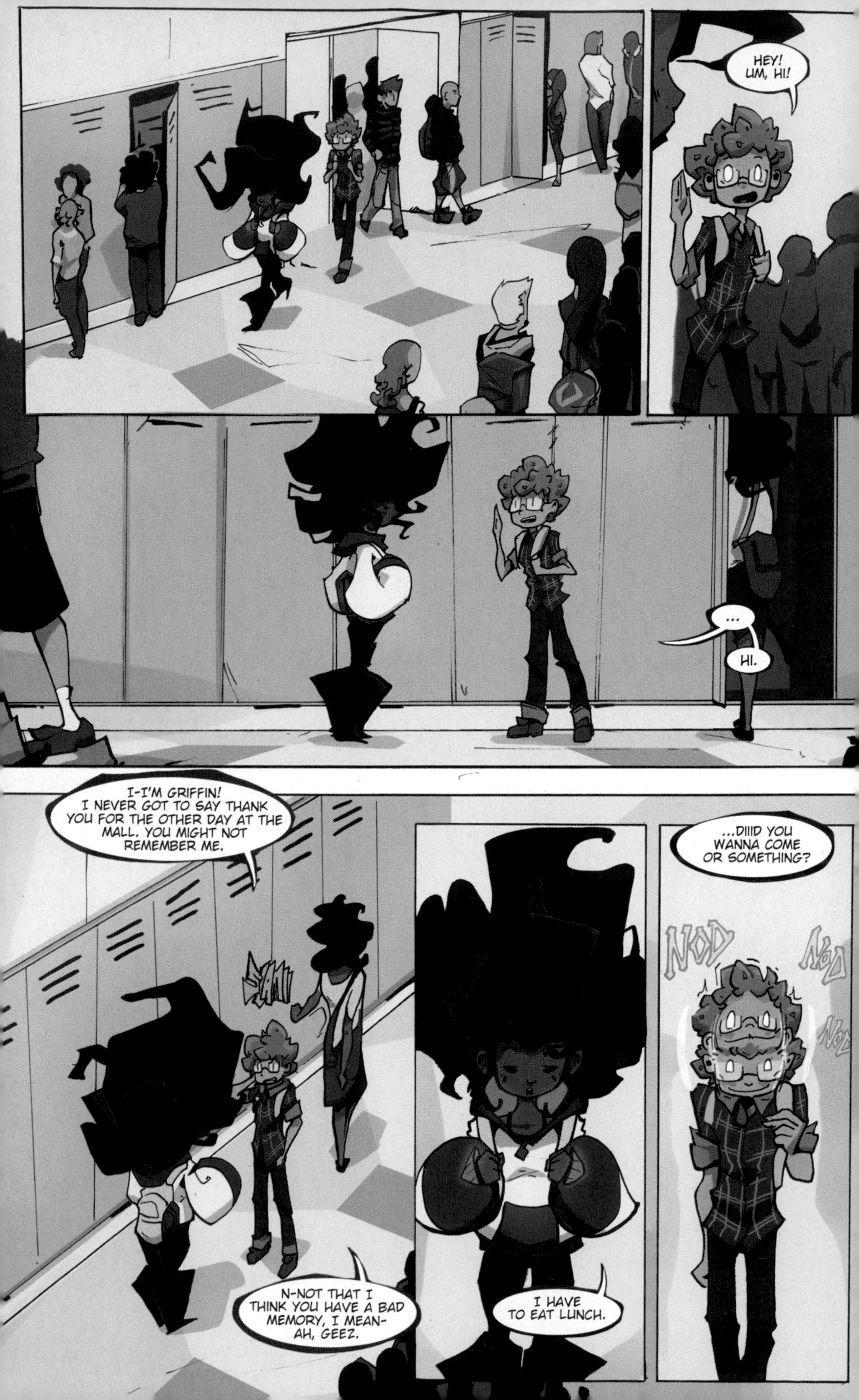
HEY! UM, HI!
...
HI.
I-I'M GRIFFIN! I NEVER GOT TO SAY THANK YOU FOR THE OTHER DAY AT THE MALL. YOU MIGHT NOT REMEMBER ME.
N-NOT THAT I THINK YOU HAVE A BAD MEMORY, I MEAN- AH, GEEZ.
I HAVE TO EAT LUNCH.
...DIIID YOU WANNA COME OR SOMETHING?
NOD
NOD
NOD

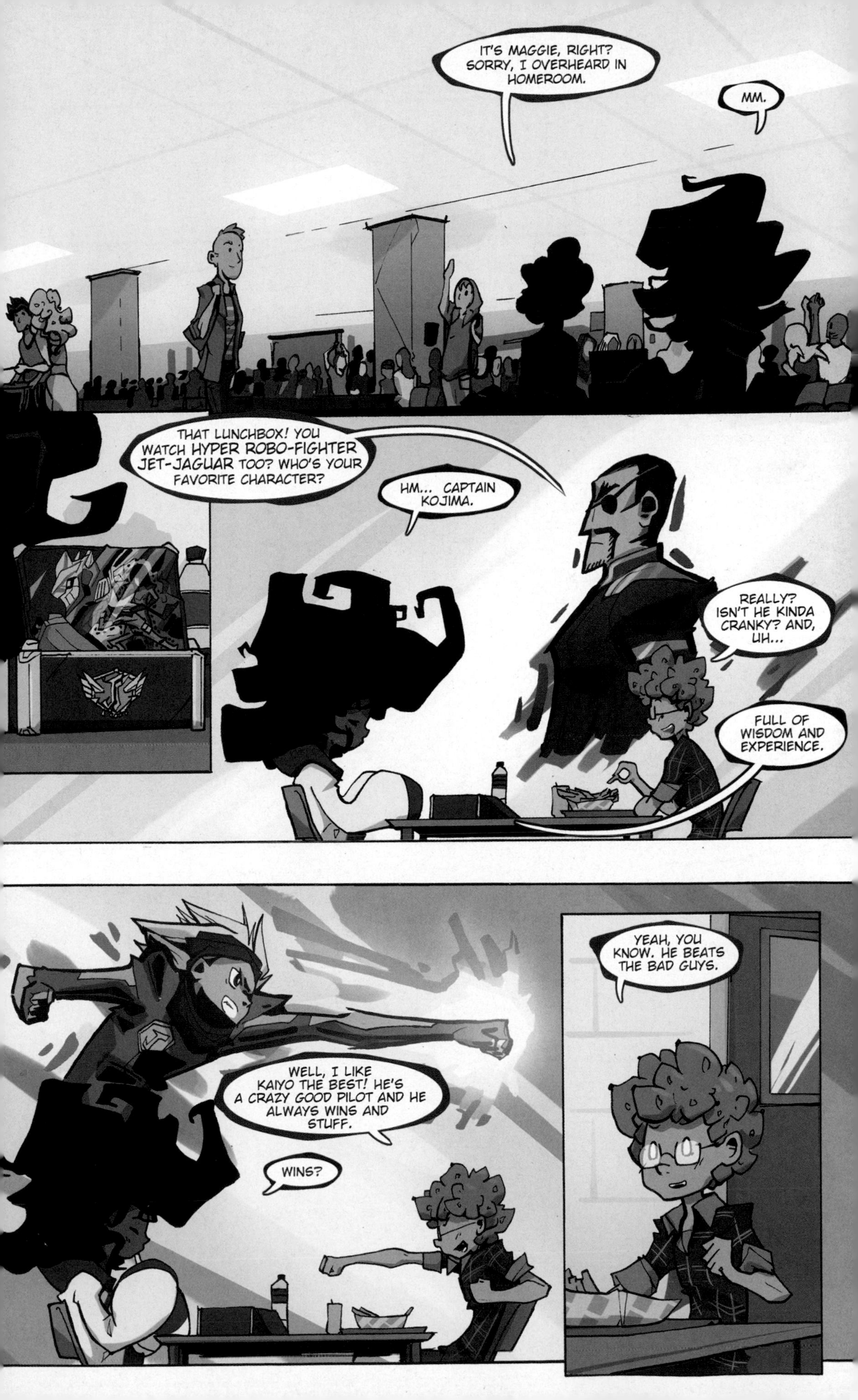
IT'S MAGGIE, RIGHT? SORRY, I OVERHEARD IN HOMEROOM.
MM.
THAT LUNCHBOX! YOU WATCH HYPER ROBO-FIGHTER JET-JAGUAR TOO? WHO'S YOUR FAVORITE CHARACTER?
HM... CAPTAIN KOJIMA.
REALLY? ISN'T HE KINDA CRANKY? AND, UH...
FULL OF WISDOM AND EXPERIENCE.
WELL, I LIKE KAIYO THE BEST! HE'S A CRAZY GOOD PILOT AND HE ALWAYS WINS AND STUFF.
WINS?
YEAH, YOU KNOW. HE BEATS THE BAD GUYS.

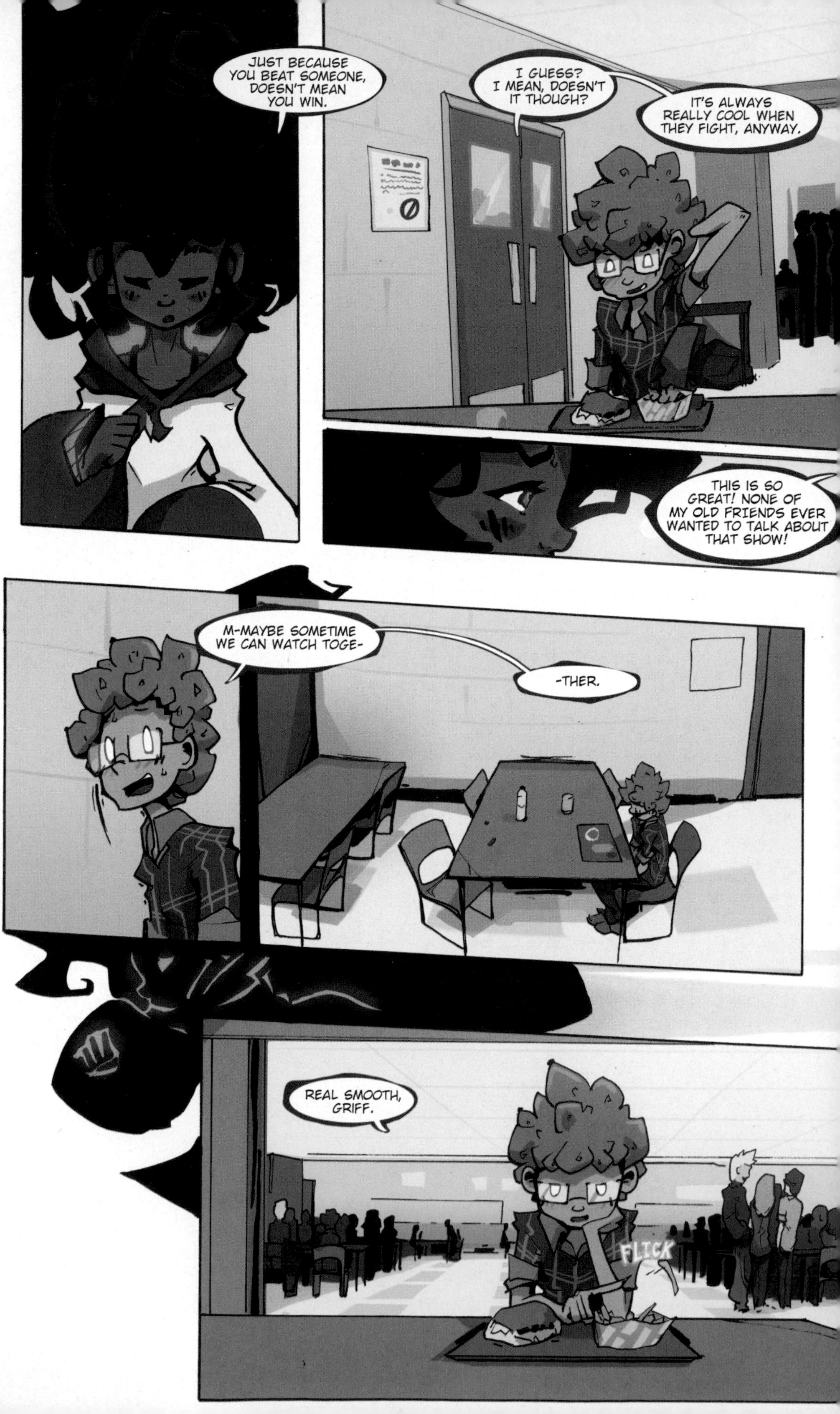
JUST BECAUSE YOU BEAT SOMEONE, DOESN'T MEAN YOU WIN.
I GUESS? I MEAN, DOESN'T IT THOUGH?
IT'S ALWAYS REALLY COOL WHEN THEY FIGHT, ANYWAY.
THIS IS SO GREAT! NONE OF MY OLD FRIENDS EVER WANTED TO TALK ABOUT THAT SHOW!
M-MAYBE SOMETIME WE CAN WATCH TOGE-
-THER.
REAL SMOOTH, GRIFF.
FLICK

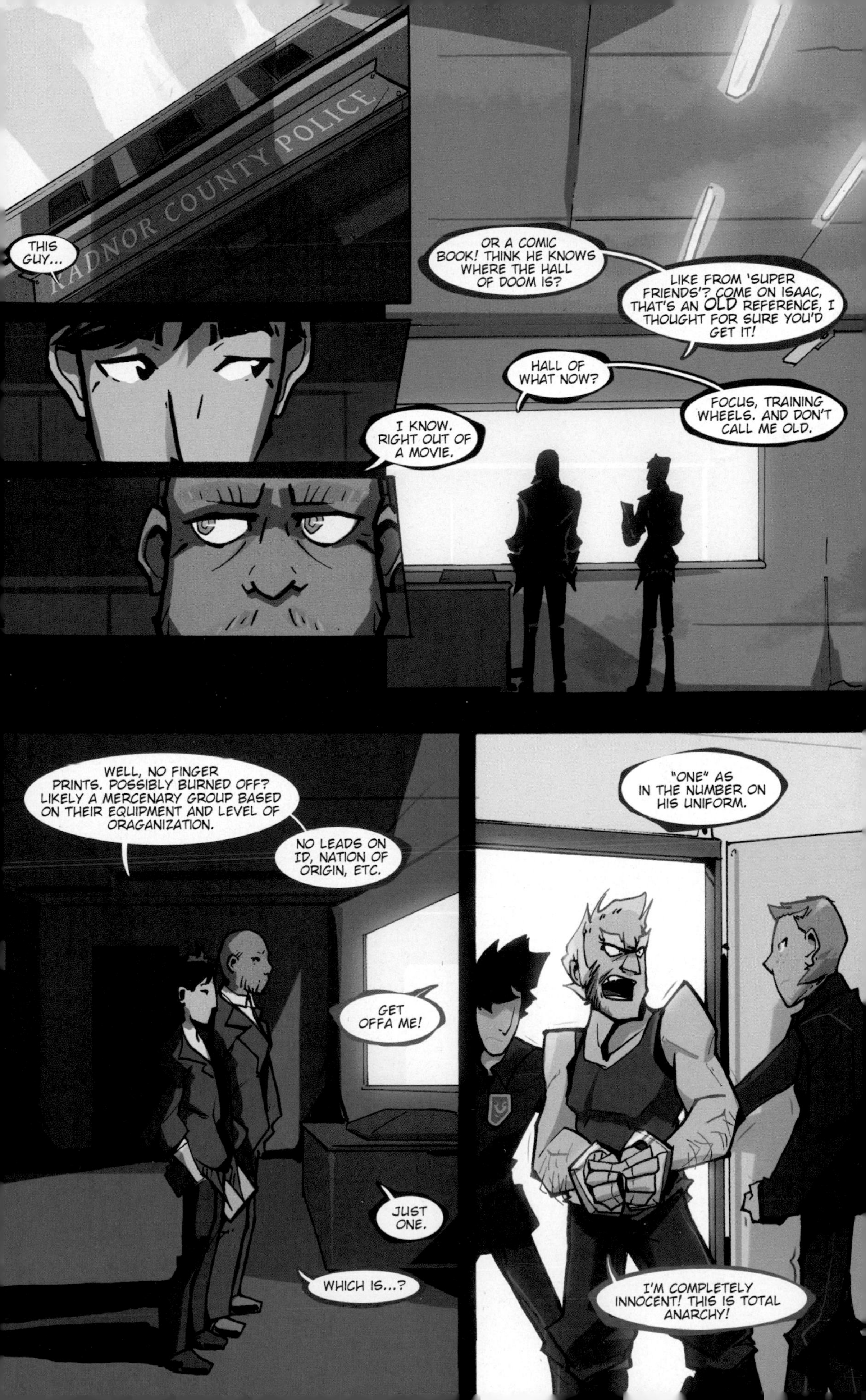
RADNOR COUNTY POLICE
THIS GUY...
I KNOW. RIGHT OUT OF A MOVIE.
OR A COMIC BOOK! THINK HE KNOWS WHERE THE HALL OF DOOM IS?
LIKE FROM 'SUPER FRIENDS'? COME ON ISAAC, THAT'S AN OLD REFERENCE, I THOUGHT FOR SURE YOU'D GET IT!
HALL OF WHAT NOW?
FOCUS, TRAINING WHEELS. AND DON'T CALL ME OLD.
WELL, NO FINGER PRINTS. POSSIBLY BURNED OFF? LIKELY A MERCENARY GROUP BASED ON THEIR EQUIPMENT AND LEVEL OF ORAGANIZATION.
NO LEADS ON ID, NATION OF ORIGIN, ETC.
GET OFFA ME!
JUST ONE.
WHICH IS...?
"ONE" AS IN THE NUMBER ON HIS UNIFORM.
I'M COMPLETELY INNOCENT! THIS IS TOTAL ANARCHY!

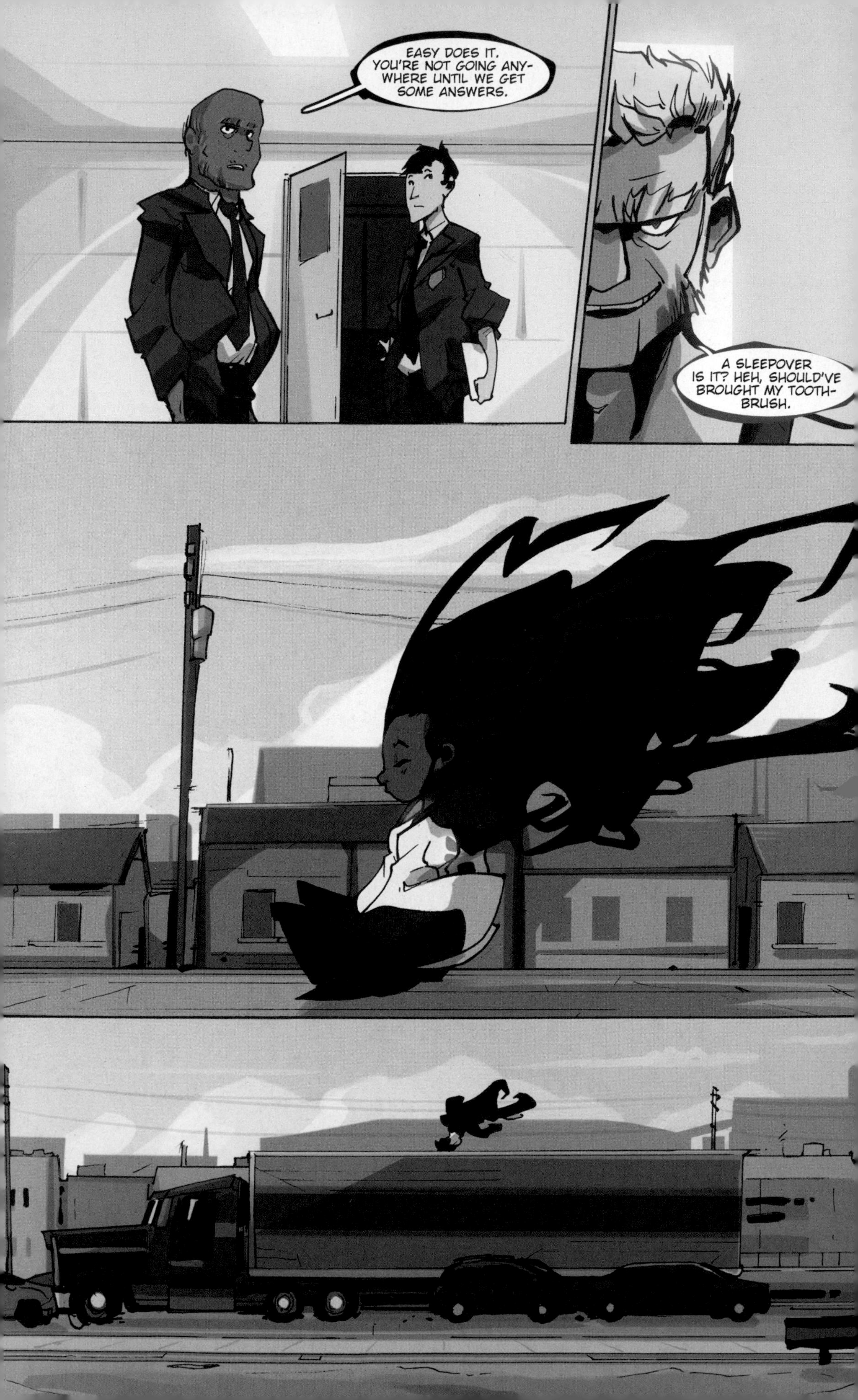
EASY DOES IT. YOU'RE NOT GOING ANY-WHERE UNTIL WE GET SOME ANSWERS.
A SLEEPOVER IS IT? HEH, SHOULD'VE BROUGHT MY TOOTH-BRUSH.

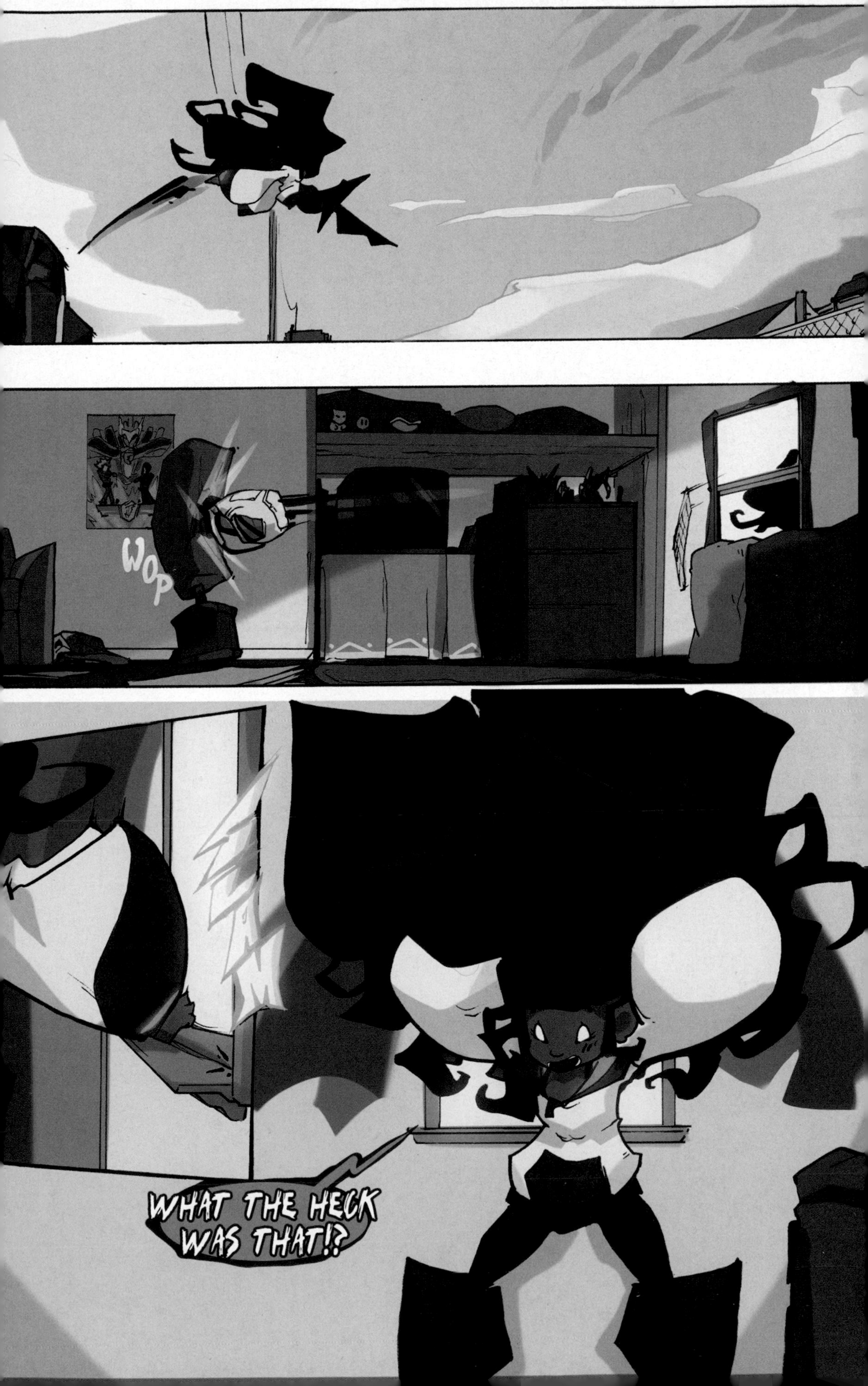
WOP
WHAT THE HECK WAS THAT!?

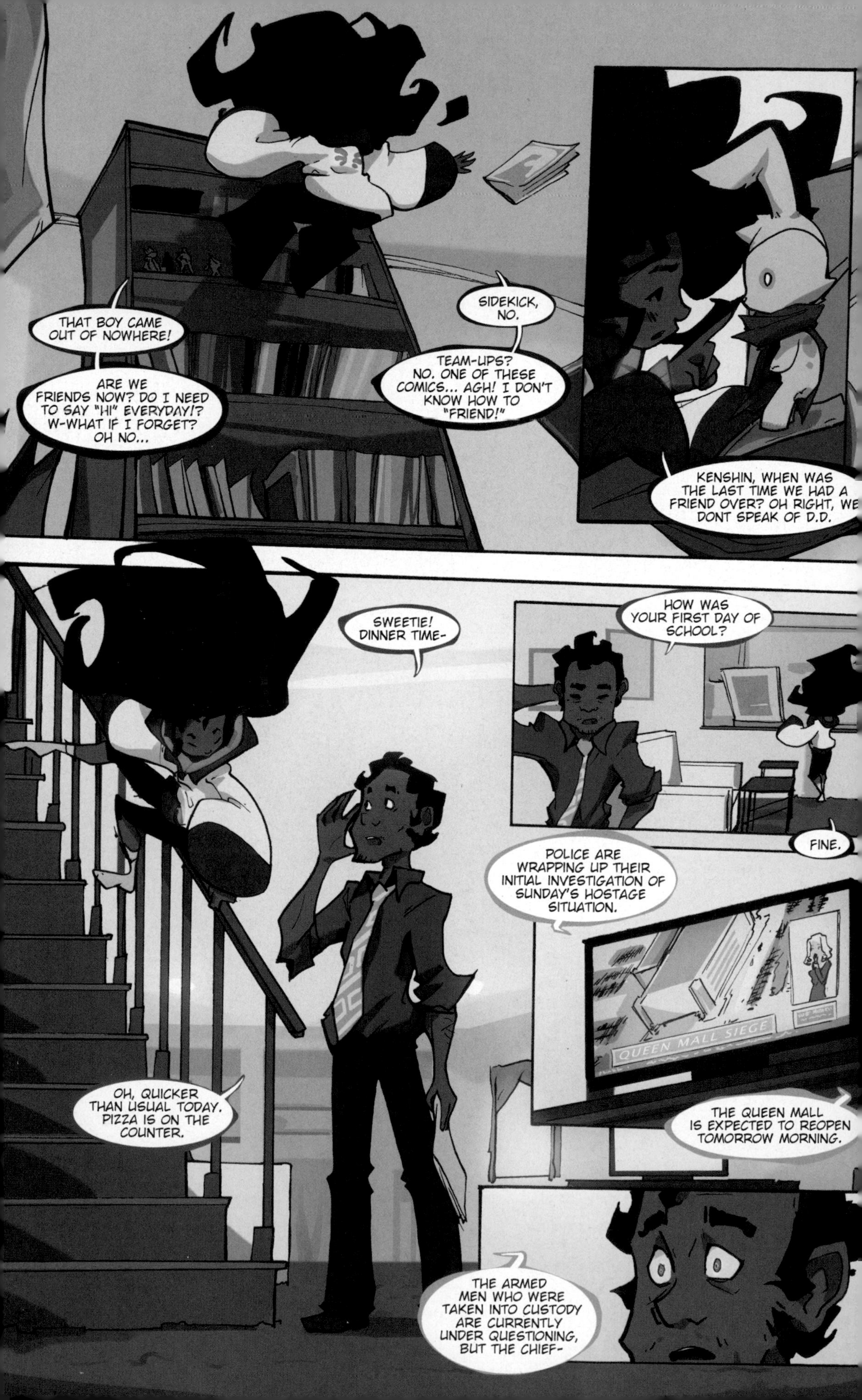

THAT BOY CAME OUT OF NOWHERE!
ARE WE FRIENDS NOW? DO I NEED TO SAY "HI" EVERYDAY!? W-WHAT IF I FORGET? OH NO...
SIDEKICK, NO.
TEAM-UPS? NO. ONE OF THESE COMICS... AGH! I DON'T KNOW HOW TO "FRIEND!"
KENSHIN, WHEN WAS THE LAST TIME WE HAD A FRIEND OVER? OH RIGHT, WE DONT SPEAK OF D.D.
SWEETIE! DINNER TIME-
HOW WAS YOUR FIRST DAY OF SCHOOL?
FINE.
POLICE ARE WRAPPING UP THEIR INITIAL INVESTIGATION OF SUNDAY'S HOSTAGE SITUATION.
QUEEN MALL SIEGE
OH, QUICKER THAN USUAL TODAY. PIZZA IS ON THE COUNTER.
THE QUEEN MALL IS EXPECTED TO REOPEN TOMORROW MORNING.
THE ARMED MEN WHO WERE TAKEN INTO CUSTODY ARE CURRENTLY UNDER QUESTIONING, BUT THE CHIEF-

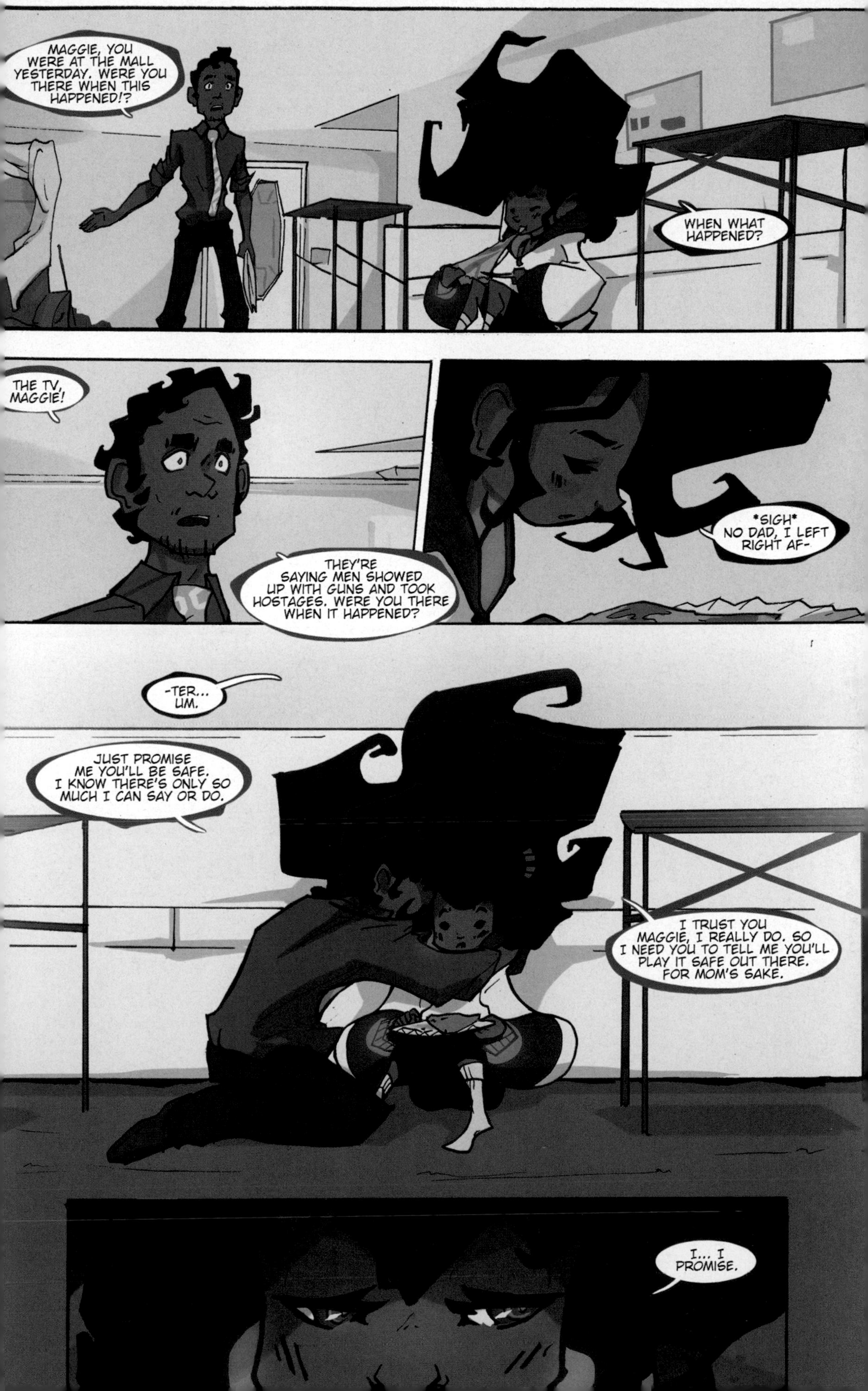
MAGGIE, YOU WERE AT THE MALL YESTERDAY. WERE YOU THERE WHEN THIS HAPPENED!?
WHEN WHAT HAPPENED?
THE TV, MAGGIE!
THEY'RE SAYING MEN SHOWED UP WITH GUNS AND TOOK HOSTAGES. WERE YOU THERE WHEN IT HAPPENED?
SIGH NO DAD, I LEFT RIGHT AF-
-TER... UM.
JUST PROMISE ME YOU'LL BE SAFE. I KNOW THERE'S ONLY SO MUCH I CAN SAY OR DO.
I TRUST YOU MAGGIE, I REALLY DO. SO I NEED YOU TO TELL ME YOU'LL PLAY IT SAFE OUT THERE. FOR MOM'S SAKE.
I... I PROMISE.

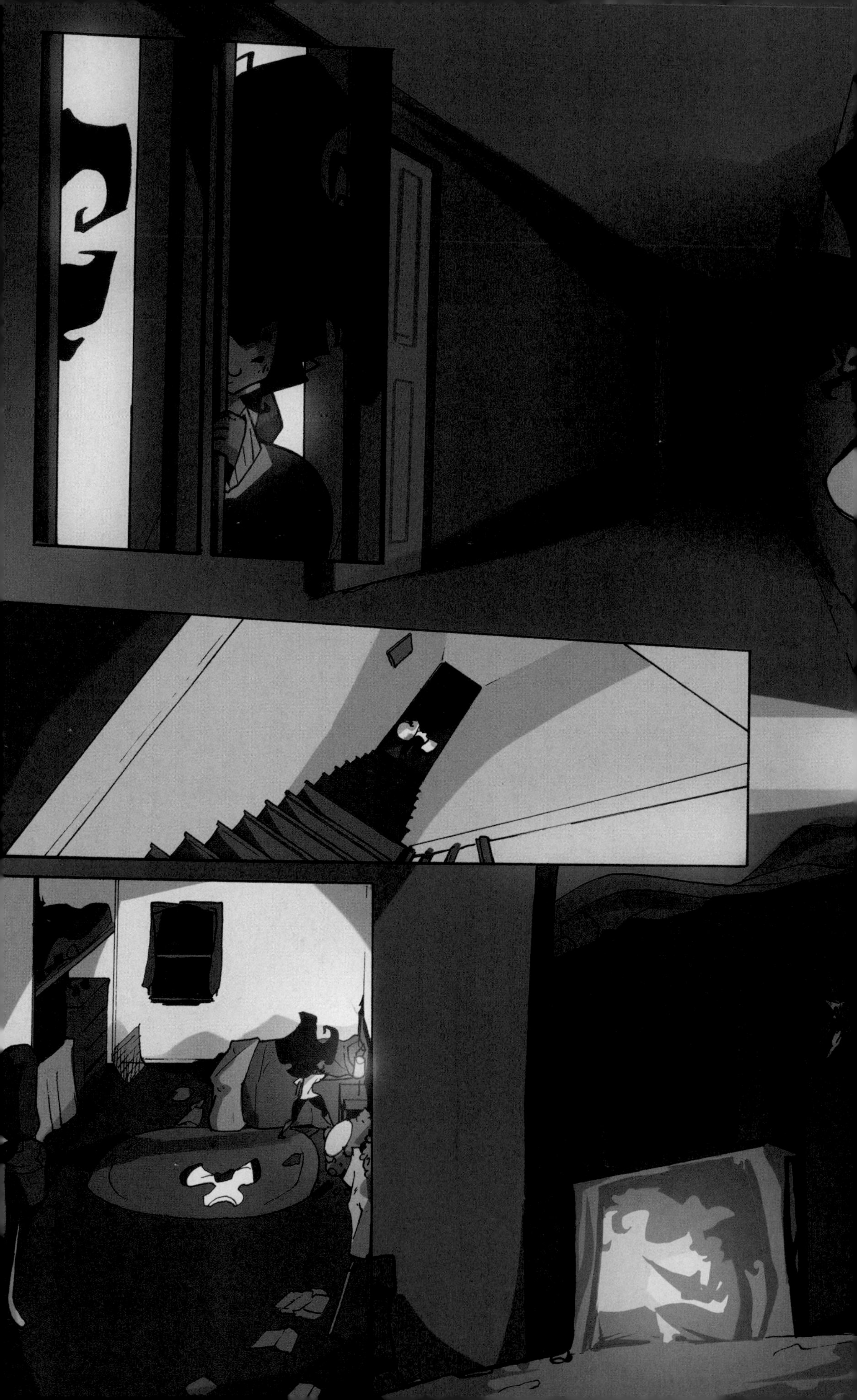

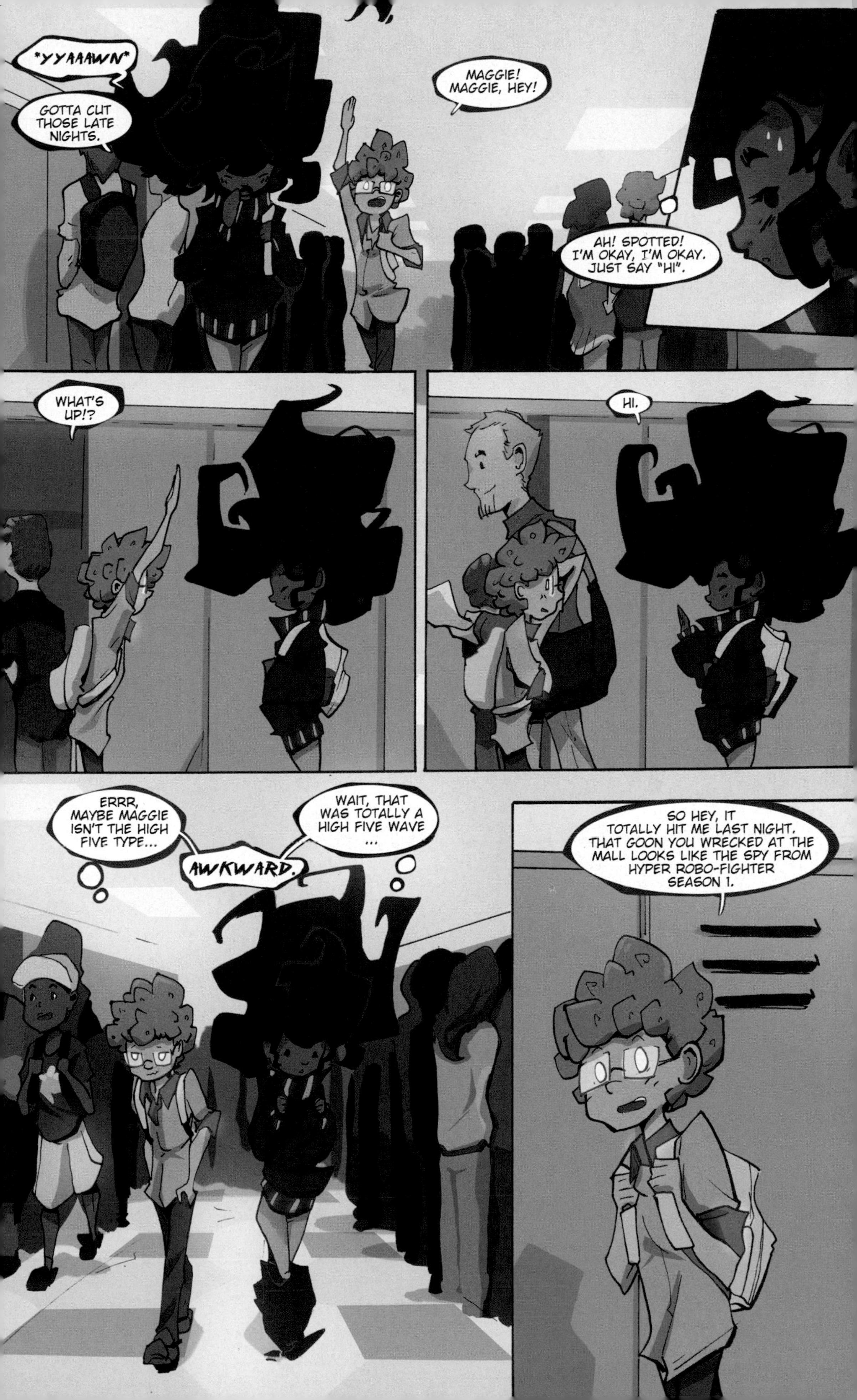
YYAAAWN
GOTTA CUT THOSE LATE NIGHTS.
MAGGIE! MAGGIE, HEY!
AH! SPOTTED! I'M OKAY, I'M OKAY. JUST SAY "HI".
WHAT'S UP!?
HI.
ERRR, MAYBE MAGGIE ISN'T THE HIGH FIVE TYPE...
AWKWARD.
WAIT, THAT WAS TOTALLY A HIGH FIVE WAVE ...
SO HEY, IT TOTALLY HIT ME LAST NIGHT. THAT GOON YOU WRECKED AT THE MALL LOOKS LIKE THE SPY FROM HYPER ROBO-FIGHTER SEASON 1.

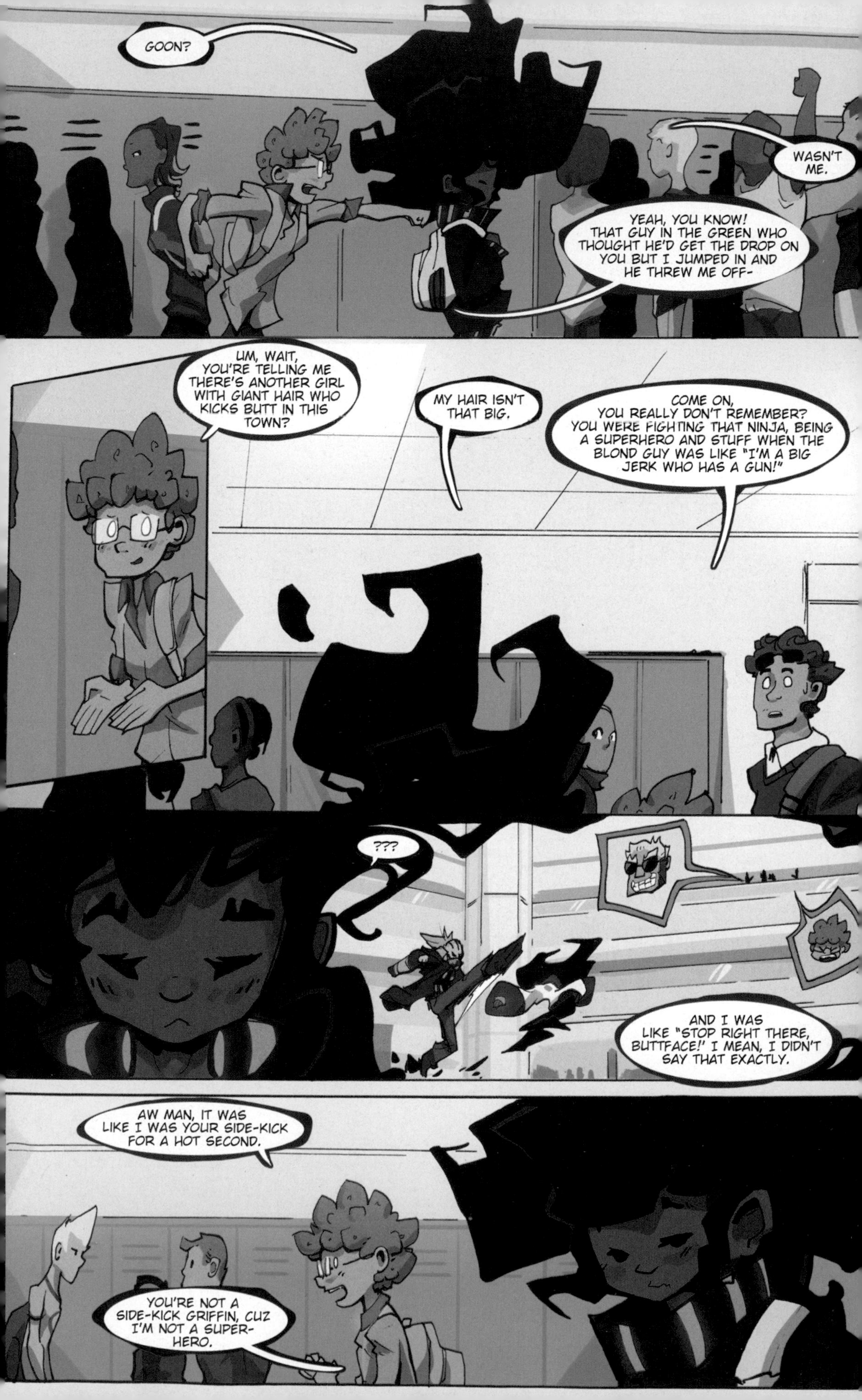
GOON?
WASN'T ME.
YEAH, YOU KNOW! THAT GUY IN THE GREEN WHO THOUGHT HE'D GET THE DROP ON YOU BUT I JUMPED IN AND HE THREW ME OFF-
UM, WAIT, YOU'RE TELLING ME THERE'S ANOTHER GIRL WITH GIANT HAIR WHO KICKS BUTT IN THIS TOWN?
MY HAIR ISN'T THAT BIG.
COME ON, YOU REALLY DON'T REMEMBER? YOU WERE FIGHTING THAT NINJA, BEING A SUPERHERO AND STUFF WHEN THE BLOND GUY WAS LIKE "I'M A BIG JERK WHO HAS A GUN!"
???
AND I WAS LIKE "STOP RIGHT THERE, BUTTFACE!" I MEAN, I DIDN'T SAY THAT EXACTLY.
AW MAN, IT WAS LIKE I WAS YOUR SIDE-KICK FOR A HOT SECOND.
YOU'RE NOT A SIDE-KICK GRIFFIN, CUZ I'M NOT A SUPER-HERO.

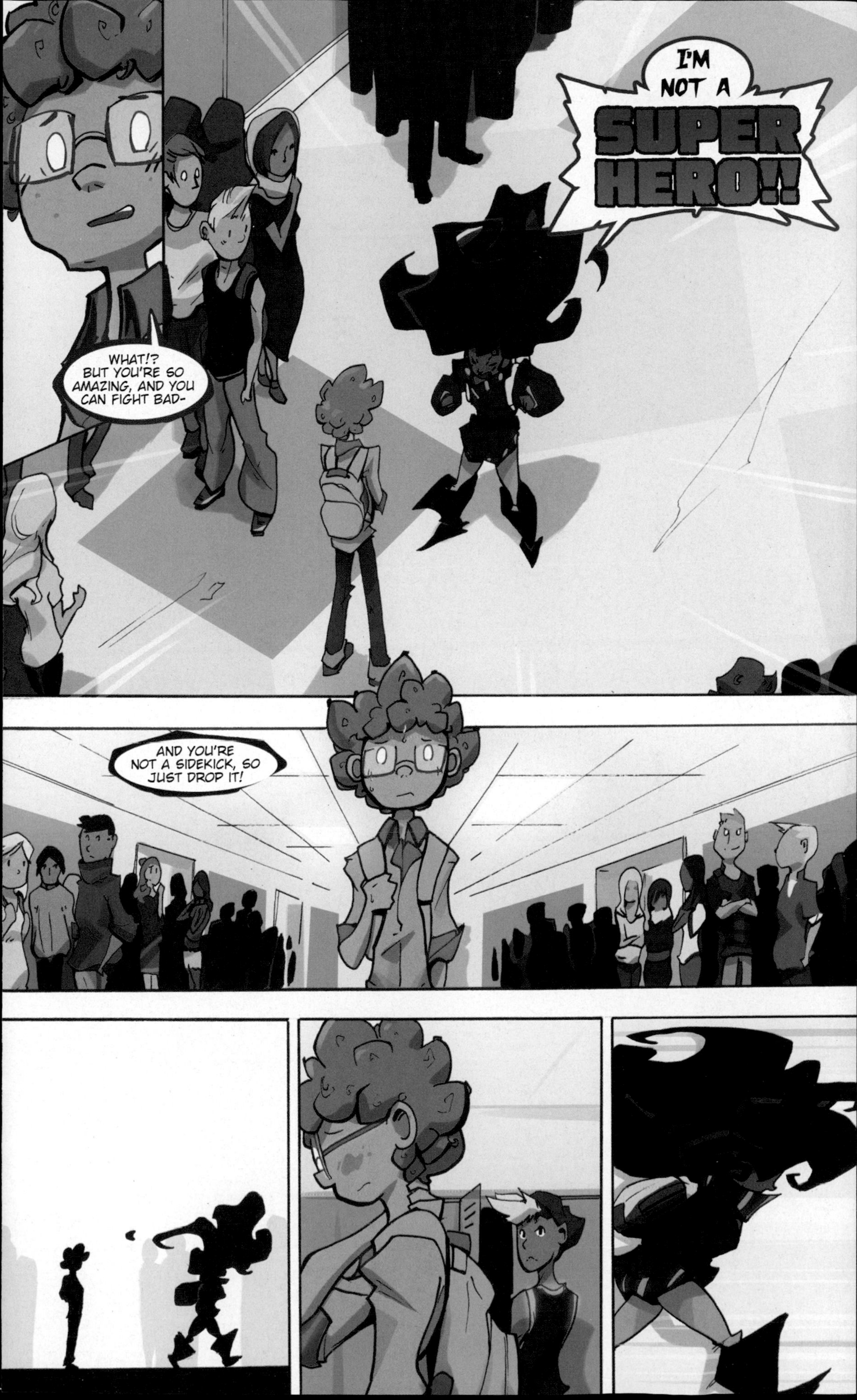
I'M NOT A SUPER HERO!!
WHAT!? BUT YOU'RE SO AMAZING, AND YOU CAN FIGHT BAD-
AND YOU'RE NOT A SIDEKICK, SO JUST DROP IT!

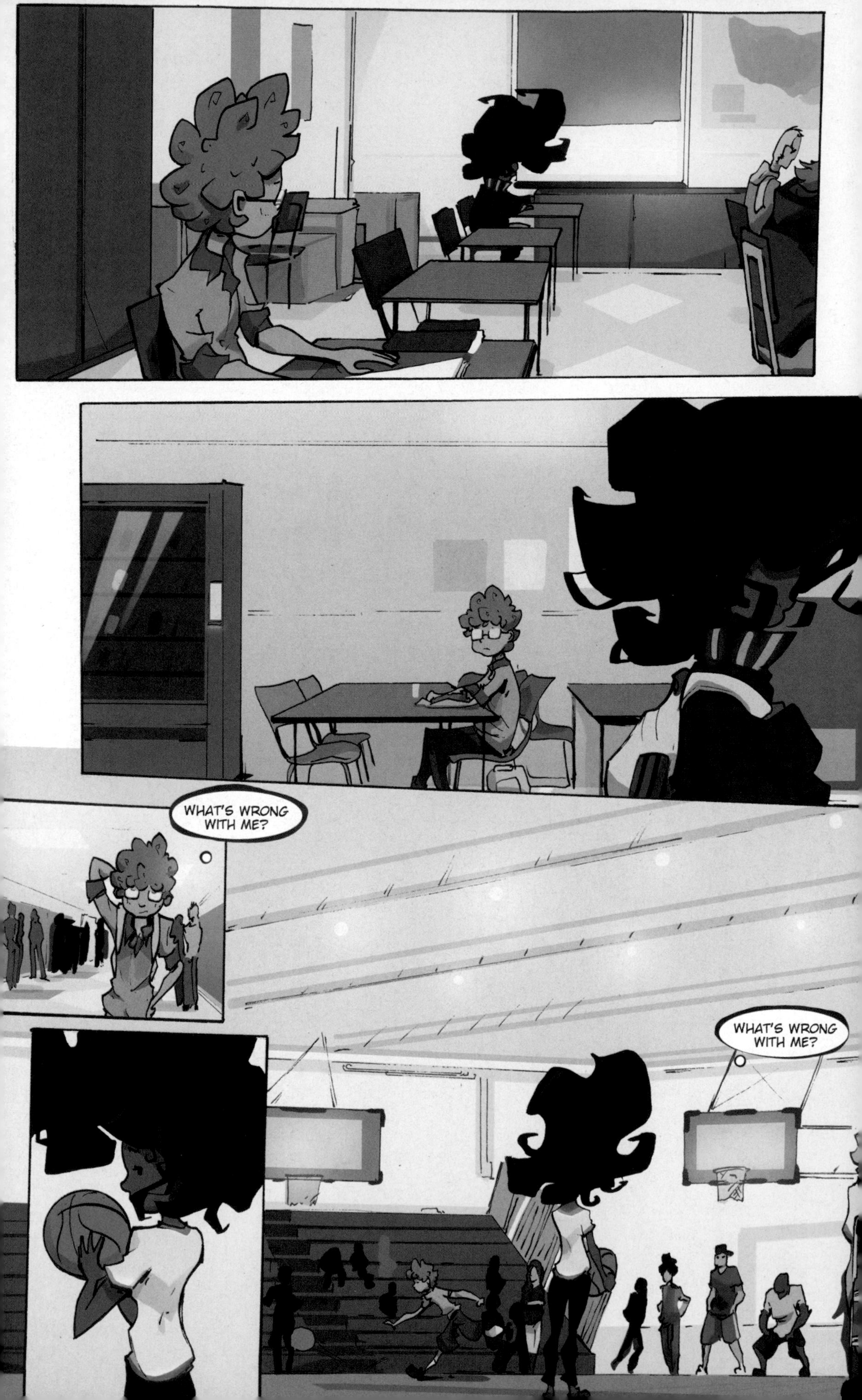
WHAT'S WRONG WITH ME?
WHAT'S WRONG WITH ME?

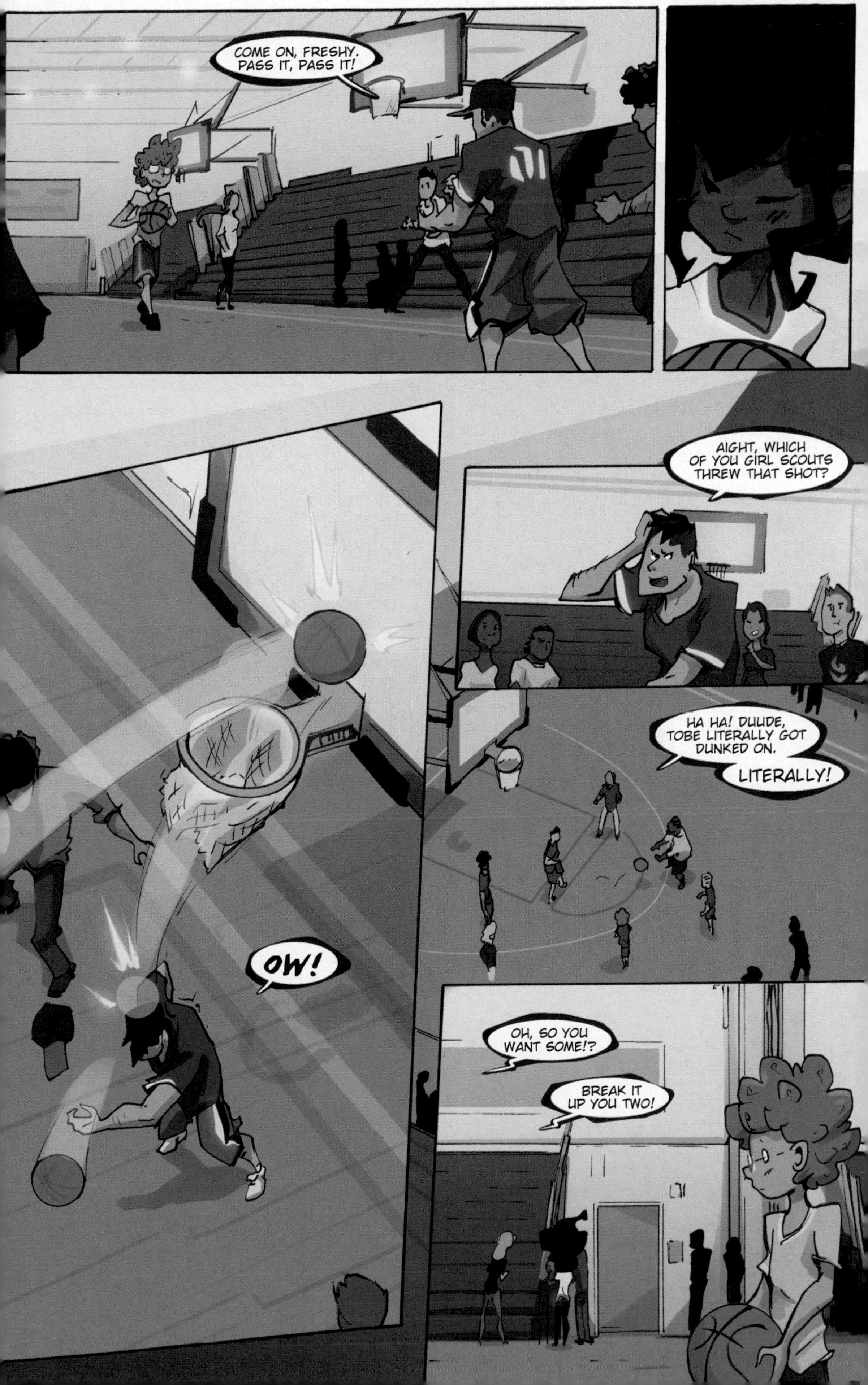

COME ON, FRESHY. PASS IT, PASS IT!
OW!
AIGHT, WHICH OF YOU GIRL SCOUTS THREW THAT SHOT?
HA HA! DUUDE, TOBE LITERALLY GOT DUNKED ON.
LITERALLY!
OH, SO YOU WANT SOME!?
BREAK IT UP YOU TWO!

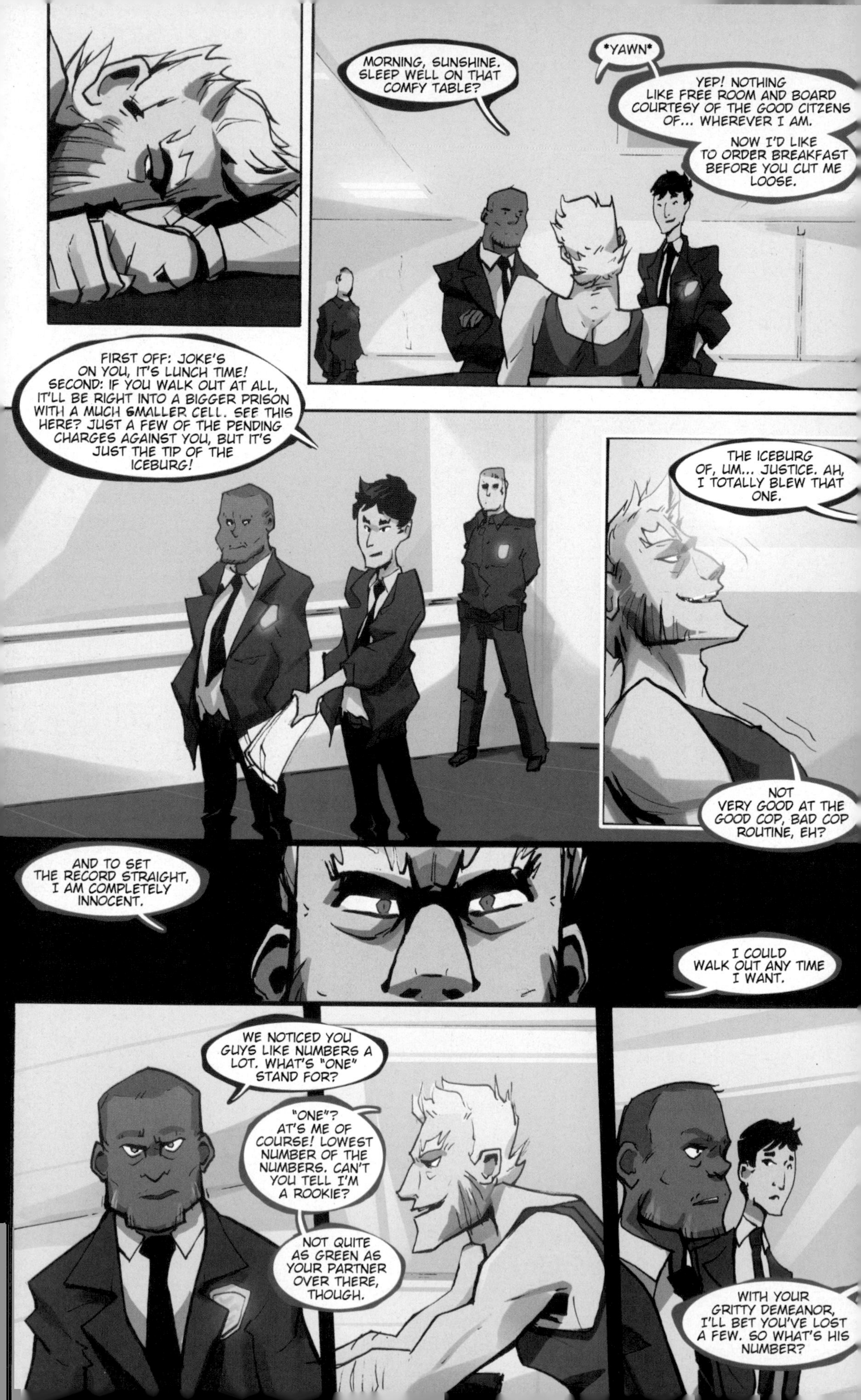
MORNING, SUNSHINE. SLEEP WELL ON THAT COMFY TABLE?
YAWN
YEP! NOTHING LIKE FREE ROOM AND BOARD COURTESY OF THE GOOD CITZENS OF... WHEREVER I AM.
NOW I'D LIKE TO ORDER BREAKFAST BEFORE YOU CUT ME LOOSE.
FIRST OFF: JOKE'S ON YOU, IT'S LUNCH TIME! SECOND: IF YOU WALK OUT AT ALL, IT'LL BE RIGHT INTO A BIGGER PRISON WITH A MUCH SMALLER CELL. SEE THIS HERE? JUST A FEW OF THE PENDING CHARGES AGAINST YOU, BUT IT'S JUST THE TIP OF THE ICEBURG!
THE ICEBURG OF, UM... JUSTICE. AH, I TOTALLY BLEW THAT ONE.
NOT VERY GOOD AT THE GOOD COP, BAD COP ROUTINE, EH?
AND TO SET THE RECORD STRAIGHT, I AM COMPLETELY INNOCENT.
I COULD WALK OUT ANY TIME I WANT.
WE NOTICED YOU GUYS LIKE NUMBERS A LOT. WHAT'S "ONE" STAND FOR?
"ONE"? AT'S ME OF COURSE! LOWEST NUMBER OF THE NUMBERS. CAN'T YOU TELL I'M A ROOKIE?
NOT QUITE AS GREEN AS YOUR PARTNER OVER THERE, THOUGH.
WITH YOUR GRITTY DEMEANOR, I'LL BET YOU'VE LOST A FEW. SO WHAT'S HIS NUMBER?

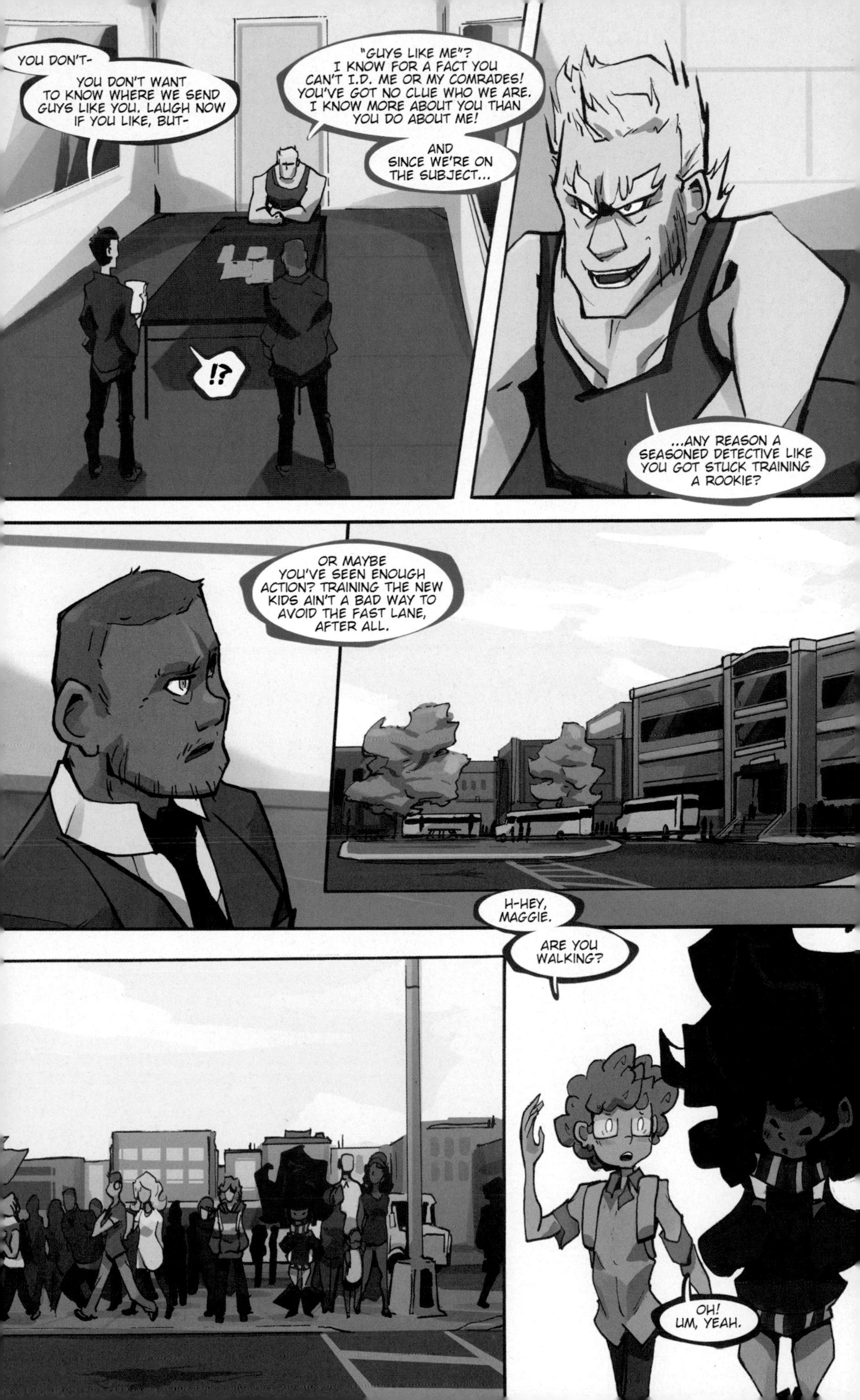
YOU DON'T-
YOU DON'T WANT TO KNOW WHERE WE SEND GUYS LIKE YOU. LAUGH NOW IF YOU LIKE, BUT-
"GUYS LIKE ME"? I KNOW FOR A FACT YOU CAN'T I.D. ME OR MY COMRADES! YOU'VE GOT NO CLUE WHO WE ARE. I KNOW MORE ABOUT YOU THAN YOU DO ABOUT ME!
AND SINCE WE'RE ON THE SUBJECT...
!?
...ANY REASON A SEASONED DETECTIVE LIKE YOU GOT STUCK TRAINING A ROOKIE?
OR MAYBE YOU'VE SEEN ENOUGH ACTION? TRAINING THE NEW KIDS AIN'T A BAD WAY TO AVOID THE FAST LANE, AFTER ALL.
H-HEY, MAGGIE.
ARE YOU WALKING?
OH! UM, YEAH.

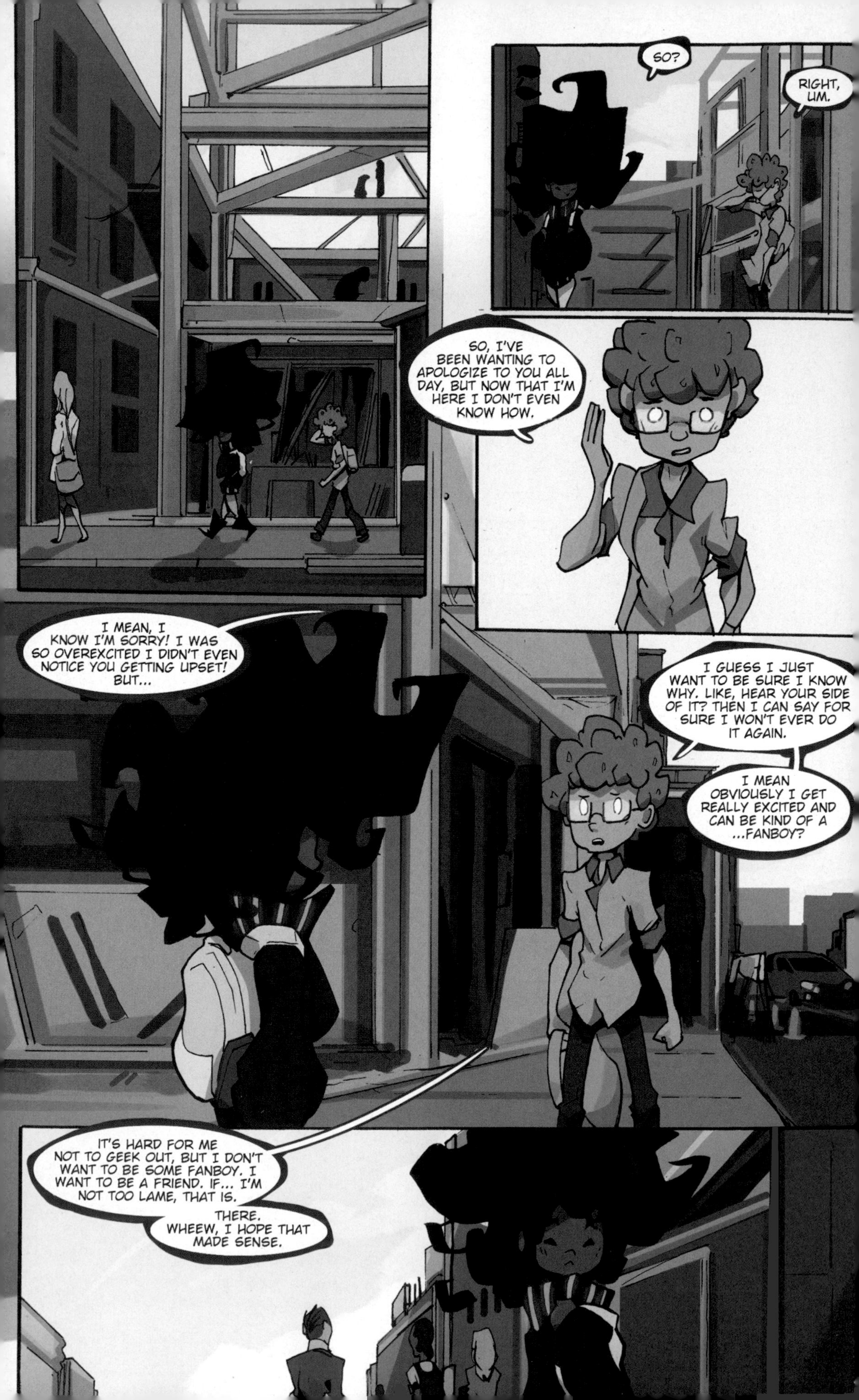
SO?
RIGHT, UM.
SO, I'VE BEEN WANTING TO APOLOGIZE TO YOU ALL DAY, BUT NOW THAT I'M HERE I DON'T EVEN KNOW HOW.
I MEAN, I KNOW I'M SORRY! I WAS SO OVEREXCITED I DIDN'T EVEN NOTICE YOU GETTING UPSET! BUT...
I GUESS I JUST WANT TO BE SURE I KNOW WHY. LIKE, HEAR YOUR SIDE OF IT? THEN I CAN SAY FOR SURE I WON'T EVER DO IT AGAIN.
I MEAN OBVIOUSLY I GET REALLY EXCITED AND CAN BE KIND OF A ...FANBOY?
IT'S HARD FOR ME NOT TO GEEK OUT, BUT I DON'T WANT TO BE SOME FANBOY. I WANT TO BE A FRIEND. IF... I'M NOT TOO LAME, THAT IS.
THERE. WHEEW, I HOPE THAT MADE SENSE.

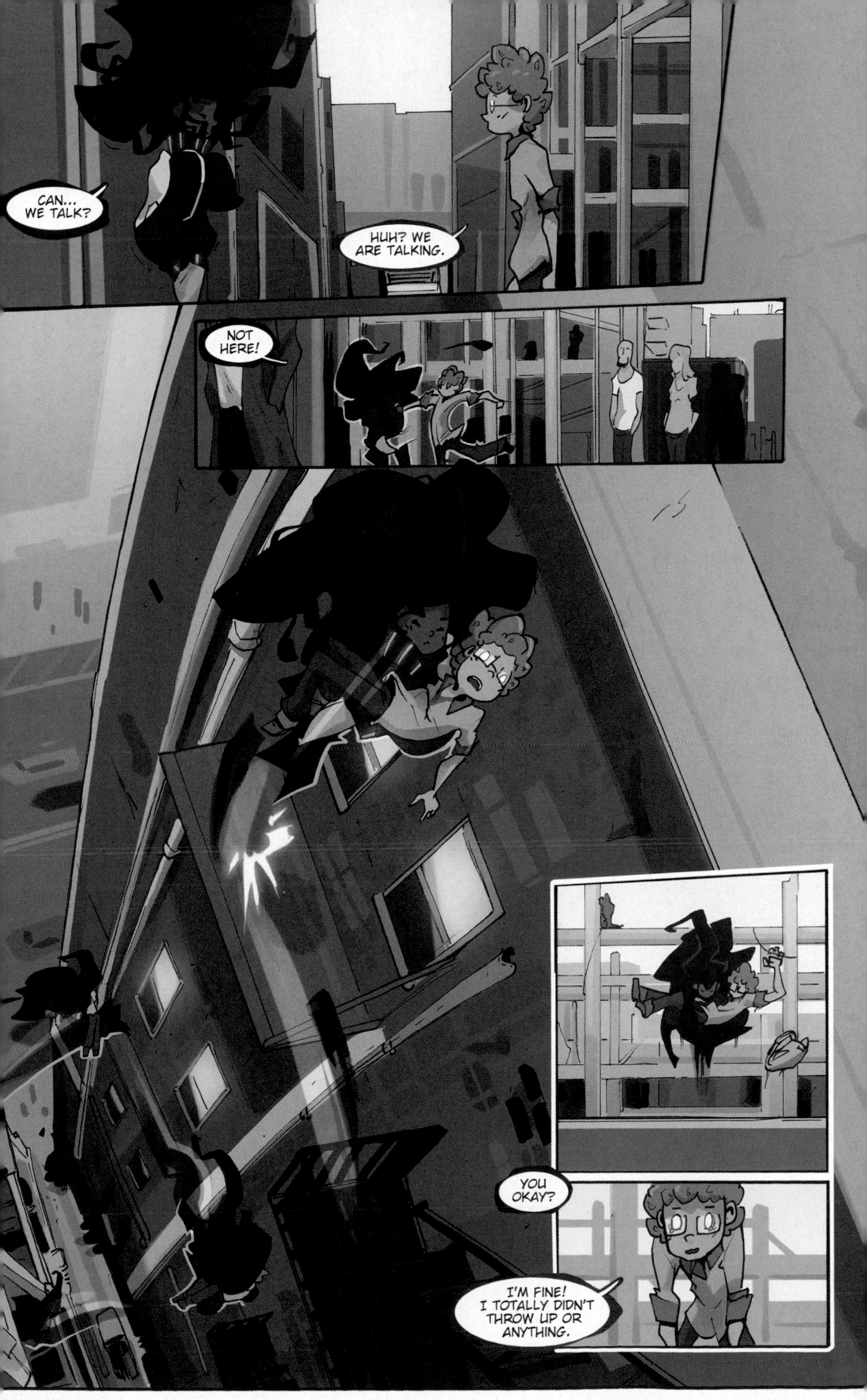
CAN... WE TALK?
HUH? WE ARE TALKING.
NOT HERE!
YOU OKAY?
I'M FINE! I TOTALLY DIDN'T THROW UP OR ANYTHING.

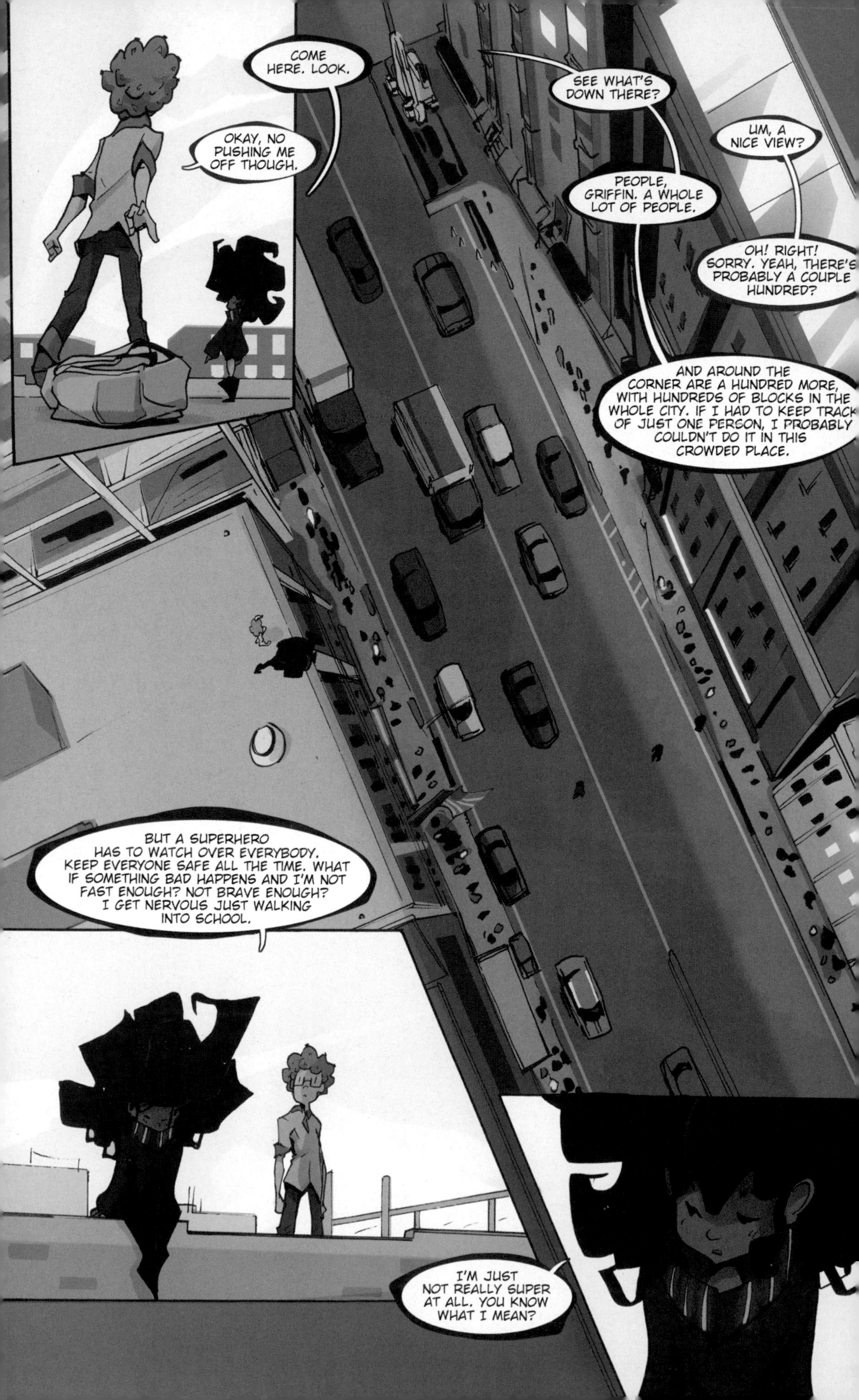

COME HERE. LOOK.
OKAY, NO PUSHING ME OFF THOUGH.
SEE WHAT'S DOWN THERE?
UM, A NICE VIEW?
PEOPLE, GRIFFIN. A WHOLE LOT OF PEOPLE.
OH! RIGHT! SORRY. YEAH, THERE'S PROBABLY A COUPLE HUNDRED?
AND AROUND THE CORNER ARE A HUNDRED MORE, WITH HUNDREDS OF BLOCKS IN THE WHOLE CITY. IF I HAD TO KEEP TRACK OF JUST ONE PERSON, I PROBABLY COULDN'T DO IT IN THIS CROWDED PLACE.
BUT A SUPERHERO HAS TO WATCH OVER EVERYBODY. KEEP EVERYONE SAFE ALL THE TIME. WHAT IF SOMETHING BAD HAPPENS AND I'M NOT FAST ENOUGH? NOT BRAVE ENOUGH? I GET NERVOUS JUST WALKING INTO SCHOOL.
I'M JUST NOT REALLY SUPER AT ALL. YOU KNOW WHAT I MEAN?

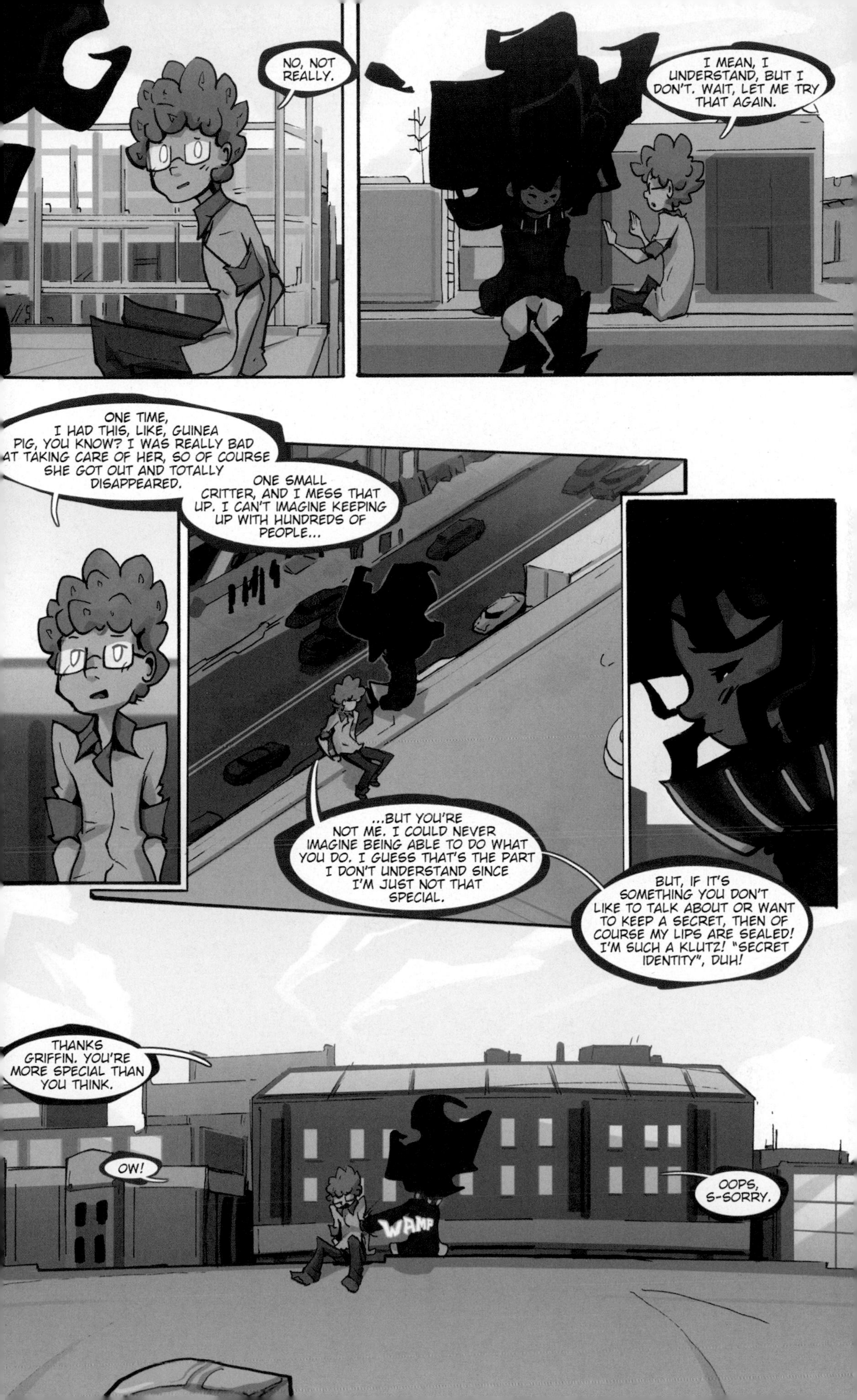
NO, NOT REALLY.
I MEAN, I UNDERSTAND, BUT I DON'T. WAIT, LET ME TRY THAT AGAIN.
ONE TIME, I HAD THIS, LIKE, GUINEA PIG, YOU KNOW? I WAS REALLY BAD AT TAKING CARE OF HER, SO OF COURSE SHE GOT OUT AND TOTALLY DISAPPEARED.
ONE SMALL CRITTER, AND I MESS THAT UP. I CAN'T IMAGINE KEEPING UP WITH HUNDREDS OF PEOPLE...
...BUT YOU'RE NOT ME. I COULD NEVER IMAGINE BEING ABLE TO DO WHAT YOU DO. I GUESS THAT'S THE PART I DON'T UNDERSTAND SINCE I'M JUST NOT THAT SPECIAL.
BUT, IF IT'S SOMETHING YOU DON'T LIKE TO TALK ABOUT OR WANT TO KEEP A SECRET, THEN OF COURSE MY LIPS ARE SEALED! I'M SUCH A KLUTZ! "SECRET IDENTITY", DUH!
THANKS GRIFFIN. YOU'RE MORE SPECIAL THAN YOU THINK.
OW!
WAMP
OOPS, S-SORRY.

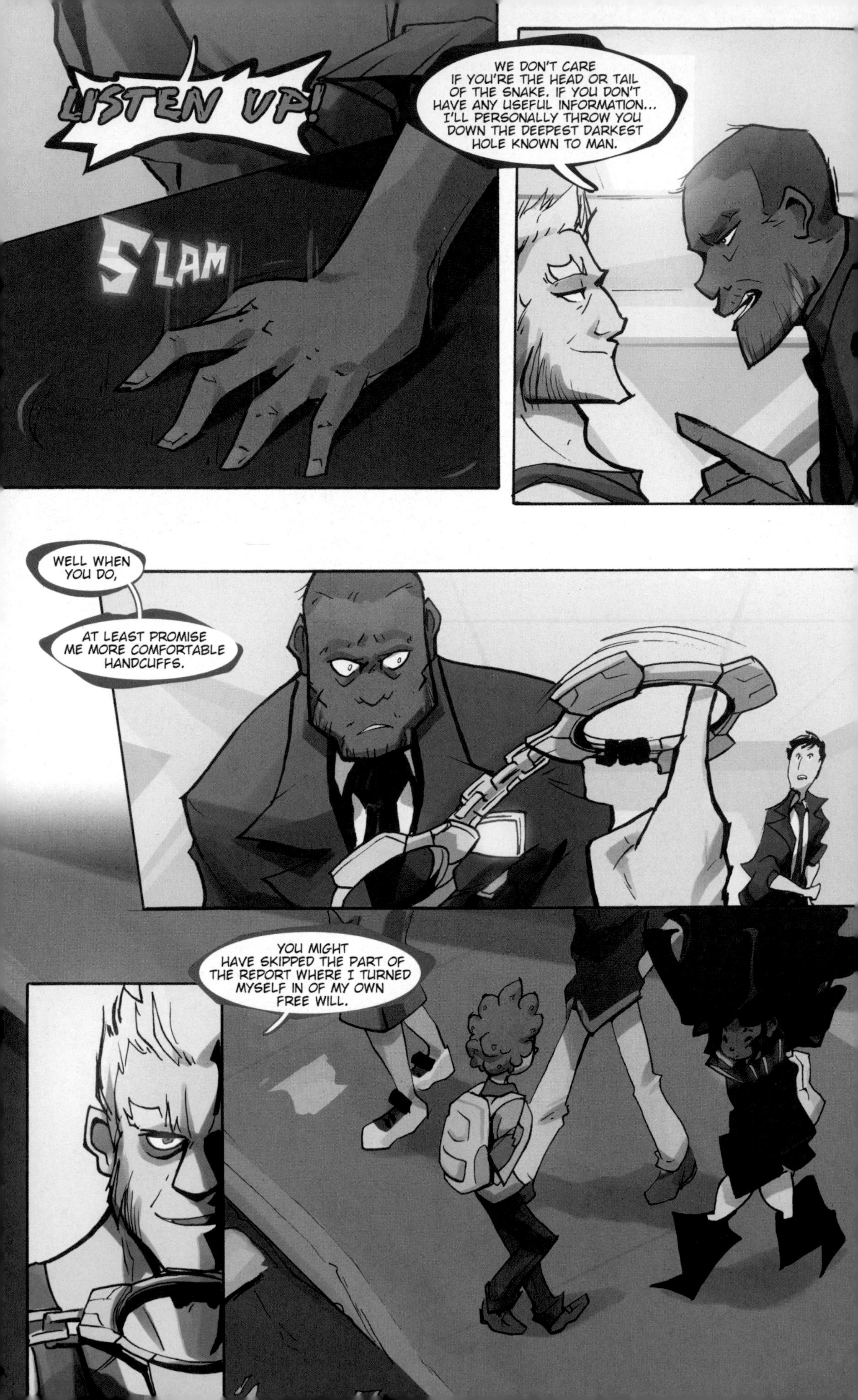
LISTEN UP!
SLAM
WE DON'T CARE IF YOU'RE THE HEAD OR TAIL OF THE SNAKE. IF YOU DON'T HAVE ANY USEFUL INFORMATION... I'LL PERSONALLY THROW YOU DOWN THE DEEPEST DARKEST HOLE KNOWN TO MAN.
WELL WHEN YOU DO,
AT LEAST PROMISE ME MORE COMFORTABLE HANDCUFFS.
YOU MIGHT HAVE SKIPPED THE PART OF THE REPORT WHERE I TURNED MYSELF IN OF MY OWN FREE WILL.

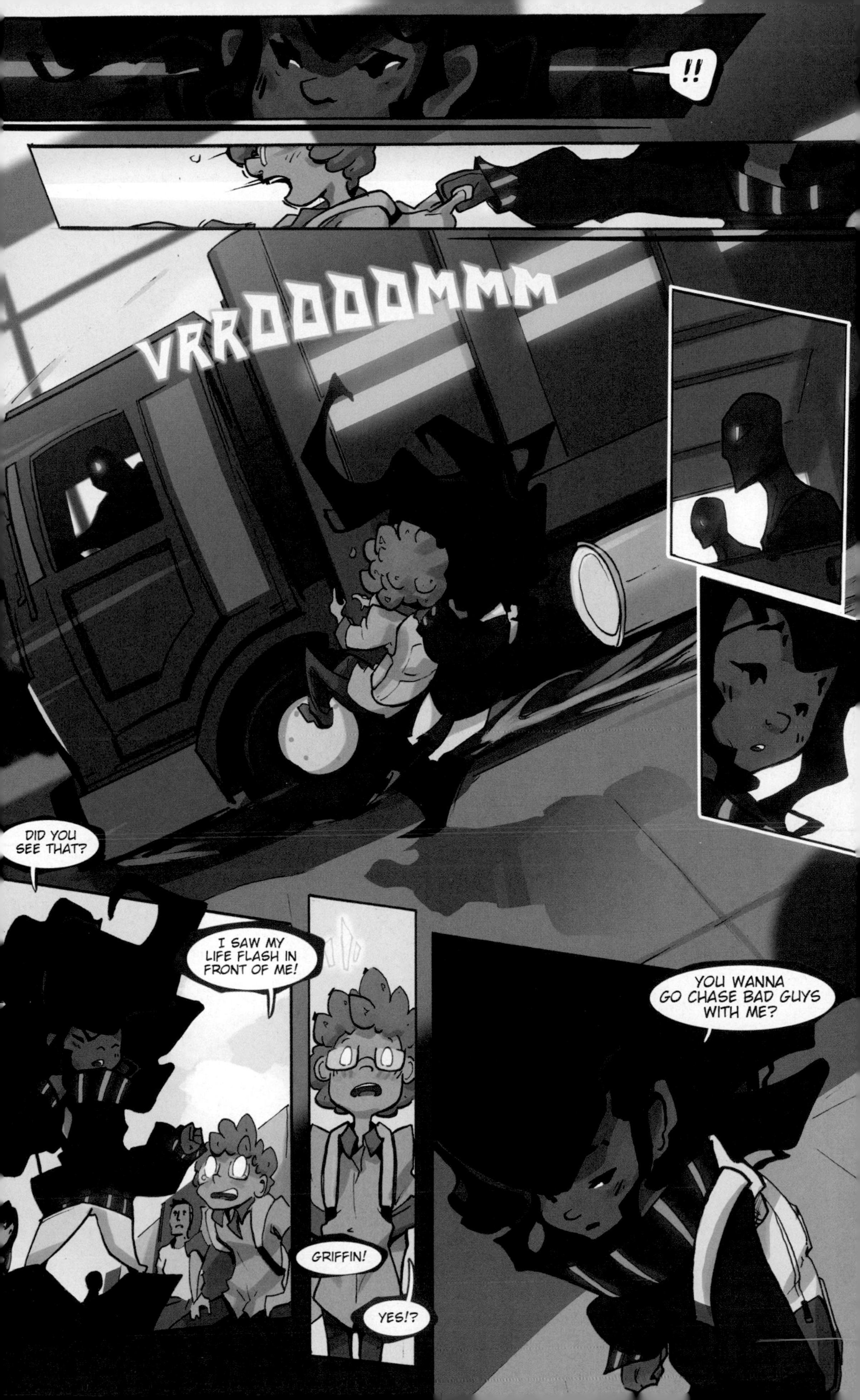
!!
VRROOOOMMM
DID YOU SEE THAT?
I SAW MY LIFE FLASH IN FRONT OF ME!
GRIFFIN!
YES!?
YOU WANNA GO CHASE BAD GUYS WITH ME?

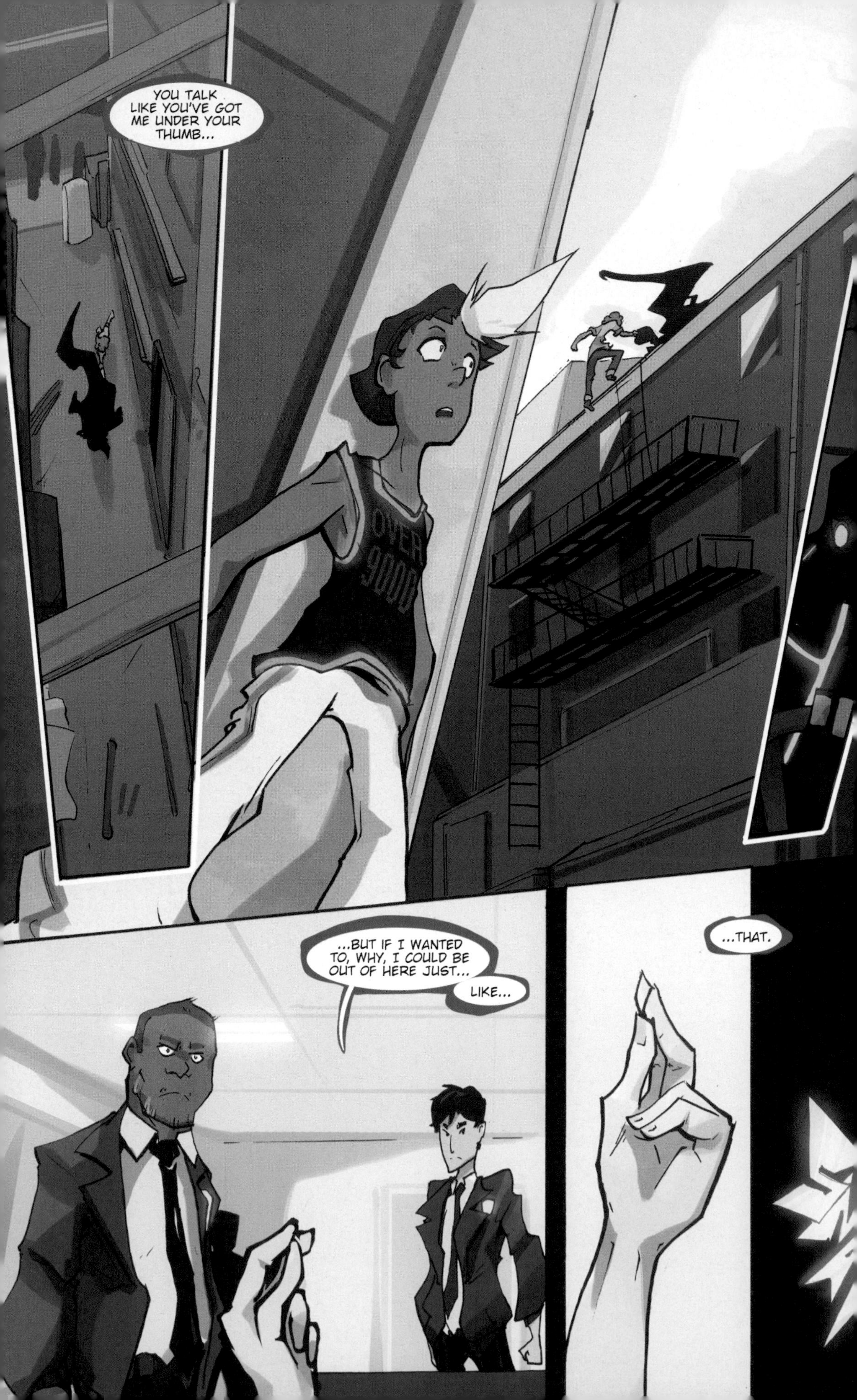
YOU TALK LIKE YOU'VE GOT ME UNDER YOUR THUMB...
...BUT IF I WANTED TO, WHY, I COULD BE OUT OF HERE JUST...
LIKE...
...THAT.

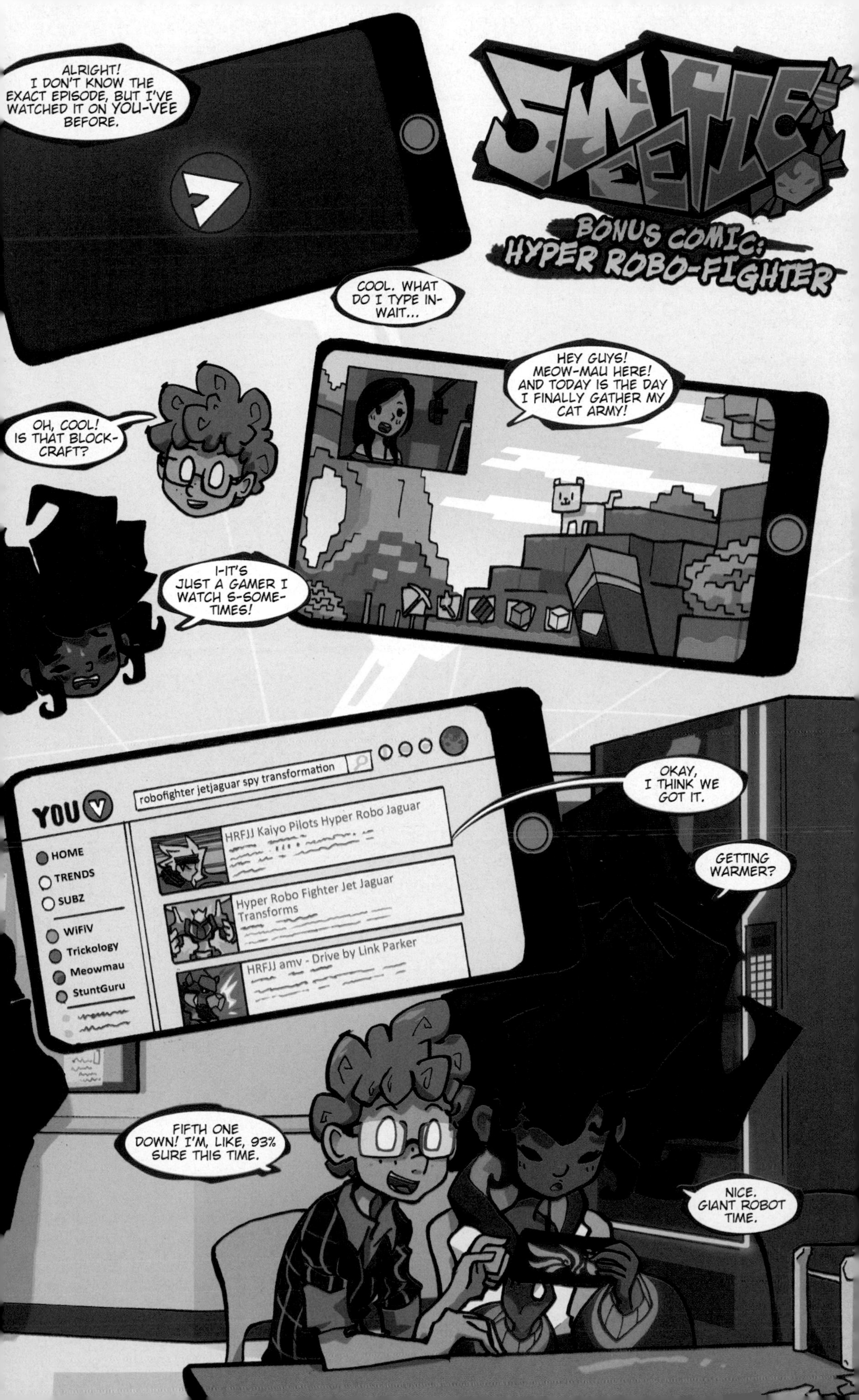
BONUS COMIC: HYPER ROBO-FIGHTER
ALRIGHT! I DON'T KNOW THE EXACT EPISODE, BUT I'VE WATCHED IT ON YOU-VEE BEFORE.
COOL. WHAT DO I TYPE IN- WAIT...
HEY GUYS! MEOW-MAU HERE! AND TODAY IS THE DAY I FINALLY GATHER MY CAT ARMY!
OH, COOL! IS THAT BLOCK-CRAFT?
I-IT'S JUST A GAMER I WATCH S-SOME-TIMES!
YOU V
robofighter jetjaguar spy transformation
HOME
TRENDS
SUBZ
WiFiV
Trickology
Meowmau
StuntGuru
HRFJJ Kaiyo Pilots Hyper Robo Jaguar
Hyper Robo Fighter Jet Jaguar Transforms
HRFJJ amv - Drive by Link Parker
OKAY, I THINK WE GOT IT.
GETTING WARMER?
FIFTH ONE DOWN! I'M, LIKE, 93% SURE THIS TIME.
NICE. GIANT ROBOT TIME.

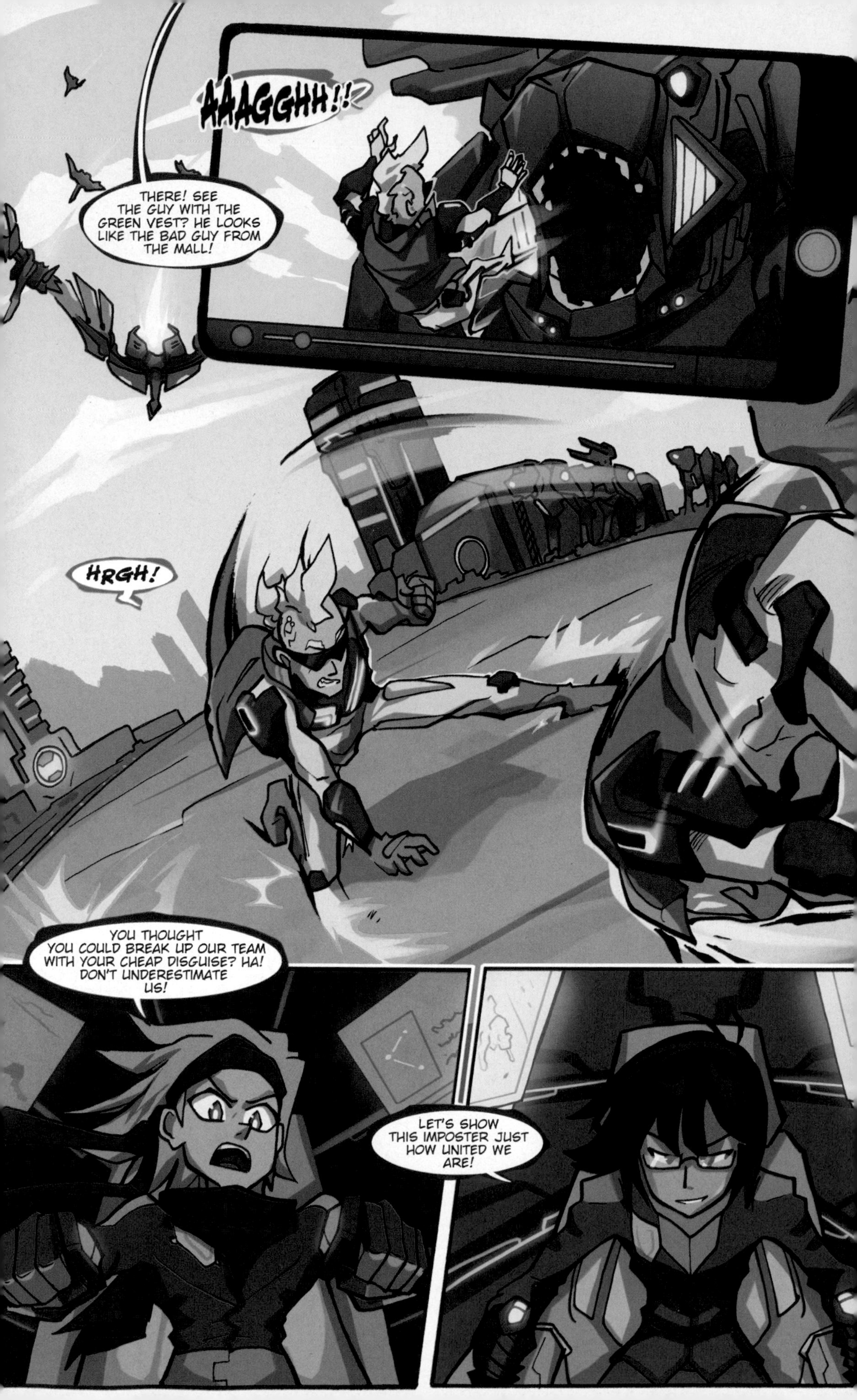
AAAGGHH!!?
THERE! SEE THE GUY WITH THE GREEN VEST? HE LOOKS LIKE THE BAD GUY FROM THE MALL!
HRGH!
YOU THOUGHT YOU COULD BREAK UP OUR TEAM WITH YOUR CHEAP DISGUISE? HA! DON'T UNDERESTIMATE US!
LET'S SHOW THIS IMPOSTER JUST HOW UNITED WE ARE!

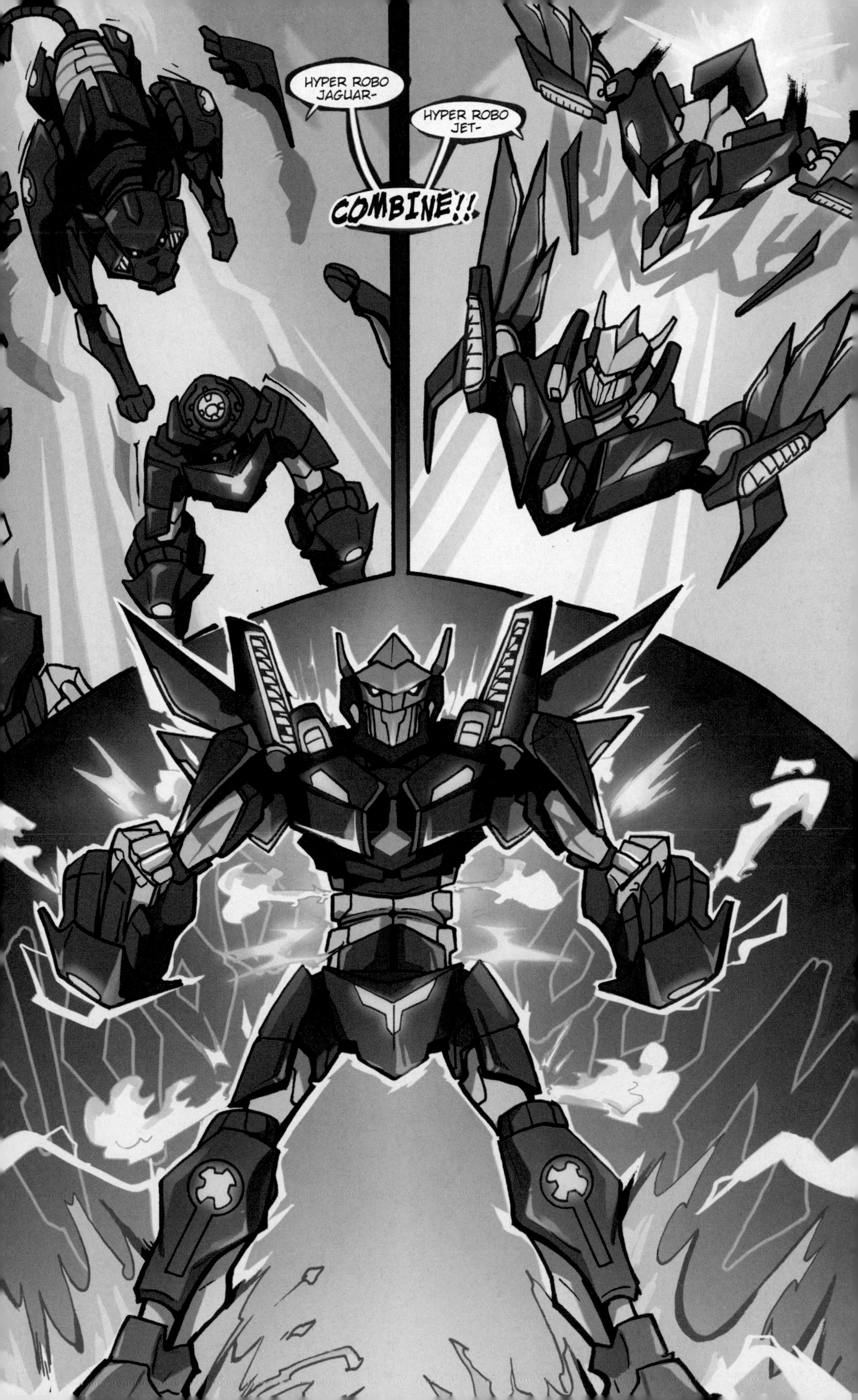
HYPER ROBO JAGUAR-
HYPER ROBO JET-
COMBINE!!

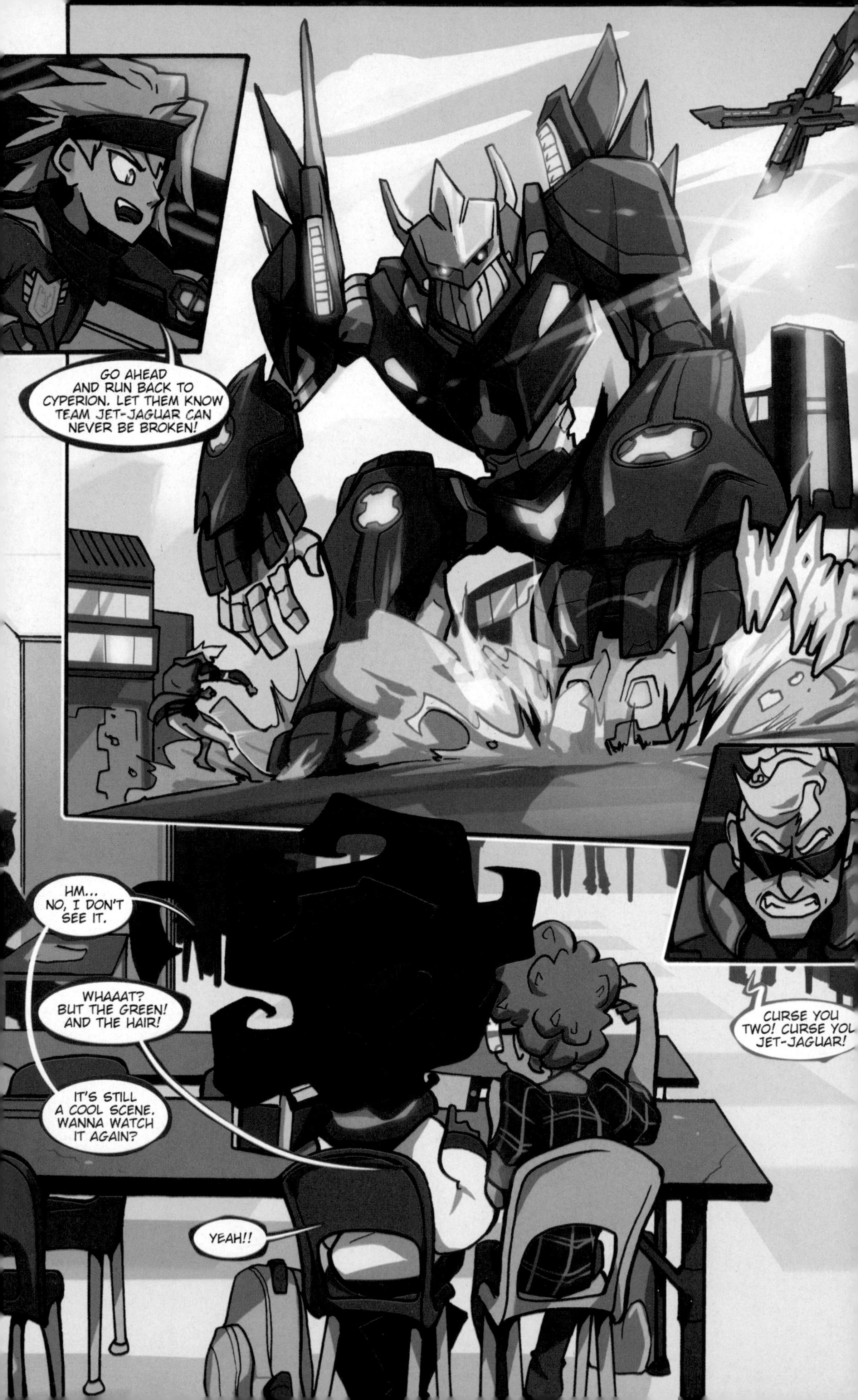
GO AHEAD AND RUN BACK TO CYPERION. LET THEM KNOW TEAM JET-JAGUAR CAN NEVER BE BROKEN!
CURSE YOU TWO! CURSE YOU JET-JAGUAR!
HM... NO, I DON'T SEE IT.
WHAAAT? BUT THE GREEN! AND THE HAIR!
IT'S STILL A COOL SCENE. WANNA WATCH IT AGAIN?
YEAH!!

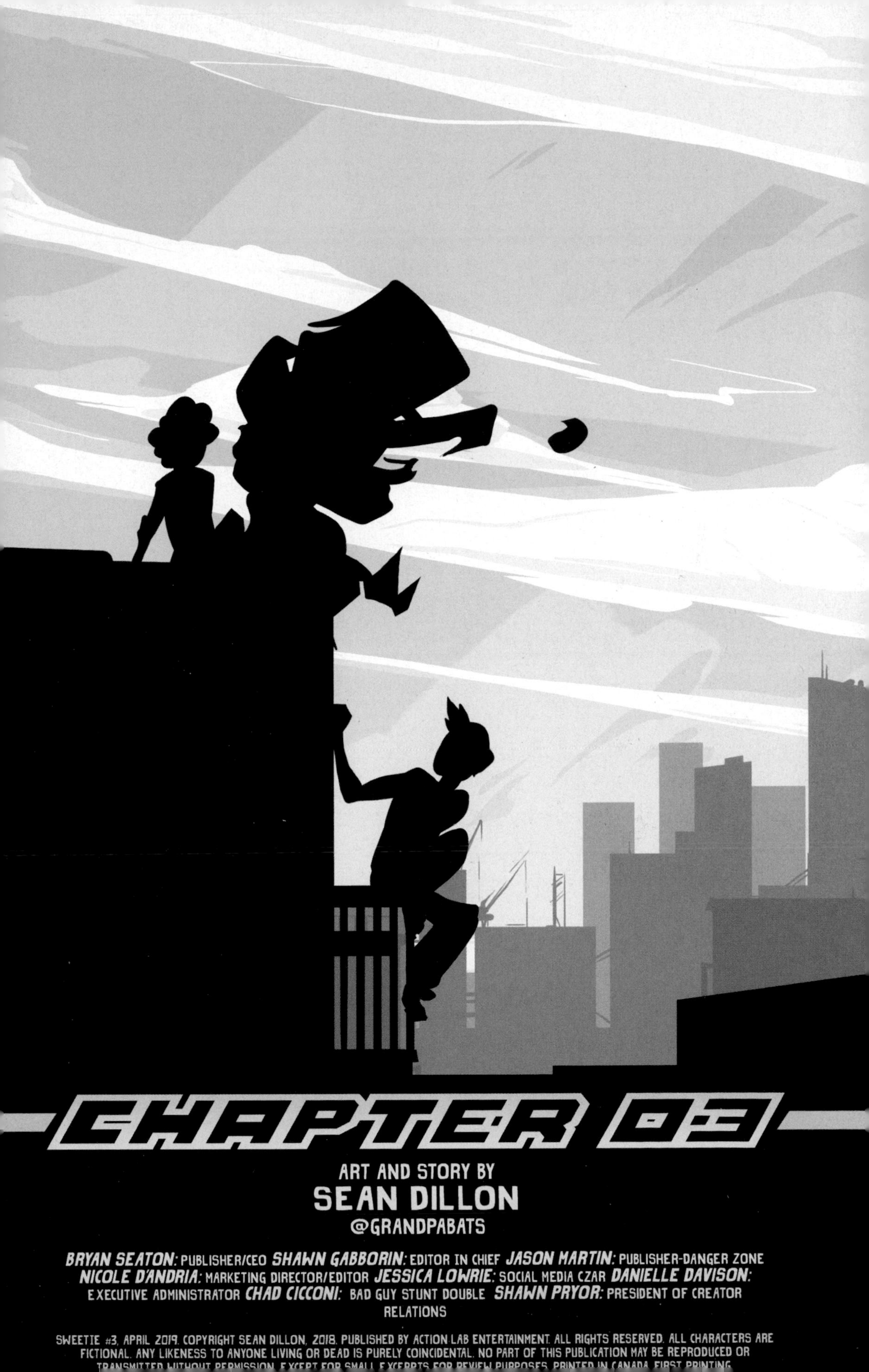

CHAPTER 03

ART AND STORY BY

SEAN DILLON

@GRANDPABATS

BRYAN SEATON: PUBLISHER/CEO ***SHAWN GABBORIN:*** EDITOR IN CHIEF ***JASON MARTIN:*** PUBLISHER-DANGER ZONE ***NICOLE D'ANDRIA:*** MARKETING DIRECTOR/EDITOR ***JESSICA LOWRIE:*** SOCIAL MEDIA CZAR ***DANIELLE DAVISON:*** EXECUTIVE ADMINISTRATOR ***CHAD CICCONI:*** BAD GUY STUNT DOUBLE ***SHAWN PRYOR:*** PRESIDENT OF CREATOR RELATIONS

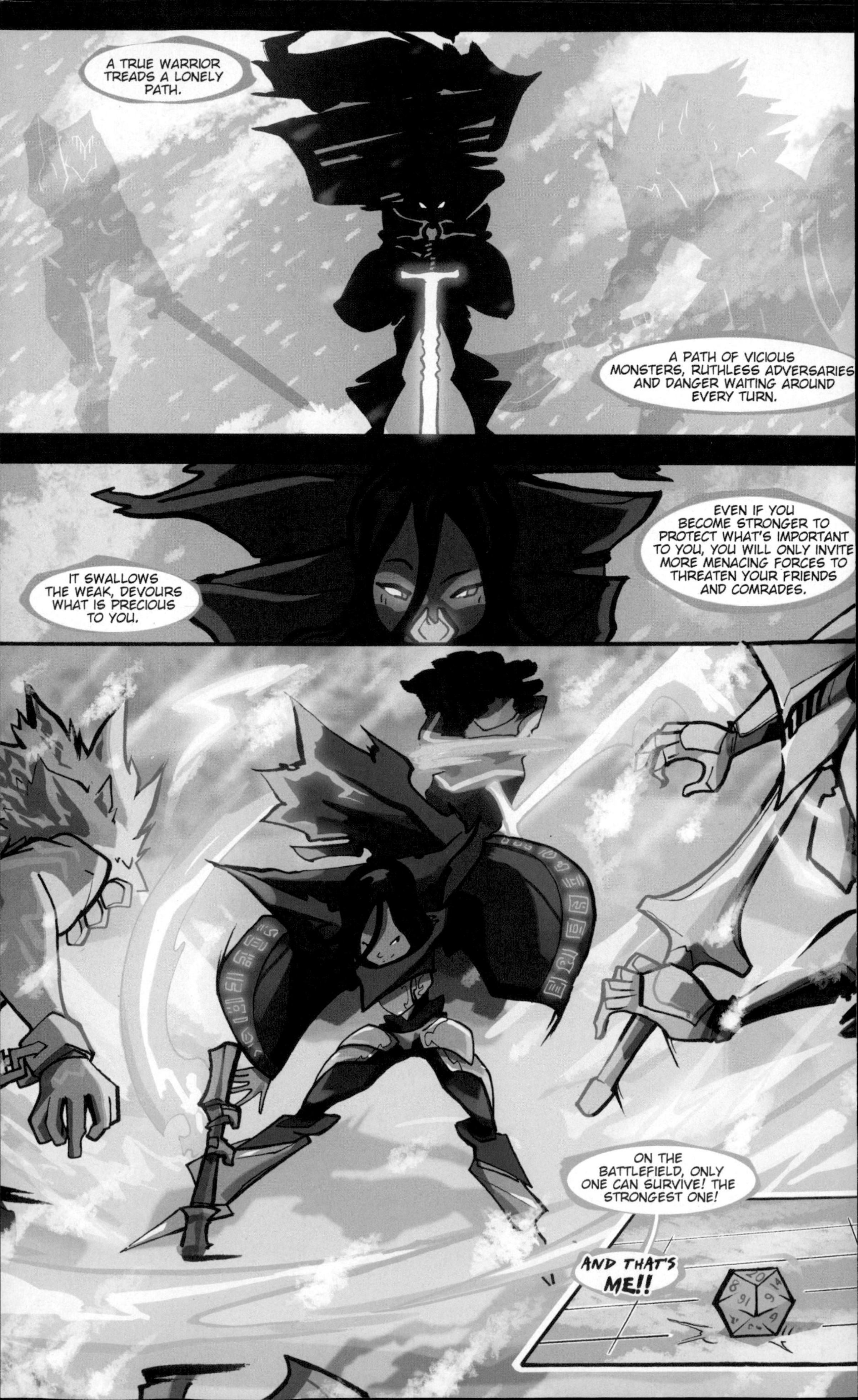
A TRUE WARRIOR TREADS A LONELY PATH.
A PATH OF VICIOUS MONSTERS, RUTHLESS ADVERSARIES AND DANGER WAITING AROUND EVERY TURN.
IT SWALLOWS THE WEAK, DEVOURS WHAT IS PRECIOUS TO YOU.
EVEN IF YOU BECOME STRONGER TO PROTECT WHAT'S IMPORTANT TO YOU, YOU WILL ONLY INVITE MORE MENACING FORCES TO THREATEN YOUR FRIENDS AND COMRADES.
ON THE BATTLEFIELD, ONLY ONE CAN SURVIVE! THE STRONGEST ONE!
AND THAT'S ME!!

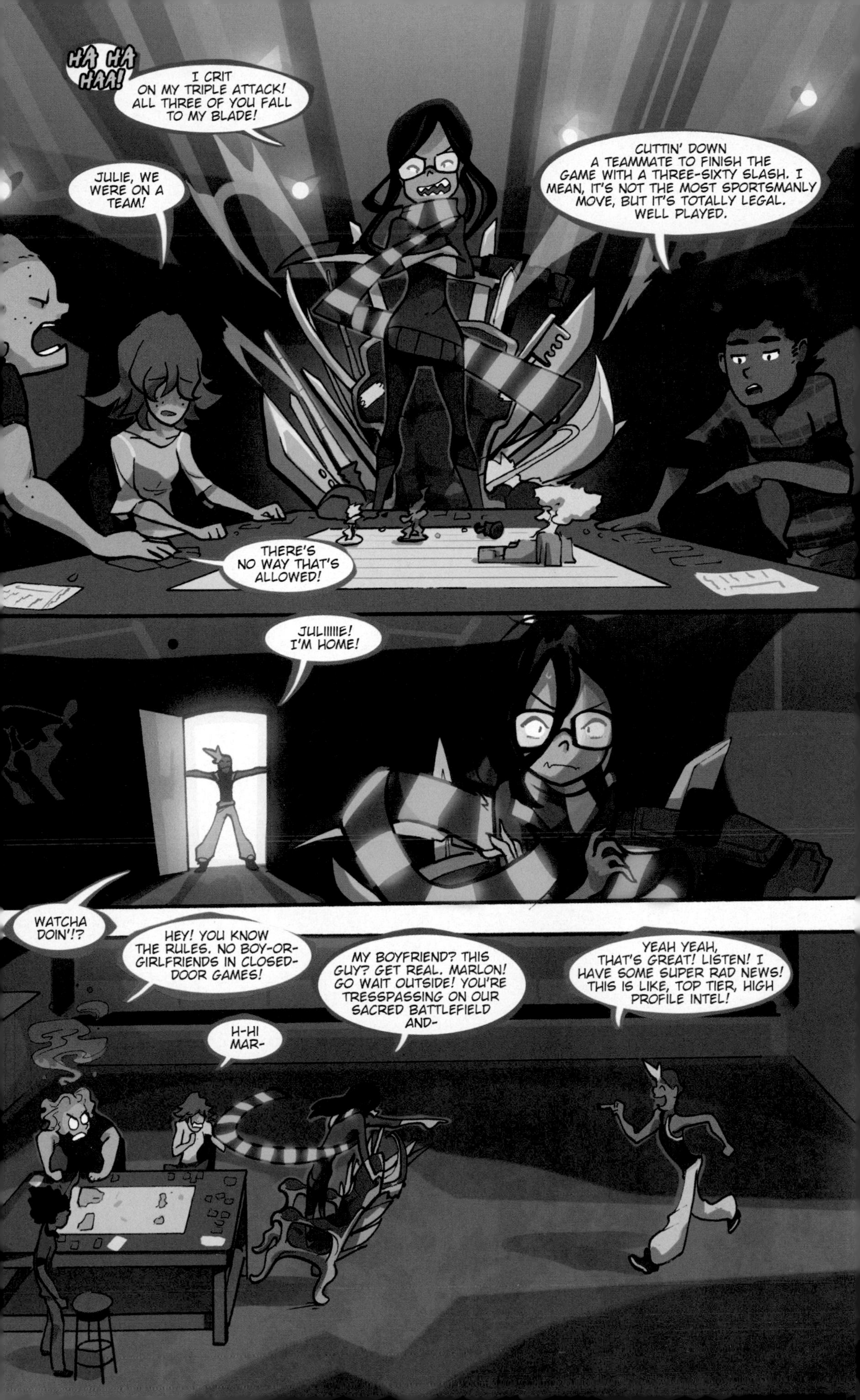
HA HA HAA!
I CRIT ON MY TRIPLE ATTACK! ALL THREE OF YOU FALL TO MY BLADE!
JULIE, WE WERE ON A TEAM!
CUTTIN' DOWN A TEAMMATE TO FINISH THE GAME WITH A THREE-SIXTY SLASH. I MEAN, IT'S NOT THE MOST SPORTSMANLY MOVE, BUT IT'S TOTALLY LEGAL. WELL PLAYED.
THERE'S NO WAY THAT'S ALLOWED!
JULIIIIIE! I'M HOME!
WATCHA DOIN'!?
HEY! YOU KNOW THE RULES. NO BOY-OR-GIRLFRIENDS IN CLOSED-DOOR GAMES!
H-HI MAR-
MY BOYFRIEND? THIS GUY? GET REAL. MARLON! GO WAIT OUTSIDE! YOU'RE TRESSPASSING ON OUR SACRED BATTLEFIELD AND-
YEAH YEAH, THAT'S GREAT! LISTEN! I HAVE SOME SUPER RAD NEWS! THIS IS LIKE, TOP TIER, HIGH PROFILE INTEL!

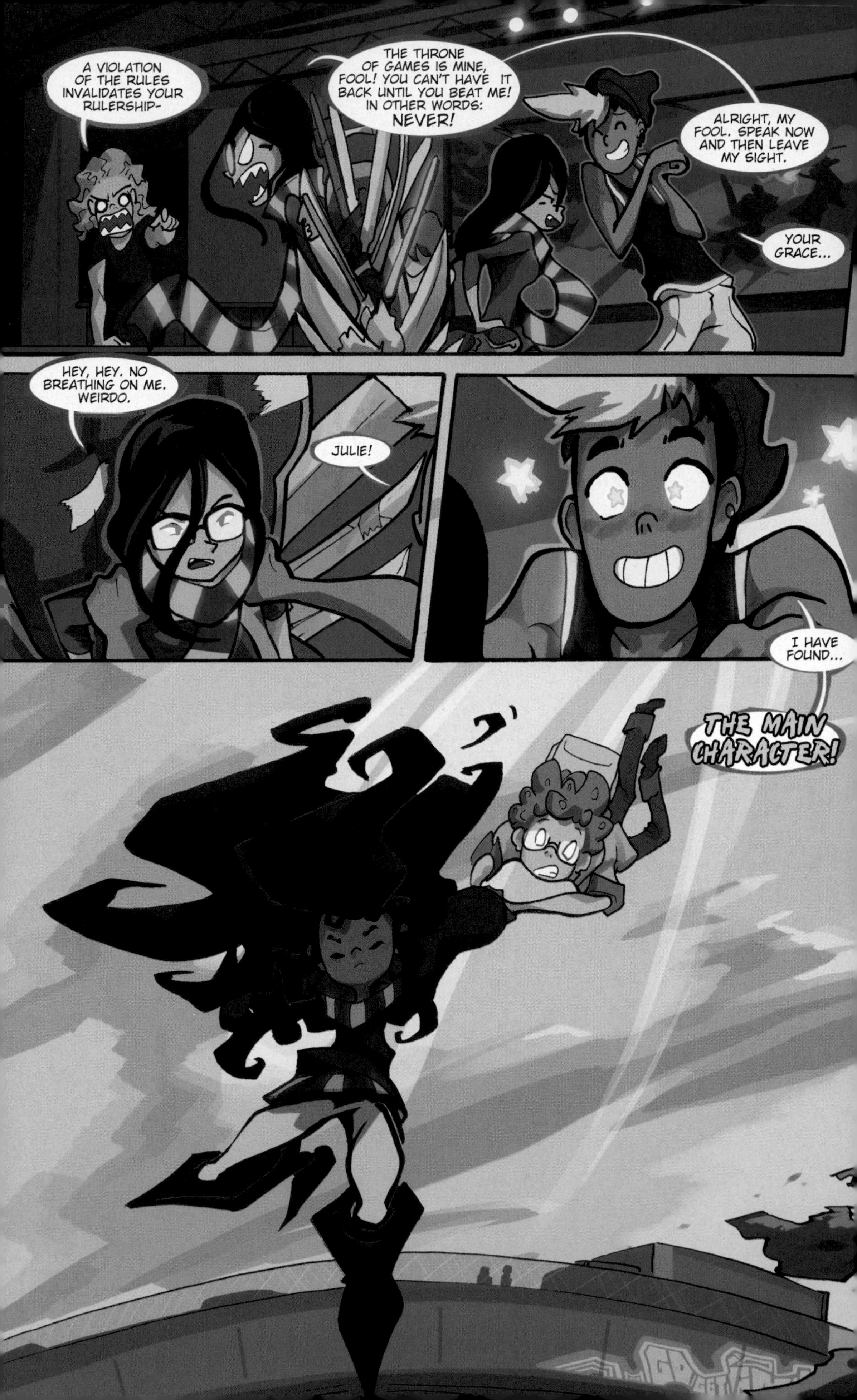
A VIOLATION OF THE RULES INVALIDATES YOUR RULERSHIP-
THE THRONE OF GAMES IS MINE, FOOL! YOU CAN'T HAVE IT BACK UNTIL YOU BEAT ME! IN OTHER WORDS: NEVER!
ALRIGHT, MY FOOL. SPEAK NOW AND THEN LEAVE MY SIGHT.
YOUR GRACE...
HEY, HEY. NO BREATHING ON ME. WEIRDO.
JULIE!
I HAVE FOUND...
THE MAIN CHARACTER!

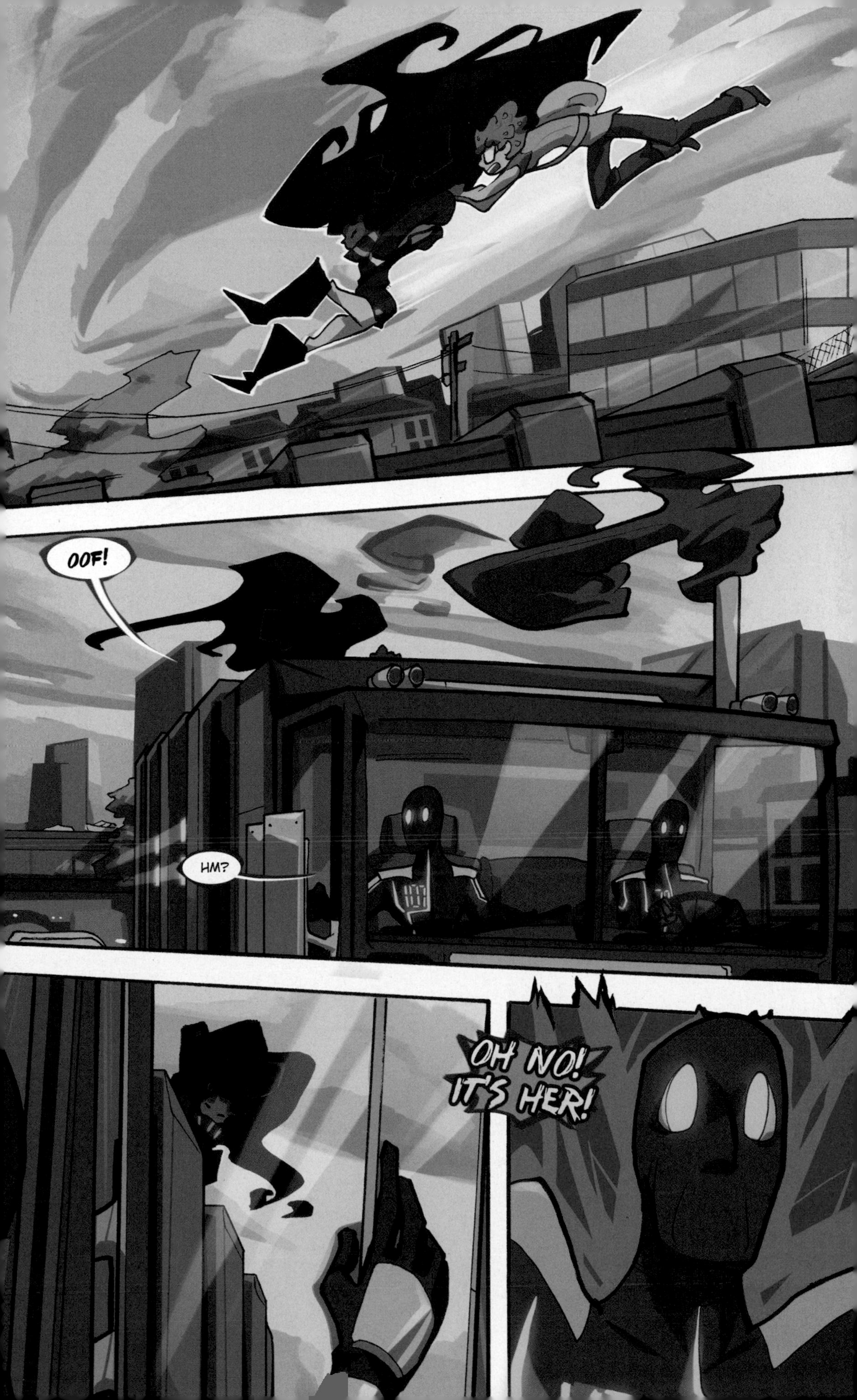
OOF!
HM?
OH NO! IT'S HER!

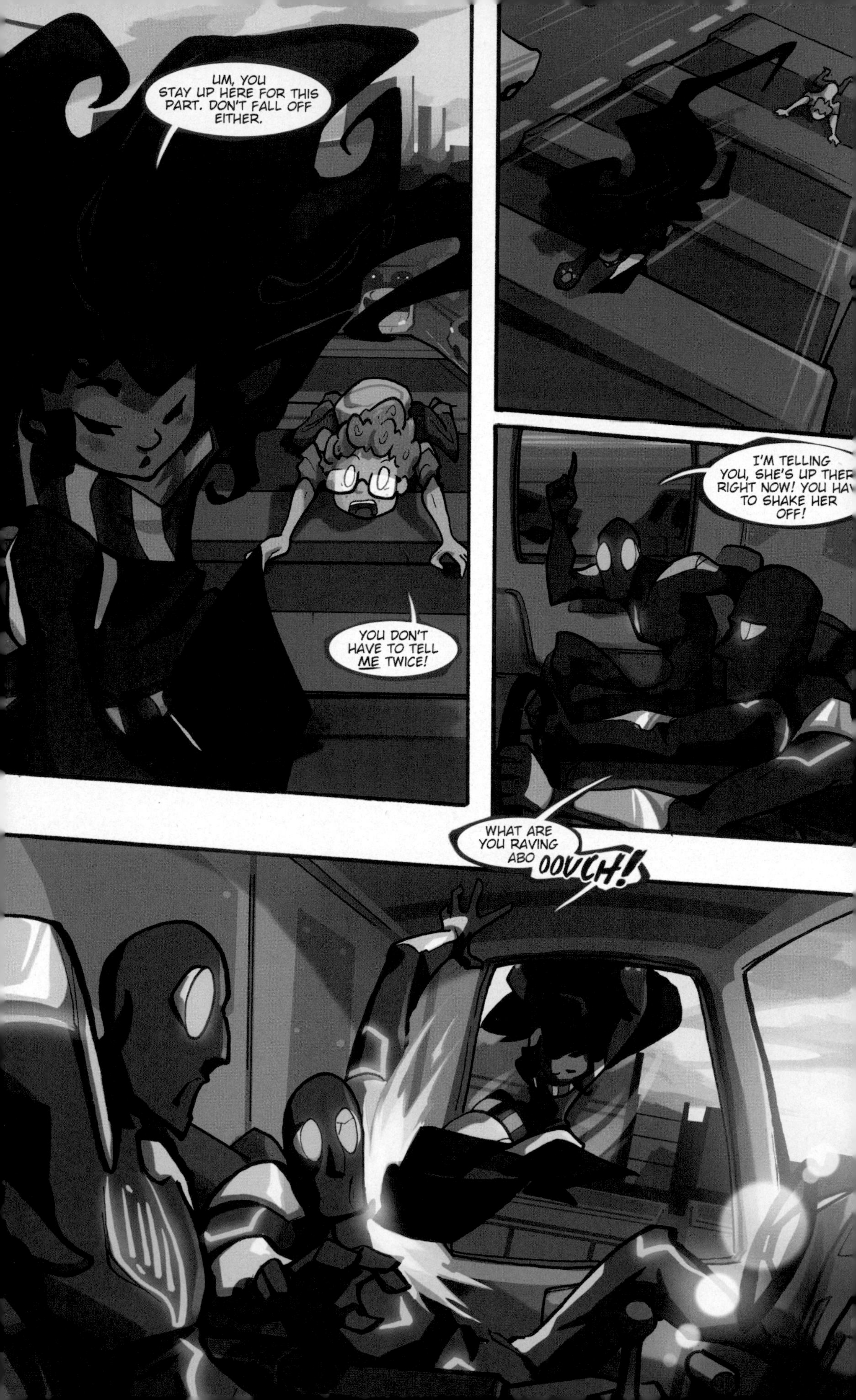
UM, YOU STAY UP HERE FOR THIS PART. DON'T FALL OFF EITHER.
YOU DON'T HAVE TO TELL ME TWICE!
I'M TELLING YOU, SHE'S UP THER RIGHT NOW! YOU HAV TO SHAKE HER OFF!
WHAT ARE YOU RAVING ABO OOUCH!

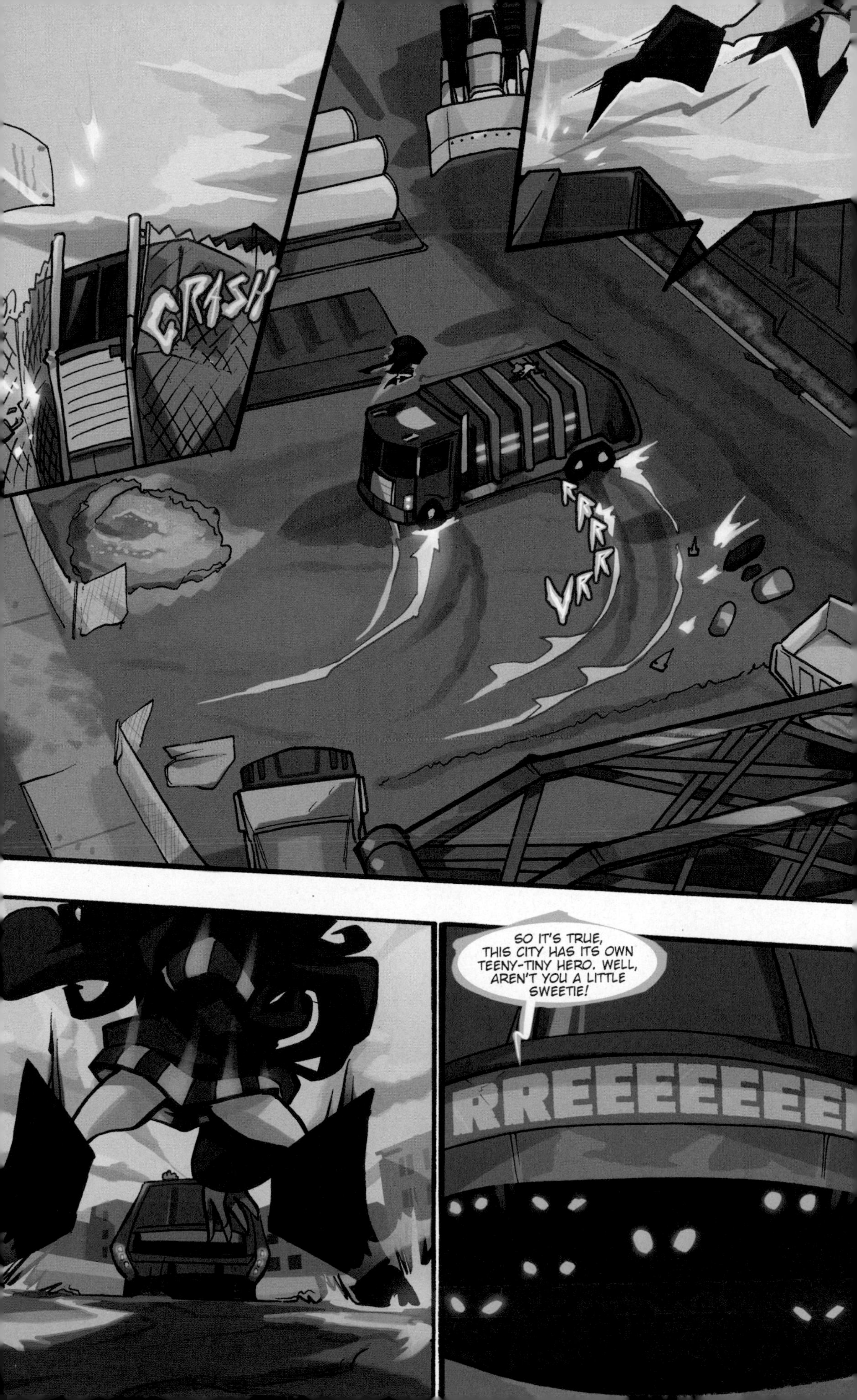
CRASH
RRRRRVRR
SO IT'S TRUE, THIS CITY HAS ITS OWN TEENY-TINY HERO. WELL, AREN'T YOU A LITTLE SWEETIE!
RREEEEEEEE

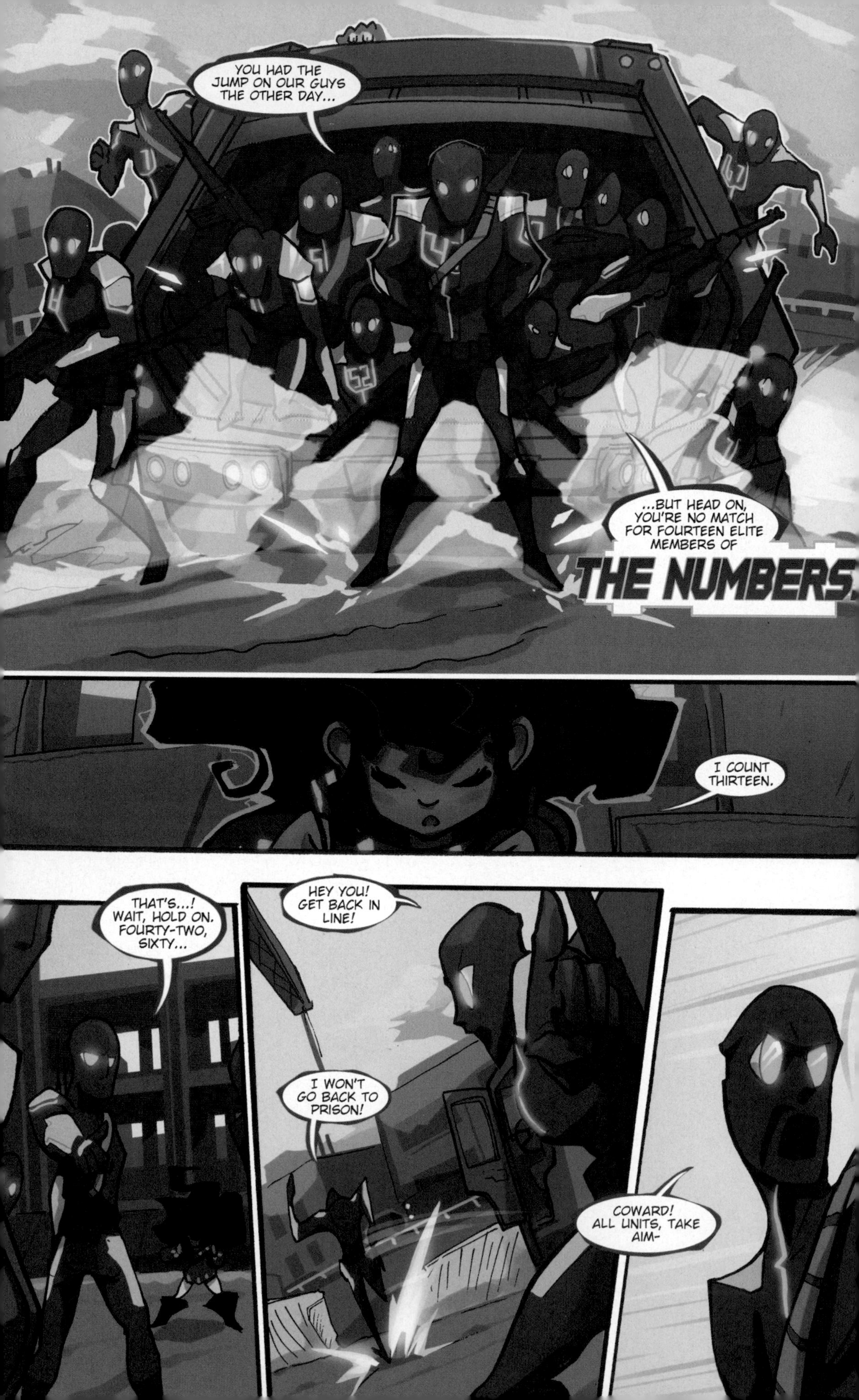
YOU HAD THE JUMP ON OUR GUYS THE OTHER DAY...
...BUT HEAD ON, YOU'RE NO MATCH FOR FOURTEEN ELITE MEMBERS OF
THE NUMBERS.
I COUNT THIRTEEN.
THAT'S...! WAIT, HOLD ON. FOURTY-TWO, SIXTY...
HEY YOU! GET BACK IN LINE!
I WON'T GO BACK TO PRISON!
COWARD! ALL UNITS, TAKE AIM-

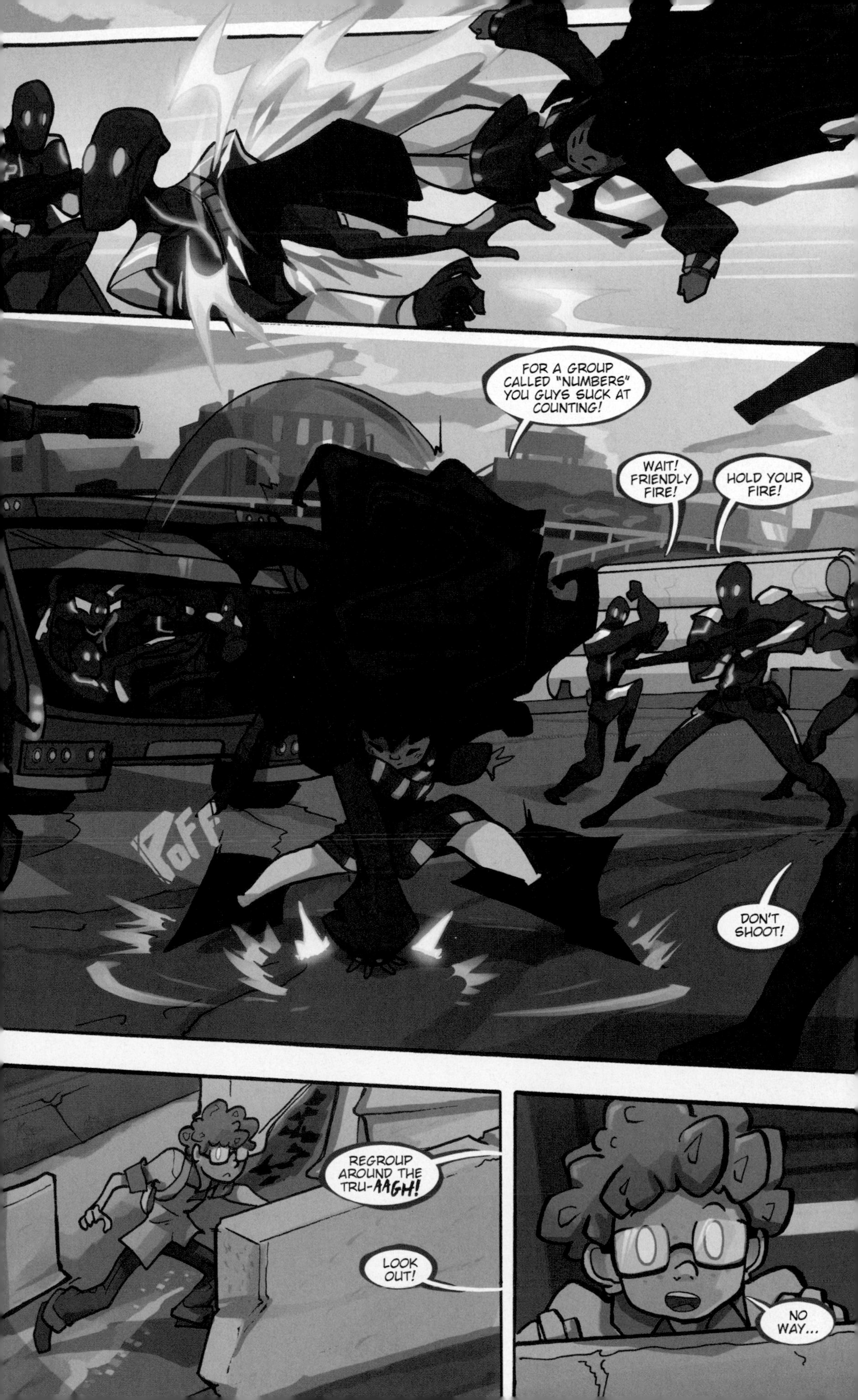
FOR A GROUP CALLED "NUMBERS" YOU GUYS SUCK AT COUNTING!
WAIT! FRIENDLY FIRE!
HOLD YOUR FIRE!
POFF
DON'T SHOOT!
REGROUP AROUND THE TRU-AAGH!
LOOK OUT!
NO WAY...

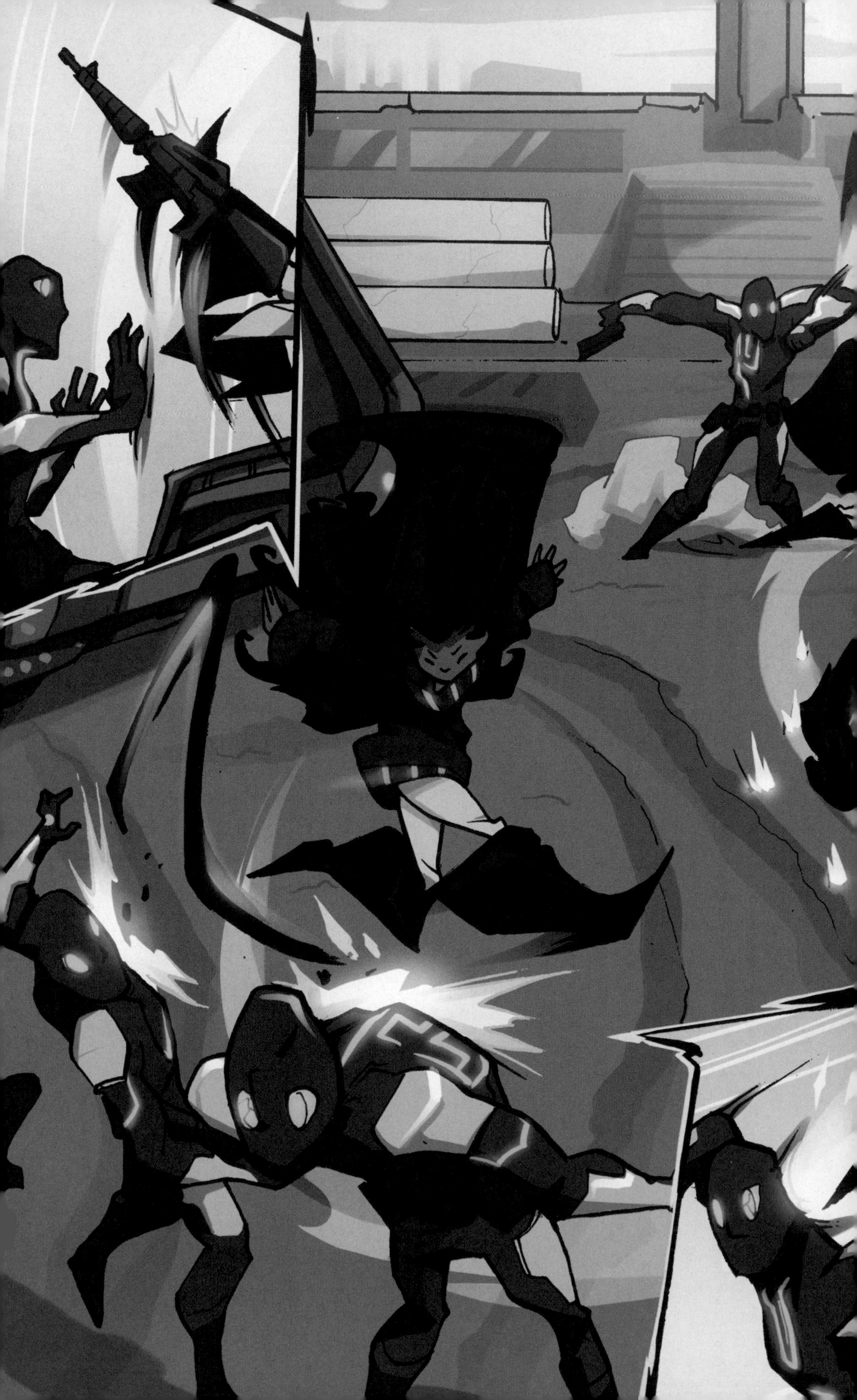

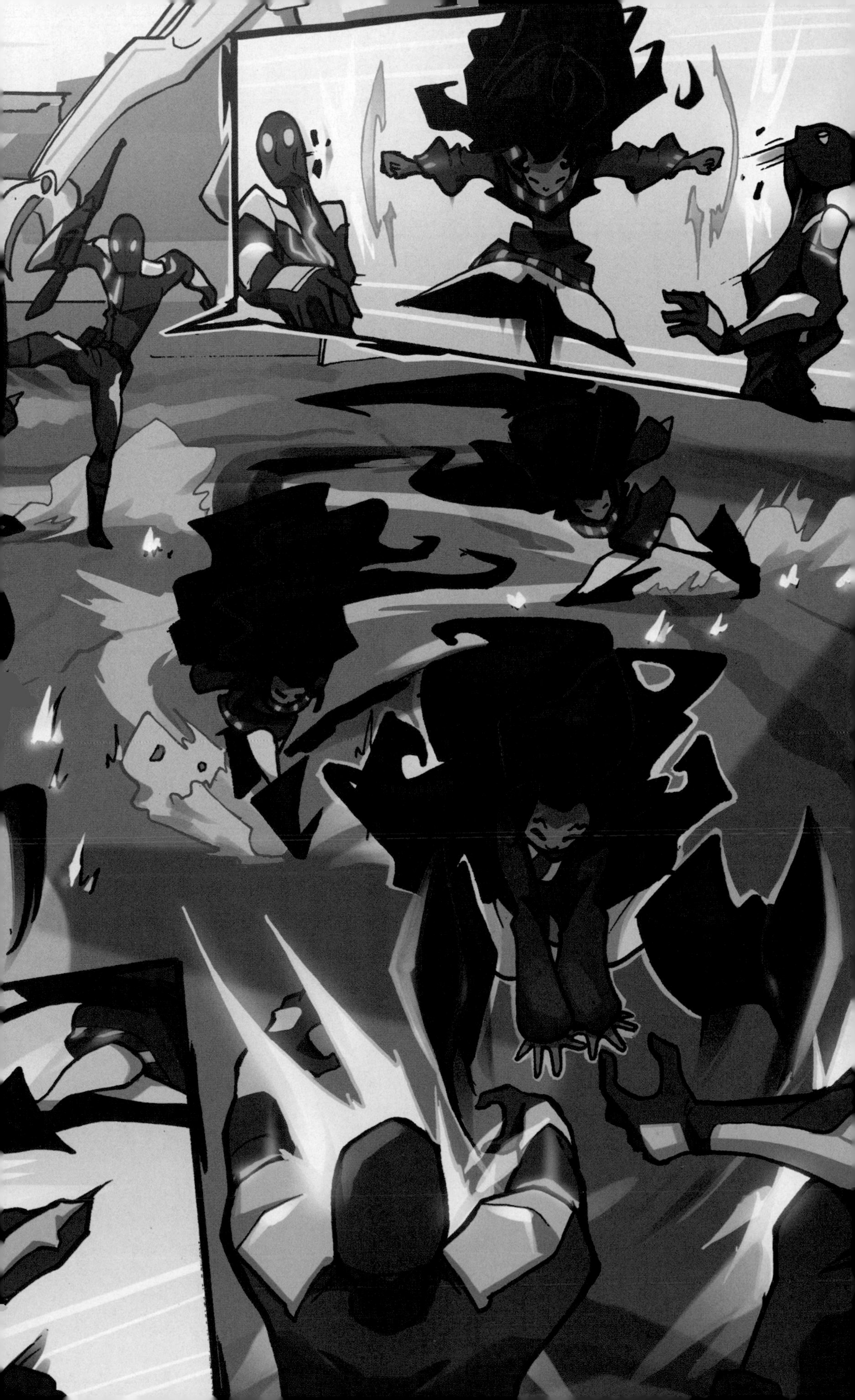

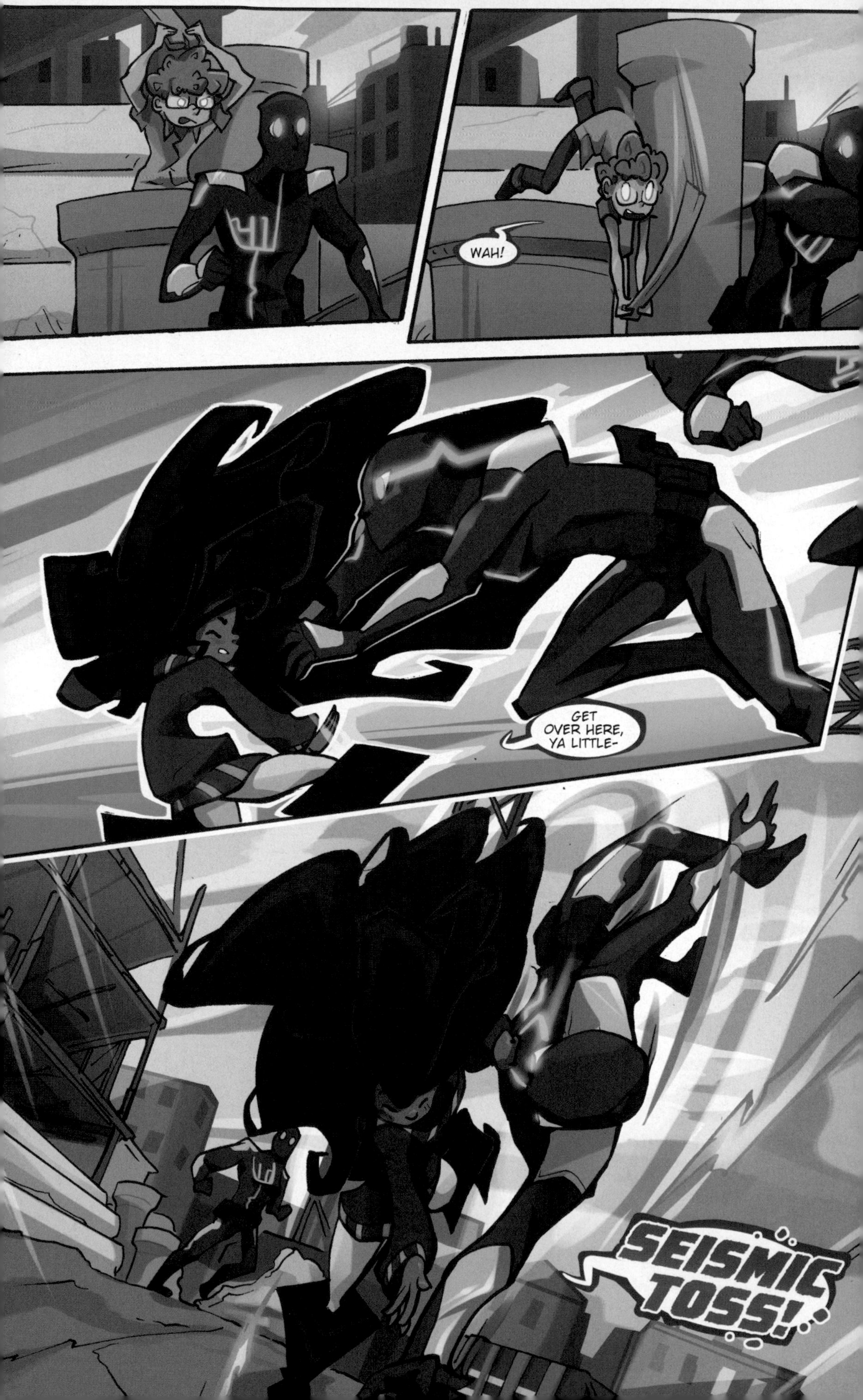
WAH!
GET OVER HERE, YA LITTLE-
SEISMIC TOSS!

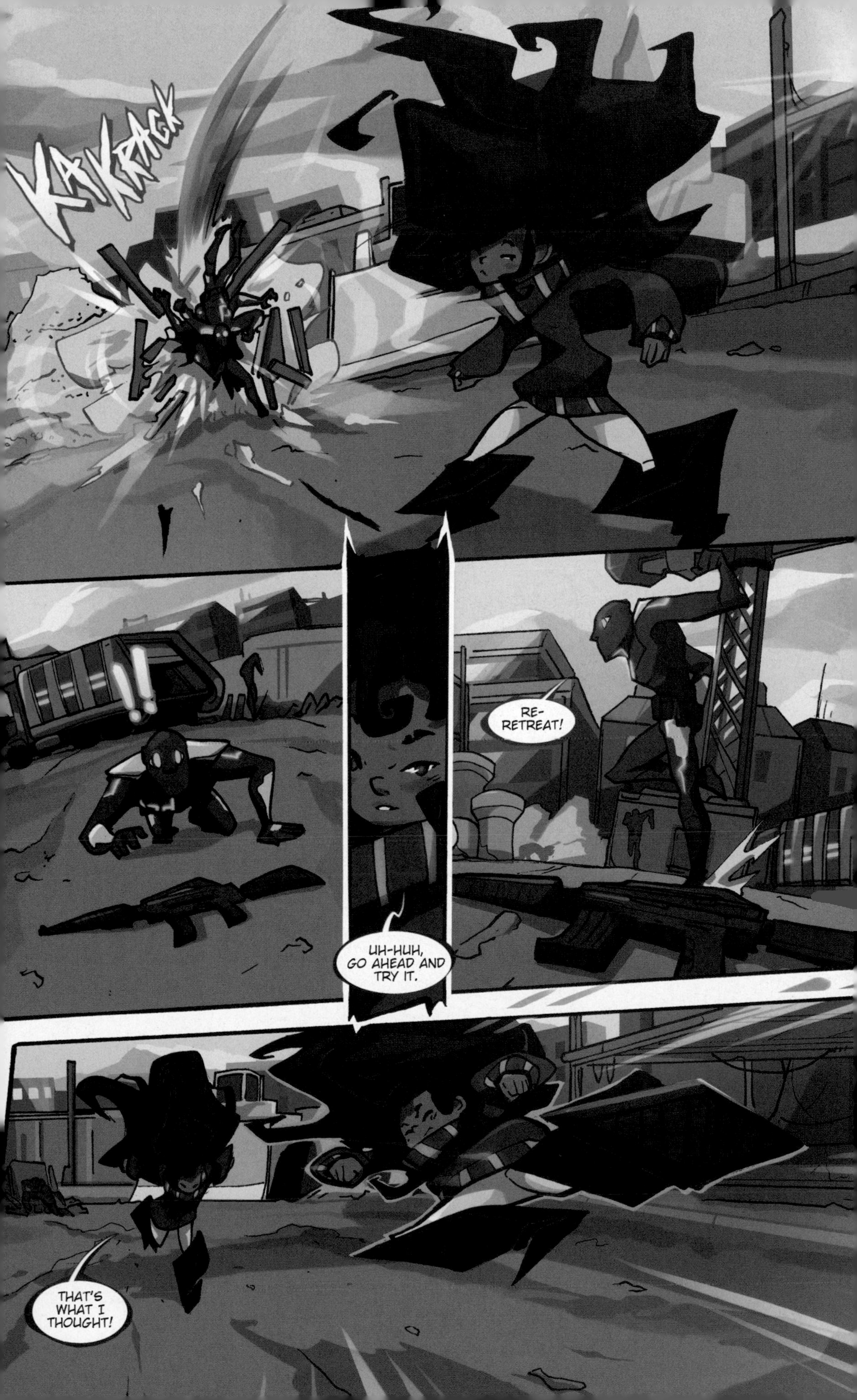
KA KRACK
RE-RETREAT!
UH-HUH, GO AHEAD AND TRY IT.
THAT'S WHAT I THOUGHT!

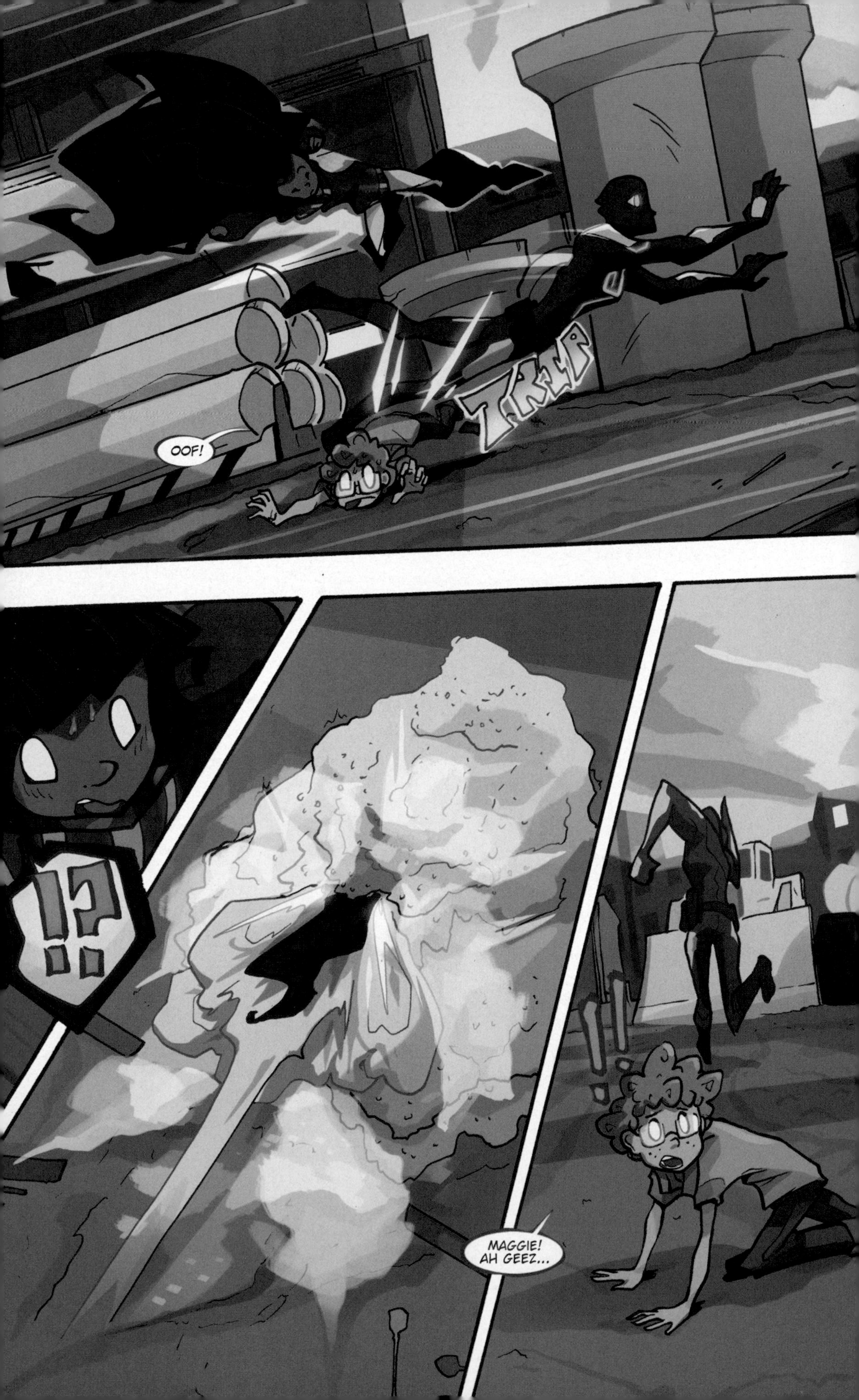
TRIP
OOF!
!?
MAGGIE!
AH GEEZ...

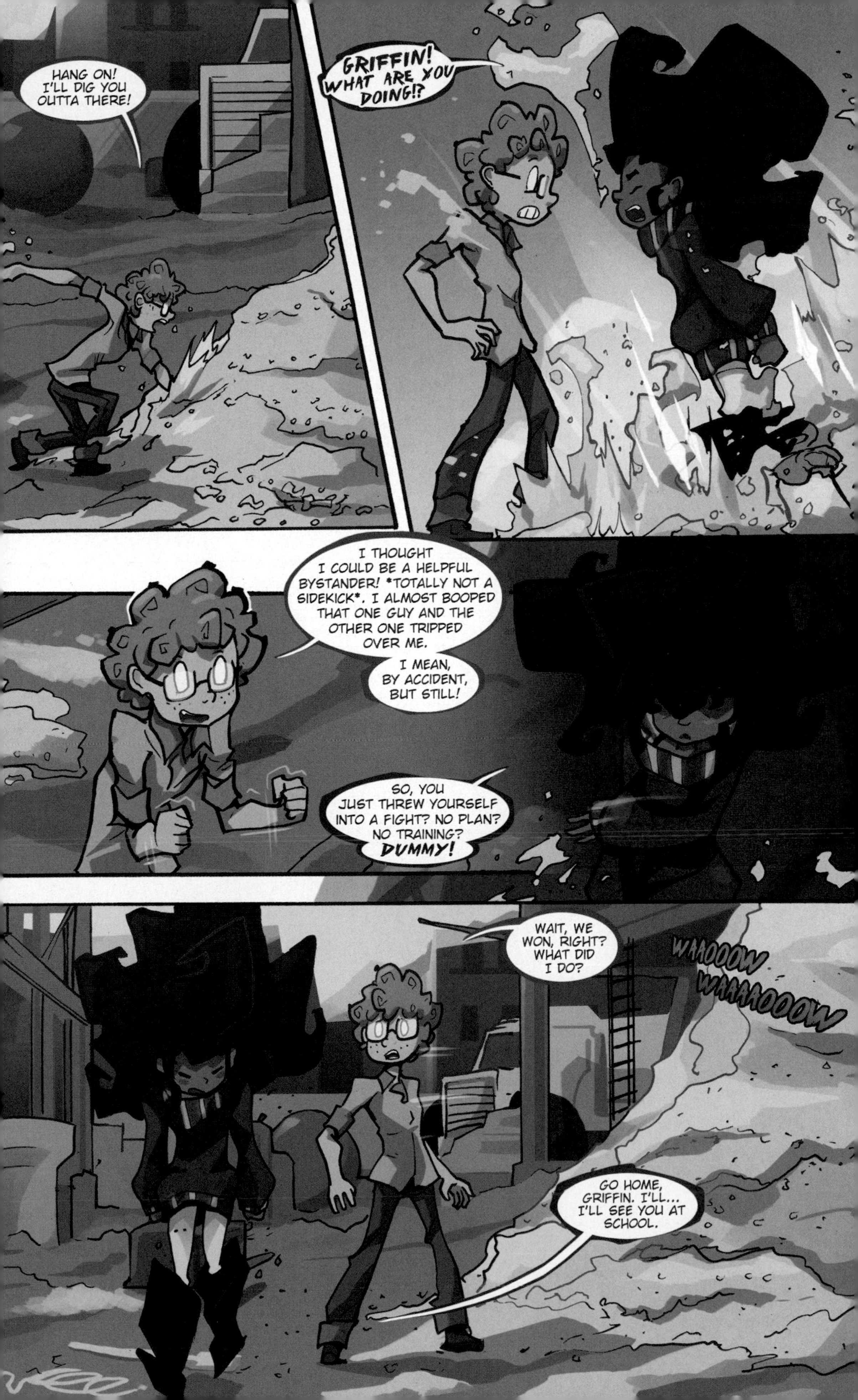
HANG ON! I'LL DIG YOU OUTTA THERE!
GRIFFIN! WHAT ARE YOU DOING!?
I THOUGHT I COULD BE A HELPFUL BYSTANDER! *TOTALLY NOT A SIDEKICK*. I ALMOST BOOPED THAT ONE GUY AND THE OTHER ONE TRIPPED OVER ME.
I MEAN, BY ACCIDENT, BUT STILL!
SO, YOU JUST THREW YOURSELF INTO A FIGHT? NO PLAN? NO TRAINING? DUMMY!
WAIT, WE WON, RIGHT? WHAT DID I DO?
WAAOOOW WAAAAOOOW
GO HOME, GRIFFIN. I'LL... I'LL SEE YOU AT SCHOOL.

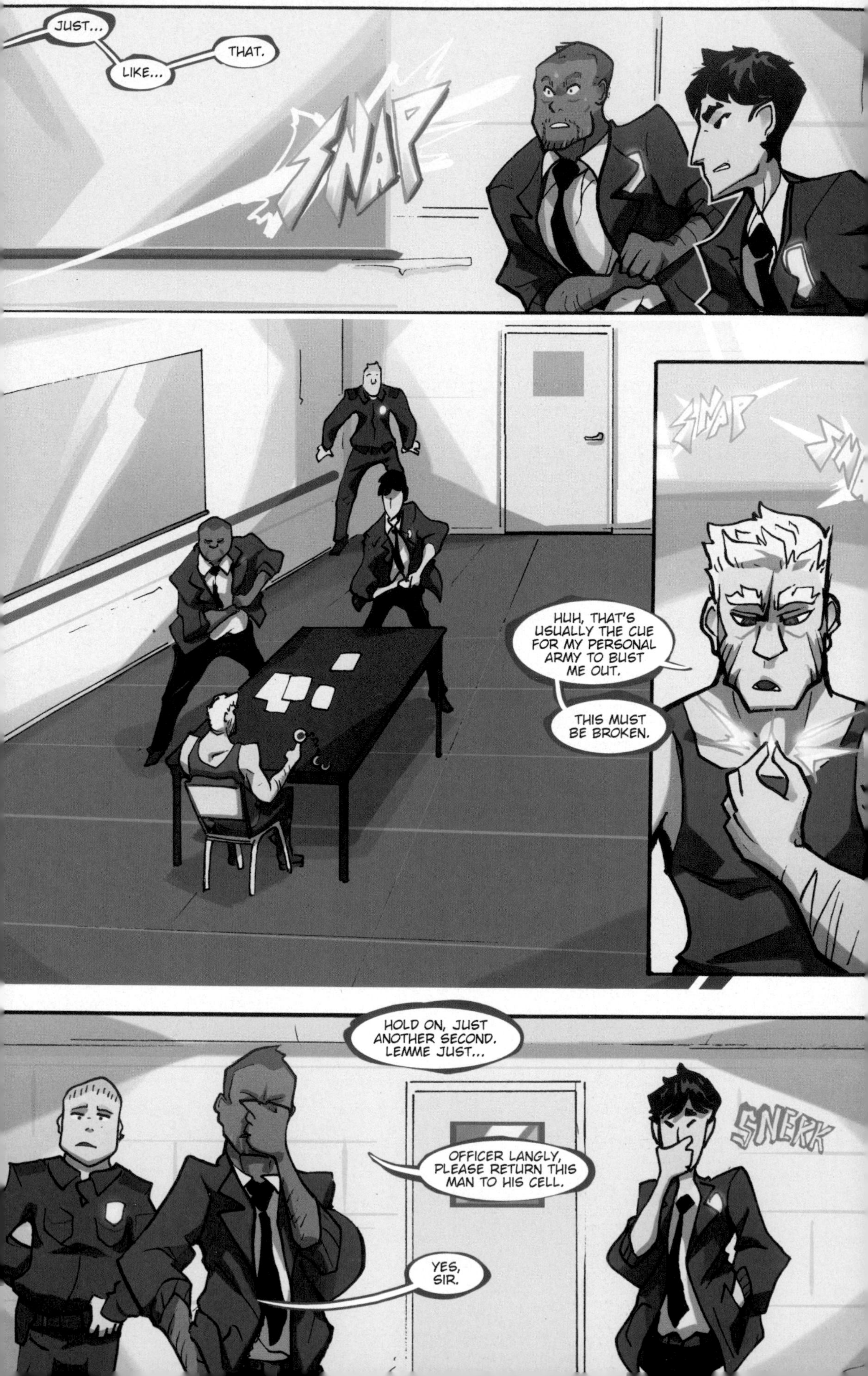
JUST...
LIKE...
THAT.
SNAP
SNAP
SNAP
HUH, THAT'S USUALLY THE CUE FOR MY PERSONAL ARMY TO BUST ME OUT.
THIS MUST BE BROKEN.
HOLD ON, JUST ANOTHER SECOND. LEMME JUST...
SNERK
OFFICER LANGLY, PLEASE RETURN THIS MAN TO HIS CELL.
YES, SIR.

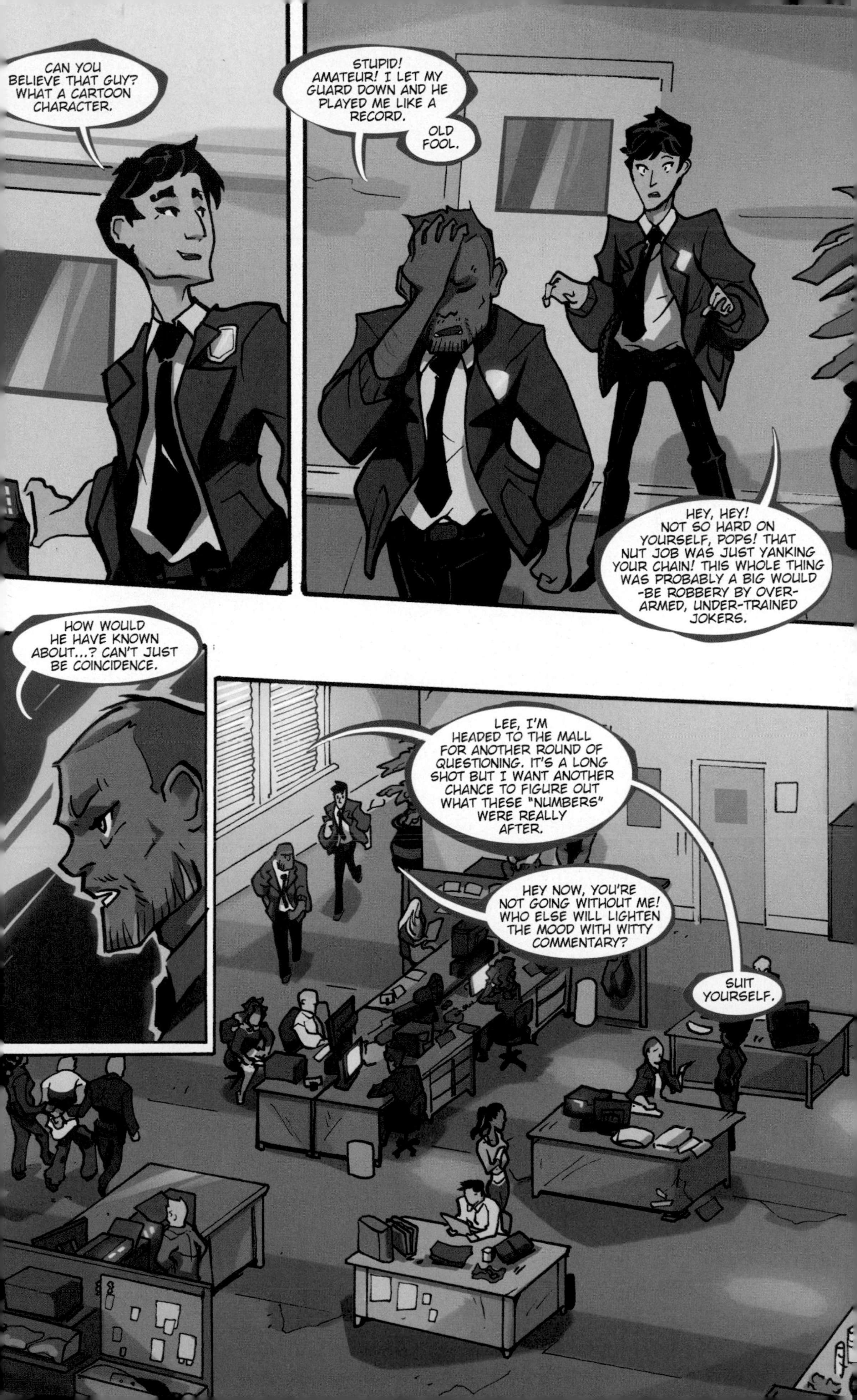
CAN YOU BELIEVE THAT GUY? WHAT A CARTOON CHARACTER.
STUPID! AMATEUR! I LET MY GUARD DOWN AND HE PLAYED ME LIKE A RECORD.
OLD FOOL.
HEY, HEY! NOT SO HARD ON YOURSELF, POPS! THAT NUT JOB WAS JUST YANKING YOUR CHAIN! THIS WHOLE THING WAS PROBABLY A BIG WOULD-BE ROBBERY BY OVER-ARMED, UNDER-TRAINED JOKERS.
HOW WOULD HE HAVE KNOWN ABOUT...? CAN'T JUST BE COINCIDENCE.
LEE, I'M HEADED TO THE MALL FOR ANOTHER ROUND OF QUESTIONING. IT'S A LONG SHOT BUT I WANT ANOTHER CHANCE TO FIGURE OUT WHAT THESE "NUMBERS" WERE REALLY AFTER.
HEY NOW, YOU'RE NOT GOING WITHOUT ME! WHO ELSE WILL LIGHTEN THE MOOD WITH WITTY COMMENTARY?
SUIT YOURSELF.

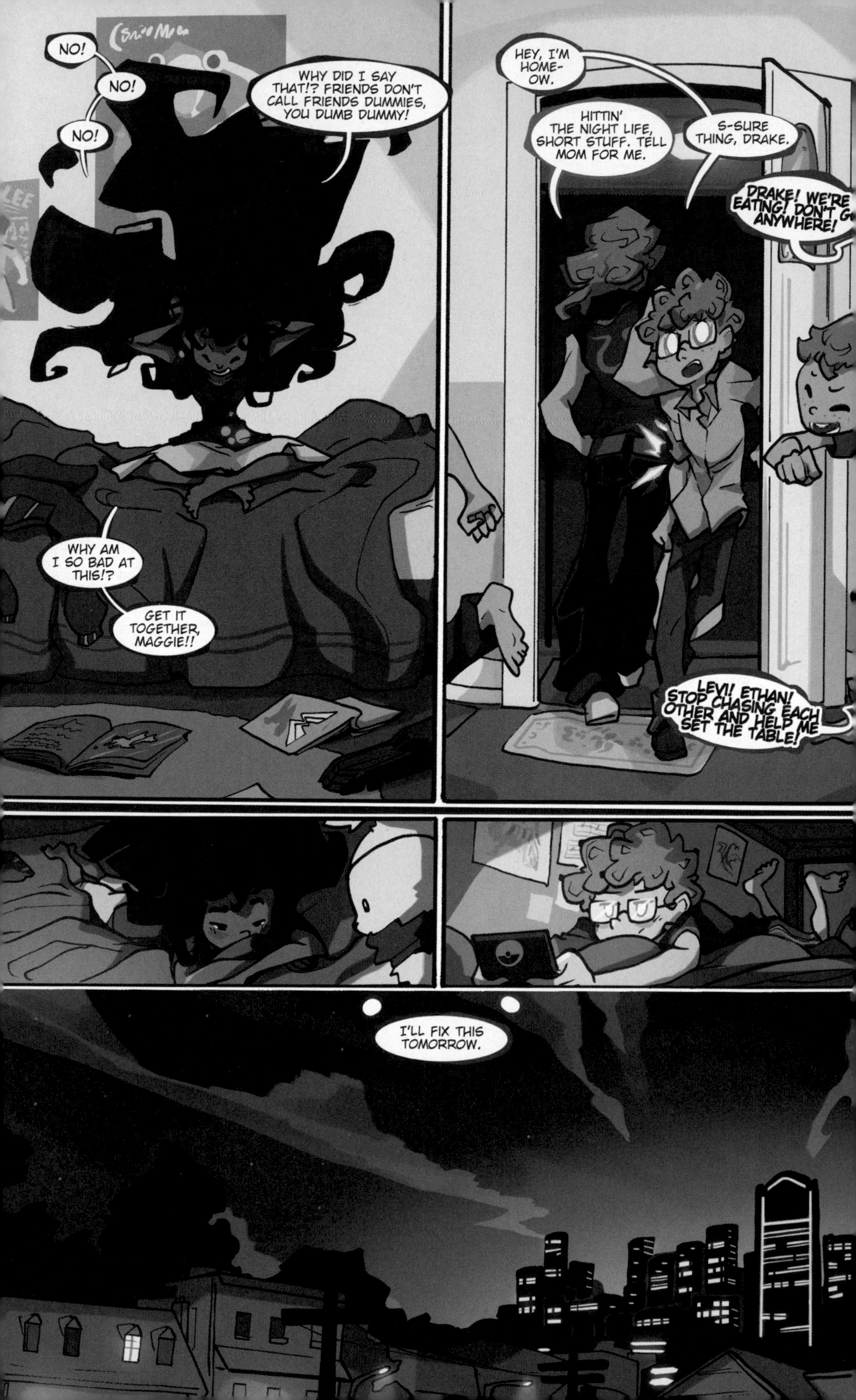
NO!
NO!
NO!
WHY DID I SAY THAT!? FRIENDS DON'T CALL FRIENDS DUMMIES, YOU DUMB DUMMY!
WHY AM I SO BAD AT THIS!?
GET IT TOGETHER, MAGGIE!!
HEY, I'M HOME-OW.
HITTIN' THE NIGHT LIFE, SHORT STUFF. TELL MOM FOR ME.
S-SURE THING, DRAKE.
DRAKE! WE'RE EATING! DON'T G ANYWHERE!
LEVI! ETHAN! STOP CHASING EACH OTHER AND HELP ME SET THE TABLE!
I'LL FIX THIS TOMORROW.

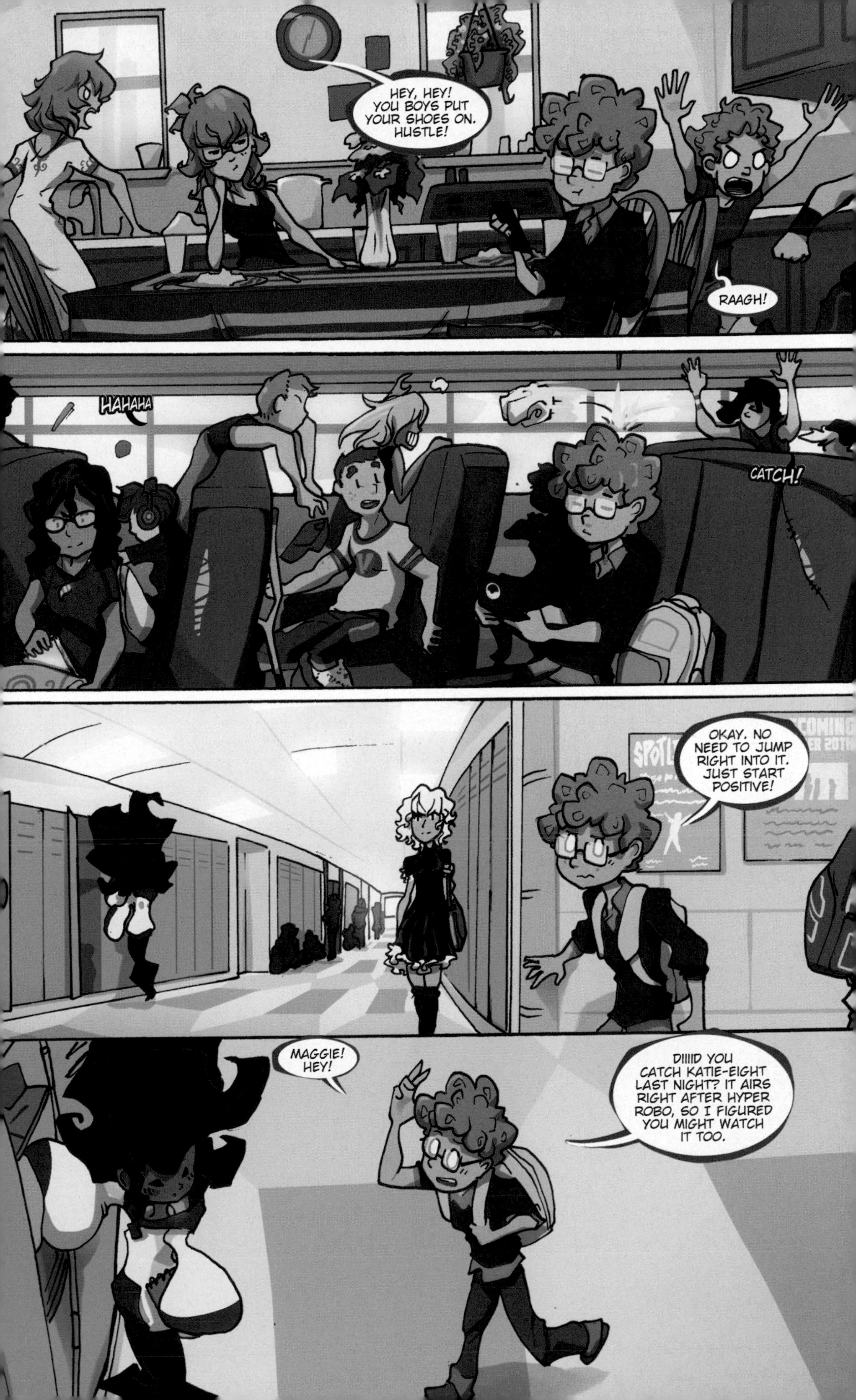
HEY, HEY! YOU BOYS PUT YOUR SHOES ON. HUSTLE!
RAAGH!
HAHAHA
CATCH!
OKAY. NO NEED TO JUMP RIGHT INTO IT. JUST START POSITIVE!
MAGGIE! HEY!
DIIIID YOU CATCH KATIE-EIGHT LAST NIGHT? IT AIRS RIGHT AFTER HYPER ROBO, SO I FIGURED YOU MIGHT WATCH IT TOO.

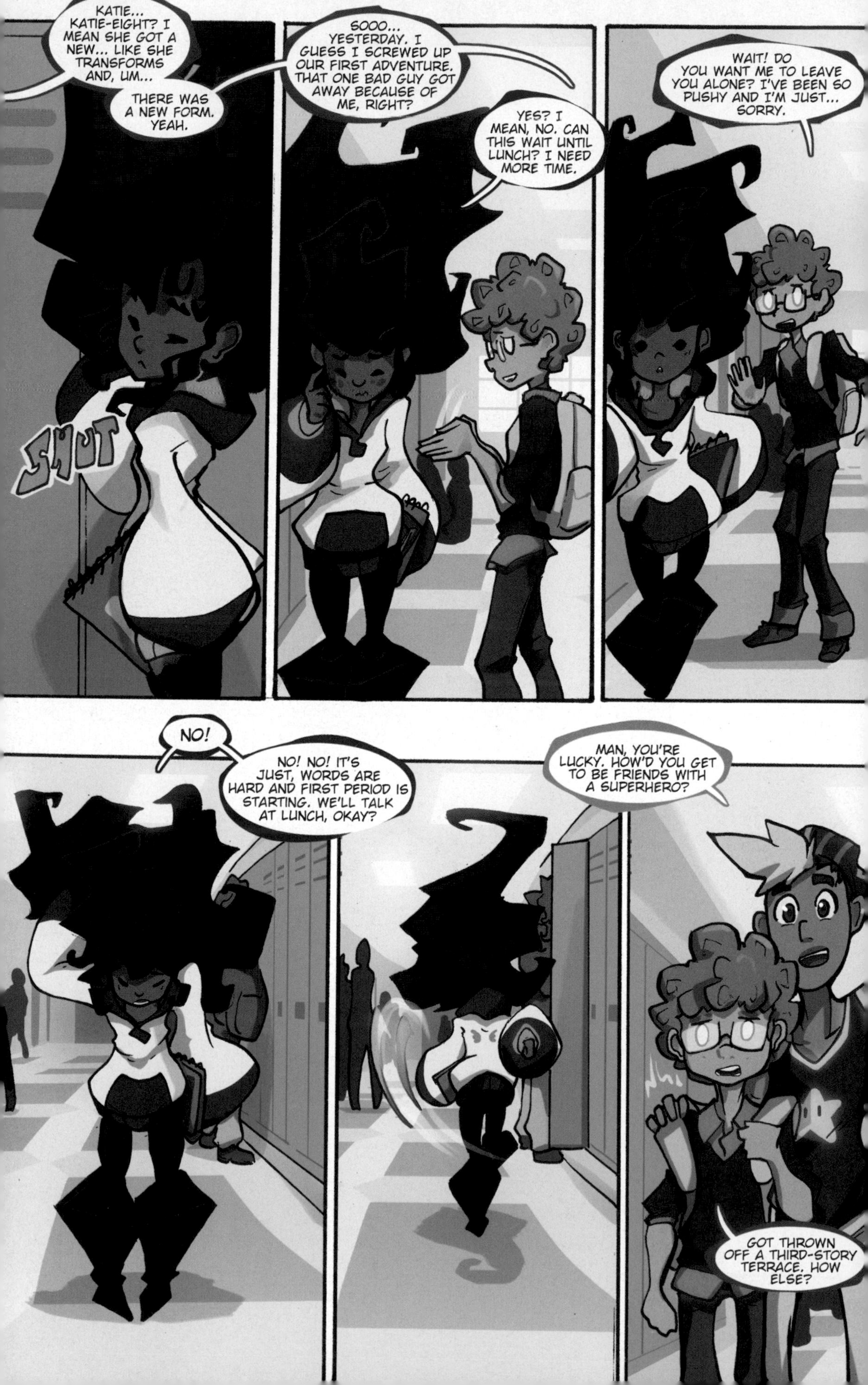
KATIE... KATIE-EIGHT? I MEAN SHE GOT A NEW... LIKE SHE TRANSFORMS AND, UM...
THERE WAS A NEW FORM. YEAH.
SHUT
SOOO... YESTERDAY. I GUESS I SCREWED UP OUR FIRST ADVENTURE. THAT ONE BAD GUY GOT AWAY BECAUSE OF ME, RIGHT?
YES? I MEAN, NO. CAN THIS WAIT UNTIL LUNCH? I NEED MORE TIME.
WAIT! DO YOU WANT ME TO LEAVE YOU ALONE? I'VE BEEN SO PUSHY AND I'M JUST... SORRY.
NO!
NO! NO! IT'S JUST, WORDS ARE HARD AND FIRST PERIOD IS STARTING. WE'LL TALK AT LUNCH, OKAY?
MAN, YOU'RE LUCKY. HOW'D YOU GET TO BE FRIENDS WITH A SUPERHERO?
GOT THROWN OFF A THIRD-STORY TERRACE. HOW ELSE?

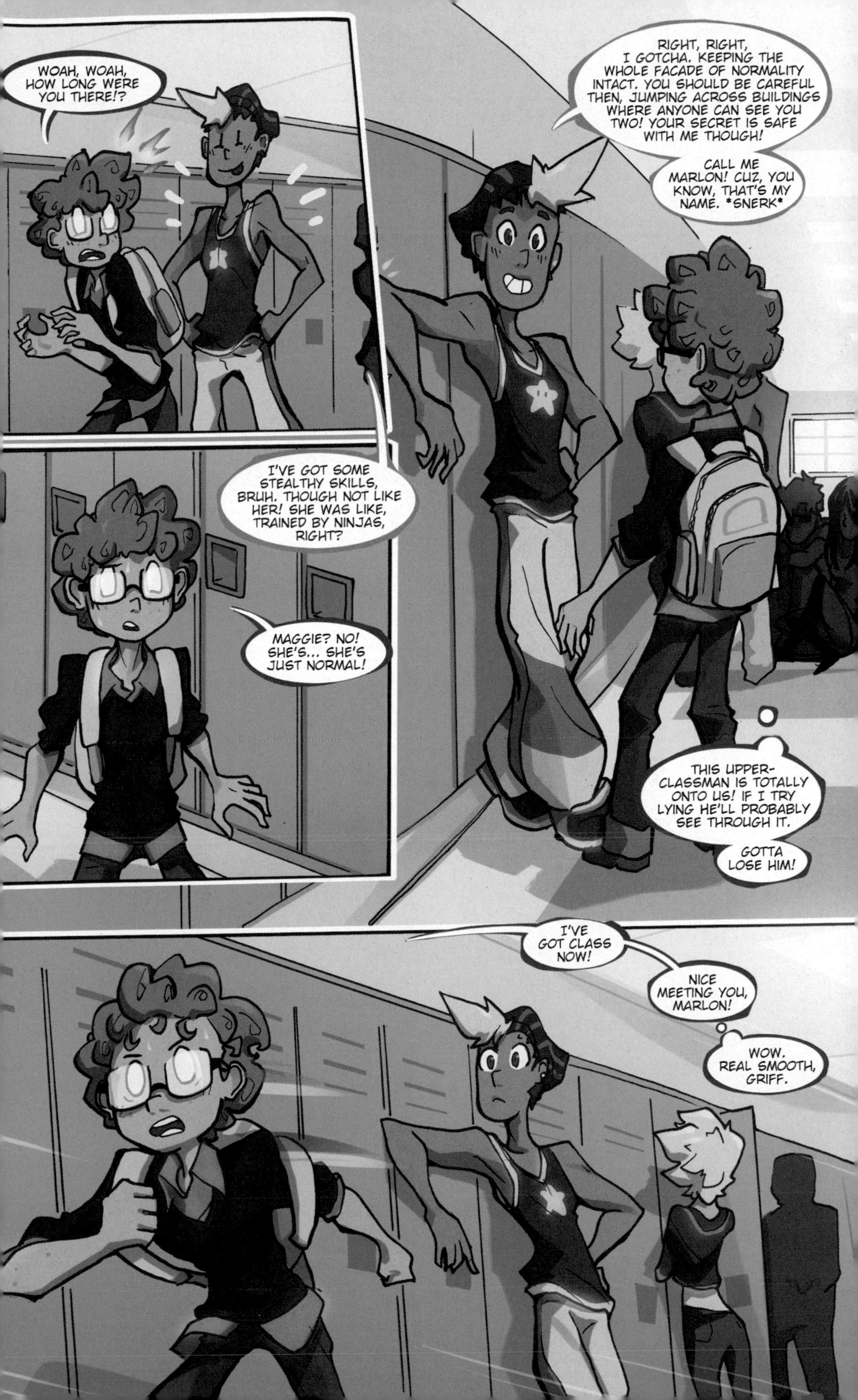
WOAH, WOAH, HOW LONG WERE YOU THERE!?
RIGHT, RIGHT, I GOTCHA. KEEPING THE WHOLE FACADE OF NORMALITY INTACT. YOU SHOULD BE CAREFUL THEN, JUMPING ACROSS BUILDINGS WHERE ANYONE CAN SEE YOU TWO! YOUR SECRET IS SAFE WITH ME THOUGH!
CALL ME MARLON! CUZ, YOU KNOW, THAT'S MY NAME. *SNERK*
I'VE GOT SOME STEALTHY SKILLS, BRUH. THOUGH NOT LIKE HER! SHE WAS LIKE, TRAINED BY NINJAS, RIGHT?
MAGGIE? NO! SHE'S... SHE'S JUST NORMAL!
THIS UPPER-CLASSMAN IS TOTALLY ONTO US! IF I TRY LYING HE'LL PROBABLY SEE THROUGH IT.
GOTTA LOSE HIM!
I'VE GOT CLASS NOW!
NICE MEETING YOU, MARLON!
WOW. REAL SMOOTH, GRIFF.

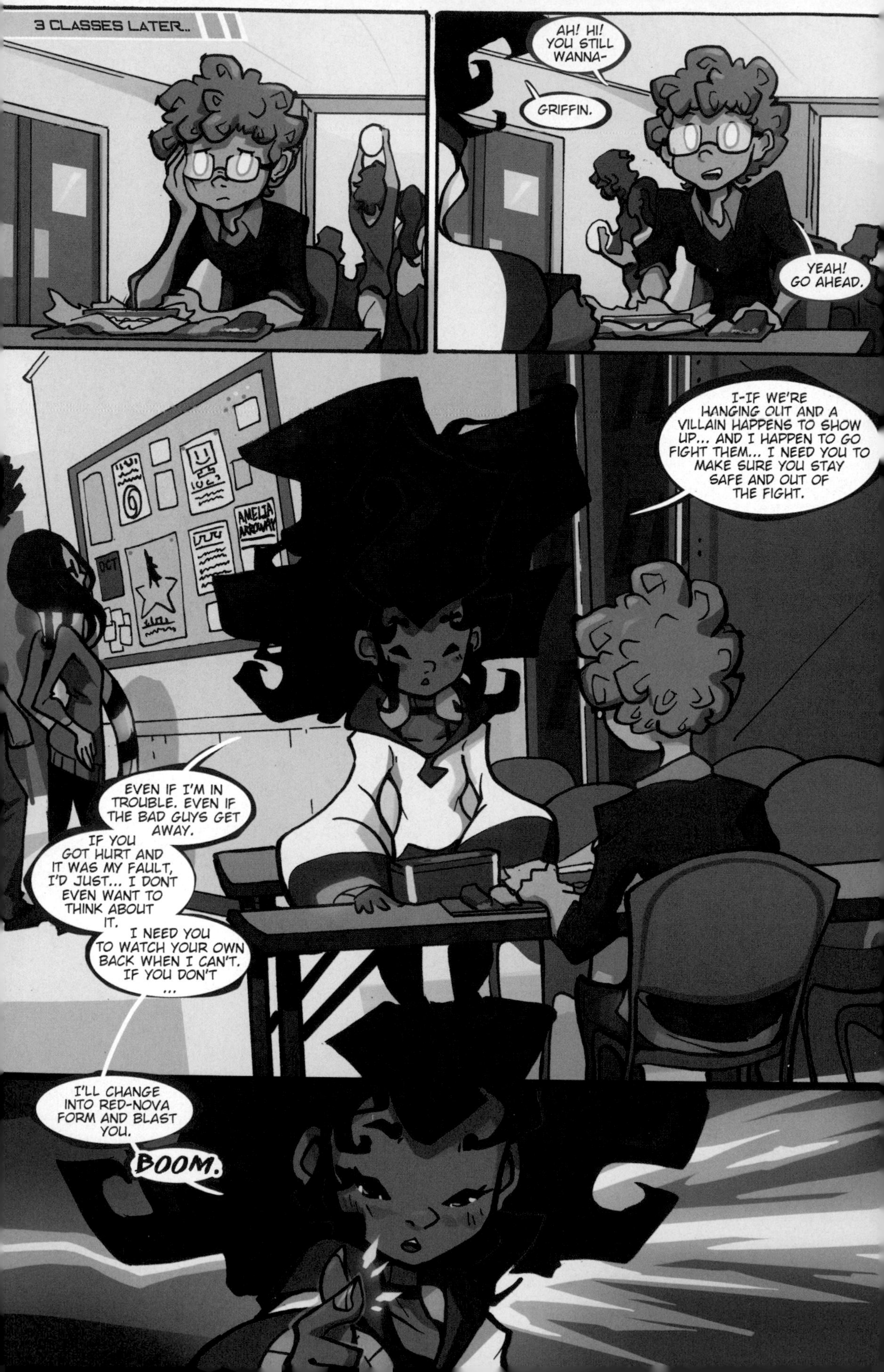

3 CLASSES LATER..
AH! HI! YOU STILL WANNA-
GRIFFIN.
YEAH! GO AHEAD.
I-IF WE'RE HANGING OUT AND A VILLAIN HAPPENS TO SHOW UP... AND I HAPPEN TO GO FIGHT THEM... I NEED YOU TO MAKE SURE YOU STAY SAFE AND OUT OF THE FIGHT.
EVEN IF I'M IN TROUBLE. EVEN IF THE BAD GUYS GET AWAY.
IF YOU GOT HURT AND IT WAS MY FAULT, I'D JUST... I DONT EVEN WANT TO THINK ABOUT IT.
I NEED YOU TO WATCH YOUR OWN BACK WHEN I CAN'T. IF YOU DON'T ...
I'LL CHANGE INTO RED-NOVA FORM AND BLAST YOU.
BOOM.
AMELIA ARROWAY
OCT

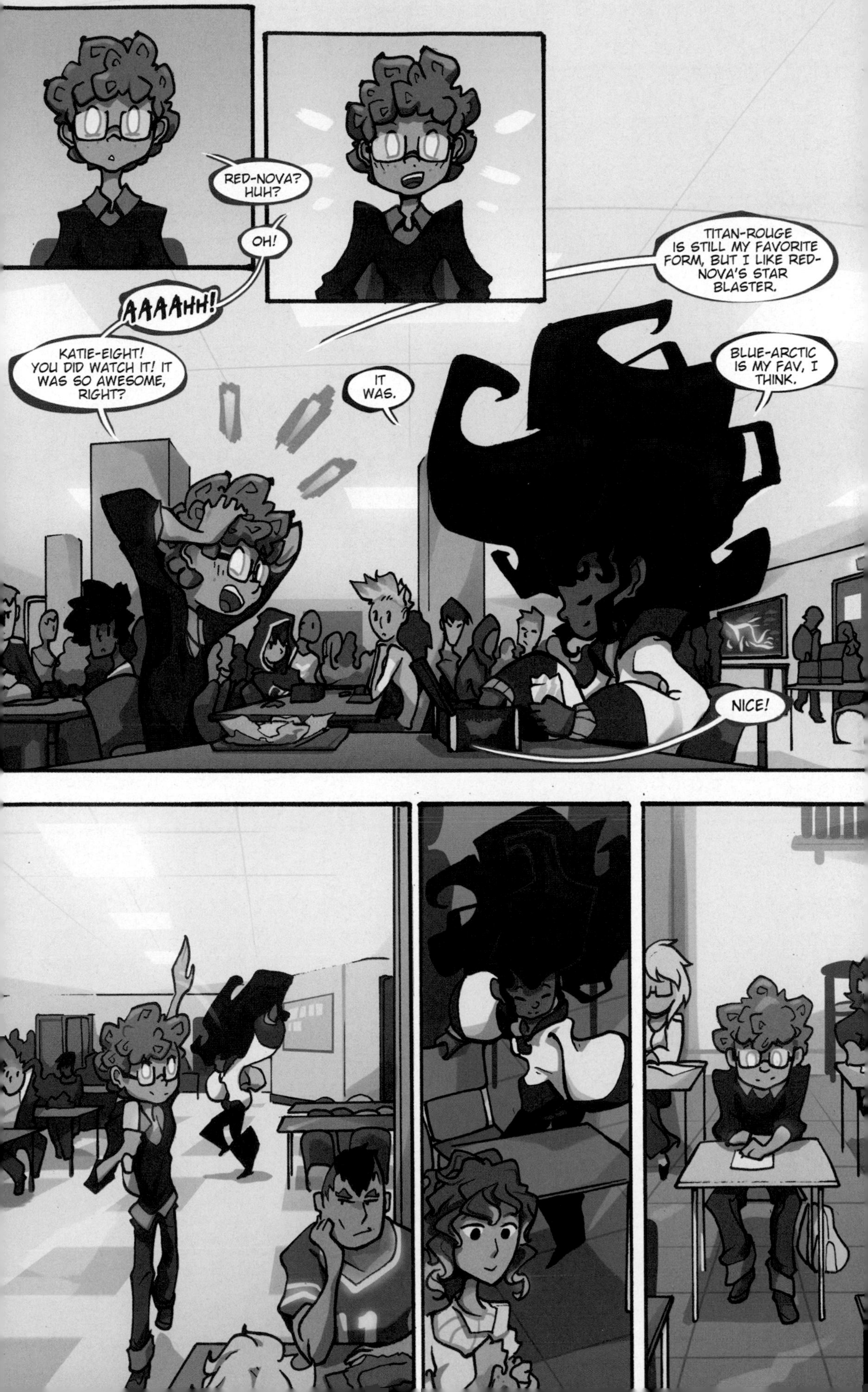
RED-NOVA? HUH?
OH!
TITAN-ROUGE IS STILL MY FAVORITE FORM, BUT I LIKE RED-NOVA'S STAR BLASTER.
AAAAHH!
KATIE-EIGHT! YOU DID WATCH IT! IT WAS SO AWESOME, RIGHT?
IT WAS.
BLUE-ARCTIC IS MY FAV, I THINK.
NICE!

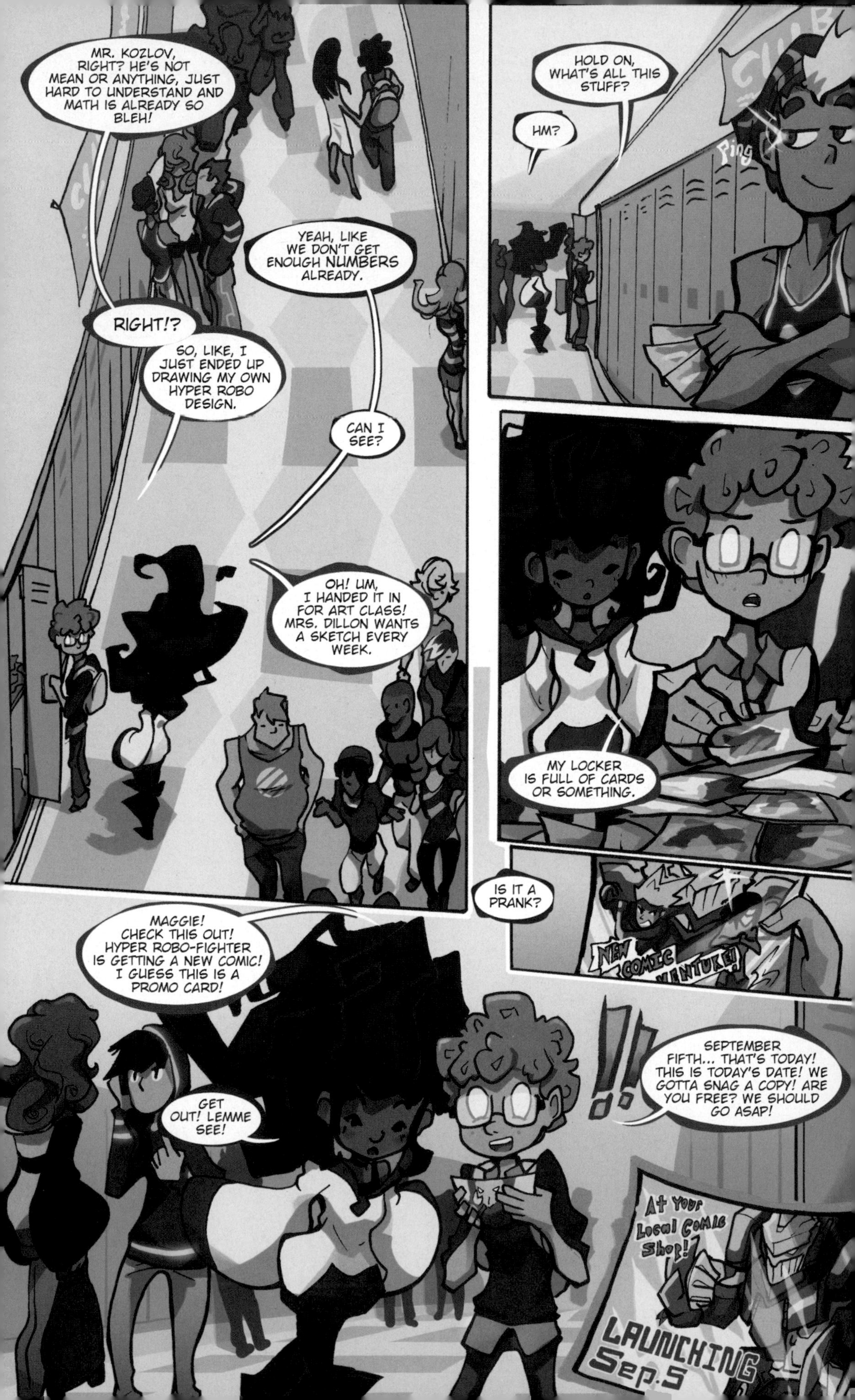
MR. KOZLOV, RIGHT? HE'S NOT MEAN OR ANYTHING, JUST HARD TO UNDERSTAND AND MATH IS ALREADY SO BLEH!
YEAH, LIKE WE DON'T GET ENOUGH NUMBERS ALREADY.
RIGHT!?
SO, LIKE, I JUST ENDED UP DRAWING MY OWN HYPER ROBO DESIGN.
CAN I SEE?
OH! UM, I HANDED IT IN FOR ART CLASS! MRS. DILLON WANTS A SKETCH EVERY WEEK.
HOLD ON, WHAT'S ALL THIS STUFF?
HM?
PING
MY LOCKER IS FULL OF CARDS OR SOMETHING.
IS IT A PRANK?
NEW COMIC
MAGGIE! CHECK THIS OUT! HYPER ROBO-FIGHTER IS GETTING A NEW COMIC! I GUESS THIS IS A PROMO CARD!
GET OUT! LEMME SEE!
SEPTEMBER FIFTH... THAT'S TODAY! THIS IS TODAY'S DATE! WE GOTTA SNAG A COPY! ARE YOU FREE? WE SHOULD GO ASAP!
At Your Local Comic Shop!
LAUNCHING Sep. 5

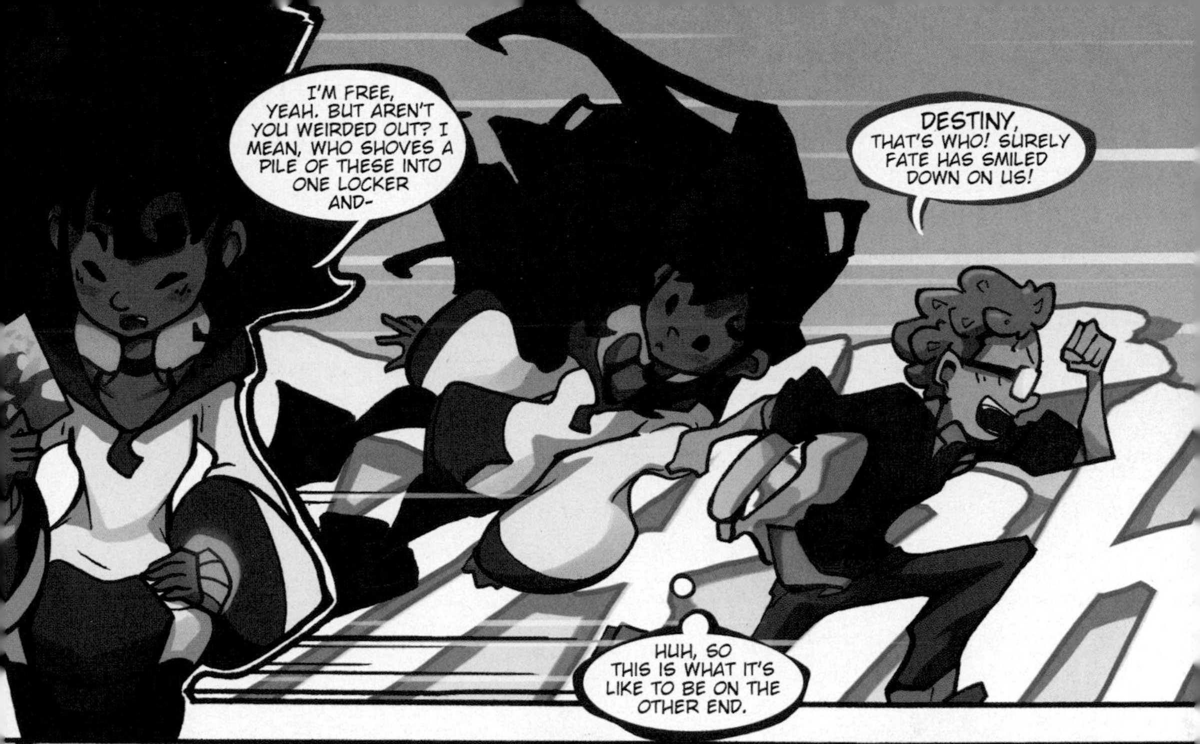
I'M FREE, YEAH. BUT AREN'T YOU WEIRDED OUT? I MEAN, WHO SHOVES A PILE OF THESE INTO ONE LOCKER AND-
DESTINY, THAT'S WHO! SURELY FATE HAS SMILED DOWN ON US!
HUH, SO THIS IS WHAT IT'S LIKE TO BE ON THE OTHER END.

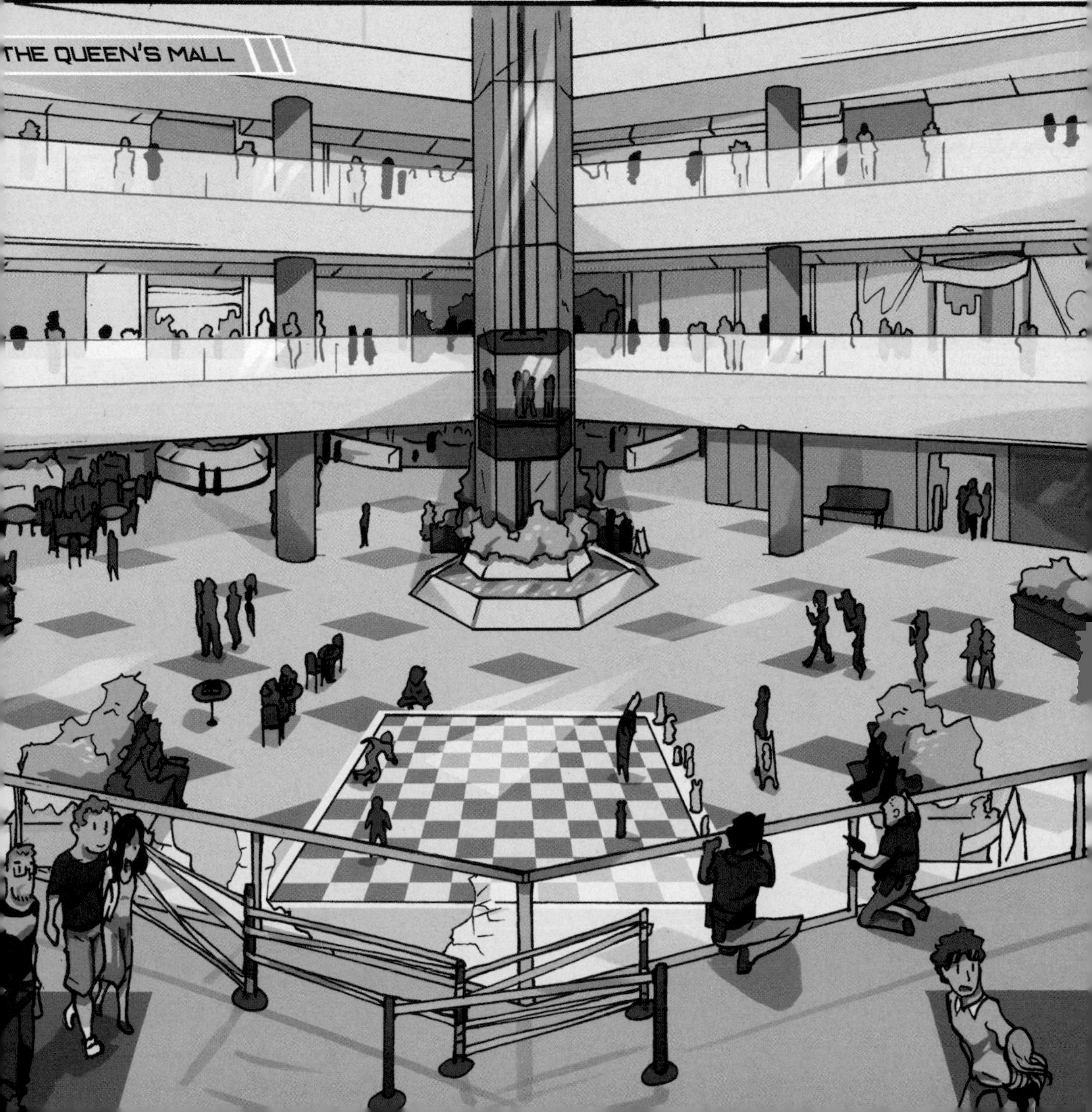
THE QUEEN'S MALL

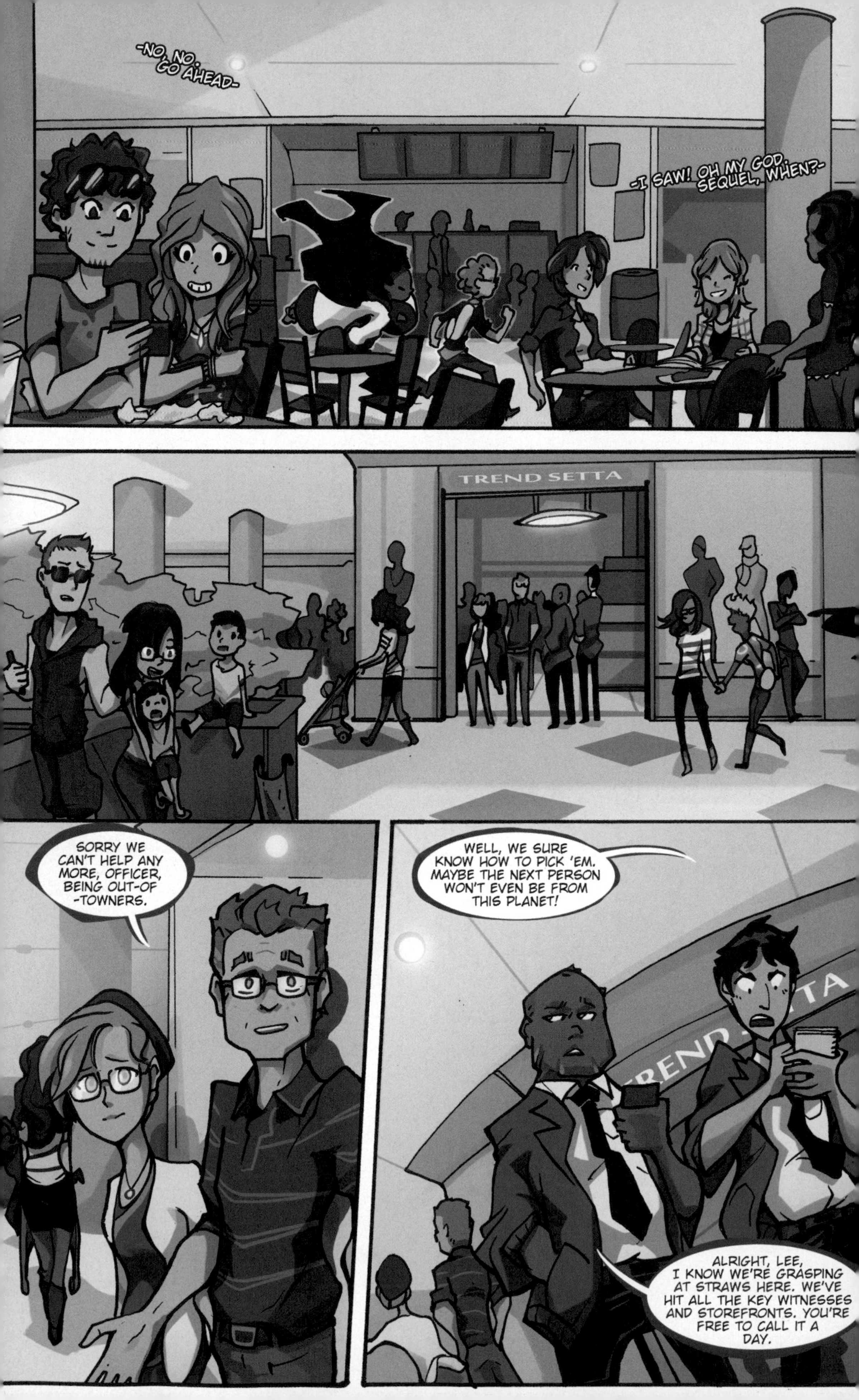
-NO, NO. GO AHEAD-
-I SAW! OH MY GOD. SEQUEL, WHEN?-
TREND SETTA
SORRY WE CAN'T HELP ANY MORE, OFFICER, BEING OUT-OF -TOWNERS.
WELL, WE SURE KNOW HOW TO PICK 'EM. MAYBE THE NEXT PERSON WON'T EVEN BE FROM THIS PLANET!
ALRIGHT, LEE, I KNOW WE'RE GRASPING AT STRAWS HERE. WE'VE HIT ALL THE KEY WITNESSES AND STOREFRONTS. YOU'RE FREE TO CALL IT A DAY.

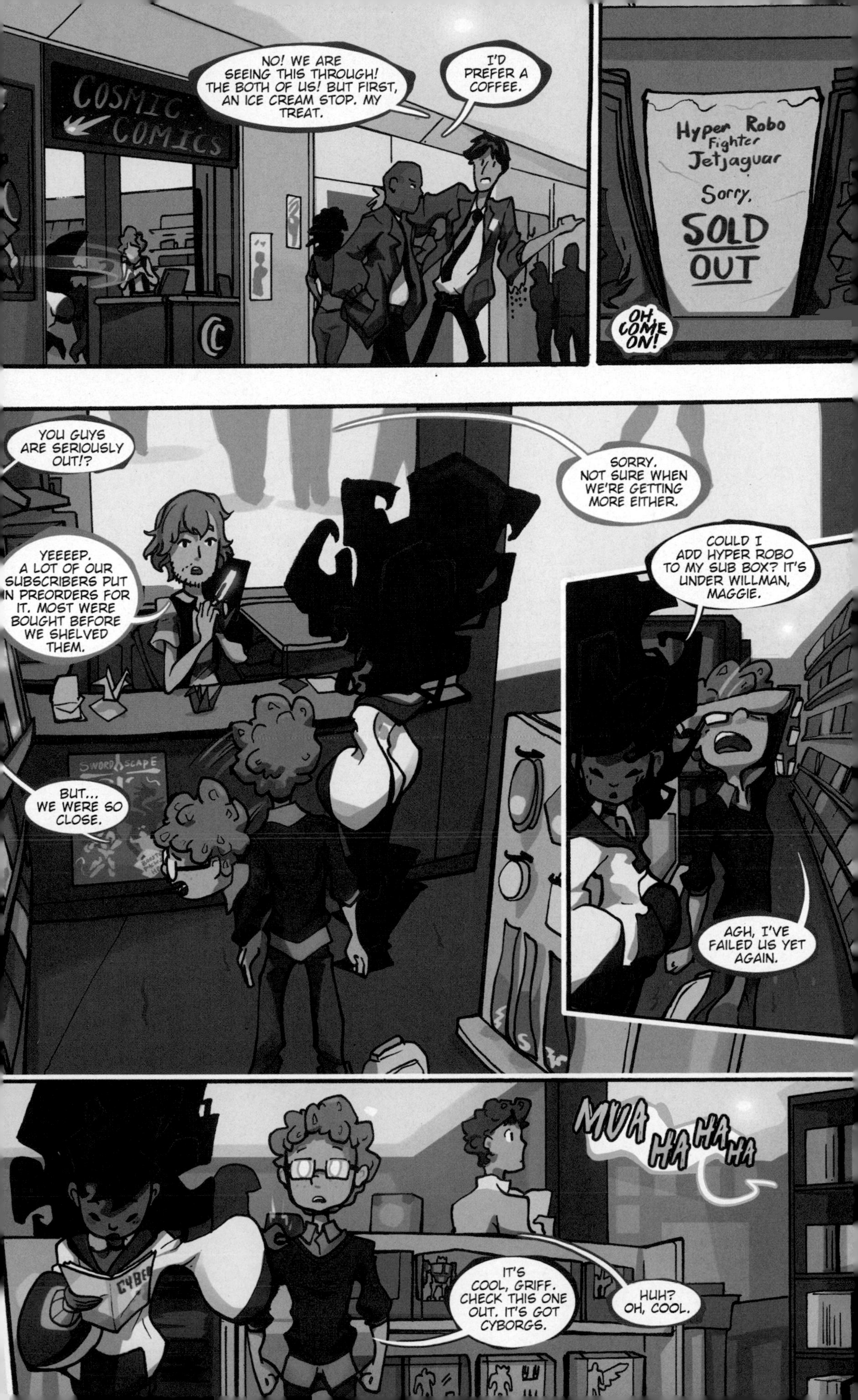
COSMIC COMICS
NO! WE ARE SEEING THIS THROUGH! THE BOTH OF US! BUT FIRST, AN ICE CREAM STOP. MY TREAT.
I'D PREFER A COFFEE.
Hyper Robo Fighter Jetjaguar
Sorry.
SOLD OUT
OH, COME ON!
YOU GUYS ARE SERIOUSLY OUT!?
SORRY. NOT SURE WHEN WE'RE GETTING MORE EITHER.
YEEEEP. A LOT OF OUR SUBSCRIBERS PUT IN PREORDERS FOR IT. MOST WERE BOUGHT BEFORE WE SHELVED THEM.
COULD I ADD HYPER ROBO TO MY SUB BOX? IT'S UNDER WILLMAN, MAGGIE.
SWORDSCAPE
BUT... WE WERE SO CLOSE.
AGH, I'VE FAILED US YET AGAIN.
MUA HA HA HA HA
IT'S COOL, GRIFF. CHECK THIS ONE OUT. IT'S GOT CYBORGS.
HUH? OH, COOL.

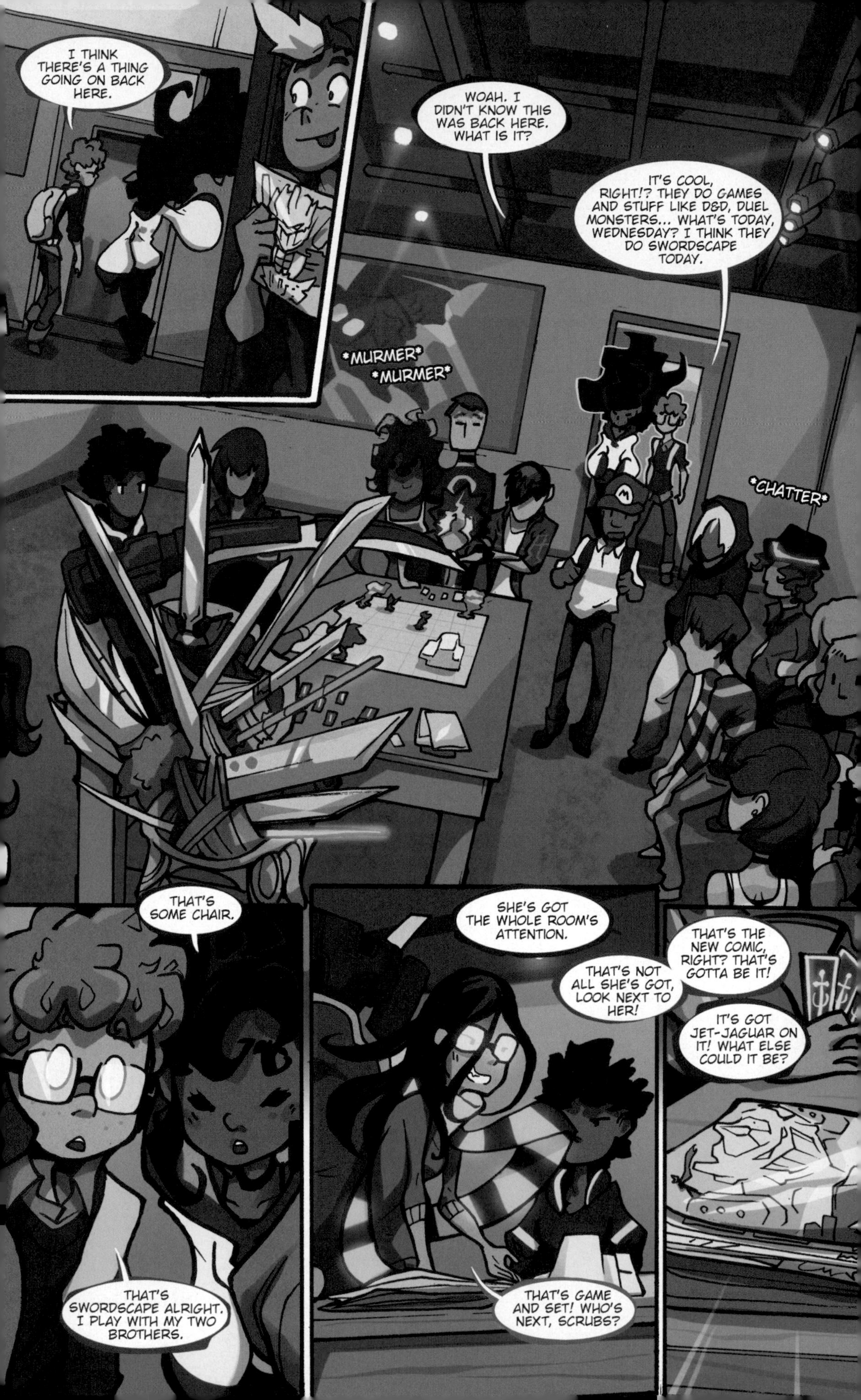
I THINK THERE'S A THING GOING ON BACK HERE.
WOAH. I DIDN'T KNOW THIS WAS BACK HERE. WHAT IS IT?
IT'S COOL, RIGHT!? THEY DO GAMES AND STUFF LIKE D&D, DUEL MONSTERS... WHAT'S TODAY, WEDNESDAY? I THINK THEY DO SWORDSCAPE TODAY.
MURMER
MURMER
CHATTER
THAT'S SOME CHAIR.
THAT'S SWORDSCAPE ALRIGHT. I PLAY WITH MY TWO BROTHERS.
SHE'S GOT THE WHOLE ROOM'S ATTENTION.
THAT'S NOT ALL SHE'S GOT, LOOK NEXT TO HER!
THAT'S GAME AND SET! WHO'S NEXT, SCRUBS?
THAT'S THE NEW COMIC, RIGHT? THAT'S GOTTA BE IT!
IT'S GOT JET-JAGUAR ON IT! WHAT ELSE COULD IT BE?

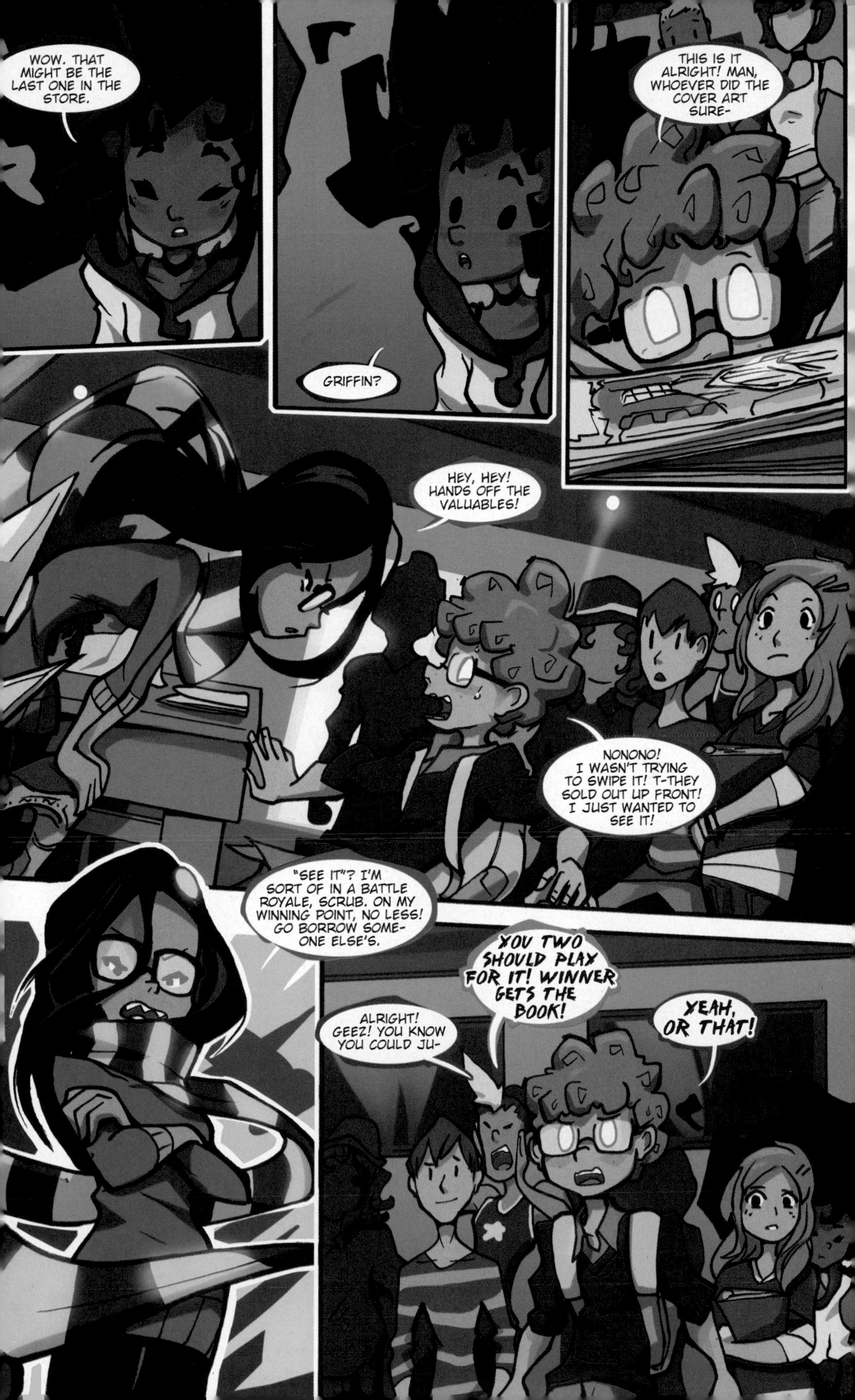
WOW. THAT MIGHT BE THE LAST ONE IN THE STORE.
GRIFFIN?
THIS IS IT ALRIGHT! MAN, WHOEVER DID THE COVER ART SURE-
HEY, HEY! HANDS OFF THE VALUABLES!
NONONO! I WASN'T TRYING TO SWIPE IT! T-THEY SOLD OUT UP FRONT! I JUST WANTED TO SEE IT!
"SEE IT"? I'M SORT OF IN A BATTLE ROYALE, SCRUB. ON MY WINNING POINT, NO LESS! GO BORROW SOME-ONE ELSE'S.
ALRIGHT! GEEZ! YOU KNOW YOU COULD JU-
YOU TWO SHOULD PLAY FOR IT! WINNER GETS THE BOOK!
YEAH, OR THAT!

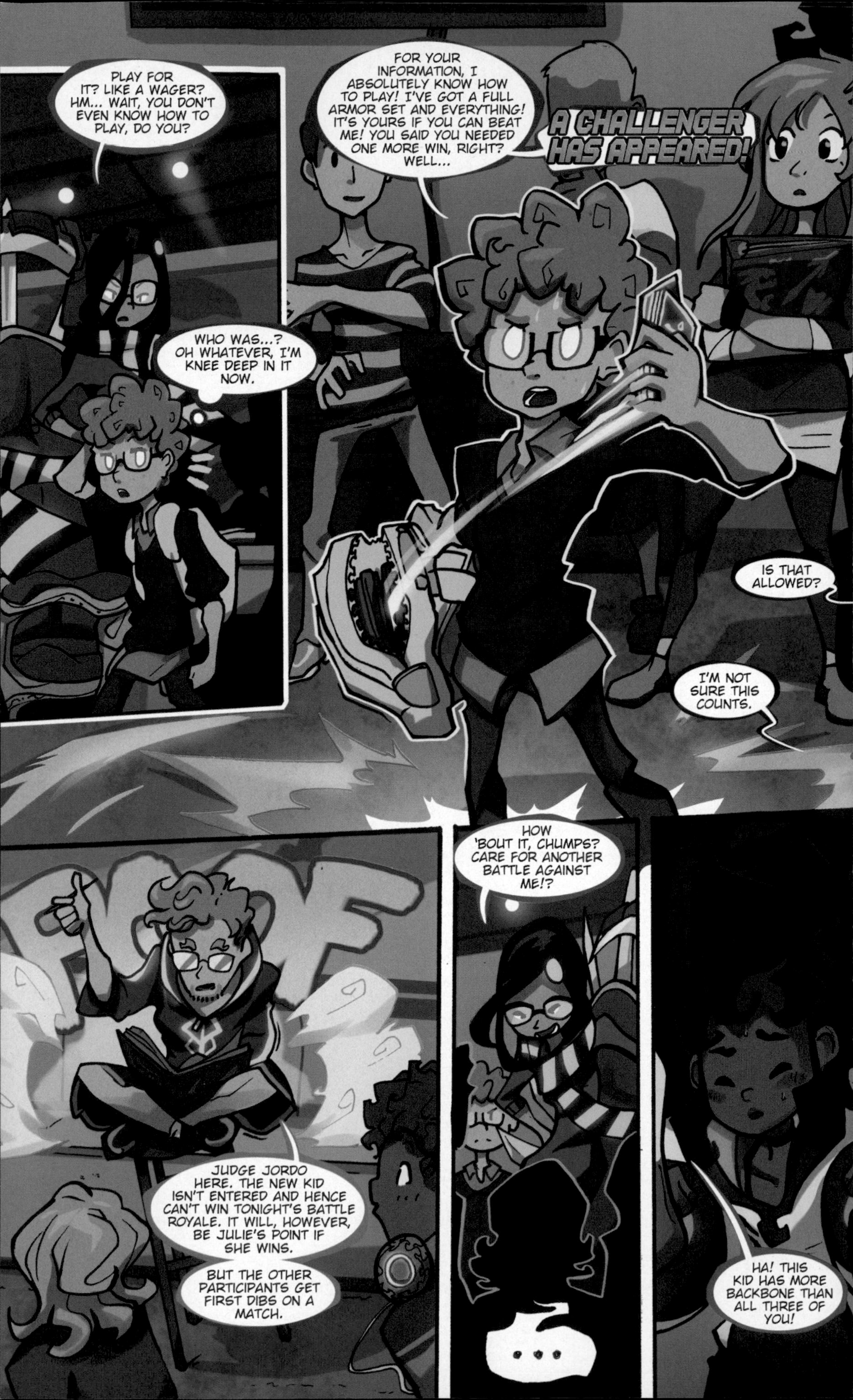
PLAY FOR IT? LIKE A WAGER? HM... WAIT, YOU DON'T EVEN KNOW HOW TO PLAY, DO YOU?
FOR YOUR INFORMATION, I ABSOLUTELY KNOW HOW TO PLAY! I'VE GOT A FULL ARMOR SET AND EVERYTHING! IT'S YOURS IF YOU CAN BEAT ME! YOU SAID YOU NEEDED ONE MORE WIN, RIGHT? WELL...
A CHALLENGER HAS APPEARED!
WHO WAS...? OH WHATEVER, I'M KNEE DEEP IN IT NOW.
IS THAT ALLOWED?
I'M NOT SURE THIS COUNTS.
JUDGE JORDO HERE. THE NEW KID ISN'T ENTERED AND HENCE CAN'T WIN TONIGHT'S BATTLE ROYALE. IT WILL, HOWEVER, BE JULIE'S POINT IF SHE WINS.
BUT THE OTHER PARTICIPANTS GET FIRST DIBS ON A MATCH.
HOW 'BOUT IT, CHUMPS? CARE FOR ANOTHER BATTLE AGAINST ME!?
...
HA! THIS KID HAS MORE BACKBONE THAN ALL THREE OF YOU!

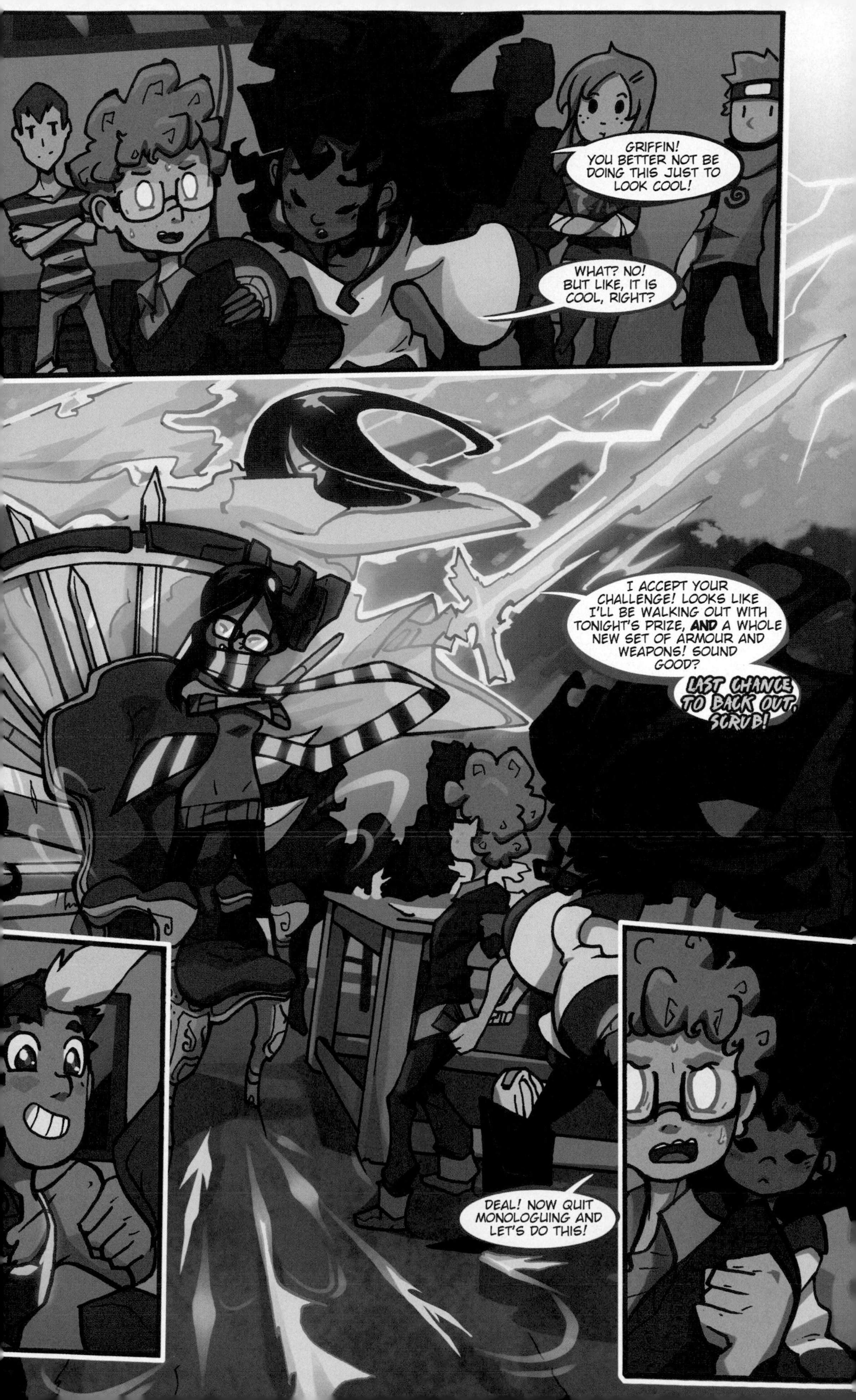
GRIFFIN! YOU BETTER NOT BE DOING THIS JUST TO LOOK COOL!
WHAT? NO! BUT LIKE, IT IS COOL, RIGHT?
I ACCEPT YOUR CHALLENGE! LOOKS LIKE I'LL BE WALKING OUT WITH TONIGHT'S PRIZE, AND A WHOLE NEW SET OF ARMOUR AND WEAPONS! SOUND GOOD?
LAST CHANCE TO BACK OUT, SCRUB!
DEAL! NOW QUIT MONOLOGUING AND LET'S DO THIS!

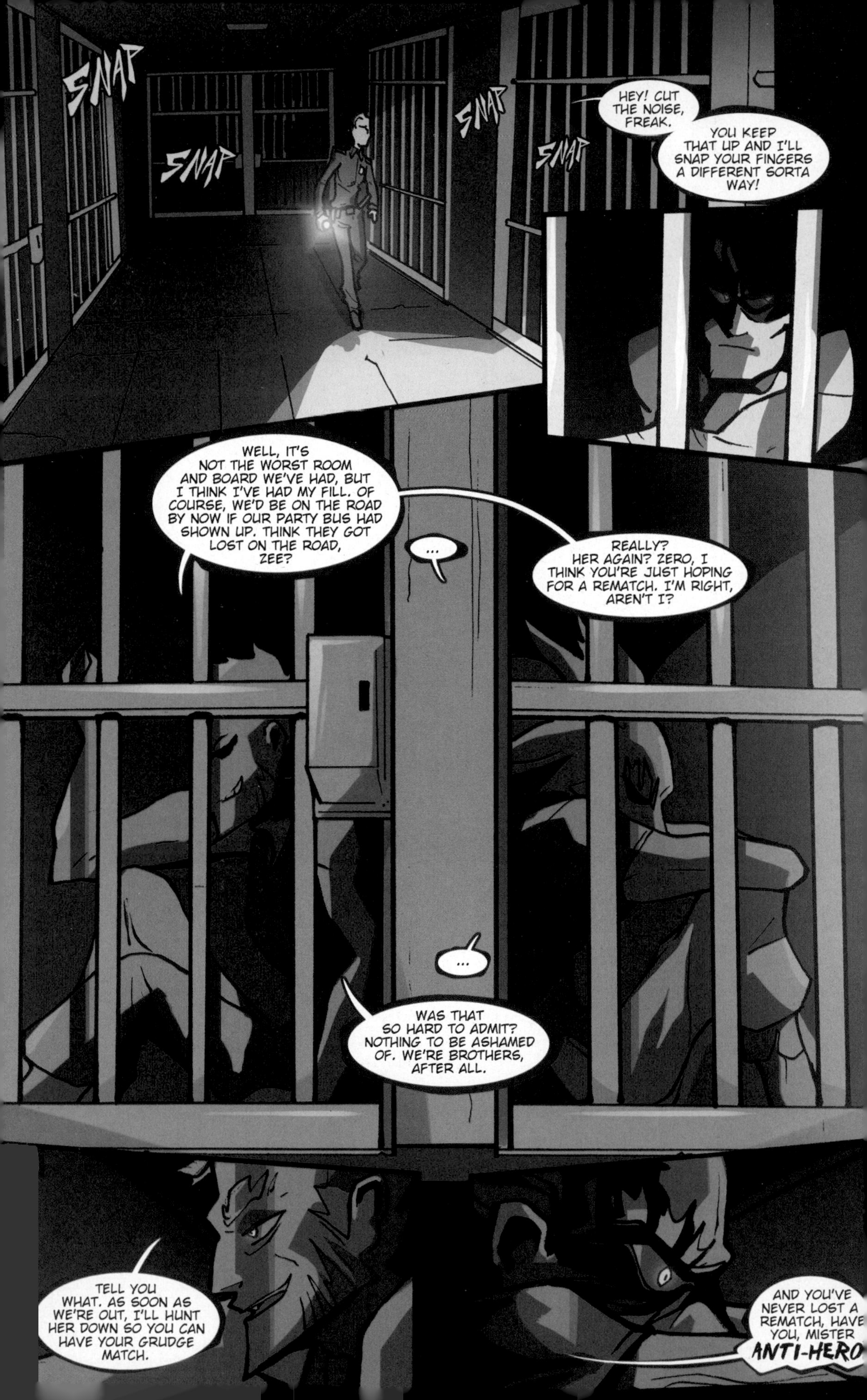
SNAP
SNAP
SNAP
SNAP
HEY! CUT THE NOISE, FREAK.
YOU KEEP THAT UP AND I'LL SNAP YOUR FINGERS A DIFFERENT SORTA WAY!
WELL, IT'S NOT THE WORST ROOM AND BOARD WE'VE HAD, BUT I THINK I'VE HAD MY FILL. OF COURSE, WE'D BE ON THE ROAD BY NOW IF OUR PARTY BUS HAD SHOWN UP. THINK THEY GOT LOST ON THE ROAD, ZEE?
...
REALLY? HER AGAIN? ZERO, I THINK YOU'RE JUST HOPING FOR A REMATCH. I'M RIGHT, AREN'T I?
...
WAS THAT SO HARD TO ADMIT? NOTHING TO BE ASHAMED OF. WE'RE BROTHERS, AFTER ALL.
TELL YOU WHAT. AS SOON AS WE'RE OUT, I'LL HUNT HER DOWN SO YOU CAN HAVE YOUR GRUDGE MATCH.
AND YOU'VE NEVER LOST A REMATCH, HAVE YOU, MISTER ANTI-HERO

CHAPTER 04

ART AND STORY BY
SEAN DILLON
@GRANDPABATS

BRYAN SEATON: PUBLISHER/CEO **SHAWN GABBORIN:** EDITOR IN CHIEF **JASON MARTIN:** PUBLISHER-DANGER ZONE
NICOLE D'ANDRIA: MARKETING DIRECTOR/EDITOR **JESSICA LOWRIE:** SOCIAL MEDIA CZAR **DANIELLE DAVISON:**
EXECUTIVE ADMINISTRATOR **CHAD CICCONI:** BAD GUY STUNT DOUBLE **SHAWN PRYOR:** PRESIDENT OF CREATOR
RELATIONS

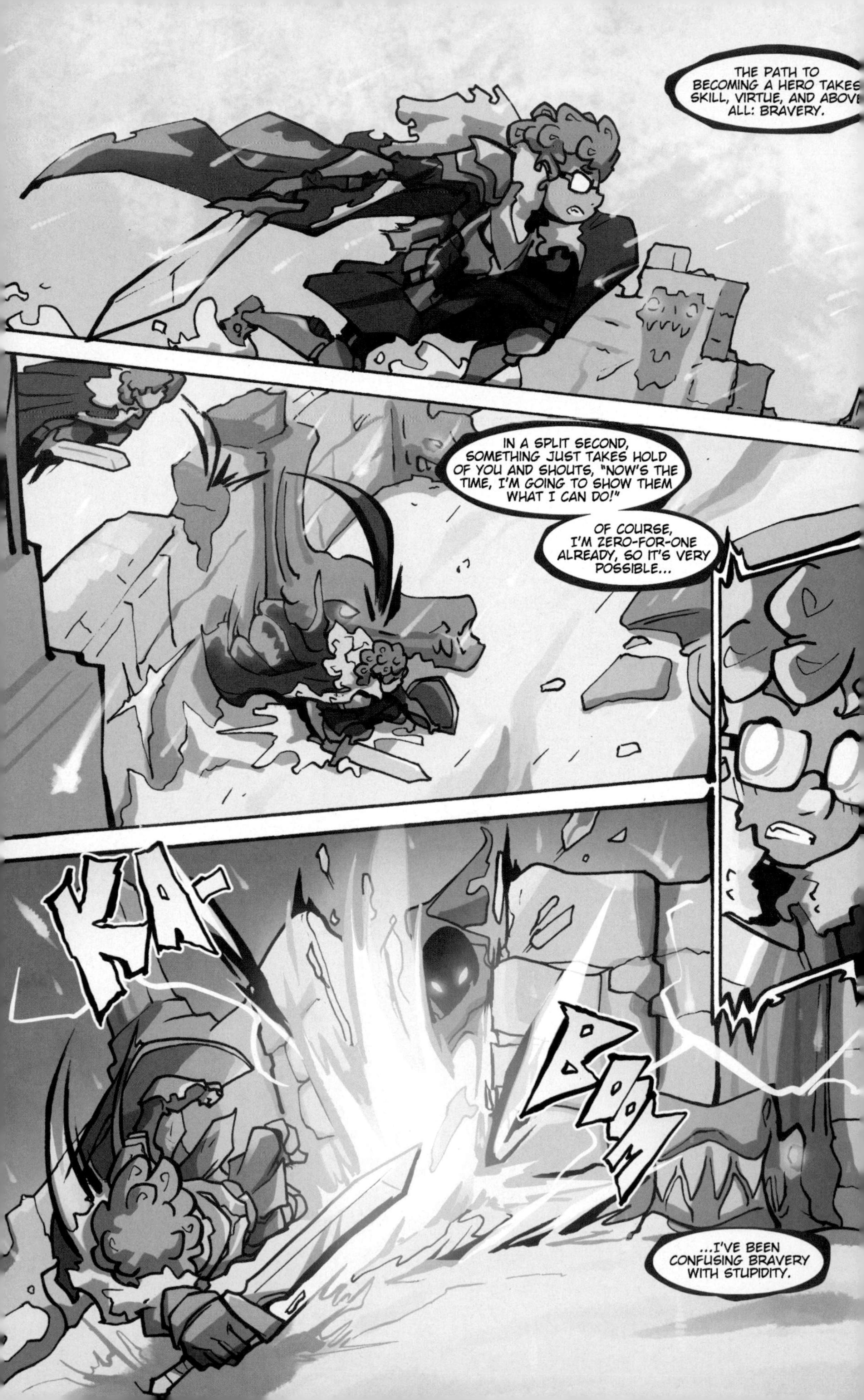
THE PATH TO BECOMING A HERO TAKES SKILL, VIRTUE, AND ABOVE ALL: BRAVERY.
IN A SPLIT SECOND, SOMETHING JUST TAKES HOLD OF YOU AND SHOUTS, "NOW'S THE TIME, I'M GOING TO SHOW THEM WHAT I CAN DO!"
OF COURSE, I'M ZERO-FOR-ONE ALREADY, SO IT'S VERY POSSIBLE...
KA-
BOOM
...I'VE BEEN CONFUSING BRAVERY WITH STUPIDITY.

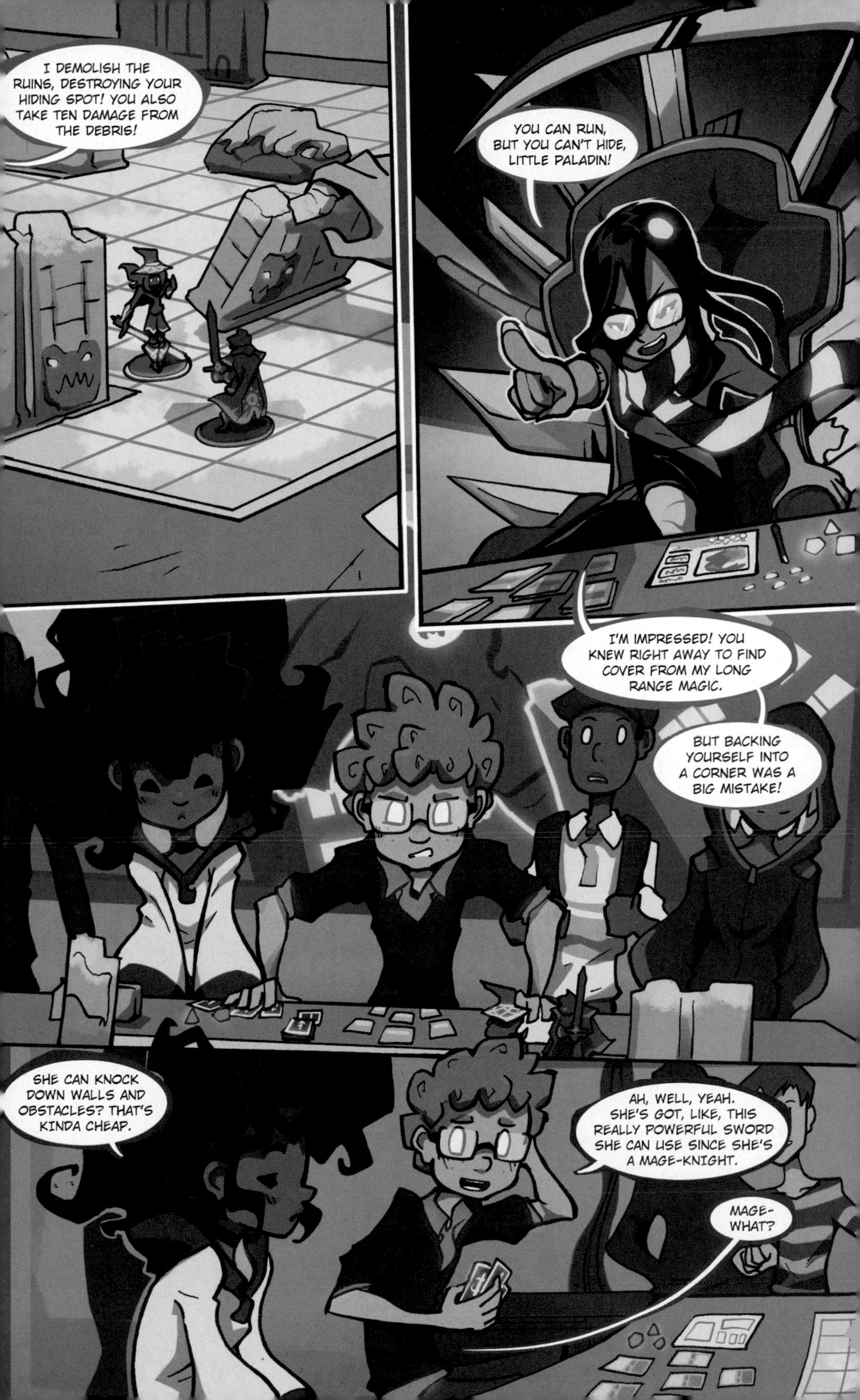
I DEMOLISH THE RUINS, DESTROYING YOUR HIDING SPOT! YOU ALSO TAKE TEN DAMAGE FROM THE DEBRIS!
YOU CAN RUN, BUT YOU CAN'T HIDE, LITTLE PALADIN!
I'M IMPRESSED! YOU KNEW RIGHT AWAY TO FIND COVER FROM MY LONG RANGE MAGIC.
BUT BACKING YOURSELF INTO A CORNER WAS A BIG MISTAKE!
SHE CAN KNOCK DOWN WALLS AND OBSTACLES? THAT'S KINDA CHEAP.
AH, WELL, YEAH. SHE'S GOT, LIKE, THIS REALLY POWERFUL SWORD SHE CAN USE SINCE SHE'S A MAGE-KNIGHT.
MAGE-WHAT?

SHE'S GOT TO HAVE CARDS THAT WORK WITH HER CLASS. THAT'S THE FIRST THING YOU F... YOU CAN BE A KNI... A MAGE OR A RAR... OUR CLASS... ...EATS...

SO... T... YOU HAV... A DIE OR S... AL ATTACKS OU P... Y NEED TO READ ...WHAT'S ON YOUR CARDS... R STRONG LIKE POTION AN ONLY BE USE ONCE BUT EQUIP RDS AND SKILL CARDS YOU CA... TO KEEP THROUG... THE WHOLE GAME.

BASICALLY YOU'VE ...OT ...HEALTH... MANA, AND MOBILITY. I HAVE HIGH HEALTH... MOVE A LOT OF SPACES... BUT ... LI... MANA. SO ...

YOU PICK EQ... ...DS LIKE ARMOU... SWORDS AND ST... ...ERYTHING GIVES... ...EFENCE OR DOES DAMAGE OR HAS SOME PE... THAT SWORD SHE'S USING HAS A LOT OF B... ABILITIES LIKE BEING ABLE TO DESTROY OBS... ON THE FIELD. SHE'S A MAGE-KNIGHT SO SH... USE BO... ...D MAGIC BUT SHE SHOU... HAVE... LOW HEALTH... I THINK.

IT CAN BE A LOT, BACK AND FOR... BUT BASICALLY OU WANT YOUR OPPONENT'S LIFE POINT... TO HIT ZER...

EXCUSE ME! WE ARE MID-GAME HERE! TEACH YOUR FRIEND ON YOUR OWN TIME.

IT'S A LOT SIMPLER THAN I'M MAKING IT SOUND.

OH...

JUST THINK OF IT AS AN EPIC HIGH-FANTASY BATTLE!

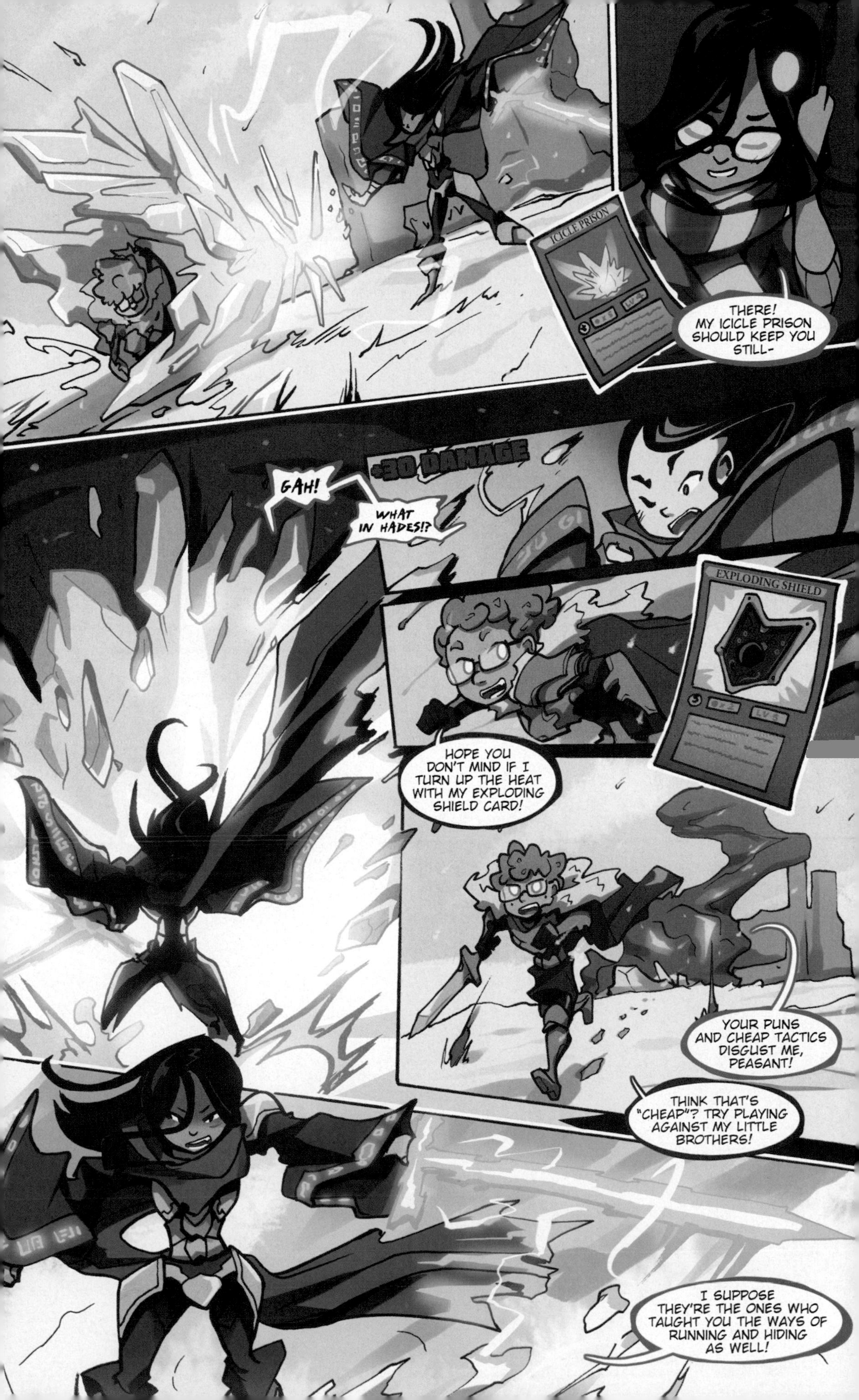
ICICLE PRISON
THERE! MY ICICLE PRISON SHOULD KEEP YOU STILL-
+30 DAMAGE
GAH!
WHAT IN HADES!?
EXPLODING SHIELD
HOPE YOU DON'T MIND IF I TURN UP THE HEAT WITH MY EXPLODING SHIELD CARD!
YOUR PUNS AND CHEAP TACTICS DISGUST ME, PEASANT!
THINK THAT'S "CHEAP"? TRY PLAYING AGAINST MY LITTLE BROTHERS!
I SUPPOSE THEY'RE THE ONES WHO TAUGHT YOU THE WAYS OF RUNNING AND HIDING AS WELL!

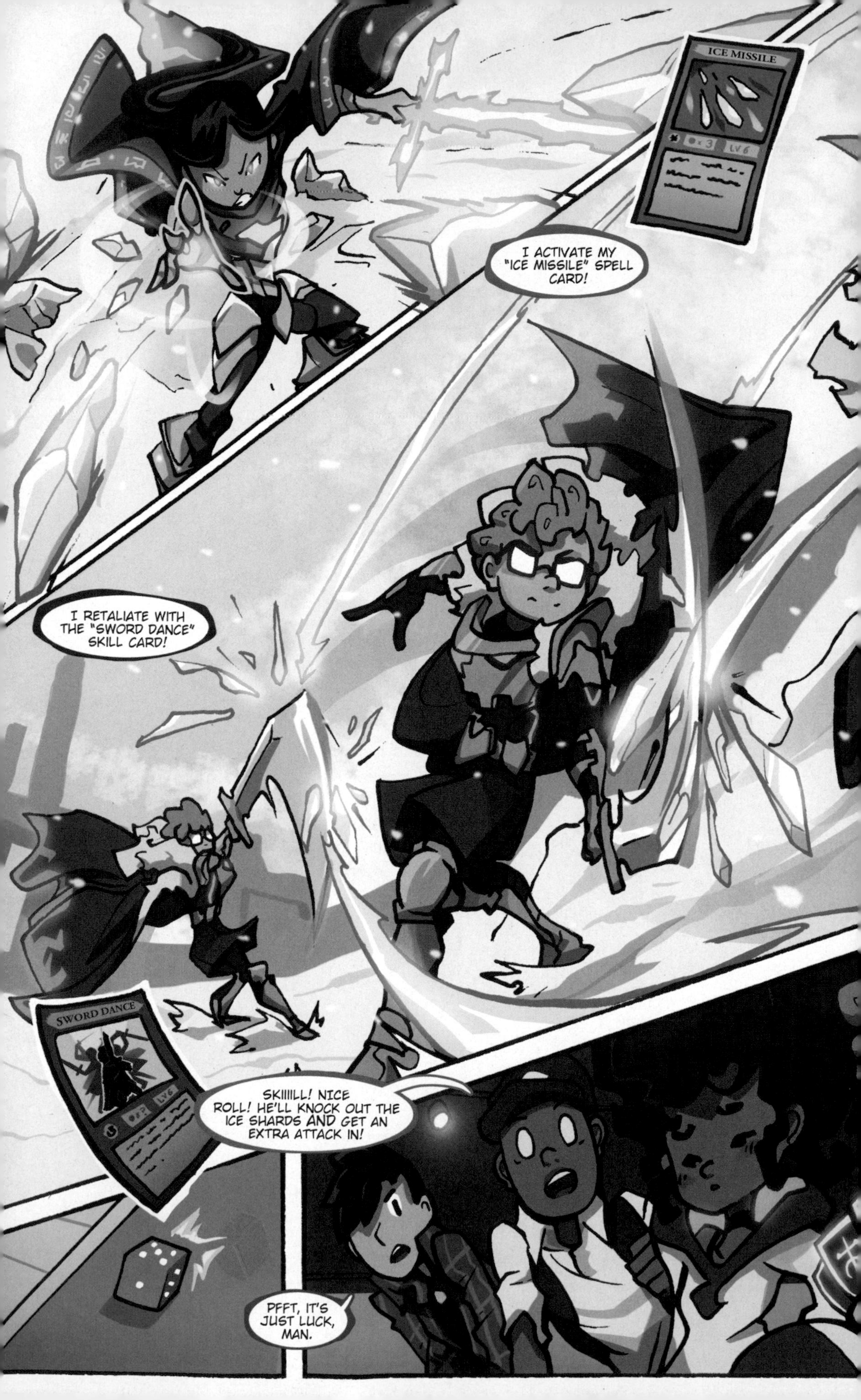
ICE MISSILE
I ACTIVATE MY "ICE MISSILE" SPELL CARD!
I RETALIATE WITH THE "SWORD DANCE" SKILL CARD!
SWORD DANCE
SKIIIILL! NICE ROLL! HE'LL KNOCK OUT THE ICE SHARDS AND GET AN EXTRA ATTACK IN!
PFFT, IT'S JUST LUCK, MAN.

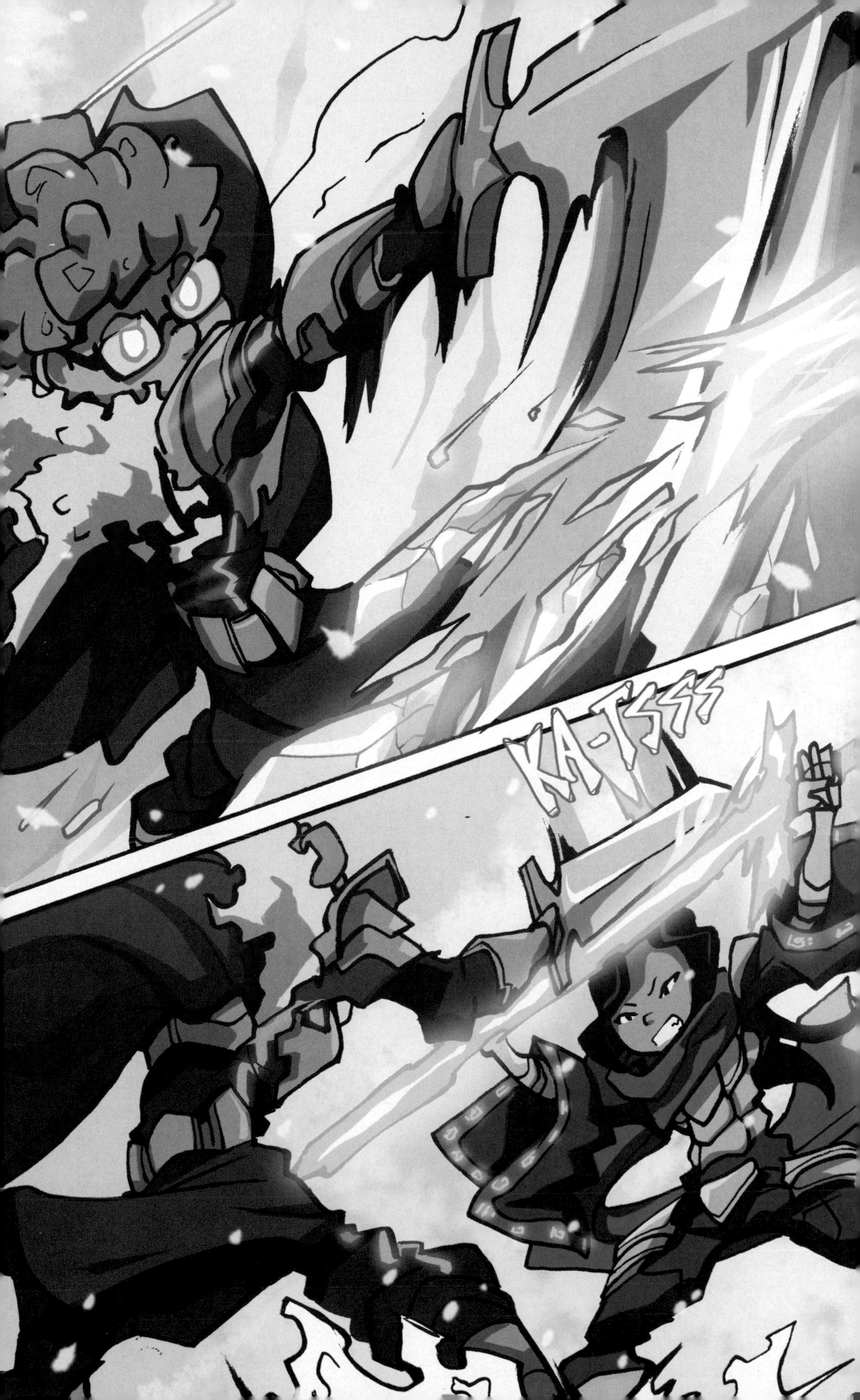
KA-TSSS

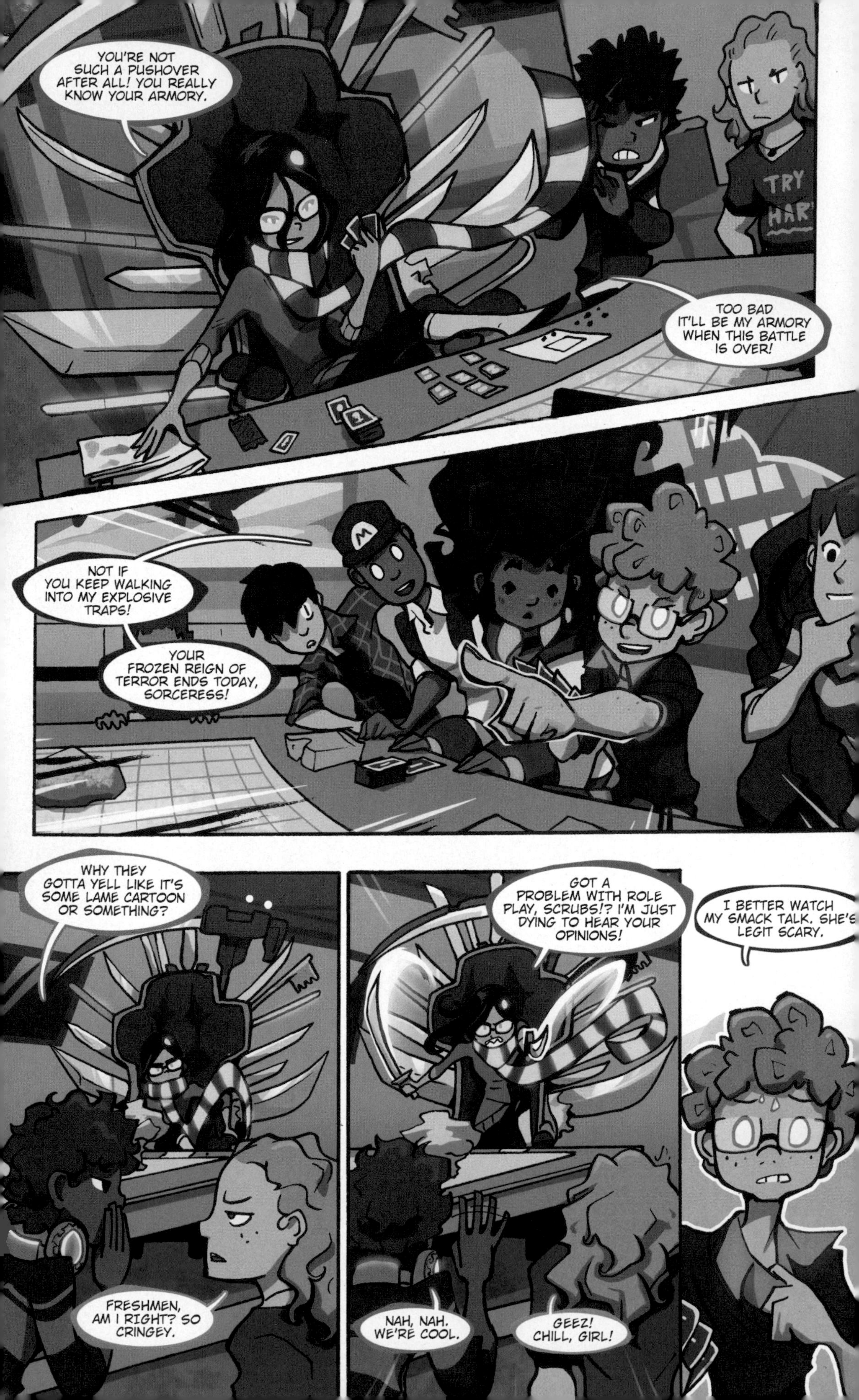
YOU'RE NOT SUCH A PUSHOVER AFTER ALL! YOU REALLY KNOW YOUR ARMORY.
TOO BAD IT'LL BE MY ARMORY WHEN THIS BATTLE IS OVER!
TRY HAR
NOT IF YOU KEEP WALKING INTO MY EXPLOSIVE TRAPS!
YOUR FROZEN REIGN OF TERROR ENDS TODAY, SORCERESS!
WHY THEY GOTTA YELL LIKE IT'S SOME LAME CARTOON OR SOMETHING?
FRESHMEN, AM I RIGHT? SO CRINGEY.
GOT A PROBLEM WITH ROLE PLAY, SCRUBS!? I'M JUST DYING TO HEAR YOUR OPINIONS!
NAH, NAH. WE'RE COOL.
GEEZ! CHILL, GIRL!
I BETTER WATCH MY SMACK TALK. SHE'S LEGIT SCARY.

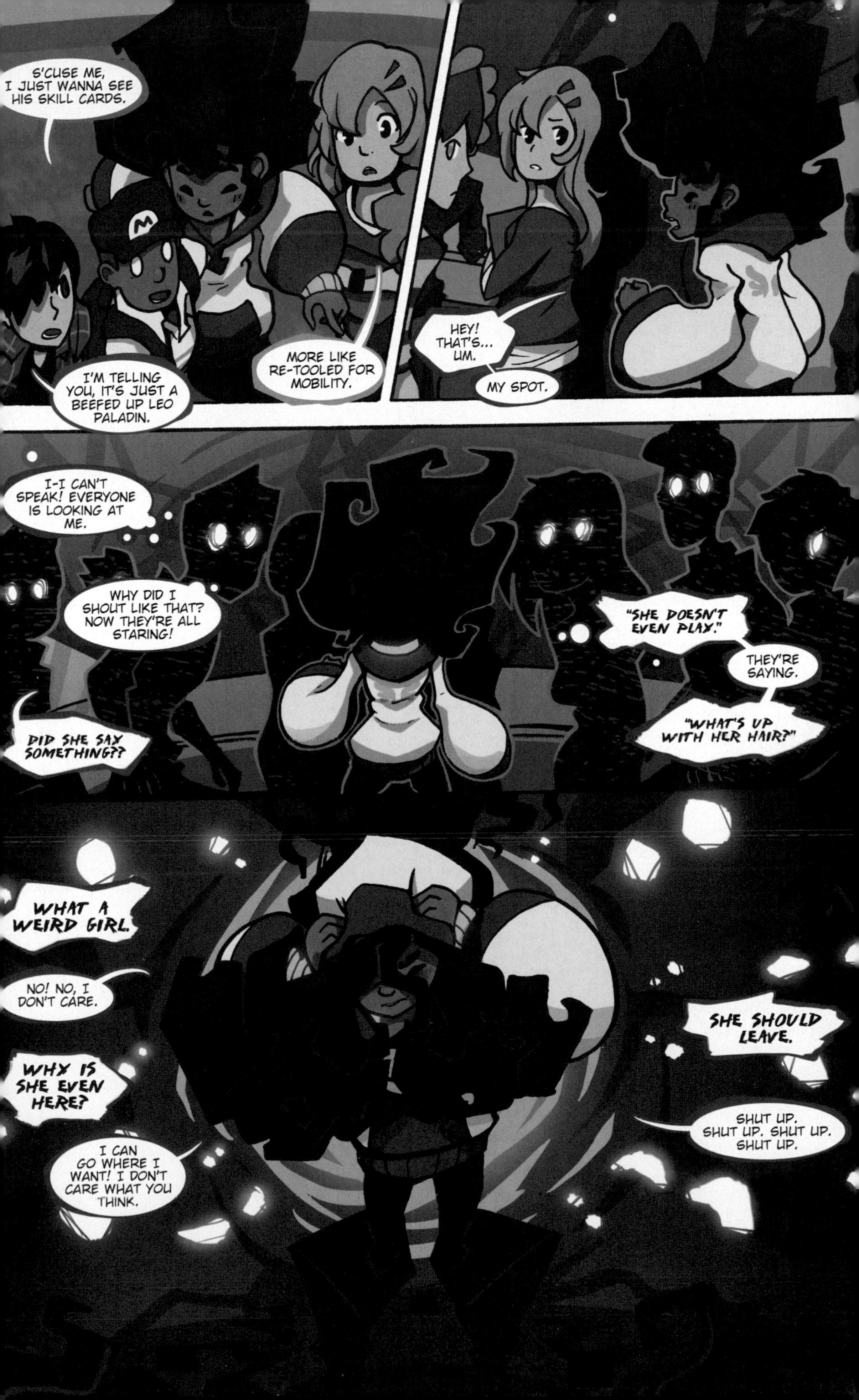
S'CUSE ME, I JUST WANNA SEE HIS SKILL CARDS.
I'M TELLING YOU, IT'S JUST A BEEFED UP LEO PALADIN.
MORE LIKE RE-TOOLED FOR MOBILITY.
HEY! THAT'S... UM.
MY SPOT.
I-I CAN'T SPEAK! EVERYONE IS LOOKING AT ME.
WHY DID I SHOUT LIKE THAT? NOW THEY'RE ALL STARING!
DID SHE SAY SOMETHING??
"SHE DOESN'T EVEN PLAY."
THEY'RE SAYING.
"WHAT'S UP WITH HER HAIR?"
WHAT A WEIRD GIRL.
NO! NO, I DON'T CARE.
WHY IS SHE EVEN HERE?
I CAN GO WHERE I WANT! I DON'T CARE WHAT YOU THINK.
SHE SHOULD LEAVE.
SHUT UP. SHUT UP. SHUT UP. SHUT UP.

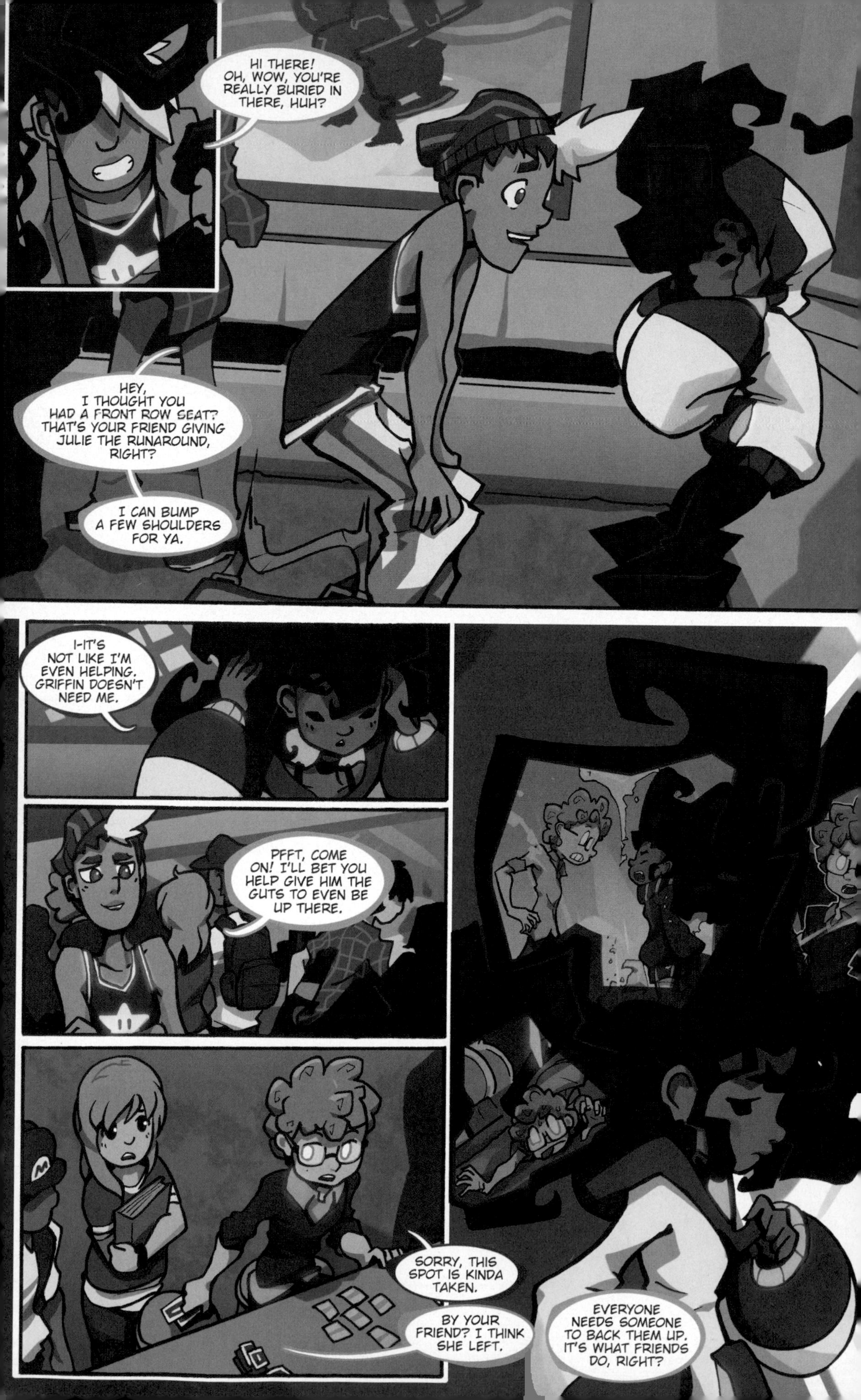
HI THERE! OH, WOW, YOU'RE REALLY BURIED IN THERE, HUH?
HEY, I THOUGHT YOU HAD A FRONT ROW SEAT? THAT'S YOUR FRIEND GIVING JULIE THE RUNAROUND, RIGHT?
I CAN BUMP A FEW SHOULDERS FOR YA.
I-IT'S NOT LIKE I'M EVEN HELPING. GRIFFIN DOESN'T NEED ME.
PFFT, COME ON! I'LL BET YOU HELP GIVE HIM THE GUTS TO EVEN BE UP THERE.
SORRY, THIS SPOT IS KINDA TAKEN.
BY YOUR FRIEND? I THINK SHE LEFT.
EVERYONE NEEDS SOMEONE TO BACK THEM UP. IT'S WHAT FRIENDS DO, RIGHT?

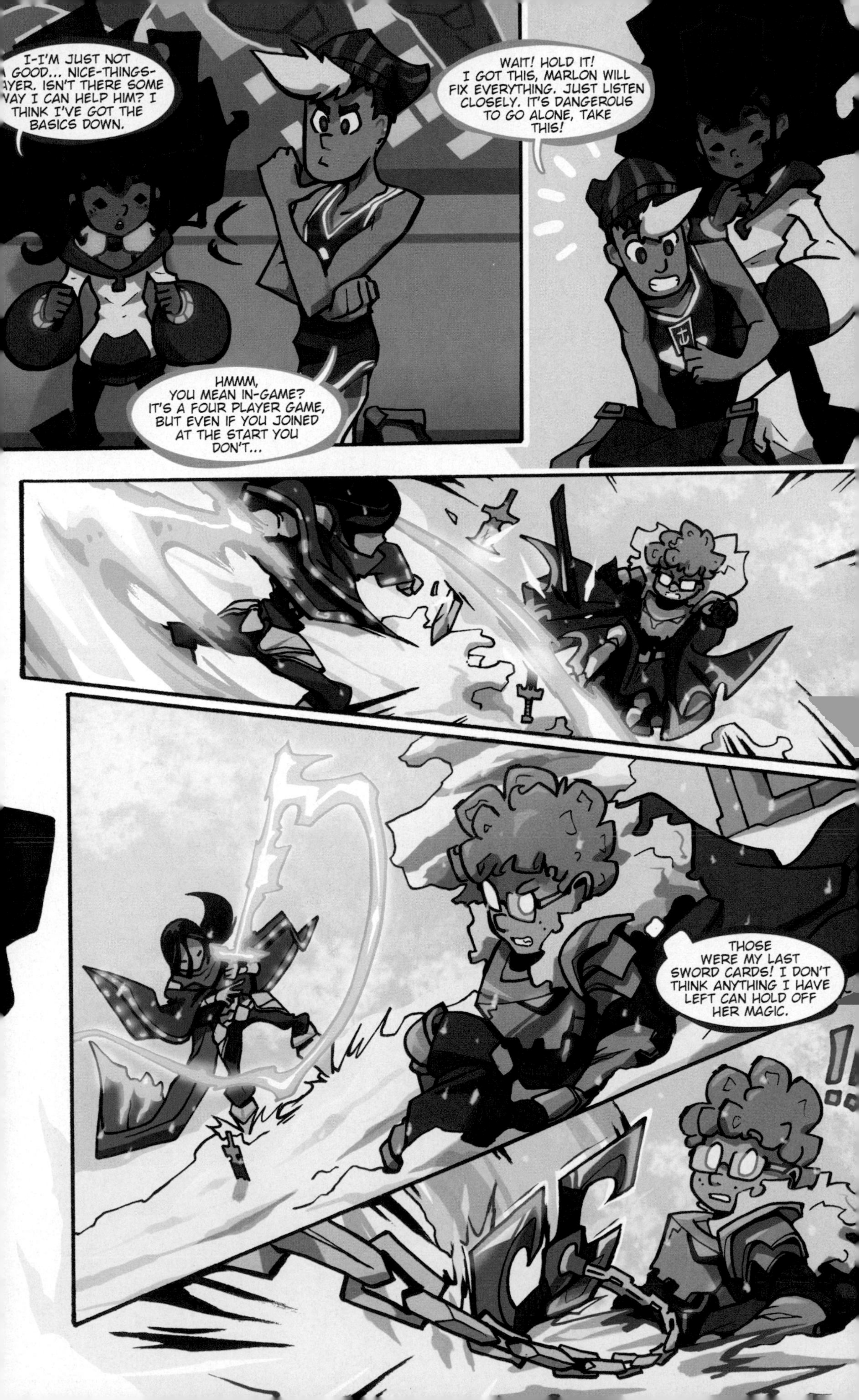
I-I'M JUST NOT
GOOD... NICE-THINGS-
AYER. ISN'T THERE SOME
VAY I CAN HELP HIM? I
THINK I'VE GOT THE
BASICS DOWN.
HMMM,
YOU MEAN IN-GAME?
IT'S A FOUR PLAYER GAME,
BUT EVEN IF YOU JOINED
AT THE START YOU
DON'T...
WAIT! HOLD IT!
I GOT THIS, MARLON WILL
FIX EVERYTHING. JUST LISTEN
CLOSELY. IT'S DANGEROUS
TO GO ALONE, TAKE
THIS!
THOSE
WERE MY LAST
SWORD CARDS! I DON'T
THINK ANYTHING I HAVE
LEFT CAN HOLD OFF
HER MAGIC.
!!

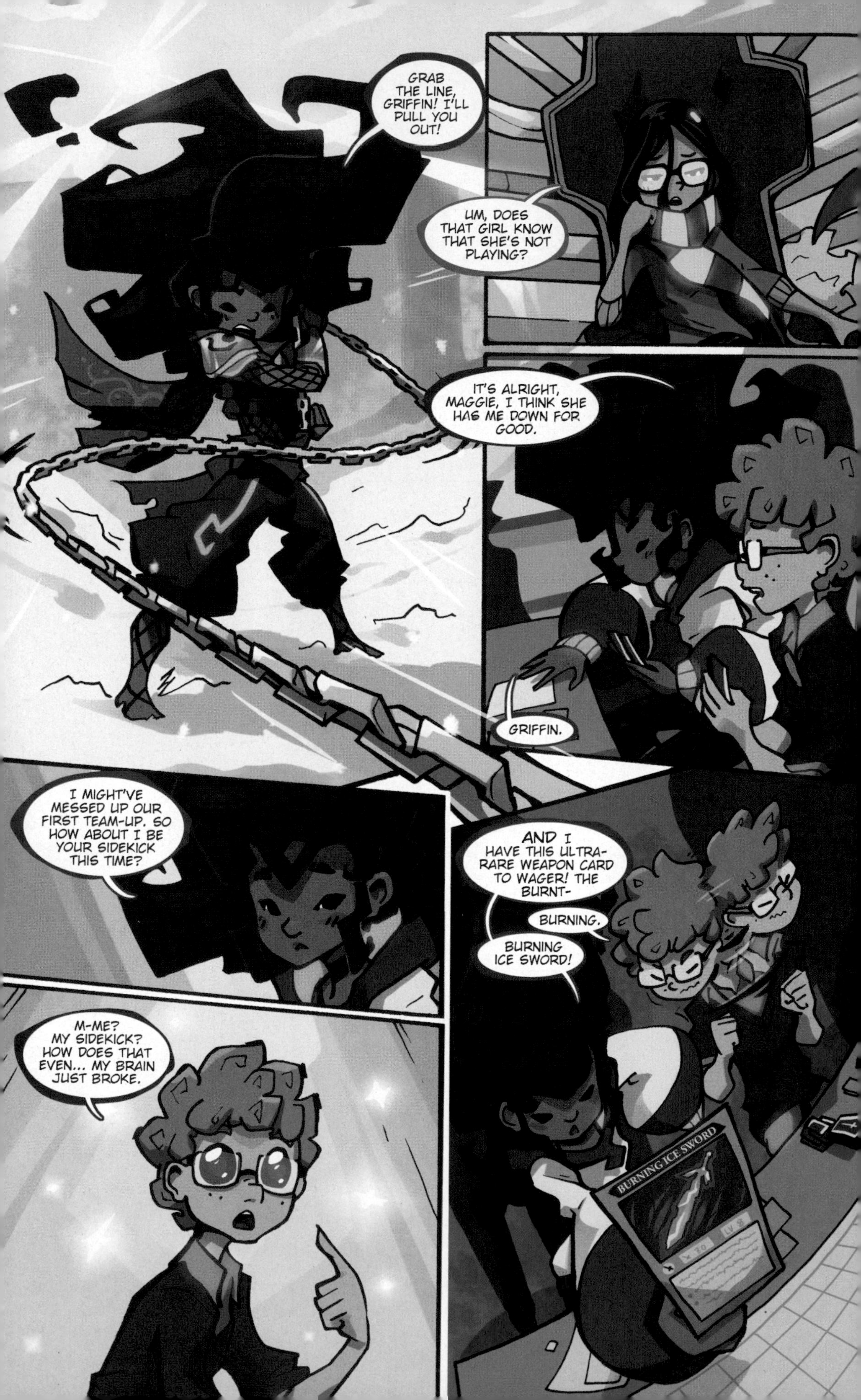
GRAB THE LINE, GRIFFIN! I'LL PULL YOU OUT!
UM, DOES THAT GIRL KNOW THAT SHE'S NOT PLAYING?
IT'S ALRIGHT, MAGGIE, I THINK SHE HAS ME DOWN FOR GOOD.
GRIFFIN.
I MIGHT'VE MESSED UP OUR FIRST TEAM-UP. SO HOW ABOUT I BE YOUR SIDEKICK THIS TIME?
AND I HAVE THIS ULTRA-RARE WEAPON CARD TO WAGER! THE BURNT-
BURNING.
BURNING ICE SWORD!
BURNING ICE SWORD
M-ME? MY SIDEKICK? HOW DOES THAT EVEN... MY BRAIN JUST BROKE.

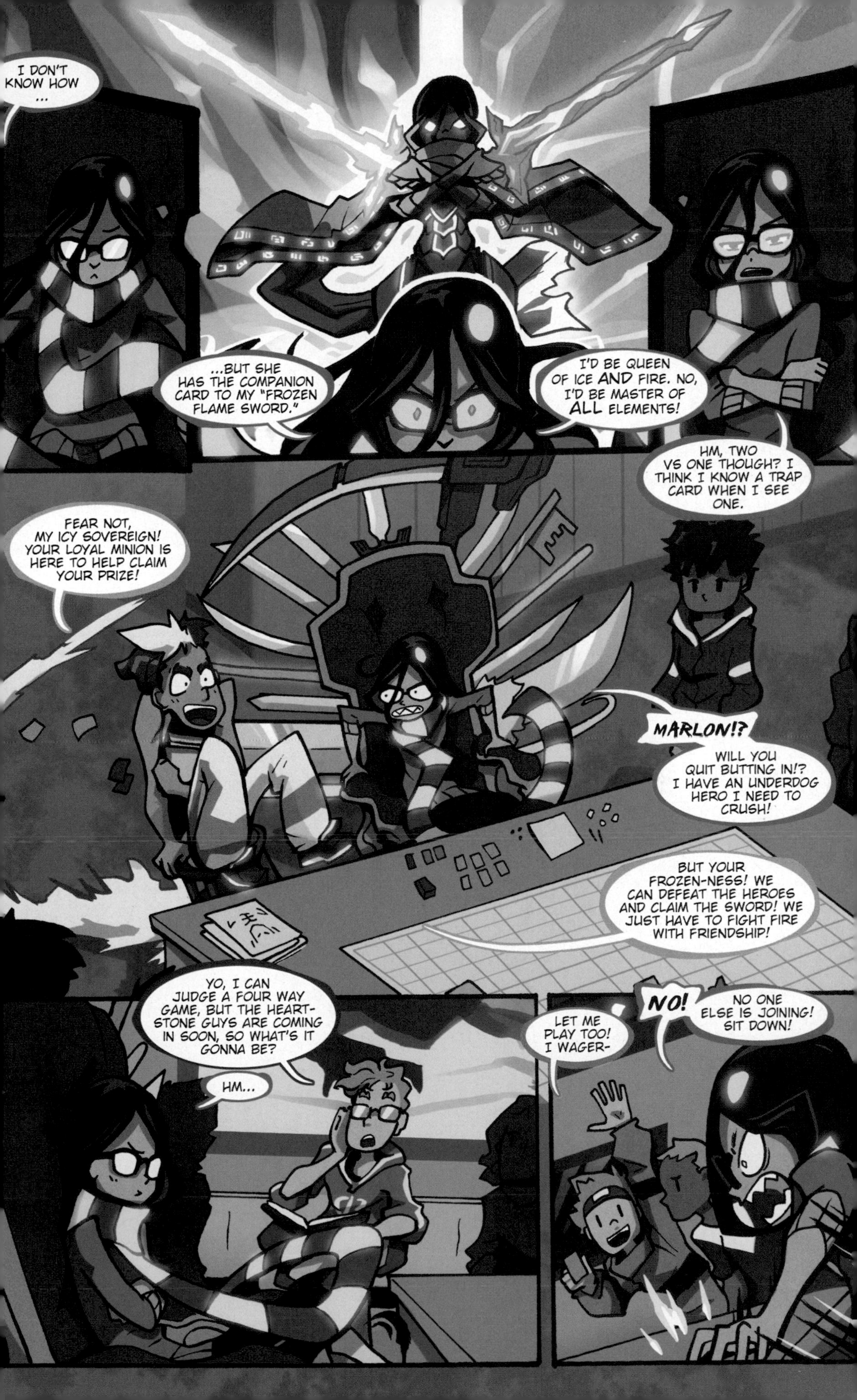
I DON'T KNOW HOW ...
...BUT SHE HAS THE COMPANION CARD TO MY "FROZEN FLAME SWORD."
I'D BE QUEEN OF ICE AND FIRE. NO, I'D BE MASTER OF ALL ELEMENTS!
HM, TWO VS ONE THOUGH? I THINK I KNOW A TRAP CARD WHEN I SEE ONE.
FEAR NOT, MY ICY SOVEREIGN! YOUR LOYAL MINION IS HERE TO HELP CLAIM YOUR PRIZE!
MARLON!?
WILL YOU QUIT BUTTING IN!? I HAVE AN UNDERDOG HERO I NEED TO CRUSH!
BUT YOUR FROZEN-NESS! WE CAN DEFEAT THE HEROES AND CLAIM THE SWORD! WE JUST HAVE TO FIGHT FIRE WITH FRIENDSHIP!
YO, I CAN JUDGE A FOUR WAY GAME, BUT THE HEART-STONE GUYS ARE COMING IN SOON, SO WHAT'S IT GONNA BE?
HM...
LET ME PLAY TOO! I WAGER-
NO!
NO ONE ELSE IS JOINING! SIT DOWN!

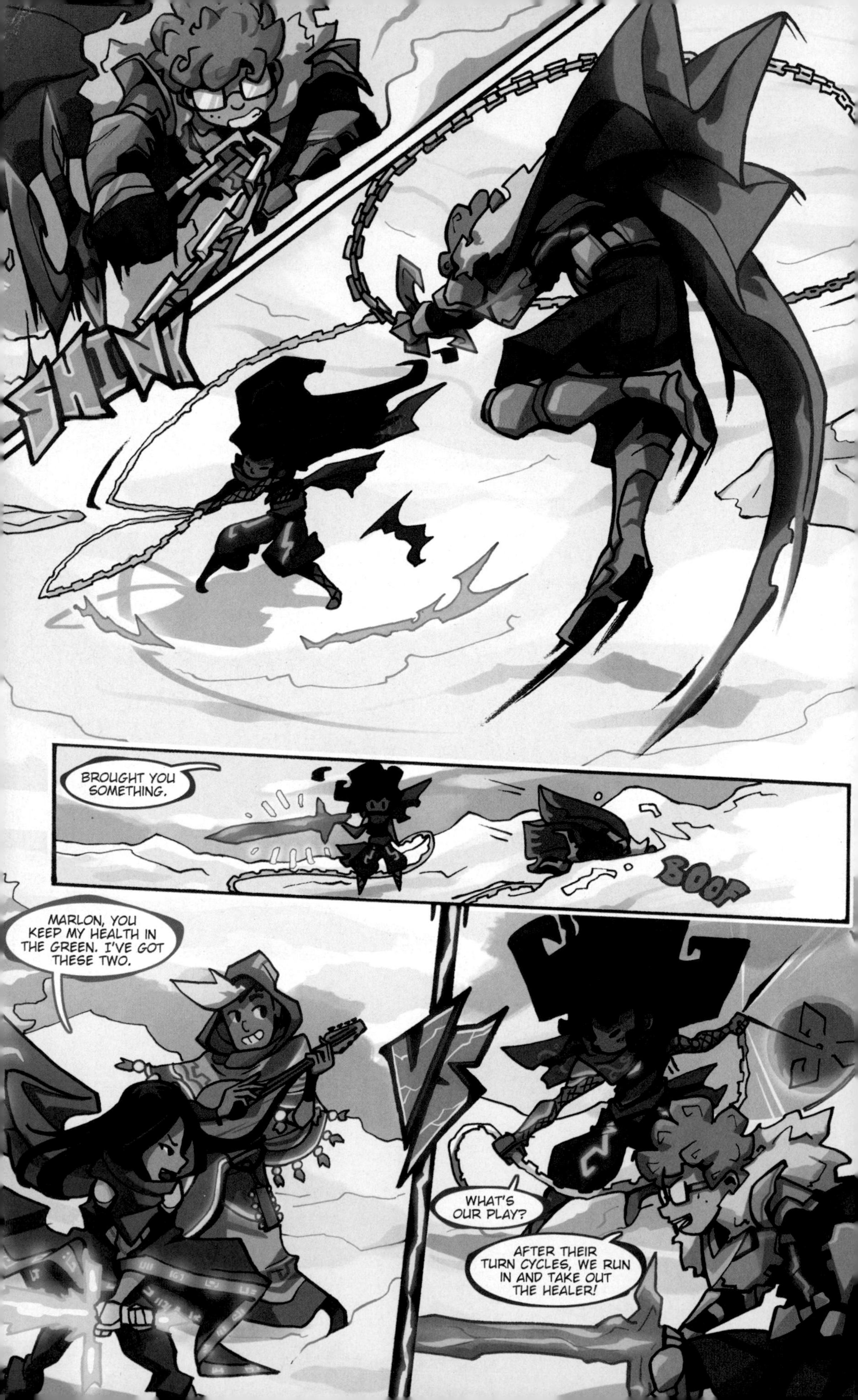
SHINK
BROUGHT YOU SOMETHING.
BOOF
MARLON, YOU KEEP MY HEALTH IN THE GREEN. I'VE GOT THESE TWO.
WHAT'S OUR PLAY?
AFTER THEIR TURN CYCLES, WE RUN IN AND TAKE OUT THE HEALER!

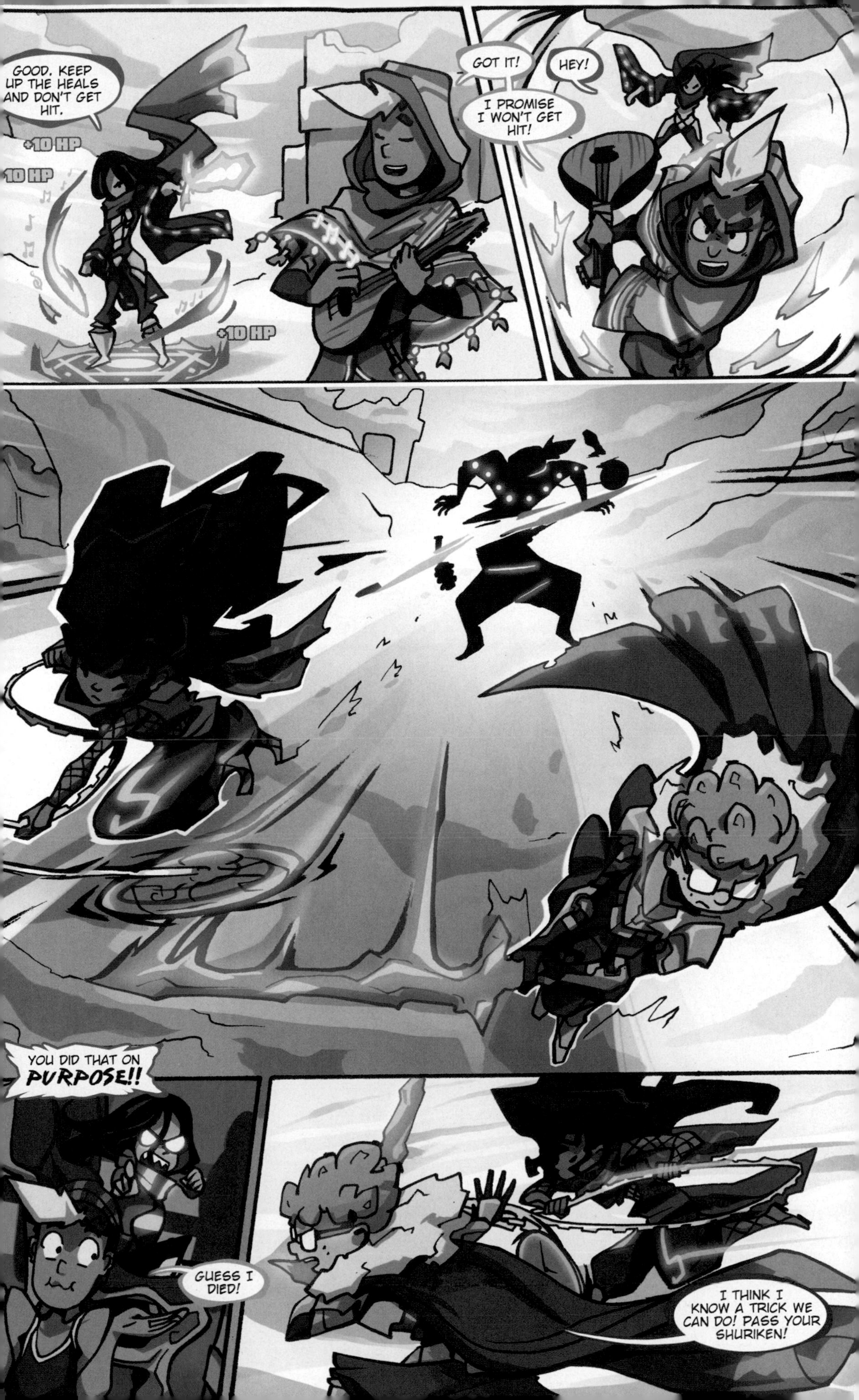
GOOD. KEEP UP THE HEALS AND DON'T GET HIT.
+10 HP
10 HP
+10 HP
GOT IT!
I PROMISE I WON'T GET HIT!
HEY!
YOU DID THAT ON PURPOSE!!
GUESS I DIED!
I THINK I KNOW A TRICK WE CAN DO! PASS YOUR SHURIKEN!

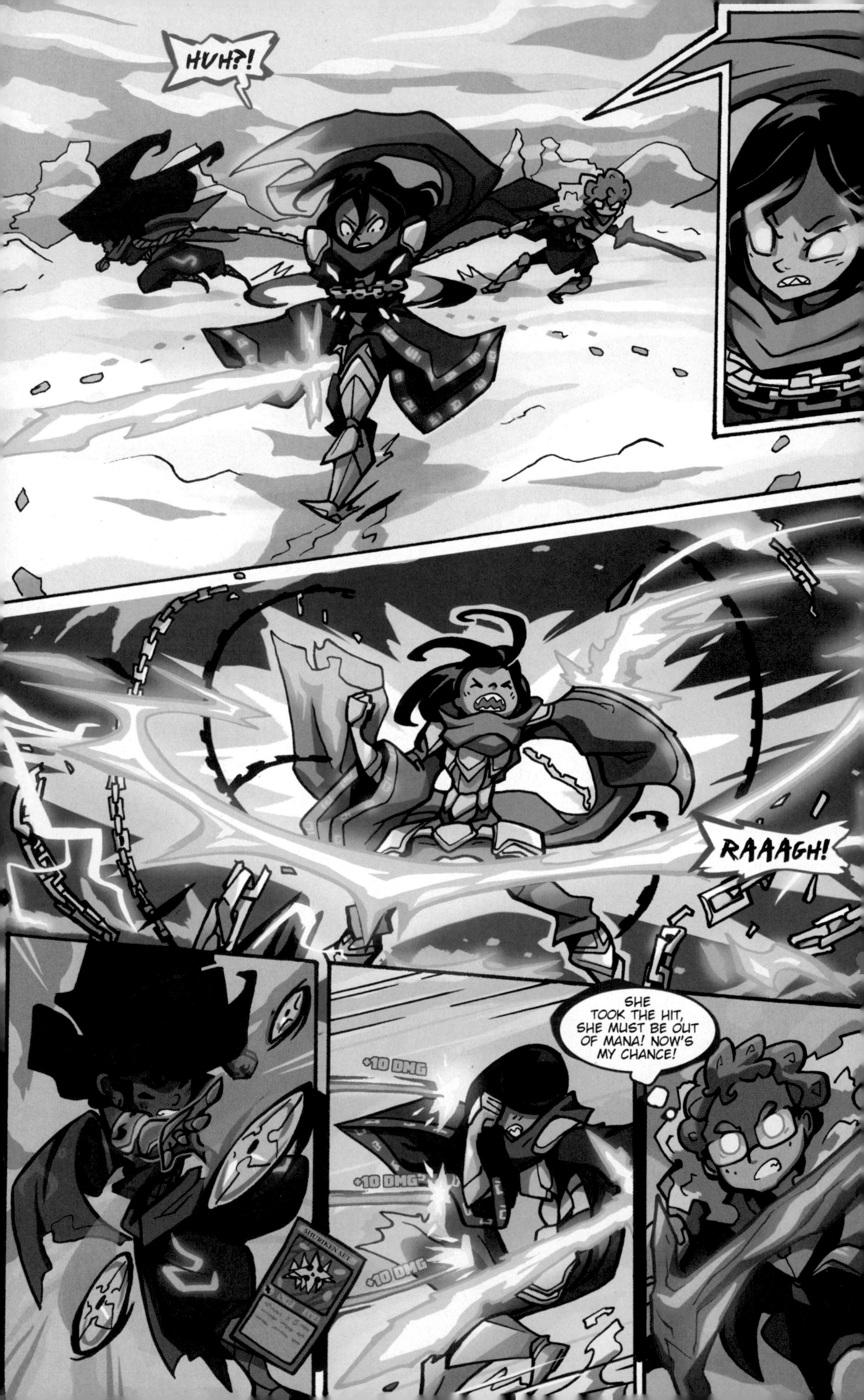
HUH?!
RAAAGH!
SHURIKEN SET
+10 DMG
+10 DMG
+10 DMG
SHE TOOK THE HIT, SHE MUST BE OUT OF MANA! NOW'S MY CHANCE!

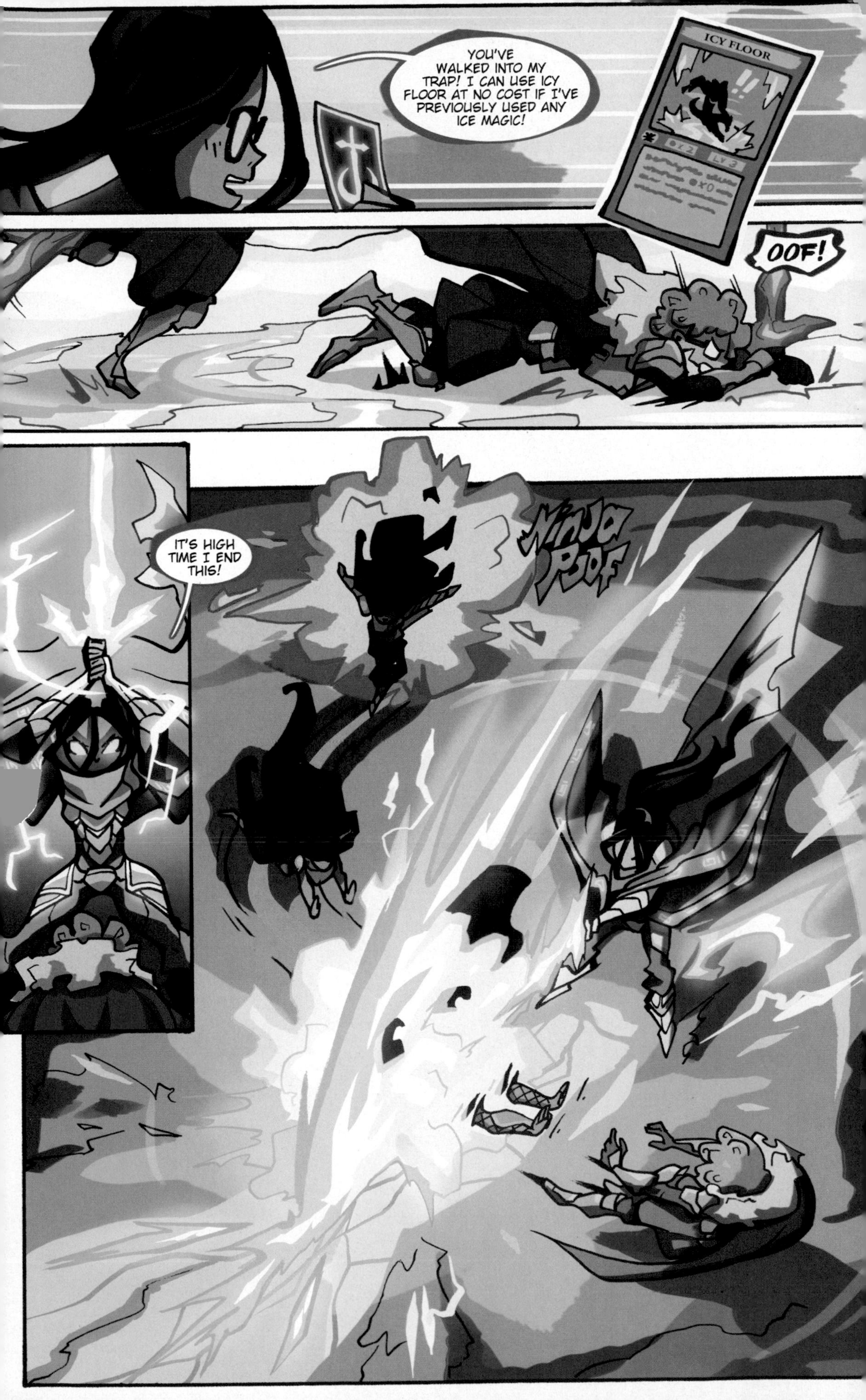
YOU'VE WALKED INTO MY TRAP! I CAN USE ICY FLOOR AT NO COST IF I'VE PREVIOUSLY USED ANY ICE MAGIC!
ICY FLOOR
LV 3
OOF!
IT'S HIGH TIME I END THIS!
NINJA POOF

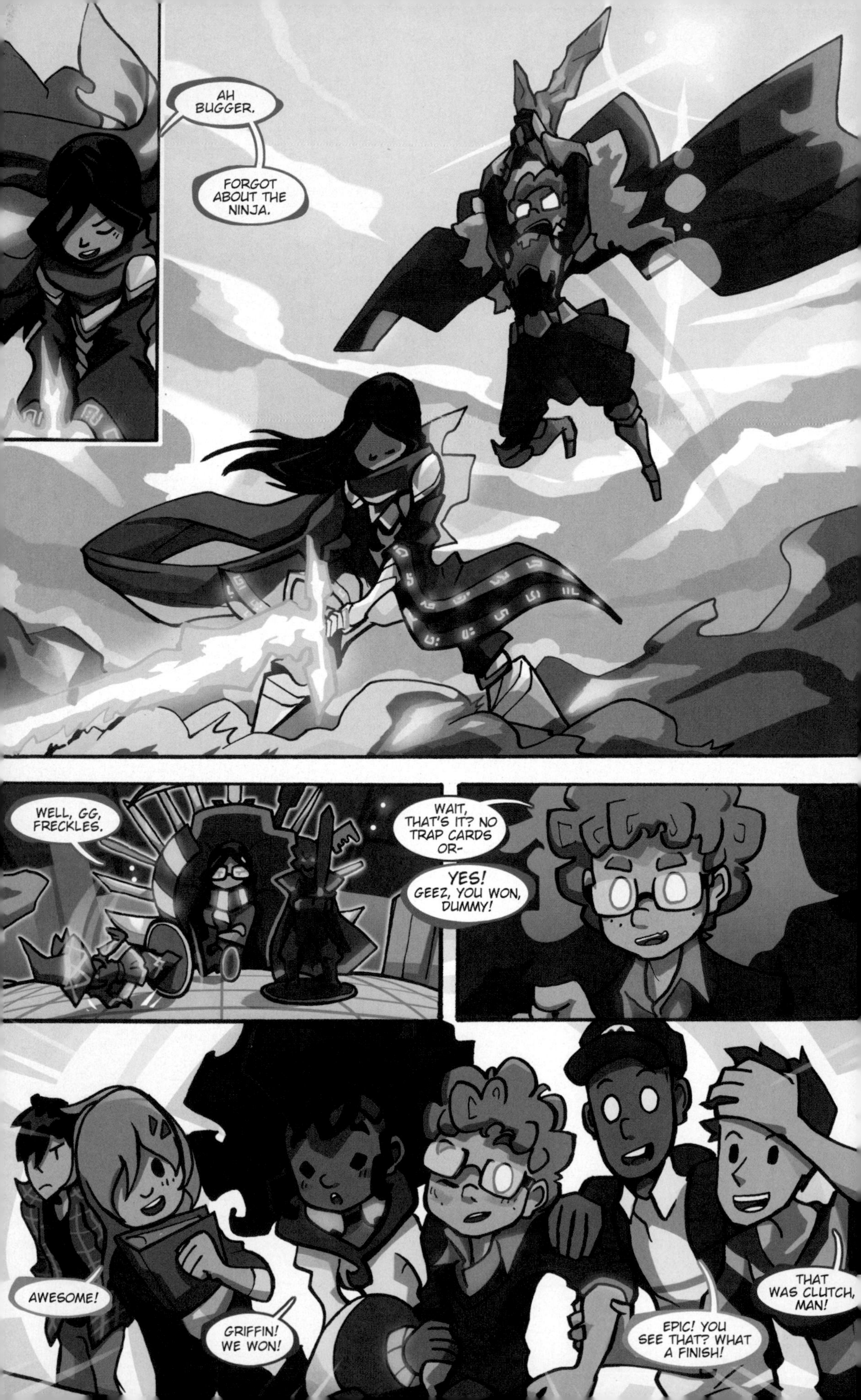
AH BUGGER.
FORGOT ABOUT THE NINJA.
WELL, GG, FRECKLES.
WAIT, THAT'S IT? NO TRAP CARDS OR-
YES! GEEZ, YOU WON, DUMMY!
AWESOME!
GRIFFIN! WE WON!
EPIC! YOU SEE THAT? WHAT A FINISH!
THAT WAS CLUTCH, MAN!

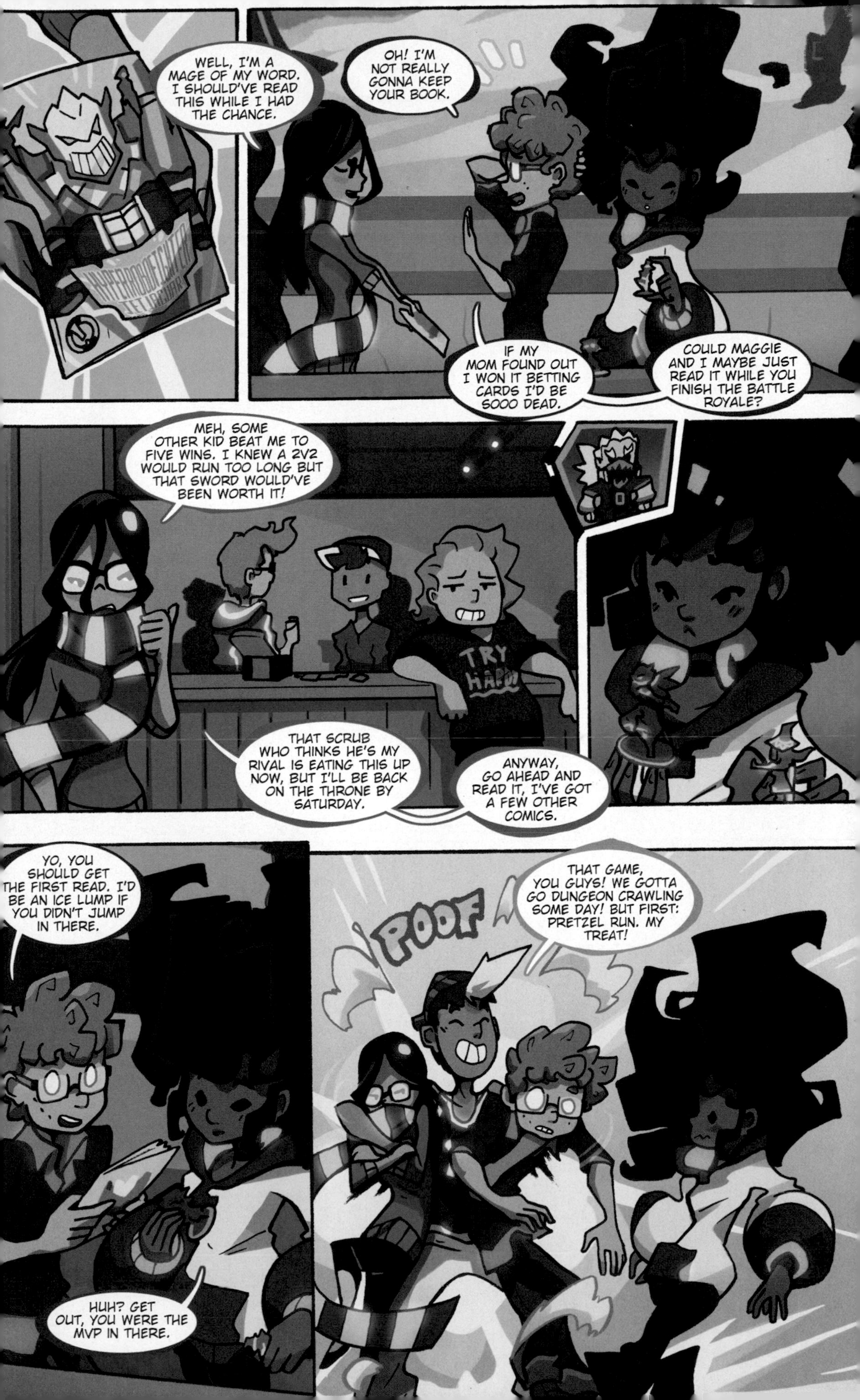

HYPERROBOTFIGHTER JET JAGUAR
WELL, I'M A MAGE OF MY WORD. I SHOULD'VE READ THIS WHILE I HAD THE CHANCE.
OH! I'M NOT REALLY GONNA KEEP YOUR BOOK.
IF MY MOM FOUND OUT I WON IT BETTING CARDS I'D BE SOOO DEAD.
COULD MAGGIE AND I MAYBE JUST READ IT WHILE YOU FINISH THE BATTLE ROYALE?
MEH, SOME OTHER KID BEAT ME TO FIVE WINS. I KNEW A 2V2 WOULD RUN TOO LONG BUT THAT SWORD WOULD'VE BEEN WORTH IT!
TRY HARD
THAT SCRUB WHO THINKS HE'S MY RIVAL IS EATING THIS UP NOW, BUT I'LL BE BACK ON THE THRONE BY SATURDAY.
ANYWAY, GO AHEAD AND READ IT, I'VE GOT A FEW OTHER COMICS.
YO, YOU SHOULD GET THE FIRST READ. I'D BE AN ICE LUMP IF YOU DIDN'T JUMP IN THERE.
HUH? GET OUT, YOU WERE THE MVP IN THERE.
POOF
THAT GAME, YOU GUYS! WE GOTTA GO DUNGEON CRAWLING SOME DAY! BUT FIRST: PRETZEL RUN. MY TREAT!

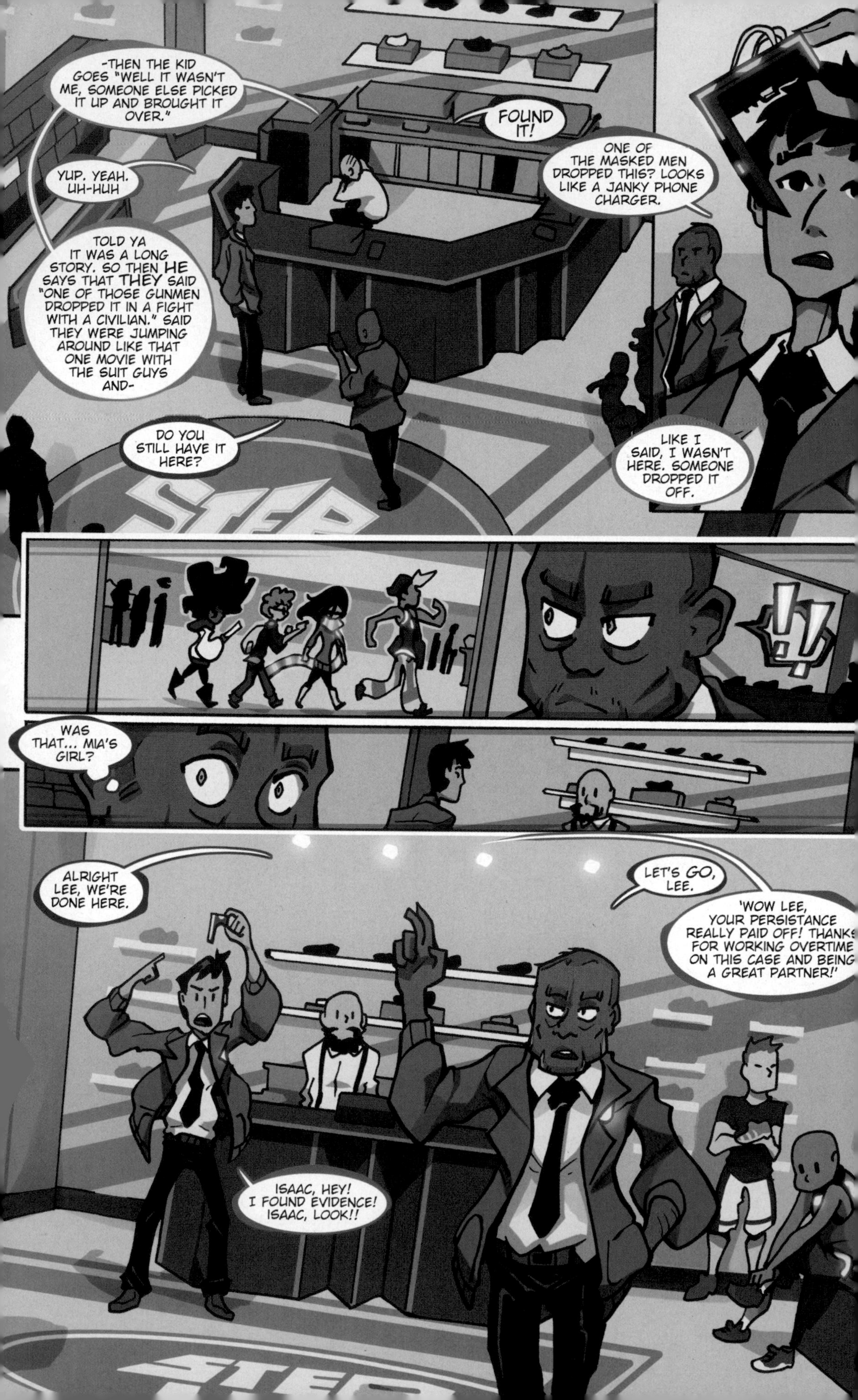
-THEN THE KID GOES "WELL IT WASN'T ME, SOMEONE ELSE PICKED IT UP AND BROUGHT IT OVER."
FOUND IT!
YUP. YEAH. UH-HUH
TOLD YA IT WAS A LONG STORY. SO THEN HE SAYS THAT THEY SAID "ONE OF THOSE GUNMEN DROPPED IT IN A FIGHT WITH A CIVILIAN." SAID THEY WERE JUMPING AROUND LIKE THAT ONE MOVIE WITH THE SUIT GUYS AND-
ONE OF THE MASKED MEN DROPPED THIS? LOOKS LIKE A JANKY PHONE CHARGER.
DO YOU STILL HAVE IT HERE?
LIKE I SAID, I WASN'T HERE. SOMEONE DROPPED IT OFF.
!!
WAS THAT... MIA'S GIRL?
ALRIGHT LEE, WE'RE DONE HERE.
LET'S GO, LEE.
'WOW LEE, YOUR PERSISTANCE REALLY PAID OFF! THANKS FOR WORKING OVERTIME ON THIS CASE AND BEING A GREAT PARTNER!'
ISAAC, HEY! I FOUND EVIDENCE! ISAAC, LOOK!!

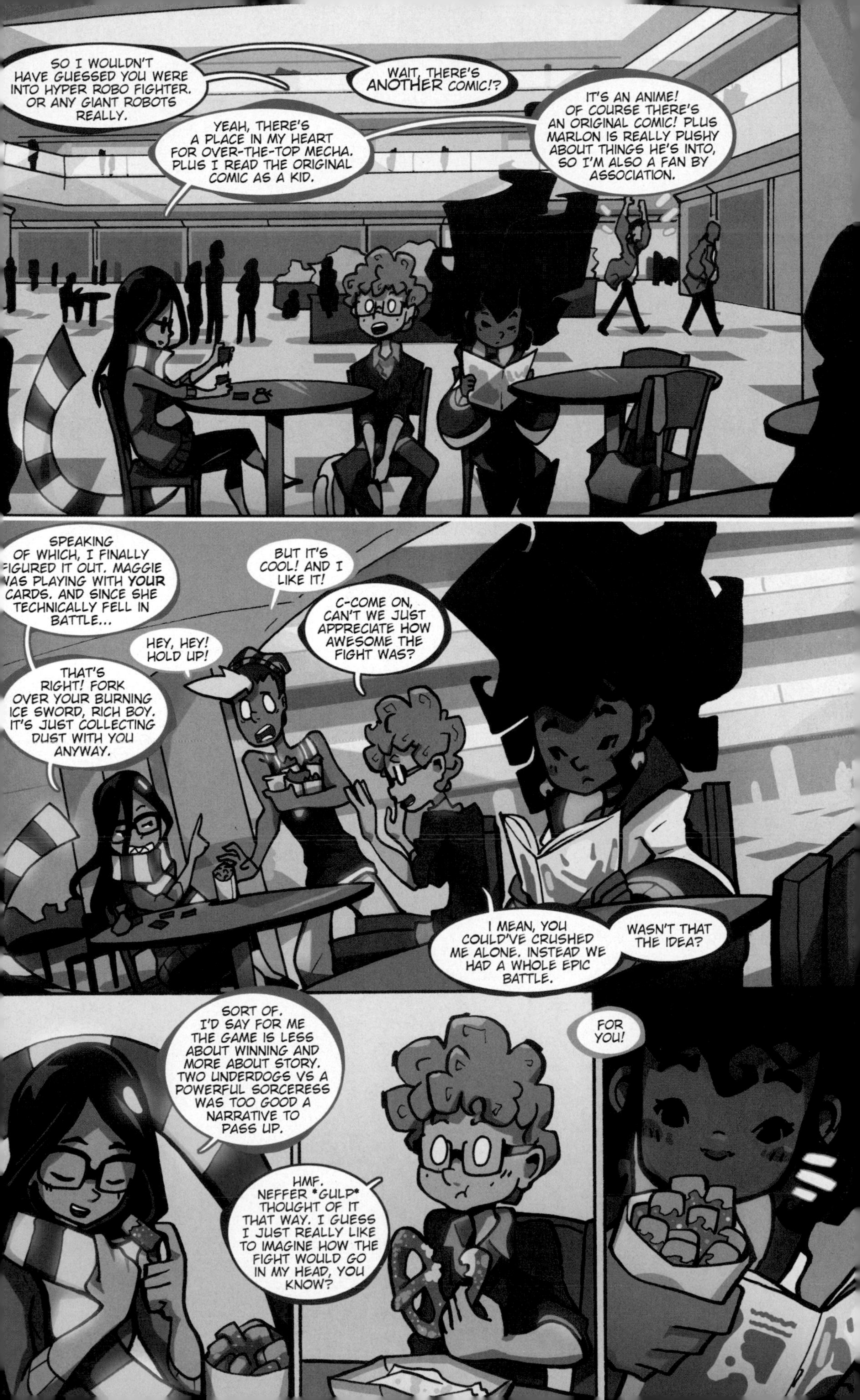
SO I WOULDN'T HAVE GUESSED YOU WERE INTO HYPER ROBO FIGHTER. OR ANY GIANT ROBOTS REALLY.
WAIT, THERE'S ANOTHER COMIC!?
YEAH, THERE'S A PLACE IN MY HEART FOR OVER-THE-TOP MECHA. PLUS I READ THE ORIGINAL COMIC AS A KID.
IT'S AN ANIME! OF COURSE THERE'S AN ORIGINAL COMIC! PLUS MARLON IS REALLY PUSHY ABOUT THINGS HE'S INTO, SO I'M ALSO A FAN BY ASSOCIATION.
SPEAKING OF WHICH, I FINALLY FIGURED IT OUT. MAGGIE WAS PLAYING WITH YOUR CARDS. AND SINCE SHE TECHNICALLY FELL IN BATTLE...
BUT IT'S COOL! AND I LIKE IT!
HEY, HEY! HOLD UP!
THAT'S RIGHT! FORK OVER YOUR BURNING ICE SWORD, RICH BOY. IT'S JUST COLLECTING DUST WITH YOU ANYWAY.
C-COME ON, CAN'T WE JUST APPRECIATE HOW AWESOME THE FIGHT WAS?
I MEAN, YOU COULD'VE CRUSHED ME ALONE. INSTEAD WE HAD A WHOLE EPIC BATTLE.
WASN'T THAT THE IDEA?
SORT OF. I'D SAY FOR ME THE GAME IS LESS ABOUT WINNING AND MORE ABOUT STORY. TWO UNDERDOGS VS A POWERFUL SORCERESS WAS TOO GOOD A NARRATIVE TO PASS UP.
HMF. NEFFER *GULP* THOUGHT OF IT THAT WAY. I GUESS I JUST REALLY LIKE TO IMAGINE HOW THE FIGHT WOULD GO IN MY HEAD, YOU KNOW?
FOR YOU!

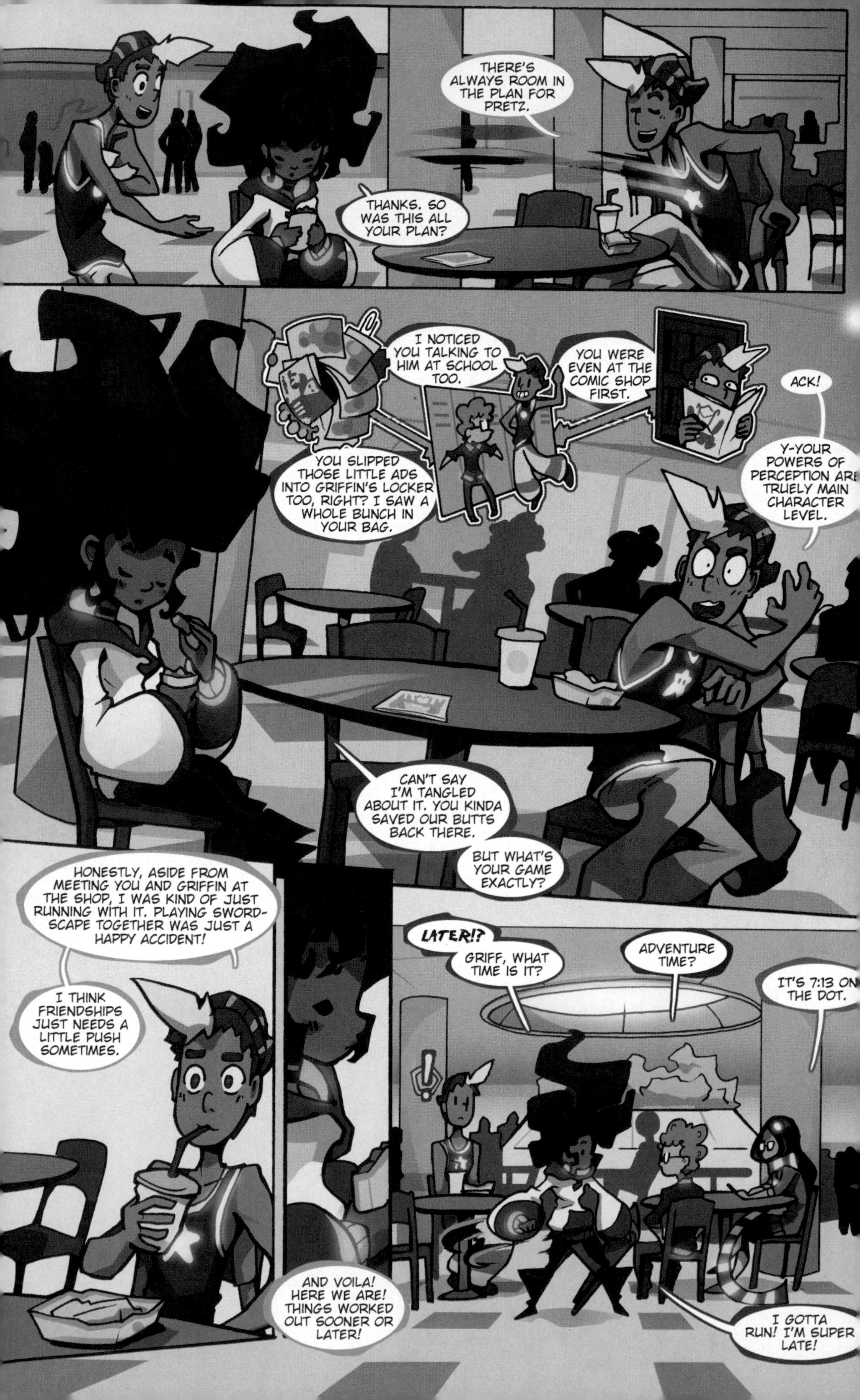
THERE'S ALWAYS ROOM IN THE PLAN FOR PRETZ.
THANKS. SO WAS THIS ALL YOUR PLAN?
I NOTICED YOU TALKING TO HIM AT SCHOOL TOO.
YOU WERE EVEN AT THE COMIC SHOP FIRST.
YOU SLIPPED THOSE LITTLE ADS INTO GRIFFIN'S LOCKER TOO, RIGHT? I SAW A WHOLE BUNCH IN YOUR BAG.
ACK!
Y-YOUR POWERS OF PERCEPTION ARE TRUELY MAIN CHARACTER LEVEL.
CAN'T SAY I'M TANGLED ABOUT IT. YOU KINDA SAVED OUR BUTTS BACK THERE.
BUT WHAT'S YOUR GAME EXACTLY?
HONESTLY, ASIDE FROM MEETING YOU AND GRIFFIN AT THE SHOP, I WAS KIND OF JUST RUNNING WITH IT. PLAYING SWORD-SCAPE TOGETHER WAS JUST A HAPPY ACCIDENT!
I THINK FRIENDSHIPS JUST NEEDS A LITTLE PUSH SOMETIMES.
AND VOILA! HERE WE ARE! THINGS WORKED OUT SOONER OR LATER!
LATER!?
GRIFF, WHAT TIME IS IT?
ADVENTURE TIME?
IT'S 7:13 ON THE DOT.
I GOTTA RUN! I'M SUPER LATE!

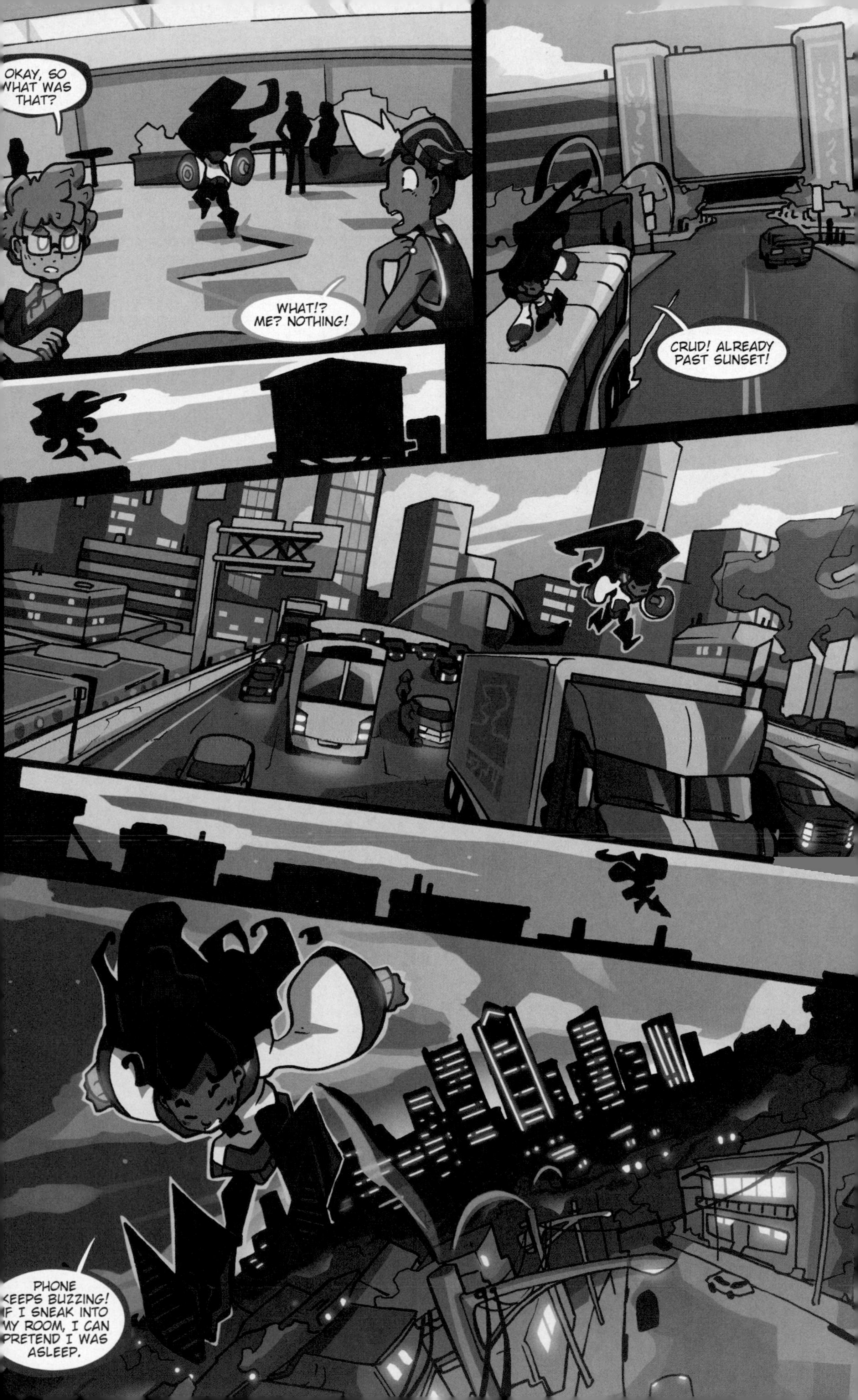
OKAY, SO WHAT WAS THAT?
WHAT!? ME? NOTHING!
CRUD! ALREADY PAST SUNSET!
PHONE KEEPS BUZZING! IF I SNEAK INTO MY ROOM, I CAN PRETEND I WAS ASLEEP.

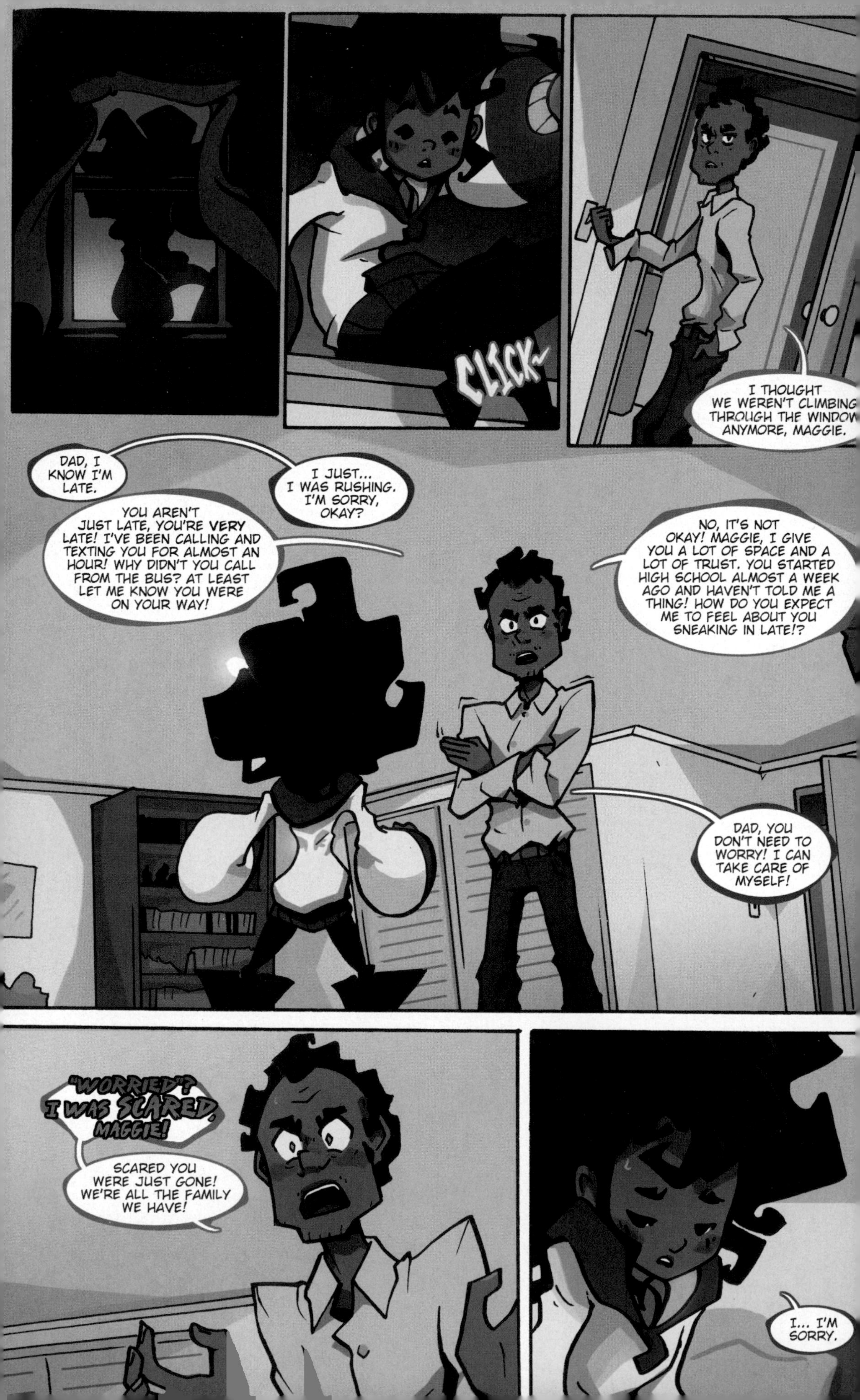
CLICK~
I THOUGHT WE WEREN'T CLIMBING THROUGH THE WINDOW ANYMORE, MAGGIE.
DAD, I KNOW I'M LATE.
I JUST... I WAS RUSHING. I'M SORRY, OKAY?
YOU AREN'T JUST LATE, YOU'RE **VERY** LATE! I'VE BEEN CALLING AND TEXTING YOU FOR ALMOST AN HOUR! WHY DIDN'T YOU CALL FROM THE BUS? AT LEAST LET ME KNOW YOU WERE ON YOUR WAY!
NO, IT'S NOT OKAY! MAGGIE, I GIVE YOU A LOT OF SPACE AND A LOT OF TRUST. YOU STARTED HIGH SCHOOL ALMOST A WEEK AGO AND HAVEN'T TOLD ME A THING! HOW DO YOU EXPECT ME TO FEEL ABOUT YOU SNEAKING IN LATE!?
DAD, YOU DON'T NEED TO WORRY! I CAN TAKE CARE OF MYSELF!
"WORRIED"? I WAS SCARED, MAGGIE!
SCARED YOU WERE JUST GONE! WE'RE ALL THE FAMILY WE HAVE!
I... I'M SORRY.

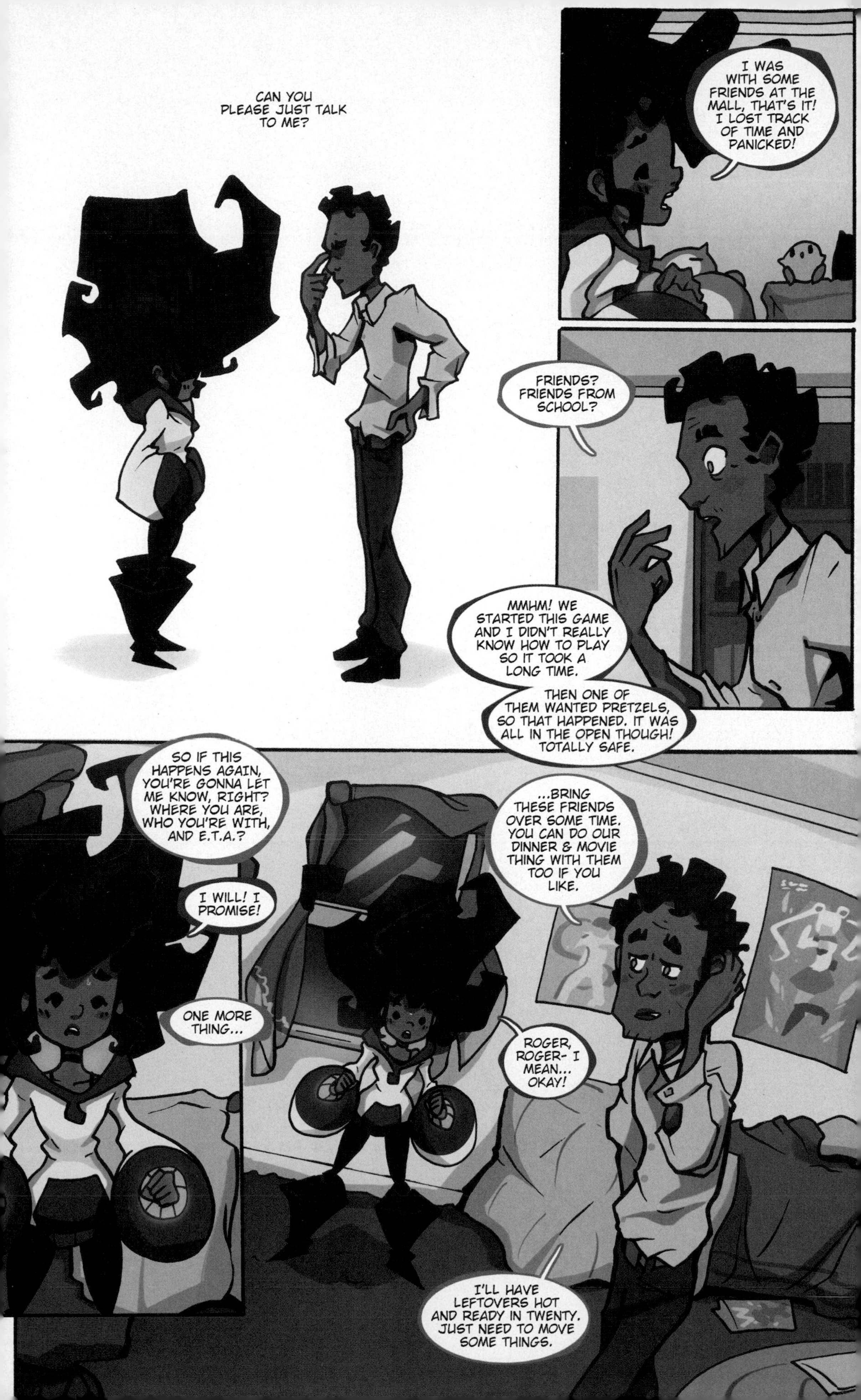
CAN YOU PLEASE JUST TALK TO ME?
I WAS WITH SOME FRIENDS AT THE MALL, THAT'S IT! I LOST TRACK OF TIME AND PANICKED!
FRIENDS? FRIENDS FROM SCHOOL?
MMHM! WE STARTED THIS GAME AND I DIDN'T REALLY KNOW HOW TO PLAY SO IT TOOK A LONG TIME.
THEN ONE OF THEM WANTED PRETZELS, SO THAT HAPPENED. IT WAS ALL IN THE OPEN THOUGH! TOTALLY SAFE.
SO IF THIS HAPPENS AGAIN, YOU'RE GONNA LET ME KNOW, RIGHT? WHERE YOU ARE, WHO YOU'RE WITH, AND E.T.A.?
I WILL! I PROMISE!
ONE MORE THING...
...BRING THESE FRIENDS OVER SOME TIME. YOU CAN DO OUR DINNER & MOVIE THING WITH THEM TOO IF YOU LIKE.
ROGER, ROGER- I MEAN... OKAY!
I'LL HAVE LEFTOVERS HOT AND READY IN TWENTY. JUST NEED TO MOVE SOME THINGS.

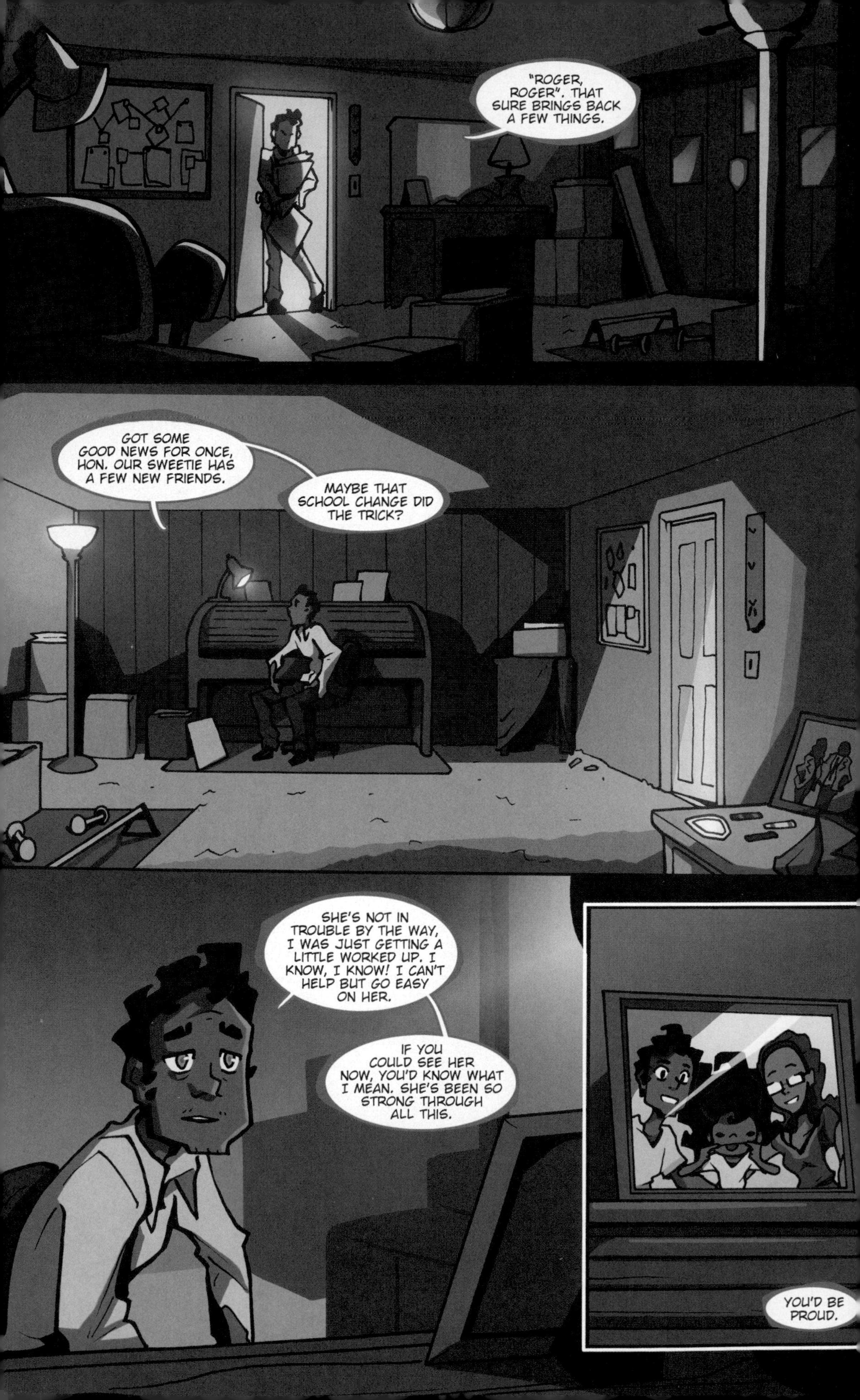
"ROGER, ROGER". THAT SURE BRINGS BACK A FEW THINGS.
GOT SOME GOOD NEWS FOR ONCE, HON. OUR SWEETIE HAS A FEW NEW FRIENDS.
MAYBE THAT SCHOOL CHANGE DID THE TRICK?
SHE'S NOT IN TROUBLE BY THE WAY, I WAS JUST GETTING A LITTLE WORKED UP. I KNOW, I KNOW! I CAN'T HELP BUT GO EASY ON HER.
IF YOU COULD SEE HER NOW, YOU'D KNOW WHAT I MEAN. SHE'S BEEN SO STRONG THROUGH ALL THIS.
YOU'D BE PROUD.

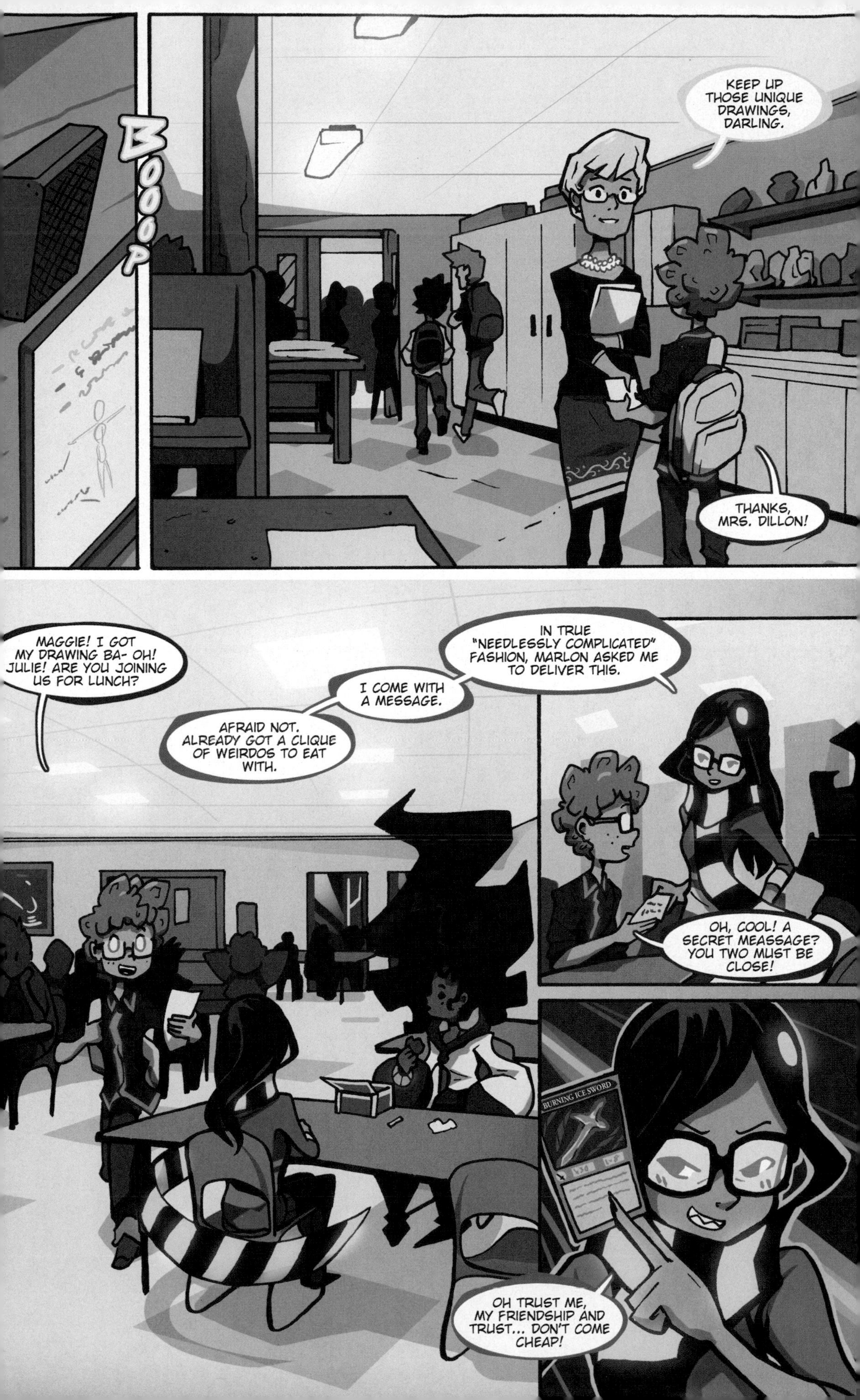
BOOOOP
KEEP UP THOSE UNIQUE DRAWINGS, DARLING.
THANKS, MRS. DILLON!
MAGGIE! I GOT MY DRAWING BA- OH! JULIE! ARE YOU JOINING US FOR LUNCH?
AFRAID NOT. ALREADY GOT A CLIQUE OF WEIRDOS TO EAT WITH.
I COME WITH A MESSAGE.
IN TRUE "NEEDLESSLY COMPLICATED" FASHION, MARLON ASKED ME TO DELIVER THIS.
OH, COOL! A SECRET MEASSAGE? YOU TWO MUST BE CLOSE!
BURNING ICE SWORD
OH TRUST ME, MY FRIENDSHIP AND TRUST... DON'T COME CHEAP!

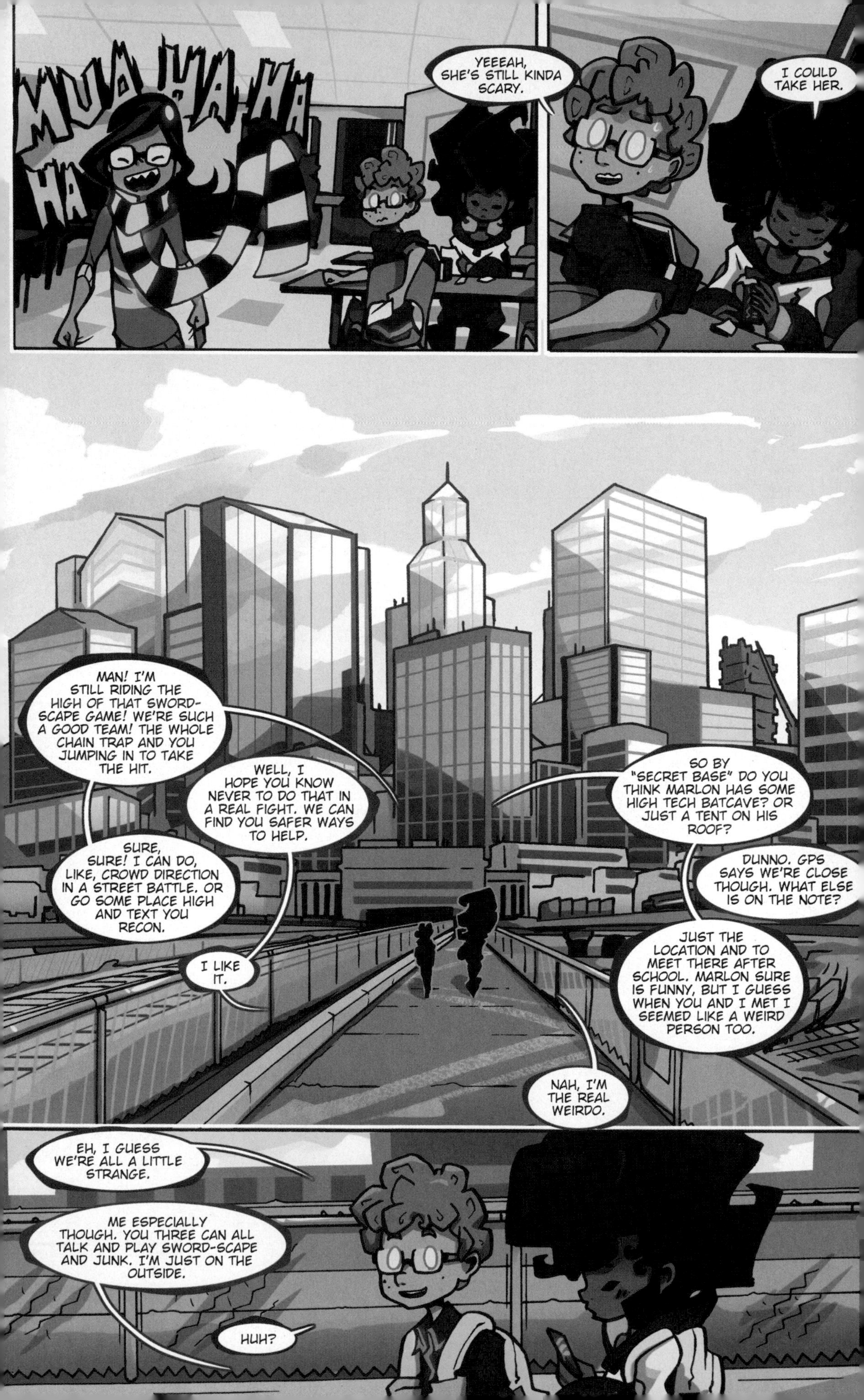
MUA HA HA HA
YEEEAH, SHE'S STILL KINDA SCARY.
I COULD TAKE HER.
MAN! I'M STILL RIDING THE HIGH OF THAT SWORD-SCAPE GAME! WE'RE SUCH A GOOD TEAM! THE WHOLE CHAIN TRAP AND YOU JUMPING IN TO TAKE THE HIT.
WELL, I HOPE YOU KNOW NEVER TO DO THAT IN A REAL FIGHT. WE CAN FIND YOU SAFER WAYS TO HELP.
SURE, SURE! I CAN DO, LIKE, CROWD DIRECTION IN A STREET BATTLE. OR GO SOME PLACE HIGH AND TEXT YOU RECON.
I LIKE IT.
SO BY "SECRET BASE" DO YOU THINK MARLON HAS SOME HIGH TECH BATCAVE? OR JUST A TENT ON HIS ROOF?
DUNNO. GPS SAYS WE'RE CLOSE THOUGH. WHAT ELSE IS ON THE NOTE?
JUST THE LOCATION AND TO MEET THERE AFTER SCHOOL. MARLON SURE IS FUNNY, BUT I GUESS WHEN YOU AND I MET I SEEMED LIKE A WEIRD PERSON TOO.
NAH, I'M THE REAL WEIRDO.
EH, I GUESS WE'RE ALL A LITTLE STRANGE.
ME ESPECIALLY THOUGH. YOU THREE CAN ALL TALK AND PLAY SWORD-SCAPE AND JUNK. I'M JUST ON THE OUTSIDE.
HUH?

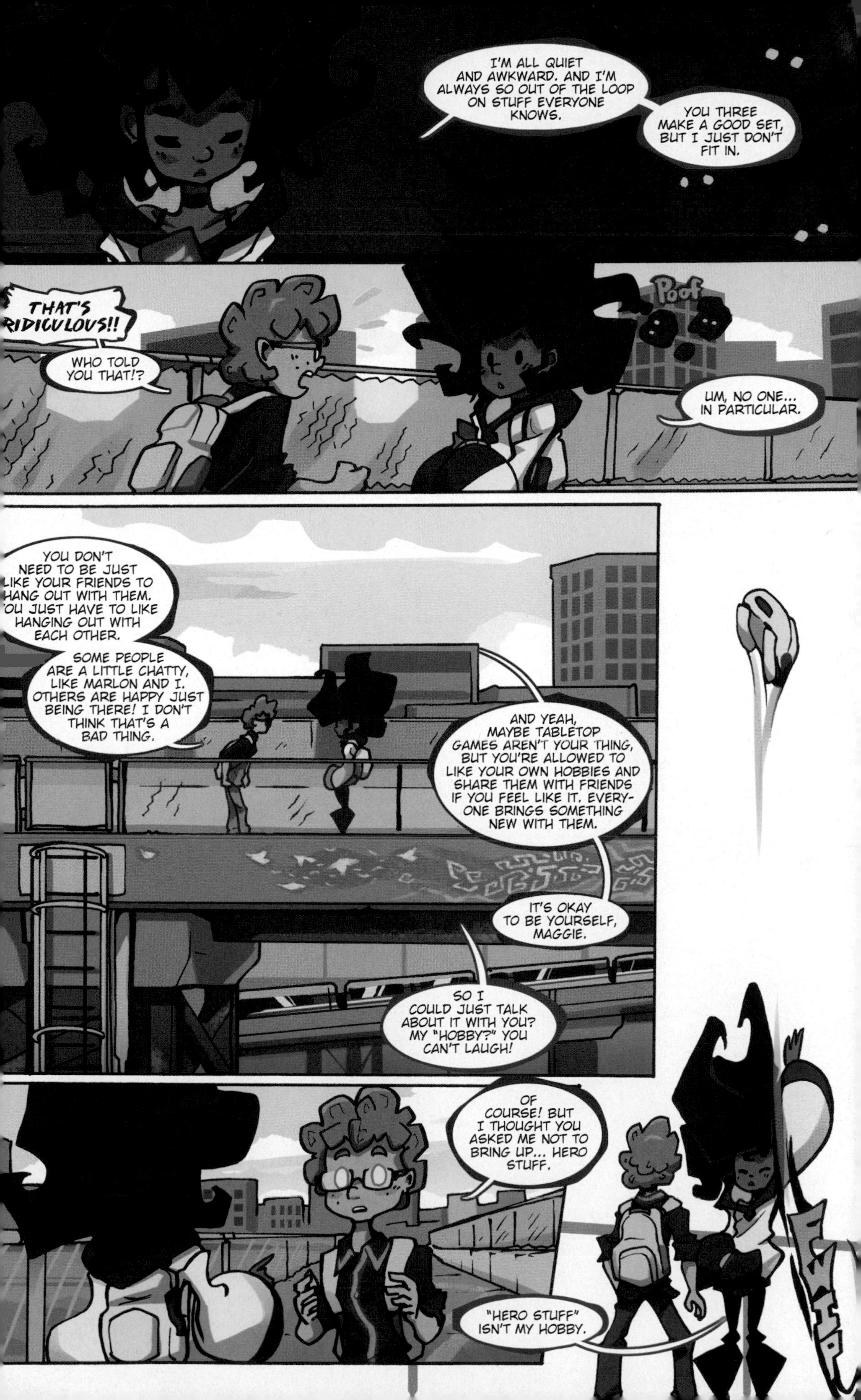
I'M ALL QUIET AND AWKWARD. AND I'M ALWAYS SO OUT OF THE LOOP ON STUFF EVERYONE KNOWS.
YOU THREE MAKE A GOOD SET, BUT I JUST DON'T FIT IN.
THAT'S RIDICULOUS!!
WHO TOLD YOU THAT!?
Poof
UM, NO ONE... IN PARTICULAR.
YOU DON'T NEED TO BE JUST LIKE YOUR FRIENDS TO HANG OUT WITH THEM. YOU JUST HAVE TO LIKE HANGING OUT WITH EACH OTHER.
SOME PEOPLE ARE A LITTLE CHATTY, LIKE MARLON AND I. OTHERS ARE HAPPY JUST BEING THERE! I DON'T THINK THAT'S A BAD THING.
AND YEAH, MAYBE TABLETOP GAMES AREN'T YOUR THING, BUT YOU'RE ALLOWED TO LIKE YOUR OWN HOBBIES AND SHARE THEM WITH FRIENDS IF YOU FEEL LIKE IT. EVERY-ONE BRINGS SOMETHING NEW WITH THEM.
IT'S OKAY TO BE YOURSELF, MAGGIE.
SO I COULD JUST TALK ABOUT IT WITH YOU? MY "HOBBY?" YOU CAN'T LAUGH!
OF COURSE! BUT I THOUGHT YOU ASKED ME NOT TO BRING UP... HERO STUFF.
"HERO STUFF" ISN'T MY HOBBY.
FWIP

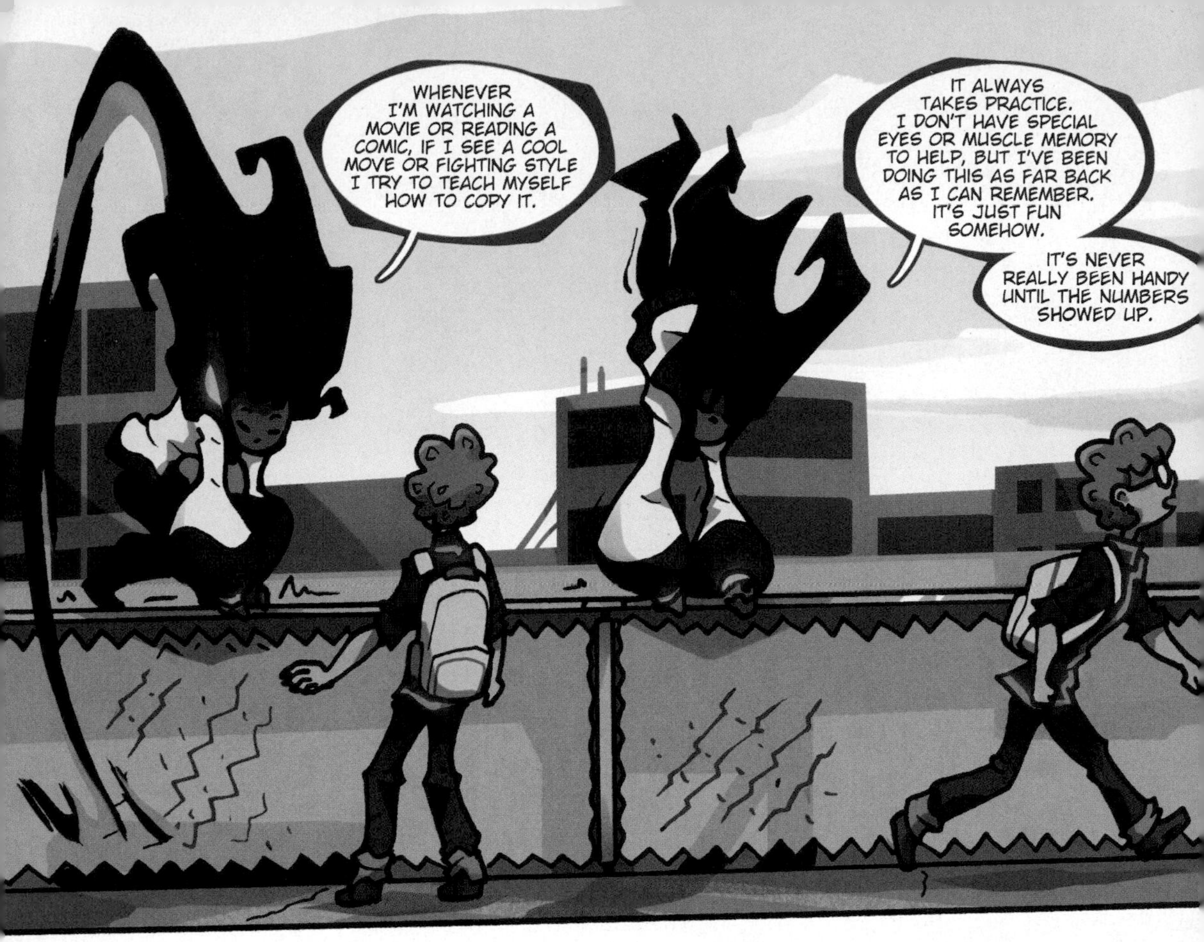
WHENEVER I'M WATCHING A MOVIE OR READING A COMIC, IF I SEE A COOL MOVE OR FIGHTING STYLE I TRY TO TEACH MYSELF HOW TO COPY IT.
IT ALWAYS TAKES PRACTICE. I DON'T HAVE SPECIAL EYES OR MUSCLE MEMORY TO HELP, BUT I'VE BEEN DOING THIS AS FAR BACK AS I CAN REMEMBER. IT'S JUST FUN SOMEHOW.
IT'S NEVER REALLY BEEN HANDY UNTIL THE NUMBERS SHOWED UP.

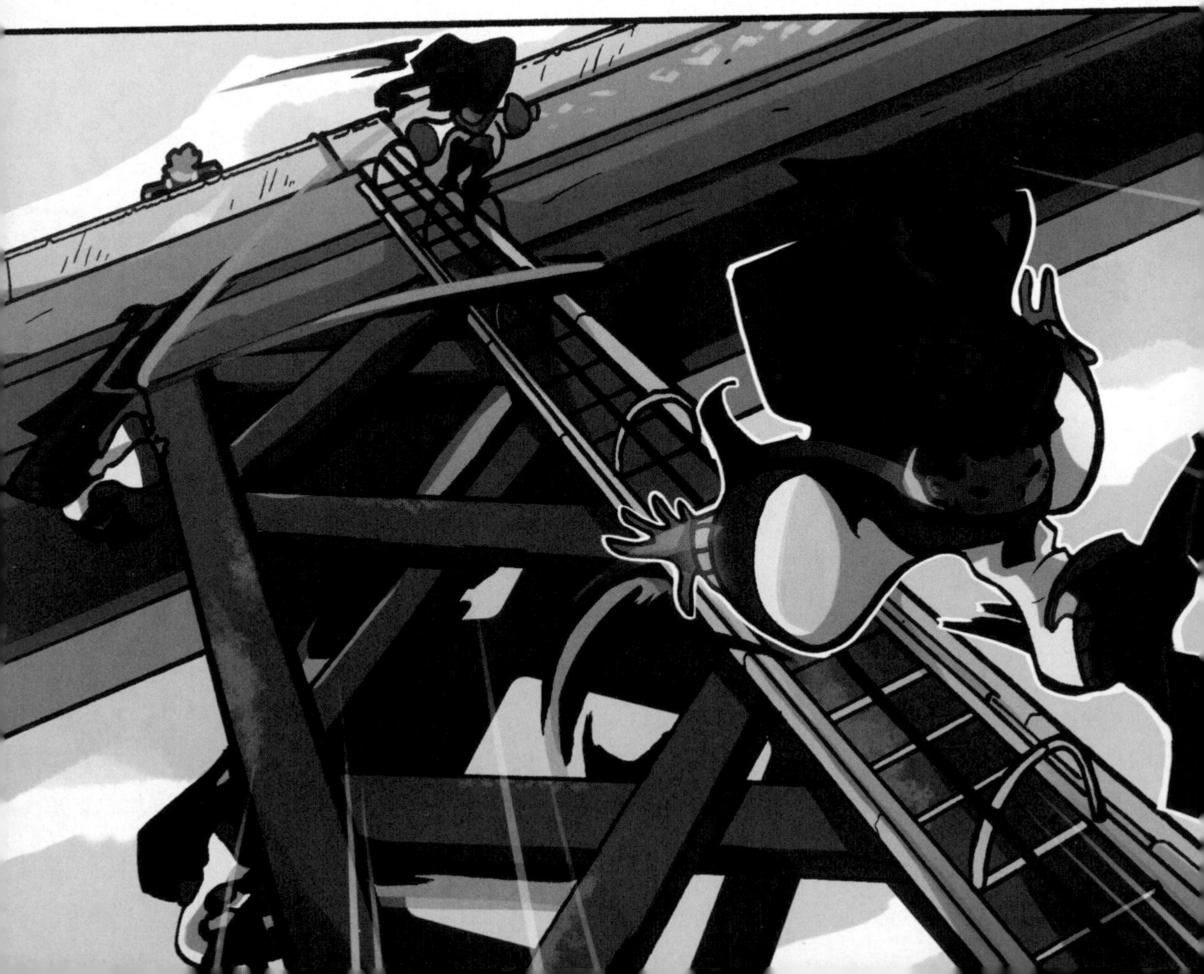

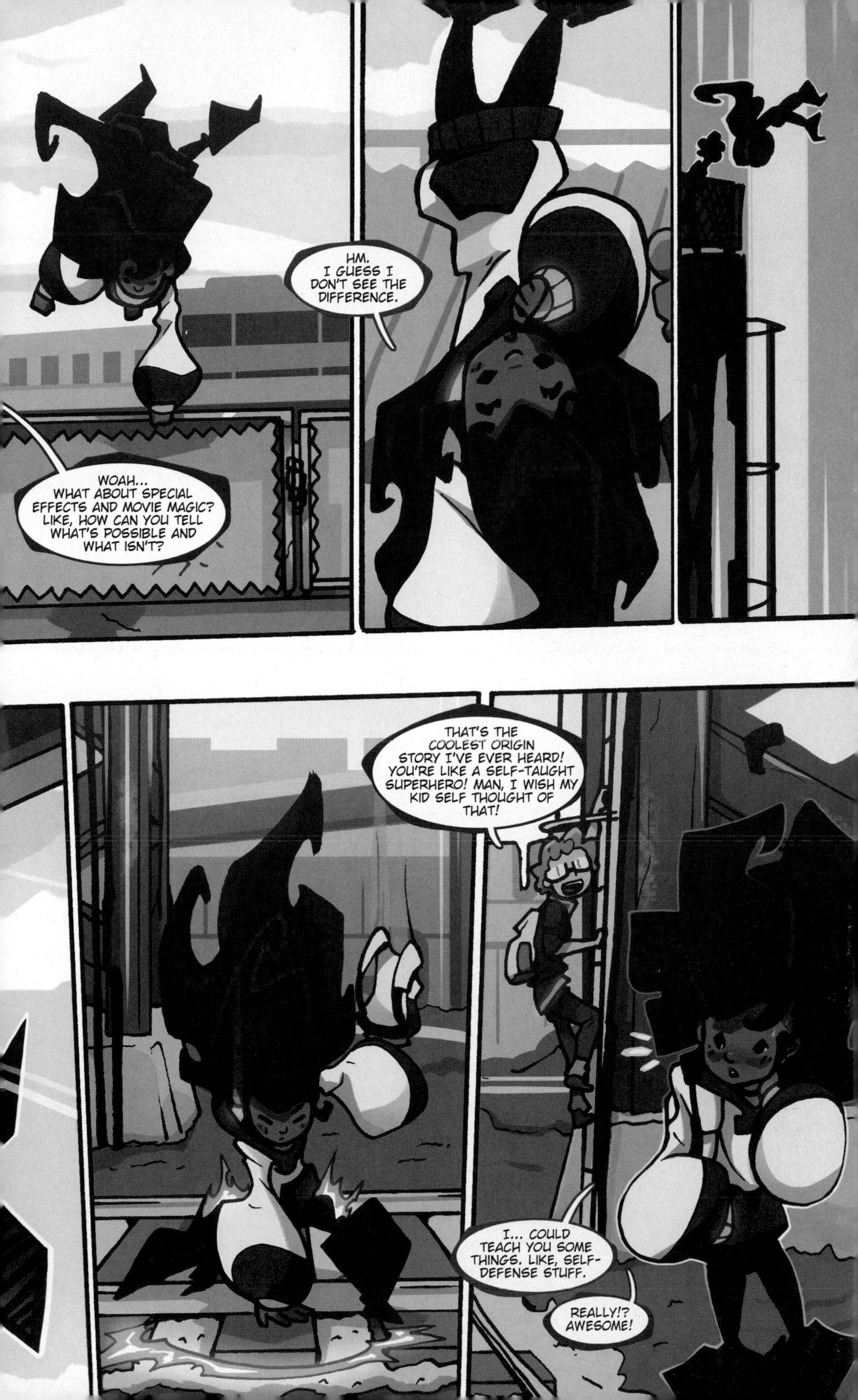
WOAH... WHAT ABOUT SPECIAL EFFECTS AND MOVIE MAGIC? LIKE, HOW CAN YOU TELL WHAT'S POSSIBLE AND WHAT ISN'T?
HM. I GUESS I DON'T SEE THE DIFFERENCE.
THAT'S THE COOLEST ORIGIN STORY I'VE EVER HEARD! YOU'RE LIKE A SELF-TAUGHT SUPERHERO! MAN, I WISH MY KID SELF THOUGHT OF THAT!
I... COULD TEACH YOU SOME THINGS. LIKE, SELF-DEFENSE STUFF.
REALLY!? AWESOME!

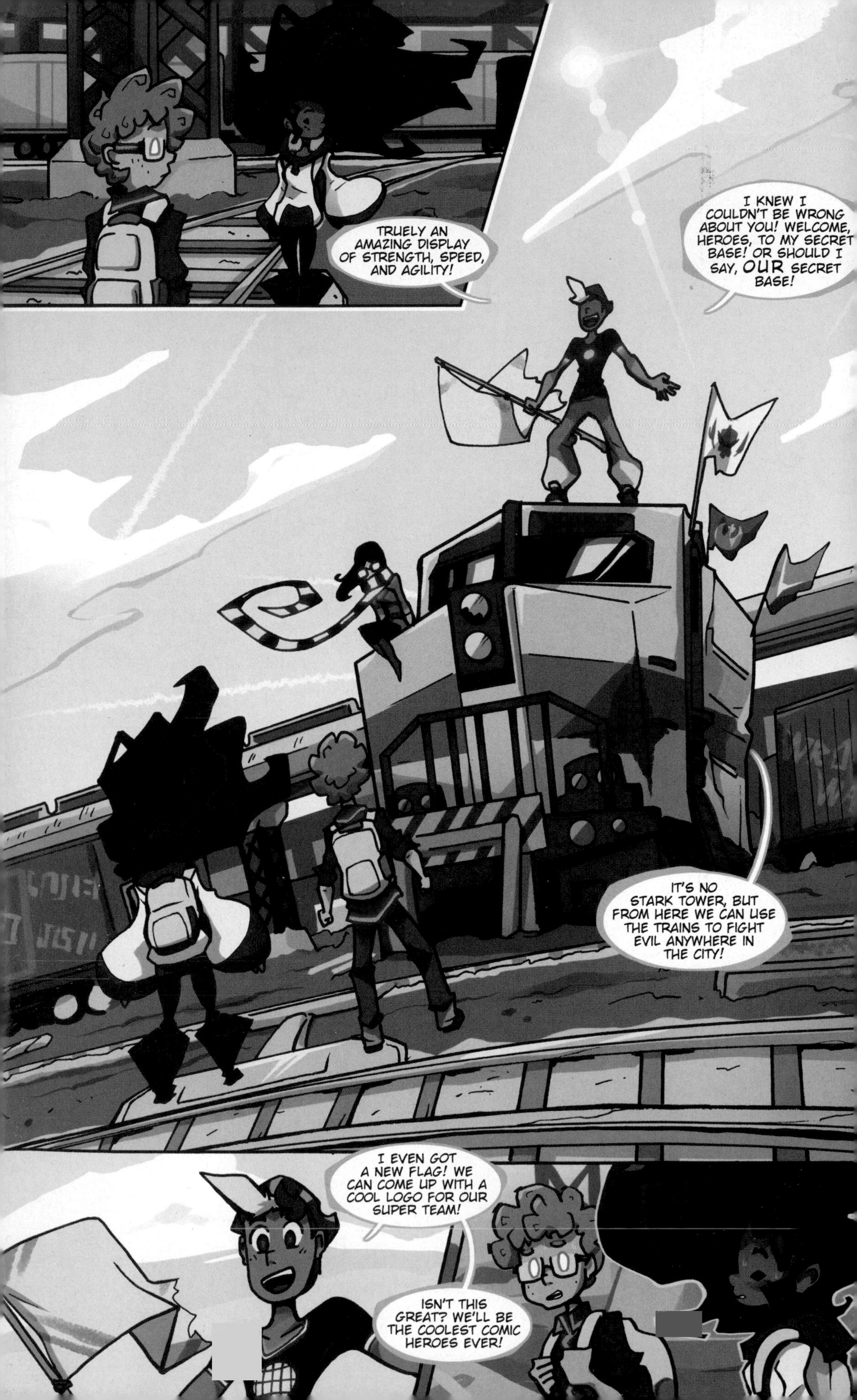
TRUELY AN AMAZING DISPLAY OF STRENGTH, SPEED, AND AGILITY!
I KNEW I COULDN'T BE WRONG ABOUT YOU! WELCOME, HEROES, TO MY SECRET BASE! OR SHOULD I SAY, OUR SECRET BASE!
IT'S NO STARK TOWER, BUT FROM HERE WE CAN USE THE TRAINS TO FIGHT EVIL ANYWHERE IN THE CITY!
I EVEN GOT A NEW FLAG! WE CAN COME UP WITH A COOL LOGO FOR OUR SUPER TEAM!
ISN'T THIS GREAT? WE'LL BE THE COOLEST COMIC HEROES EVER!